Tease Me *Once*

A Three Peaks Romantic Comedy

Romance with Altitude - Book 1

JODY A. KESSLER

Please visit: www.JodyAKessler.com
Sign up for the newsletter

ISBN: 9798557784450

Edited by Marianne Hull - MarianneHull.com
& Emily A. Lawrence - LawrenceEditing.com

Cover Art by Coverinked
www.coverinked.com

Manufactured in the United States of America
First Edition

Other Works Available

<u>Granite Lake Romance</u>
Unwrapping Treasure - 1
Chasing Treasure - 2
Reclaiming Melanie - 3
Divining Elise - 4
Detecting Autumn - 5
Catching Kiera - 6

An Angel Falls series

Death Lies Between Us - 1
Angel Dreams - 2
Haunting Me - 3
Destined to Fall - 4
The Misplaced – An Angel Falls Novella with Chris Abeyta
The Call – An Angel Falls Novella with Chris Abeyta

<u>Historical Time Travel series</u>
The Night Medicine

<u>Witches of Lane County</u>
Heart of the Secret - 1
A Witch's Fate - 2

&

<u>A New Adult Coming of Age Novel</u>

When We're Entwined

Dedication

To my muse.

One

MALEAH HALE STEPPED OUT of her basement and smashed her knee against the concrete. Tripping over her doorstep was oh-so becoming. It was still early. Too early to be on the move, but today was the big day, and she didn't want to miss a single second. She pried herself off the ground, no little feat in high heels and a pencil skirt, and was fairly certain she'd broken something—other than her dignity. This should have been Maleah's first clue that today wasn't going to turn out the way she'd imagined.

She turned around and reentered her one-room studio apartment. Somehow, during her ungainly stumble, her phone stayed clutched in her hand and nothing had fallen out of her purse. Maybe if she hadn't been checking her phone for new messages from Holden, she wouldn't have tripped. But where was he? She'd messaged her boss-slash-friend-slash-future-life-partner the day before and hadn't heard back from him. It wasn't like Holden to ignore his messages. He must be distracted with everything happening at his company. Everyone had been busier than normal for the last two months. Even this morning, Maleah was going into the office an hour early to double-check her files, documents, and reports, take care of emails, straighten up the common room and break room, and otherwise make sure True Green Bioplastics was ready and sparkling before her bosses and the other interns arrived for the most important business meeting of her young career.

Apparently, her internal clock felt that the simple act of being awake, coherent, and able to walk out the door at the butt-crack of dawn was too much to ask. The heel on her favorite double strap, blue suede, sexiest shoes she owned—shoes she rarely ever let herself wear, but today was special and she wanted to look fantastic— caught on the rug and she fell again. Shooting, fiery pain radiated from her knee. "Holy Toledo! Ow!" At least the ancient squishy carpet—the basement had been flooded one too many times—cushioned her second fall exceedingly better than the concrete had. Maleah caught herself before she face-planted into the shag and ruined her makeup. This time, her phone went flying and the contents of her purse poured out. *Figures.* Maleah climbed off the floor, leaving behind any remaining dignity. She didn't have time for this. Humbled and wondering if she was putting way too much emphasis on the importance of her morning—today was only the day she'd been working toward her entire life—she carefully hobbled to the bathroom to clean, disinfect, and bandage her bruised and bleeding knee.

There were no cabinets in the tiny bathroom and just enough square footage to accommodate a pedestal sink, the toilet, and a poor excuse of a shower. She rooted inside the bottom drawer of the cheap plastic rolling storage bin that held her first aid supplies, toiletries, and other bathroom necessities. By the time she had the implements in hand and stood up again, blood had leaked down her shin and almost onto her foot. Blood on the perfect, cerulean blue suede of her favorite shoes was not going to happen, so help her.

Distress about the blood racing toward her shoe wasn't the only problem. A dizzying wooziness overcame Maleah and clouded her vision. She sank down and planted herself on the toilet. Maleah gripped the edge of the sink. The bottle of disinfectant clattered inside the bowl. The porcelain felt cool and solid and gave her something to hang onto and helped her stay conscious. She tore some tissue from the roll and pressed the wadded-up paper against the blood now running over the ankle strap. Deep breaths moved in and out of her lungs until the need to hurl the toast and coffee she'd eaten for breakfast had passed.

Maleah wasn't fond of seeing blood, especially her blood, but her hands remained steady as she cleaned her leg and knee and then poured the disinfectant over the small gash. The bruise was going to be worse than the cut, but she would live.

She rose from the seat and felt something wet against her leg. Maleah craned her neck around to look for the problem. The slit in the rear of her skirt had landed in the water. She should have closed the lid, but there hadn't been time as she was blacking out, and there wasn't a lid. The missing seat cover was one of a hundred small inconveniences in her overpriced hole-in-the-wall shanty.

"Nooo..." she whined. Maleah reached behind her back and released the hook on the waistband and lowered the zipper. "Why me? Why today?" She shimmied out of the soiled skirt and took a step toward the door. Not one to forget easily, she halted before stepping back onto the carpet that loved to tangle with the spiked heels of her shoes.

Maleah started to unbuckle the straps on the high heels and realized bending her knee wasn't going to happen without pain. Keeping her leg mostly straight, she worked on unfastening the straps with her backside high in the air and wearing nothing but the sexy blue heels, a navy-blue lace thong with matching strapless bra, and a semi-sheer blouse and camisole. A sigh fell from her lips as she stepped out of the shoes. If only Holden were here to appreciate the view and maybe kiss her knee all better. But that was a fantasy she had to keep to herself for the time being.

She wanted to be with Holden in every sense of the word, but until she was no longer his intern, she knew they could never do more than flirt. Holden McNutt was too professional and respectful to jeopardize her chances of becoming a full-time employee at True Green Bioplastics. Soon, she told herself. Soon she and Holden would go on a date, out in the open, where everyone would know they were meant to be together. They would take over the biodegradable and compostable plastics industry and change the world for the better.

Today was her day. She was sure of it. She'd done everything Holden and his business partner had asked of her for ten straight months. Maleah had contributed to the company as if it were her business baby. She'd gone above and beyond and had grown True Green Bioplastics' online presence from virtually nothing to being everywhere on the internet. She'd learned everything she could about biobased polyester plastics, polyhydroxyalkanoate, blended starch/cellulose plastics, biodegradation, polylactide acid, cellulose acetate, and ASTM specifications. Holden had been sharing the bioplastic chemistry secrets with her. Every day at work was exciting and what she had dreamed of. Well, not the part of her days tied to a computer for hours on end doing data entry and marketing, or running into town for lunches and coffee. But she loved being part of a team that could make a positive difference for the environment.

The ticking clock taunted Maleah's early morning plans. She still had to change clothes and get herself safely to the office. The mad rush to find pants that looked phenomenal with her blouse and choosing a new pair of shoes resulted in a closet explosion.

She managed to make it to her car and submerse herself in morning traffic fifteen minutes later... and then she remembered why she normally went to work at the time she did. Early eager beavers and university students traveled into town this time of the day, and the heavy congestion made driving an exercise in patience. As her car crawled from stoplight to stoplight, her mind drifted as it often did to what her future life as a full-time employee would be like. She would buy a bicycle. Cycling would be good for her—well, not on snowy days—and a bike would be faster than sitting in traffic. At this rate, walking would get her there faster. She sighed for at least the fiftieth time and pulled into the parking lot at True Green Bioplastics—right on time. Her intention of arriving early had disappeared much like Dorothy and Toto in a Kansas tornado. *You know what they say about good intentions; they're the road to hell.* Her subconscious whispered the words... in a super-loud voice, but she shoved all doubts aside. *Nope. Nope. Nope. Today is going to be great!* She was having a rough start, that's all.

As she continued to self-narrate and talk herself up, she made it safely out of the car and into the building.

"Why are you limping?" Davis Kapoor, one of the four interns working at True Green Bioplastics, asked after she entered the common room.

"I'm not limping," she said and immediately realized she was in fact favoring her sore knee.

Davis's gaze dropped to her leg and then glanced up again. "Sorry, my bad."

Davis was a brilliant scientist, but preferred to work alone and only collaborated when forced to. Maleah knew he sometimes annoyed Holden. On more than one occasion, Holden had come to her with specific requests and then asked if she would pass the information along to Davis, thereby avoiding the intern completely. Holden trusted her to relay important information to her co-intern, work together exclusively on the latest project, and report their findings back to him.

Davis's self-important, know-it-all douchebaggery tendencies were mentally taxing, to say the least. Maleah put up with him because Holden thought they worked well together. Her boss had not been wrong. She and Davis made a breakthrough in the lab that had Holden speechless. They had delivered their news and turned in their report last week. Holden said he would present their findings to the other business partner and get back to them, but he had been ecstatic. He mentioned he thought they had earned their permanent positions at True Green. That was the last time Maleah had spoken with her boss, and she didn't understand why he hadn't gotten back to her even by text message. *He's busy,* she told herself again. He'd announce her and Davis's accomplishment in the hemp and mycelium-based biopolymers project to the rest of the staff and interns this morning. She was sure of it.

Maleah shifted her laptop bag from one arm to the other and glanced at her favorite seat at the conference table where everyone would be gathering in the next few minutes. She took a step in that direction, and was about to ask Davis if Holden had said anything to him about their report, but her knee buckled.

"Ow!" The sound escaped from her before she could stop it. Davis didn't reach out to steady her but instead leaned away as if she were contagious. Maleah winced and regained her balance on her own.

"But you're not limping," Davis said flatly.

"And you're not helping," she threw back at him. This brought a slight quirk to the corners of his mouth. "I forgot," she lied. "I had a minor accident this morning. I'm not hurt, though."

"I don't really care." He walked over to the table where he planted himself in her favorite spot, two seats to the right of where Holden always sat.

Jerk. She should be more annoyed, but she had worked with Davis long enough to know he was unapologetically honest and blunt. He claimed he had little to no empathy and had even warned and apologized to her about his sometimes-brash personality. Maleah suspected Davis was a genius, but if being a genius meant you were also an ass then she'd take a hard pass.

Maleah set up her laptop on the opposite side of the table from Davis and opened her notes. Holden McNutt and Terence Zhang, her bosses and the owners of True Green Bioplastics, entered the common space from the direction of their offices. Terence wore a kind smile, but the pinched creases around Holden's eyes and lips didn't give Maleah a good feeling. He also wouldn't make eye contact with her. Something was wrong, and she wasn't sure if she wanted to know what it was.

"Good morning, everyone," Terence said as he approached the table.

They took their places, one on either end of the conference table. The rest of the seats were already taken. Maleah noticed the entire staff and all interns were in attendance for the meeting.

Terence Zhang started. "As you know, today's meeting is not our regular weekly update. We have a lot to share with you, including some exciting progress on the hemp polymer project."

Maleah felt a burst of pride at the mention of her and Davis's project. She glanced at Holden, but his eyes were trained on his business partner.

"Unfortunately, we also have bad news that we received yesterday. I'd like to start with the good news. Holden was able to combine two of our interns' hemp polymer findings with his research and the results are exactly what we have been looking for. We are now going to be able to take the new mycelium hemp polymer plastic into the final stages of development. With Davis's preliminary findings, we are ninety-nine-point-nine percent certain we have found the missing link we have been looking for. Without our incredibly talented interns, this breakthrough would have never happened. Which is why our bad news is such a shock and a hugely disappointing blow to Holden and me." Terence stared down the length of the table at his partner. Maleah watched Terence let out a deep breath before compressing his lips into a frown.

Her head swiveled to look at her boss, her potential soon-to-be boyfriend. He stared at his phone. She'd never seen him so disconnected. *What's going on?* She couldn't imagine what could be so terrible.

Terence continued, "Let me preface this by letting you know that we have been trying to work out this turn of events for our company since receiving the news. We have gone over every possibility. We haven't slept." He looked at every person sitting around the table and said, "We've barely eaten as we've been too busy working on finding a solution to these new challenges. Our team has been the most dedicated group of individuals we could have ever hoped to bring together, and we have been thriving day in and day out. For that we are more grateful than you will ever know. Unfortunately, there are aspects of working with government-funded grants that are out of our control. Holden, will you take it from here, please?"

The sinking feeling in Maleah's gut hit bottom like an anchor. *Oh no.* Terence's bad news had to do with their funding. She turned to face Holden and steeled herself to hear the rest.

Holden rose to his feet and stuffed his hands in the pockets of his slacks. He made eye contact for a fleeting moment and then looked skyward as if searching for the right words. The creases of concern and stress softened, and he smiled before speaking.

"Well, Terence sounds rather ominous, and while it's true this is the hardest thing we have had to do since we started True Green, hang in there with me as I go over the worst of it first. Then I will share the solution we have come up with." He smiled again, but there was an obvious element of sadness and stress. "We've had an excellent run, and I know everyone here believes in our company's mission and what we are attempting to do with bioplastics. Before I go any further, I want to tell you we have lost our grants. With the current administration in the White House, this should not have come as a surprise, but we thought our funding was secure for at least two more years. That is no longer the case. We are definitely not the only ones affected by current politics. I'm sorry for it and for everyone else who has lost their funding."

Holden took a deep breath, then continued. "True Green is on the verge of making a substantial profit in bioplastics within one to two more years, but without our grant money, we have to cut back by fifty percent. What this means to you is that we have to eliminate all paid internships. All staff members will remain in their current positions, and we will review contracts as they come up. Terence and I have chosen to take considerable pay decreases. We are offering one new position to an intern because Melissa is leaving us. Her husband is being deployed to Korea and she is going with him. We're sorry to see Melissa leave but happy to offer her position to one of our incredibly talented interns." Holden paused.

This is it. Maleah worked the hardest of any of the interns. She knew everything about True Green, and she had earned her place at the company. Tears threatened to make an appearance. She needed this job and really needed the increase in pay. Living on an intern's salary had been worse than making minimum wage, but she loved what she was doing and the sacrifices had been worth it. But Holden wasn't looking at her.

"Davis. We think the work you've done over the last year, and especially the progress you made with the hemp polymers, has earned your right to be a full-time chemist with True Green. I sent you our offer. If you will look it over and give us an answer as soon as possible, then Terence and I will know how we are going to move forward."

Holden finally looked at Maleah and then the other interns. Sadness and stress emanated from his sapphire-blue eyes, or maybe he was only mirroring Maleah's inner turmoil. *Davis? They want Davis?*

Davis said, "I'll all in, McNutt. I'm sure I'll be staying with you and Terence. I'm ready to get back in the lab right now."

Davis was an extraordinary chemist, and that had to be the reason he was chosen over her, but Maleah had been equally responsible for their findings on the last project. She helped with every step and had written the entire report. Holden and Terence hadn't even acknowledged her role in the mycelium and hemp polymer project. How was that fair? If she hadn't helped Davis, he would have never made the breakthrough.

She was about to speak up when she realized Holden had been talking and she missed what he'd said.

"If you will look over the new intern contracts and let me or Terence know if you are able to stay with us, that would be great. We understand if the new terms are not a viable option for you at this time. We're terribly sorry.

Today is not how any of us imagined our third-quarter meeting would go."

What? She couldn't admit she hadn't been listening and glanced at her fellow interns. Brandy, who sat to her left, was clicking on her email, so Maleah did the same. The email heading read "True Green Bioplastics Internship Program." Maleah opened the message and read. The new internship offer was an unpaid position. She blinked and read the offer again. Images of her future flashed like a slideshow inside her head. School loans, credit card debt, and homelessness were not how she pictured her future. Her car was paid for, but she couldn't live in it. When she'd accepted the internship, the pay had been minimal, and she'd somehow managed to make it work, but working forty to fifty hours a week for zero dollars was impossible. She'd have to find a second job... at night when she was supposed to be sleeping. Maleah had put in her time with True Green. She had worked so hard. *Why is this happening?*

By the time she stopped obsessing over the email, most of the room had cleared out. Embarrassed by her lack of awareness, she closed her email app, stood, and headed to her desk. The frenzy of overbearing doom settled into a dull numbness.

She didn't notice anyone or anything until a familiar voice asked, "So, are you going to stick around, Hale?"

Maleah turned to face her rival. "I worked as hard as you did on our project. I wrote the entire report while you watched online videos. I know everything about this company."

"But I know the exact chemical composition that makes hemp polymers bond with the mycelium to decompose in one hundred and eighty days or less in both land and marine environments."

"If I hadn't been in the lab with you that day, you would have never added the fungus mycelium in the first place," she said.

"But Holden and Terence don't think so. I told them the formula was my idea."

"Why would you do that? I deserve recognition for my part of the project."

"You do, but I beat you to the punch. Now I have the job we all wanted and you don't."

"What is wrong with you?" she asked, disgusted and mystified by Davis's callous and hurtful words.

He didn't have to think about it, as the answer rolled off his tongue without hesitation. "I'm a dude. We get what we want because we're not worried about hurting the feelings of our competition. You women think you're equal to us men, but this proves you're not. If you wanted the permanent position with True Green, you would have done what it takes to get the position. We all know Holden and Terence like you more than me, yet I will be staying. With a paycheck. You didn't answer my question. Will you be sticking around? You are pretty useful, in your way."

Maleah had so much to say in response that her words tangled and made speaking coherently impossible. And truth be told, Davis didn't deserve an answer even if she could manage to spit out her response. What insulted her more was how he said everything as a simple matter-of-fact statement.

"You can piss off. I'm going to talk to Holden." She left Davis standing by her cubicle and didn't look back.

"Running to the boss won't change anything," he called.

She flipped him the bird. Davis laughed, his mockery fueling her temper.

Two

MALEAH KNOCKED ON Holden's office door and strained to hear if he was inside. The door swung open so quickly that she jumped. Brandy, her fellow intern, flashed a sympathetic look and then dropped her gaze to the floor before hurrying down the hall.

"Maleah. I knew you'd come. Close the door behind you," Holden said.

He stood in the center of his office and had the aura of someone who had been defeated but refused to stay down. Her sympathy meter shot off the charts, and she instantly wanted to make everything better. Davis's declaration of "I'm a dude that gets what he wants because he's not afraid of hurting other people's feelings" went off like an air horn inside her head. *But dammit*, she had feelings and empathy. Unlike her dipstick coworker, she couldn't turn off her emotions, especially when the person who was hurting was someone she cared about.

"Oh, Holden, I'm so sorry about losing the grants."

"You, me, and everyone. But thank you. The last couple days have been challenging."

She approached her boss and placed a hand on his arm. Holden covered her hand with his. His touch was slightly clammy and not at all what she would have thought. But still, he was touching her.

"What can I do?" she asked.

"Maleah, I know you've been living on a shoestring budget. I don't expect you to work for free. Terence and I have always been adamant about paying our interns. Having to ask people to work for free is killing me, but we can't figure out any way around it. We'll be applying for new grants and searching for investors, but for now, we are stuck." His hand fell away and he moved to the desk chair.

"I can help you with that. In fact, I have spreadsheets listing possible investors and private donors."

"Email me what you have, and I'll definitely use anything I may have missed. You're incredible. You're going to be an asset to any company that is lucky enough to have you. I can't believe this is happening right now. I thought we had another year at least, and by that time, we would be making enough to expand. Cutting back now is going to stall our progress. It's unbelievable. This couldn't have happened at a worse time."

"Everything is going to work itself out. You'll see," she said with more optimism than she felt. Holden's misery was palpable and distressing on a level she hadn't experienced before. Her heart ached, and she suddenly needed to be his cheerleader, to make him realize that when life hands you lemons, a new door opens. *Wait*, she had that all wrong.

She tried again. "When the world delivers limes, you make margaritas."

Holden's look of confusion made her blurt out another one.

"Even in your darkest hour, smile because it happened." She blinked and tried to correct herself again. "That is so wrong. It's... that... I can't find my favorite quotes. They're hiding from me. But you know, lemonade and dark nights of the soul, happiness, positivity, transformation from finding your rainbow." Mortification was setting in now, and she was messing this up on a whole new level. "I used affirmations and mental tricks to stay positive during some rough days in college. But right now, I don't know what's wrong with me."

The baffled look lessened slightly. "Are you trying to tell me it won't always be this bad?"

"Yes! And we have to keep going. You have a great team, and everyone understands that this can happen. I can help you through this trial by fire, and we're going to come out stronger and more secure than ever. What you're doing for bioplastics is going to change the future of our planet. We both know it. You said I'm incredible, but it's not me who is changing the world, it's you."

Holden's eyes closed, and she watched him breathe for a moment.

Maleah stalled. She was about to say she would continue working for the company, but the words wouldn't form. How could she survive with no income? The answer was simple, she couldn't.

He rose from the chair, came to her, and wrapped his arms around her in a tight embrace. After months of wondering and dreaming what it would feel like to have his body pressed against hers, it was finally happening. He was strong, his body firm and lean from cycling, running, and swimming. When he wasn't working at True Green, Holden trained as a triathlete, and it showed.

His hand stroked down her back. "Maleah, you always make me feel better. Even when you're babbling or talking nonsense, it helps. Thank you."

"It's one of my best skills," she said as she tried to process exactly what he meant by pointing out her flaw of babbling like an insane person. *Seriously? He likes that?* She hated when she couldn't find the right words.

Was now the time to point out that since she was no longer his intern they could go out on a date?

"Holden," she started.

His hot, damp palm stayed pressed against her back, keeping her close. She cherished the feeling of his body but couldn't help but wonder if there was a wet spot on her sheer blouse.

"You're a real-life angel. I want to keep in touch with you after this settles down."

Oh, goodness. He's thinking the same thing I am. "I want that too."

His phone rang. Holden left her standing in the middle of his office as he returned to the desk and answered. "Hey, Davis," he said and then fell quiet, listening.

The mention of Davis's name brought back the anxiety-ridden, eye-twitching frustration of her current circumstances and how Davis threw her under the bus. She waited patiently and listened to see if Holden would end the call, but instead he walked around the desk, clicked his mouse, and bent over to look closer at the computer monitor.

"Uh-huh. Yes, I have it in front of me," Holden said.

Her boss, well, former boss should know what happened. She hung out for another minute, but Holden was engrossed with his screen. Maleah moved to the door.

Holden finally glanced up. "I have to deal with this. Sorry, Maleah. Bad timing."

"It's okay," she said, agreeable as always. She attempted a smile and turned to let herself out. He was having the worst day of his life. She didn't expect him to make promises now, did she? She was being ridiculous.

Then she heard him say, "Davis, hold on one second," followed by, "Maleah?"

She turned back around. He wasn't done talking to her after all. Her heart lightened as she faced the world's sexiest and most intelligent boss.

"Thanks for helping me get through this. You are a gem. Email me those files when you can, all right?"

The smile was forced as she said, "Of course."

She let herself out and somehow made it to her car. The fallout wasn't pretty, and she didn't remember how she got home, but Maleah found herself inside her hole-in-the-wall apartment before the ugly crying started.

The part of her morning that disturbed her most was how she'd put Holden's feelings and stresses before her own. Maleah hadn't stood up for herself, and Davis received all the credit for their project. After replaying the morning's events a thousand times in her mind, she realized the day had slipped away and she was starving. Eating a frozen pizza, a pint of fudge brownie ice cream, and most of a bag of ranch-flavored potato chips, which didn't taste too great and were kind of stale, she felt bloated and had to change out of her pants because the waistband was digging into her stomach. The pig-out session didn't improve her dismal new reality either. To make matters worse, Maleah calculated that she'd consumed roughly ninety thousand calories in one sitting and felt guilty about it. Going for a run would solve everything. Running not only burned calories and released endorphins, but the physical exertion would take her mind off her problems.

She threw on joggers and a T-shirt, tied the laces on her sneakers, and headed outside—heedless of the cold and the dark. Fifteen pounding strides down the sidewalk later and she remembered vividly why there was a large Band-Aid on her knee and that she hadn't run or jogged anywhere in years. She'd been too busy trying to make True Green the top bioplastics company in the world. Maleah limped home, opened the only bottle of alcohol in the apartment, and chugged.

"Bleh." The Marsala was not meant for gulping. She took another long swig, gagged, and felt a dribble of wine leak down her chin and onto her shirt. She hobbled over to the bed, plunked down on the edge of the mattress, missed by a couple inches, and fell on the floor. Soggy carpet be damned. Maleah felt too sorry for herself to move and sat there in a pitiful heap, contemplating why Marsala tasted so good with chicken and mushrooms but not by itself.

She tasted the wine again. "Too strong," she said and coughed. Maleah wiped the back of her hand over her mouth and drank the rest.

* * *

Mistakes had been made. It was true. Maleah wasn't perfect. As much as she hated to admit it to herself, she had weaknesses. Apparently, one of her faults was that she couldn't stomach cheap wine with frozen pizza, not to mention the other mistakes she'd stuffed into her mouth the night before. However, learning from her mistakes was something she excelled at, and she swore to never drink the cooking wine ever again. Eating chicken Marsala may be off the menu permanently as well. *Shame.* That was one of her favorite meals.

Another weakness she needed to work on was checking her phone as soon as she woke up every morning. Ignoring her phone wasn't happening on this day, though. One self-improvement at a time seemed like enough work. She reached over and grabbed the phone from its customary spot on the nightstand. Her hand bumped the empty bottle of Marsala and it fell to the floor. The thick green glass bottle survived the fall on the cushy old carpet. If any wine spilled out, it hardly mattered.

Panic zoomed through her bloodstream, and her heart skipped a beat when she didn't immediately locate her phone. She peered over the side of the bed and eyeballed the space around the nightstand. Trying to remember where she'd last seen it felt like extracting answers to the mysteries of the universe. Outside? During her failed jogging attempt? When she'd thought about calling a taxi to bring her sorry ass home even though she was only one house down the street? An ambulance would have been dramatic. A taxi driver wouldn't ask questions and would have been a lot cheaper.

Maleah pushed herself up to look for her phone on the counter or in the restroom and something foreign brushed against her skin. She reached beneath the covers and pulled her phone out from under her butt. *At least my phone is getting a little action.* She used the sheet to wipe away the smudges on the phone screen—the streaks on the glass weren't really from her ass... she hoped—and then checked for new messages.

There was a voicemail from her mom. As she was about to hit the send button to listen to her message, she had a paralyzing, possibly life-altering, memory of drunken texting to Holden. Maleah's mouth went dry. She checked the text history and almost died again. Why couldn't the Marsala have just put her in a coma? Maleah groaned. She'd sent Holden gifs of funny baby elephants having a bad day. Then she invited him to come over and asked if he would bring wine because hers tasted awful. Thank God he hadn't replied. He knew where she lived and that the apartment was small, but she didn't actually want him to see how small and terrible her place was.

Closing her eyes and taking a few long, slow, and centering breaths helped ease the embarrassment that had her blood pumping as if she'd been running from a madman. She grimaced, but there was nothing she could do about the drunk texting. Holden would probably find it hilarious and totally justifiable. She did lose her job after all. He was a mess too. Maybe he drank all night and passed out before seeing her messages. Then again, he hadn't replied. She tucked her lower lip beneath her teeth and listened to the voicemail.

"Hi, sweetie. This is your mom." Jona Hale stated the obvious, as if Maleah didn't know it was her. She kept listening, hoping the familiar sound of her mother's voice would help soothe the unbearable ache that had replaced her vision of the future.

"I know yesterday was your big day. I can't wait to hear how everything went. You're probably out celebrating right now with that handsome boss of yours. I hope I'm not interrupting." Her mother's voice sweetened. "You've worked so hard for this moment. Your father and I are proud of you no matter what you do."

Maleah listened to the rising swell of emotion in her mother's tone and felt the proverbial knife twisting inside her gut. *Ugh.*

There was a slight pause, and then Jona said with a tempered and more serious voice, "When you have a few uninterrupted minutes, will you please call me back? I have some news to share with you too. Call me as soon as you get my message, okay? Talk to you soon." And she hung up.

If Maleah wasn't already overwhelmed with sudden and shocking changes in her career, life, and the domino effect of being jobless was going to create, she would have worried more about her mother's last words in the message. But in the moment, all she could think of was how she was going to settle her upset stomach, get rid of the dehydration headache, and survive on one hundred and seventy-six dollars and a maxed-out credit card.

After taking care of the bodily necessities, Maleah settled back onto her bed with a cup of ginger mint tea. The tea recipe was her mother's cure for everything, and it soothed her stomach and warmed her hands. She was about to call her mom and share the bad news when her phone rang. Her heart pinged as she thought it might be Holden checking in, but it was her mother again.

"Hi, Mom."

"Sweetheart? Thanks for answering this time," Jona said, as if Maleah had been ignoring her mother's calls. She never did. Her mom continued before Maleah pointed out that she always answered. "No one answers the phone. You have to send a text message or an email. Does anyone talk to each other anymore? It's not like that here in Waialua. Everyone enjoys seeing one another. Our neighbors are so wonderful. When can you come to visit, Maleah? It's been a long time."

Maleah cleared her throat. She hadn't gotten a word in yet.

"Sorry. Forget I asked. I know you are busy. I can't believe I have to call and ask a favor of you today of all days. But before I tell you what happened here, you tell me how it went at your plastics company yesterday."

"Wait. What's going on? Is everything okay?" Maleah remembered the change in her mother's voice in the message.

"No, no. My news can wait. Did you get the job? Is it official? Oh, and did you and your handsome man go out and celebrate last night? Your celebrations are more important than my bad news."

"Bad news?" Maleah didn't know if she could handle more disappointment or stress. She sipped the magic tea and prayed it really was a cure-all. "Please tell me and get it over with."

Jona said, "I'm sorry, sweetheart. The timing is awful, which is why I didn't call yesterday morning after your father's accident. It's just as well, though, because I received another upsetting call about an hour ago."

"Mom, please, tell me. I'm not good at holding my breath." Maleah set the cup down and clutched the phone tighter. "What happened to Dad?"

"He's okay. It's nothing major," she said, but Maleah heard the tiredness in her voice. "He had an accident pruning the palm trees and fell off the ladder yesterday. He had the long pruning pole in his hands and ended up in a terrible mess. Anyway, his left foot is broken, and he sprained his right wrist. We spent the better part of the day at the hospital. What a zoo that was. I think he might take my suggestion and hire some men to do the trees next time. Those coconut trees can be such a hassle, you know."

"Oh, no," Maleah said. "Does he need surgery on his foot?"

Mom's Japanese-American accent was getting stronger as she talked about Albert. "No, no. I don't think so. He's right here. You speak to him after we're finished." She paused, and Maleah heard a muffled exchange between her parents. Jona returned to the conversation and said, "Albert says he is fine and nothing hurts, but I can tell he's playing the tough guy. He's more upset about not being able to drive than anything. His ego is bruised more than his thick head."

"He hit his head too?" Maleah's anxiety was creeping higher and higher the longer the phone call continued. She gulped the tea, then set the cup down so hard that it splashed over the side and onto the table.

"Yep. Good thing he is so hard-headed. The doctor says Albert doesn't have a concussion, thank Wakea." Jona's exasperation was transmitted three thousand miles away to Boulder, Colorado, where Maleah sat on the bed feeling slightly befuddled on top of concerned.

She asked, "Did you just thank a Hawaiian god?"

"Wakea? Yes, yes, I did."

"But you don't practice the Hawaiian religion," Maleah said slowly.

"You're right, I don't. But you know how it goes. When in Rome, do as the Japanese Hawaiians do."

And now Maleah's mixed babbled nonsense in Holden's office yesterday was making a lot more sense. She slapped the phone to her forehead and sighed. Maleah turned on the speaker. "Okay, well, I hope you and Dad stay in Wakea's and Pele's good graces from here on out."

"Yes, that would be nice," her mother said with exasperation. "And a few minutes ago, after I got your father all settled in front of the TV. He's watching reruns of *M*A*S*H*. Can you believe he found that old show on the television? He's seen every episode, but it makes him happy, so I don't say a thing."

"Mom," Maleah interrupted. Her patience for her mother's wandering thoughts was wearing a wee bit thin. "Can you tell me your other news?"

"I'm getting to it," she said.

Maleah loved her mom dearly, but there were times when the woman tested her inner strength.

"Aunt Kiki had an episode and she is at the Mount Tenderfoot Medical Center."

"What kind of episode?"

"The nurse told me Aunt Kiki was confused and wandering around town in the middle of the night in her bathrobe. She kept saying she lost her pet turtle."

"In Three Peaks? When did this happen?"

"Last night."

Maleah thought about her great-aunt and could picture Kiki doing something like that. "I highly doubt she was confused."

"I can't say if she was or not, but the nurses didn't believe there was any turtle involved. She also didn't have shoes on. When the paramedics arrived, Aunt Kiki was sitting on the curb and she was bleeding. This isn't good, Maleah. Your great-aunt is under observation, and for now they will not release her."

"Mom, that's awful. Aunt Kiki is the most mentally sound person I know. If she said she lost her turtle, then she lost her turtle." That wasn't totally true, but once you understood her quirks, you realized Aunt Kiki's eccentricities were a normal part of her personality, not an "episode."

"She was half frozen and speaking nonsense. I don't blame the nursing facility for holding her. The whole situation is a mess. Even worse than the one here. I can't fly to Colorado to check on her. Not with your dad in his condition."

The bomb hovered over Maleah's head. Before it dropped, she asked, "Did you call Auntie Hana or Brielle?"

Maleah knew what her mom would say about her cousin Hana before the words came out of her mouth. Jona's cousin, Hana, and Aunt Kiki's only daughter, was as reliable as a canoe with a giant hole in the bottom. Hana's daughter, Brielle, who Maleah had practically grown up with in Three Peaks, was a hundred times more reliable but often hard to get ahold of.

As expected, Jona shared her findings about trying to reach her flaky family members. "Hana is working on a boat in Alaska. She's not going to be back in port in Ketchikan for another two weeks. When she does arrive, I doubt she'll come home to check on her mom. I haven't been able to speak with Brielle. I was starting to wonder if the two of you were ignoring my calls on purpose."

"I don't do that, Mom," Maleah reiterated. "I'll try to reach Brielle online. She's in Ireland, but she doesn't always check her messages."

"Oh, thank you. I know Brie will want to know about Kiki."

"Okay, sure," Maleah said, resolving herself to the current emergency. Emergencies, she corrected. Plural problems.

Jona and Maleah sighed simultaneously.

Maybe Maleah was doomed by her genetics. She thought of herself as an honest, hard-working, well-grounded woman with the highest of integrity and morals, but the weirdness gene still existed somewhere within her strands of DNA. Talking to her mother reinforced these ideas that the nature was stronger than the nurture. She had Albert for a father, though, so maybe there was some hope.

She knew what was coming next but waited for her mother to ask.

"Can you check on Aunt Kiki? She has friends, you know, but she needs someone in the family right now."

Before answering, Maleah already knew she was headed home to Three Peaks. The place she'd grown up in. Where she learned to dislike small towns for their inability to let you have any privacy whatsoever, and where you simultaneously had nothing better to do than gossip about the neighbors. After high school, Maleah couldn't move away from town fast enough. Not that Three Peaks, Colorado, was horrible, because it wasn't. The mountain town didn't suit the lifestyle she dreamed of living. She wanted activity, nightlife, and conveniences. Or did she?

Maleah had gotten her master's degree from the University of Denver and had experienced what she had longed for as a kid. Parties, diversity, city life were right outside her door. But by her senior year, she was too busy completing her graduate work to go out much. After graduation, she worked full-time at a nursery near her house while searching for the perfect job. It'd taken over a year to find and be accepted into the paid internship program at True Green.

After moving to Boulder, she'd become even more focused, and her entire social life revolved around work. It'd been months since she had gone out with friends. Maleah usually spent her limited amount of free time catching up on movies or going for a hike. If she wanted to splurge and treat herself, her grand outings involved buying a cup of coffee and taking advantage of a sale on clothes or shoes. Since graduating, she wasn't what anyone would call a social diva, partygoer, or extroverted in any sense of the meaning. Somehow, she'd morphed into a worker bee, a drone, a freaking recluse. *Wow. What happened to me?*

"Maleah? Are you still there? These cell phones are so awful, Albert..."

"I'm here, Mom. Sorry, I was just thinking. Of course I'll go see Aunt Kiki. Do you need help with Dad? Should I fly to Hawaii after I visit Three Peaks?" *What am I saying? I can't afford to fly to Hawaii.*

"You are such a sweet girl," her mother cooed. "No, no. We'll be fine. Albert will heal fast. But I would love to see you. Maybe you should come for a visit at Thanksgiving. Will you be able to take time off work? We would love that so much!"

Maleah swallowed hard. Mom didn't know she was jobless, and Maleah didn't want to deliver any more bad news.

"I can't give you an answer about the holidays right now, but I can be in Three Peaks today. I'll call you when I find out what happened to Auntie Kiki."

"Are you sure? You can take off work on short notice? Are you at work now, sweetheart?"

Maleah ignored the last question. "Yep, I can leave as soon as I pack my bag. My boss is great." *Yeah, because she is me,* Maleah thought and realized for the first time that when you don't have a boss, you are officially your own boss. The idea was both thrilling and unsettling. She was going to have to kick herself in the rear and get moving if she was going to make the four-and-a-half-hour drive home. "Taking off for a few days to take care of family is not a problem."

Her mom rambled on for a few more minutes, but Maleah missed most of the babbling about her father's need for pillows and pineapple juice. She caught the name of the hospital, nursing, and rehabilitation center where Aunt Kiki was, but she was already familiar with the medical facility. It was the only one in town and a big deal when it had opened in the high country.

They hung up and Maleah headed for the shower. She packed a couple bags with enough clothes and essentials to get her through a few days. After locking the apartment, Maleah made it to her car without tripping or falling. That had to be a sign that today would be better than the day before. Any day had to be better than yesterday, she thought as she started a playlist on her phone. A road trip couldn't begin without music. The hangover lingered like a cloud of smog polluting her brain and her bloodstream, but she had a mission to complete, and as long as she focused on helping her aunt, she could ignore her other woes.

Three

BEN CRANKED UP THE stereo and rolled the windows down in his truck. The workday had been long and productive, just the way he liked it. The heaviness of tired muscles in his arms and the stiffness in his neck meant he'd worked his ass off and had earned a beer and a few hours of relaxation before doing it all over again tomorrow.

Things were finally returning to normal after all the unnecessary drama of separation, divorce, and accompanying heartache of splitting up with Kinsey. God, that woman was something else. He shifted his thoughts to the road and the view of the mountains surrounding the Copper River Valley. His family's ranch lay behind him and to the west. The Ericksons settled here in the 1880s and found a love for the mountains that couldn't be shaken. Ranching had its ups and downs, but the Ericksons had persevered through decades of good and bad years. Ben had not been born with the call to work the cattle, and that was all right, because the ranching gene ran strong in his older brother, Jeremiah. Ben wanted—no, he needed, to make his own way and earn his own success. His roots were deep in Three Peaks and the Copper River Valley, but he wouldn't own and operate the family ranch.

Rebuilding his business after Kinsey had claimed, and been awarded by the court, half of his construction company had eaten up every ounce of his energy and all of his time. What a hellish and drawn-out nightmare she'd created with her need to destroy him. He'd offered her a cash settlement, not that he'd had the liquid assets. His money had been tied up in the business, but he would have come up with the cash to get her name off of it. Instead, she wanted to make his life as miserable as possible, and the judge had given her everything she wanted.

Rather than playing games and continuing to be manipulated by his shit-ass crazy ex, he'd sold the remaining half of his business for next to nothing and walked away, leaving her with a less-than-desirable partner. He also gave Kinsey the house. It wasn't worth the fight or the headaches. Besides, his daughter lived in that house and he wouldn't take that away from Skyla.

Kinsey had lost her freaking mind when she found out Ben had sold his share of the business to a stranger, and she'd refused to let him see his daughter for three months. He realized after the fact that the price of being cut off from his daughter was too high, but Ben had made his choice. He never thought Kinsey would take Skyla away from him. The depth of Kinsey's revenge was seemingly bottomless. Had he known Kinsey would ignore the court ordered visitation schedule, he might have chosen differently, but selling the business had been his best option at the time. Fighting his ex in court for a second time only compounded the misery. But Ben won the second round, and visitations with Skyla had finally begun again.

One step at a time. One day at a time. This was the advice his mother gave him as he experienced the hardest part of his twenty-eight years on the planet. His daughter was ten, old enough to see, hear, and know everything that transpired between her screwed up parents.

Ben didn't want to think on what his life had been like for the past two years. Today had been a great day. Despite competing against his former company, his new construction company was growing and doing well. It helped that his brother had decided to remodel the family homestead and rebuild the old bunkhouse, but that was one of his four contracted projects. He was set for the year, and he was looking forward, not back.

Looking forward, literally, Ben took in the view of the mountain range with their remaining patches of last year's snow. Fall was on the way. At the high elevation, the grass tops were heavy with seed, and the stalks turning gold. The sedge had darkened along the riverbanks and already showed tinges of burnished copper as it completed its life cycle. Back at the ranch, Jeremiah had baled the last cutting of hay for the year in the highest meadow. Ben looked forward to a break from the summer heat. Last winter brought more snow than usual and a wet summer, but the August heat had been right on target. A good thing too, as the hay needed to be dry before baling. The past weekend had brought a couple cold nights, and it had been a relief, even if he'd had to listen to a few of the older ladies downtown complain that they weren't ready for the snow or having to scrape ice off their windshields.

Ben was about five minutes outside of town when the golden hour of sunset struck the peaks and warmed the expansive views. He was caught up in appreciating the weather and the vastness of sky and land and clouds and he nearly missed the half-naked woman prancing around in the ditch next to a black car alongside the road.

Curious wasn't a strong enough word for his intrigue. He was downright captivated by what he saw. Her dark hair flew in all directions, covering most of her face as she hopped and flailed in the weeds. Her screeching and yelling overpowered the music and road noise. Something was definitely wrong. Ben stared so hard in the rearview mirror he almost missed the curve in the road. He hit the brakes as the passenger side tires went off the edge of the pavement and into the gravel.

Ben stopped the truck in the berm, executed a three-point turn, and returned to see if she needed help. Maybe an ambulance? When the dogs acted like that, he'd been known to turn the hose on them. *I could call the fire department.* She was barefoot and slapping at bare legs while yelling like a banshee. *Can people get brainworm?*

Ben stepped out of his truck and approached with caution. Her back was to him, and she didn't appear to notice his arrival on scene. Living in the sticks with a small population, few roads, and limited emergency services meant everyone depended on each other for help. This was civic duty, he told himself. Approaching a crazy lady from behind, and unarmed, might not be the smartest thing he'd ever done, but he was at least trying to be helpful. And as far as he could see, and unless she had a small weapon tucked under her shirt, she was also unarmed.

"Hey there!" he called. "You doing all right?"

No kidding, the woman didn't hear him, or she was completely deaf. She whipped off her shirt and threw it on the roof of her car. He now saw that the car had a flat tire, which helped explain why she was parked in the weeds along Route 9. As far as bodies go, hers was better than average. She was long-limbed, and her smooth curves were in all the right places. The thong back of her undergarment made his mouth go dry, and he swallowed. Her flawless skin widened his eyes and warmed him in places he shouldn't be feeling any heat when she was obviously in a vulnerable state.

Ben cleared his throat and tried again. "Yo, lady!"

Her head whipped around and her hands moved to cover up the pretty lady parts. Not that her attempt at modesty did much good. The bra and panties were tiny and some kind of colorful print he thought looked cute. He needed to stop staring now.

Ben shifted his gaze out across the field to his left. Jesus, she looked familiar, but he couldn't come up with a name. Was she an old client? An acquaintance of Kinsey's? He'd been looking at her undies and the most perfect figure he'd ever seen and hadn't taken a good look at her face, if he were being honest about it. He'd take a second look now, but he'd already been caught staring at her in a way that would make any woman uncomfortable given the circumstances.

He looked quickly and then away again as he apologized. "Sorry." Ben kept his head turned and asked, "You need some help or something?"

"Ben? Ben Erickson?"

That caught his attention. She knew him. He did his best to keep his eyes above her shoulders. She pulled her shirt back on then opened the car door and stood behind it so he couldn't see her lower half.

"Maleah?" Oh yeah, he knew that face. He couldn't believe he didn't recognize her sooner.

She was the only girl in all of his childhood who had so much exotic mystery, good looks, and smarts. They had been in the same class since she moved to Three Peaks in the first grade. They had been friends in elementary school and got along okay in middle school, but that was where their friendship had taken a turn. He didn't remember exactly why or what happened, but by high school they no longer acknowledged each other's existence. That was only partially true. He knew she was still around. There was no ignoring Maleah Hale in a graduating class of one hundred and fifteen students. To Ben, she stood out in a crowd, and she had been at the top of their class. She'd won at least three scholarships and was given awards at every academic school function. And he hadn't seen her a single time since high school graduation.

"What are you doing out here?" he asked.

"This is not what it looks like," she said with an air of horrific misunderstanding.

The tomato-red flush on her cheeks could have been from all the exertion, but Ben was fairly certain there was plenty of embarrassment in her color.

He licked his lips and hooked his thumbs in his pockets. "Well, it looks like you're suffering from brainworm, to be honest." Ben shrugged. How could he pass up the opportunity to make her squirm a bit more? He couldn't and added, "I called the sheriff before I got out of my truck. Based on my description, I suspect an ambulance is coming as well."

"What? No!" She made a sound like she was jabbed with a hot poker and jumped backward. Maleah hefted herself onto the hood of the car, pulling her feet up and wrapping her arms around her shins protectively. A second later, she yelped again and jumped back off.

Ben rushed forward with her scream, intent on assisting or saving her. From what, he didn't know, but her pain was obvious.

She held a butt cheek in each hand and cried out, "Ow! That's bloody hot! Oh my gosh!" As she rubbed her skin, Maleah stared at the hood of her car as if it'd personally assaulted her.

He hardened his jaw in an attempt to keep from laughing.

"Now I'm burned too." She craned her neck around to stare at her backside.

Ben looked too. Who wouldn't? Red ovals rosied each cheek, and it was a glorious thing to behold in the near perfect evening light. "Black paint gets pretty hot. We're about to lose the sun for the evening. Then you'll be all right to sit up there." The corners of his mouth twitched as he held back a laugh.

"That's real sage wisdom, Ben. And stop looking at me like that," she scolded. "This isn't funny." She ducked inside the car and began ranting. "My tire is flat and a stupid cow stole my skirt. But these horrible, awful—"

He cut her off. "Yo. Hold up." Ben raised a halting hand. "A cow stole your skirt?" His gaze shifted to the field beyond the barbed wire fence about seven feet from the car. There wasn't a cow to be seen. The fields belonged to the Donovans, another ranching family in the valley. Like the Ericksons, the Donovans also raised and bred Herefords.

"Yes! Give me a minute to find some pants."

"But why aren't you wearing shoes?" Ben tipped his head to the side and watched Maleah unzip a small suitcase in the back seat. He needed to clear some things up before he could move on.

"Because I threw them at the cow!" she said as if this was obvious and reasonable.

"Right," Ben agreed and wondered if it were possible that Maleah could be even crazier than his ex. Maybe it was something in the water. The three of them had grown up together after all.

"Would you like help with your tire?"

She turned in the seat as she stuffed a long, slender, and pale foot into a pant leg. Maleah glanced up at Ben. "It would be a lot more helpful than watching me get dressed. Did you really call the sheriff's office?"

"Nah," he admitted.

She frowned, and Ben grinned. *Damn.* Maleah Hale had grown into a gorgeous babe, and all that bare skin was distracting to say the least. He pivoted, both physically and mentally. His brain was fixed on helping her with her pants more than the flat tire. He rounded the back end of her small SUV to take a closer look at the problem. *What the hell am I doing? I don't ogle women.* Although he might start if Maleah was back in town for any length of time.

Ben married Kinsey the summer after high school graduation. She was pregnant, and he'd done the right thing by her and their baby. The opportunities to perfect his skills at being a pig hadn't presented themselves all too often. Ben had never been interested in other women. Kinsey was his first and only love. His daughter was the second. He'd vowed to be a faithful husband and he'd meant it. Too bad Kinsey hadn't felt the same.

Maleah continued speaking from inside the car. He thought she was warning him about the skirt-stealing cow again, but he only heard a few words. His mind was alternating between the vision of a half-naked Maleah and the way her painted toenails had the ability to make his body and mind respond in ways he hadn't experienced since before he was married. *How the hell did a cow steal her skirt?* Ben was distracted and he needed to focus on the tire.

The spare tire lay on the ground, and she'd put the jack in place and inserted the crank handle. Ben knelt down to make sure she'd placed the jack against the chassis. Everything looked good and the lug wrench lay on the ground nearby. He cranked the handle a couple times and then he caught sight of Maleah approaching the fence.

"What are you doing now?"

"I want my sandals back," she tossed over her shoulder at him. "Did you hear what I said about the—" But she was facing away from him and too far away, so he didn't hear the last part of her question.

Still thinking he could be the hero of the day, Ben stood and joined Maleah at the fence.

"Where are your shoes?"

She pointed and he squinted at the pasture. Sure enough, there was a brown leather sandal on the ground.

"The other one is a little farther up the hill." Maleah adjusted her hand a few degrees. "I'm hesitant to go in there after hitting the cow in the head with my shoe."

"You actually hit it?"

"Yeah. He didn't enjoy it either and bolted over the hill. I don't know where he's at now. I didn't want to hurt him; I wanted him to stop nibbling my skirt. The stupid cow ran off with my skirt stuck to his face."

Ben eyed Maleah with skepticism as he tried to picture the scenario she described. She smacked his stomach with the back of her hand.

"Don't give me that look. I swear it's true. I couldn't make this up if I tried. It was one of my favorite skirts too," she said.

Her look of bafflement mixed with disappointment were the only reasons Ben bought her story.

"I see your shoes. Hold the fence for me and I'll grab 'em. If I see the skirt, I'll pick it up."

"Okay, but be careful. I think I pissed off that cow."

"I was born a rancher, remember? I think I can handle myself. Besides, it appears you scared her off." Ben placed his shoe on the middle wire between the barbs and grabbed the top wire of the three-line fence. "You remember how to do this, don't you?" He pulled the top wire up and pressed down with his boot on the lower wire.

"It's been forever, but yeah, I think I can handle it," she said, mimicking his words and adding some sarcasm. She stretched the barbed wire fence open and Ben ducked through.

He stood up. "Hey, you remember that time in middle school when a whole group of us snuck onto old man Fred's property to play by his pond?"

"Yeah." She smiled. "I wanted to see the dinosaur prints that are supposed to be in the rocks over there."

"And I wanted to catch frogs. That was a good day," Ben said.

"It was until old man Fred started shooting his rifle."

"Eh." Ben shrugged. "He wasn't really tryin' to hurt anyone. He was being crotchety about us kids trespassing all the time. Everyone still visits his pond. He doesn't care anymore as long as you don't leave trash behind."

"I didn't know at the time. I thought he was trying to kill us. I was so scared about how much trouble I was going to get into at home."

"So was I," Ben admitted. "The old man never even called our parents."

"Thankfully."

Ben strolled across the meadow, smiling about the memory he hadn't thought of in years. He retrieved Maleah's sandal, but the second shoe was closer to the top of the small hillock, and sure as hell, she hadn't been lying. A dozen cattle grazed on the backside of the hill and to the north. From the road, you couldn't see them. Ben moved a couple yards farther up the shallow slope and looked around for the missing skirt.

"What color is your skirt?" he called back to Maleah.

"Dark blue with bright red flowers!" she yelled back.

Ben squinted into the setting sun, searching the hillside, but didn't see anything but cropped grass littered with cow pies. His gaze lifted and settled on the bull. Ben felt some empathy for the poor guy. Maleah's skirt was tangled on one horn and draped over the back of his head and down his neck. Ben shook his head at the predicament for both the bull and Maleah.

He'd grown up with Herefords and had known many bulls. Often, they had been like pets for him and his brother. This particular two-thousand-pound bull was out grazing with his breeding group and didn't deserve to be tangled up with Maleah's flowery skirt. Ben walked over to see if he could help the dude out.

Maleah called out, "Where are you going?"

He pointed, not wanting to yell and possibly scare the bull into a run, and then headed in his direction.

Most people might think bulls are aggressive and don't want to be messed with, and it could be true at times, but a lot of bulls were used to people and fairly tolerant of human interaction. They were raised to be so.

"Hey there, big guy," Ben said as he approached with caution. He'd feel out this bull's temperament and see if there was any way of helping him out. If not, then at least Ben had tried.

A tickling sensation moved along his inner calf and he reached down to scratch his leg. The bull eyed Ben, pawed the ground once, then twice, and went back to grazing. *So far, so good.* The bull wasn't too upset with Ben being in his zone. Ben took a couple more steps closer, but wisely kept thirty feet between them.

"You want that off your head, big guy? I can help you out." He eased in closer.

The bull ignored him. Another tickle caught his attention, this time on his shin. He ignored the sensation because the bull lifted his head and stared hard at him.

His nostrils flared slightly. Ben listened to the bull take a snorting breath.

He wasn't ready to give up yet. "How about I get that silly skirt off your horn, hmm?" Ben kept his voice and heart rate calm as he walked a little closer. "Easy there, big guy. I'm here to help."

Throughout his life, Ben had approached cattle in every type of situation. This one didn't belong to his family and wasn't used to his scent or the sight of him, but he wasn't too worried. Especially when the bull wasn't showing signs of aggression. Ben now had the attention of the nearby grazing cows, and they were curious and wary of the stranger in their pasture. They kept their eyes on him.

When Ben was within fifteen feet and the bull hadn't started walking away, he thought he might be able to pull off this miracle. The bull turned his head and eyed Ben as if suddenly deciding Ben was challenging his territory. He'd seen that look before, and it wasn't good. The bull snorted. Snot, bits of grass, and dirt huffed out of his large nostrils.

Ben moved back, respecting the animal's personal space. "Easy there. I'm going to take that skirt off your head." Ben spread his arms and hands slowly. The gesture was supposed to make himself look bigger and help discourage the bull from charging. But he forgot about the shoe missiles in his hand.

He could see and feel the exact second when the bull recognized the shoes. The bull's instinct-to-kill switch had flipped. His rear end swung around and the beast lowered his head.

"Fuck this," Ben said and paused, waiting for the exact right moment to move. The move that would save his life. The bull charged and Ben dodged to his left, evading the horns and the skirt. For a beast that weighed as much as a car, he was as nimble as a ballet dancer.

The bull ran, bucking and kicking right into the middle of his breeding group. The cows bawled, broke into two groups, and began a stampede. Four or five cows, along with the bull, were headed straight toward Ben. *Jesus*, if it were one or two cows, he could move out of the way, but with a herd coming at him, he didn't stand much of a chance. He ran like... like four tons of cattle were about to mow him down. He made it to the crest of the hill, glanced back, and saw they were gaining on him.

Ben's legs began stinging and his mind couldn't connect the sharp stabbing pains on his calves with the motion of sprinting for his life.

When he saw Maleah, he yelled, "Get back! Go! Get in the car!"

"What?" she asked, barely stepping away from the fence.

"Move!" he yelled as he barreled down the slope.

Ben veered away from Maleah as she screamed, "Cows!"

He reached for the top of a fencepost and stepped on the wire in one swift move. Vaulting over a barbed wire fence isn't a skill you learn in gym class. Ben improvised the best he could as he jumped and swung his legs over the top wire as he leaned most of his weight on one hand against the top of the post. It would have worked better if the cuff of his jeans hadn't snagged a barb.

He fell to the ground, rolled, and landed on his back. He had enough sense to glance back and make sure the cattle weren't suicidal enough to plow through the fence. Three cows went left and one went right. The others hadn't followed over the hill.

With eminent doom no longer breathing down his neck, Ben stared up at the raspberry-streaked sky. The colors of the sunset added a superb backdrop to the thundering beats of pounding hooves and his heart. A laugh moved through his chest and he felt mildly delirious. That was until Maleah's face came into view.

She stared down at him. "I tried to warn you."

He laughed a little harder until he was consumed with a sudden and voracious need to spew cuss words.

"Fucking hell! What the shit is going on?"

Maleah's eyes widened. "What? Are you hurt?"

"Yes!"

Sharp biting stings on his legs took priority of the moment. A painful stab to his inner thigh had his full attention. Ben flew off the ground and onto his feet. The distinct sensation of something crawling toward his crotch had him unbuttoning his jeans and reaching to save his boys as if he were about to be castrated. His jeans were around his knees when he caught a glimpse of the little fuckers. "Ants! Holy bejesus! Ahh!" he yelled when another red ant took a bite of his ass. He swatted and slapped. With his boots on he couldn't get out of his pants but at least he now knew what was attacking him.

"I told you there was a red ant pile next to the tire," Maleah said.

He responded with a sour look. "No, you didn't."

"I did. You may not have heard me, but I did. Twice."

Ben rolled his eyes and continued dealing with the new crisis. Bright and shiny clarity hit hard as to why Maleah had been mostly naked on the side of the road slapping herself. The bites stung like a bitch. A fiery hellish bitch.

With the knowledge that he was only battling ants, he was able to calm down enough to systematically remove them by brushing his hands over himself. He removed a lone assassin from his bunched-up jeans and then noticed the blood on his fingers.

"What kind of bloodthirsty ants are these?" He pulled up his jeans, leaving them unzipped in case he missed an ant or two. Ben inspected his work boots, looking for any more creepy buggers.

"I'm not bleeding," Maleah said unhelpfully. "The bites hurt, though."

Ben clenched his jaw and this time it didn't have anything to do with holding in a laugh.

"Oh, I see. Oh no." She flinched. "You tore your pants on the fence and the barbed wire must have cut you." Maleah squatted down for a closer look and reached toward the torn denim. Tentatively and with care, she eased the ripped jeans away from his cut. "Ooh…" She made a pained face. "That's not good."

"Stop that." Ben didn't care to be fussed over.

She glanced up. "I think we better get to town and get you cleaned up. When was your last tetanus shot?"

"Tetanus?" That was all that managed to come out of his mouth when they heard an approaching car. They both turned to look as a pickup truck crested the hill in the road, slowed, and came to a stop.

The window lowered. "Hey, Ben? I recognized your truck. Everything all right?"

The driver leaned toward the passenger side window for a better look. Ben recognized Gilbert Cantwell, an old friend from way back.

"We're good," Ben yelled back.

Gilbert's eyes widened, and his wide smile exposed the gap between his two front teeth. "Well, alrighty then. Sorry to interrupt your evening." He paused, squinting into the dimming evening light. "Is that Maleah Hale? Holy craptastic. Really?"

Maleah raised a hand and waved.

Gilbert's laughter echoed out of the truck window. "Ben and Maleah Hale. Smokin' frijoles," he said again as he sat back, honked the horn, and continued driving toward town.

Maleah looked up as Ben looked down.

"Umm." Ben reached to zip up his jeans. Maleah's face was less than a foot away from his open fly. Apparently, she hadn't caught on yet as to why Gilbert acted the way he did. He wasn't worried about his reputation, but hers. Gilbert would inform everyone and anyone what he'd witnessed out on Highway 9 next to the Donovan ranch.

Ben stepped back and buttoned his pants. "This probably doesn't look great from the road."

Watching the dawning realization hit her face was similar to seeing the clown pop out of the jack-in-the-box. Her cheeks flushed again, and the hue was nearly identical to the maroon glow on the underbelly of the clouds on the western horizon.

"But I'm… and you…" She rose to her full height. Maleah was always a little taller than most of the girls in school, and she looked him straight in the eyes and sighed. She shook her head and there was a twitch at the corner of her lips.

Ben started laughing again. He couldn't hold it in. "Shit," he said.

"Yeah. And my legs hurt. Stupid ants."

"Yeah," he agreed. "My leg hurts too. Grab your bags and I'll give you a ride into town. No one wants to fool around by that ant hill tonight. If it's all right, we'll deal with the tire tomorrow."

She took a moment to consider his offer. When she didn't answer, he asked, "You are headed into town, aren't you?"

Maleah smiled, and it softened her face and gave him a look at her for the first time since he'd pulled over that wasn't full of stress, biting ants, or angry bulls. She was beautiful in the most natural way and without heavy makeup or some fancy hairstyle.

"I was. I'm staying at my aunt Kiki's, in the Columbine Building."

That was a surprise he hadn't expected. "I'm headed downtown too," Ben said and didn't mention their other coincidence, because he had to get something off his chest first.

"Maleah?"

"Hmm?" She made the smallest of inquisitive sounds and waited for him to ask.

"Do you know there's a difference between a cow and a bull? It's kind of significant."

She jabbed him in the ribs with a pointy finger. "Of course I know the difference."

"Just checking. In case you ever have to explain how a cow stole the clothes off your ass again. Sometimes the devil's in the details. I could have benefitted from this small detail before heading into the pasture."

She had enough sense to look mildly abashed. "Don't tease me, Ben Erickson. In case you didn't notice, I was a little stressed out when you asked me why *my ass* was hanging out."

He loved how she punctuated the words "my ass." Ben smirked. *Having Maleah around is going to be fun.*

She placed a hand on her hip as one fine eyebrow lifted in a questioning glare. "Where the hell are my sandals?"

"I suspect the bull is wearing them. They match the skirt."

Four

BEN HELPED MALEAH TRANSFER her bags to his truck. They were careful to steer clear of the side of the car with the flat tire and the angry ants. Even so, Maleah checked her sneakers after sitting down on the passenger seat. No vicious red ants were to be found. She was grateful she packed more than one pair of shoes, but then again, Maleah didn't go anywhere without being overprepared.

On their drive into town, she and Ben shared more laughs over the incident by the side of the road.

Downtown Three Peaks came into view, and she said, "I think I need to stop at Franklin Drugs or the grocery store and find something to put on these bites. Do you have any antiseptic? You need to clean your cut." She hadn't packed her bottle because her knee had scabbed over.

Ben stroked his jaw and looked thoughtful. "I'm not all that concerned about my leg. I'm current on my tetanus shot. But if you want to stop, we can." He pulled into the parking lot of City Market and turned off the engine.

Maleah noticed the changes since the last time she'd shopped there. The aisles had been rearranged, and she didn't know where to go. But Ben did, and as they shopped together, it seemed every other person said hello to him or passed two or three glances their way.

"You have grass and weeds in your hair and on your back," she whispered after an elderly lady with a silver bouffant hairdo stared so hard at him she thought the woman's face might freeze in place.

Ben grabbed the bottle of antibacterial ointment off the shelf. "That's not why everyone is staring at us."

"They're not staring at us. They're staring at you."

"You can deny it if you want, but believe me when I tell you they're looking at you too."

"Am I covered in dirt and grass?" She didn't think so, and she'd shaken out her shirt and the pants were clean.

"You must have forgotten what it's like to live in Three Peaks," Ben said with a small, pitying shake of his head.

She slapped her hand to her forehead. "Oh, right. I keep forgetting."

Resigned, Maleah tried to ignore the stares as she grabbed the bites and stings relief ointment off the shelf. Then she picked up a tube of all-natural homeopathic plus essential oil remedy for bug bites and read the label. It looked promising, but the price was twice as much as the other medicine. She put it back. Her budget was so tight, she wasn't sure if she could afford to eat for the next couple days and have enough money to buy gas to get back to Boulder.

"What's that?" Ben asked.

"Another remedy. But I only need one." She couldn't admit how broke she was, and her next paycheck would be short because of losing her internship. She sighed and turned to leave the aisle.

Ben followed and they paid for their items. She noticed he bought the other bug-bite cream.

When they walked out and across the parking lot, he said, "Maleah?"

"Yeah?"

"I didn't want to say this inside, but your hair is a little wild after all the jumping around."

She groaned. The two of them must look like quite the pair. "Thanks a lot for telling me *before* we went inside the store."

"No problem." His smirk returned and she saw him holding back a laugh.

They drove three blocks down Main Street and turned left on Shavano Way. Her aunt owned three quarters of the Garden Block. After Kiki's husband died, she invested the life insurance money in real estate. She loved Three Peaks and believed the old buildings downtown needed to be saved, restored, and brought back to life. Maleah didn't know when Aunt Kiki had moved out of her house and started living downtown, but the questions were piling up.

Maleah was surprised when Ben turned into the alley and parked beside a mammoth-sized camper trailer in the shared parking lot of the Columbine and Aspen buildings.

"How did you know where to go?"

"I knew your aunt has been living here."

"Really? Did you hear she had an accident this weekend?"

"No, I didn't." Creases of concern knitted his brows. "I spent the weekend working at the ranch. Is Kiki all right?"

"I'm not sure yet. I'm back in town to be with her. She's at the hospital. I went there first, but she was napping. When she woke up, she was severely confused. I don't know if she recognized me. It was awful. The nurse suggested I come back tomorrow. I decided I would go to the overlook on Route 9 to watch the sunset and try to calm down before coming into town. That's where I was headed when you found me being attacked by the ants. I don't know how I got a flat tire."

"What you're telling me is, you're having a fantastic day and could use a drink."

"Pretty much," Maleah said, already accustomed to Ben's use of sarcasm and simple solutions. *If only he knew the rest,* she thought. "You don't have a tranquilizer gun, do you?" she mumbled.

He laughed. "That might be somewhat extreme, but if you really need it, I know someone who could hook us up."

"Maybe later. First, I should go inside and see if the bug cream works." Maleah reached for the door handle.

"I'll walk you in. It's a large building, and I know my way around."

"You do?" she asked, surprised.

"I've been doing some work for Kiki," he said and didn't elaborate before opening the door and stepping into the pale glow of the streetlights behind the Columbine Building.

Maleah grabbed the shopping bag, then retrieved her overnight bag. Ben took the suitcase from the back seat of the four-door pickup. She'd noticed his tool belt, work gloves, and duffle bag in the back seat and wondered what Ben did for a living.

Maleah looked for the flower pot that her mother said was where Aunt Kiki hid the key to the building, but Ben walked to the back door and inserted a key.

"You have your own key?" There were so many questions that needed answering, but Maleah's brain was fried and all she wanted was to soak in a hot shower and pass out. If the ointment eased the sting of the bug bites, then all the better.

"I do. Come on in." He held the door open.

They entered a pitch-black hallway, and Maleah waited for her eyes to adjust. A narrow sliver of light entered the building from the alleyway behind them. She heard and felt Ben's movements beside her.

A repetitive clicking sound penetrated the darkness before Ben said, "Electricity is off."

"Of course it is. This is my life now." She set her overnight bag down and pulled out her phone. As Maleah turned on the flashlight, it rang.

"It's my mom," she said to Ben, then answered the call.

"Maleah? Is that you?"

"Hi, Mom. I meant to call after leaving the hospital, but I got distracted. Sorry," she said.

"I already know you're distracted. That's the reason I'm calling. I thought you were in Three Peaks to take care of Aunt Kiki. Why didn't you tell me you and Ben Erickson are seeing each other? I've known his parents forever. You didn't have to keep your relationship a secret."

"I'm sorry. What?" Maleah couldn't believe what she'd just heard come out of her mother's mouth.

"Did you not tell me because of Holden? It's okay, honey. If you're no longer interested in your handsome boss, you can tell me. Ben was always a good kid. He's kind of quiet, though. Are you sure he's no longer with that Kinsey? You know, I never liked her. She's what you might call high-maintenance. They were a cute couple in high school, but—"

"Mom, stop," Maleah interrupted. "How did you know I am with Ben?" Then she realized how the question might sound. "I mean, I—" Her tongued twisted, and she stammered before getting the words out correctly. "I'm not with Ben. I mean he's standing here, but we're not together, together. I had car trouble." *And ant trouble, and cow trouble, and now electricity trouble*, but she kept that to herself. "Ben found me and my car on Route 9. He gave me a ride to town. We're at Aunt Kiki's building downtown right now."

Her mother tsked into the phone. Actually tsked, as if Maleah was doing something shameful.

"Really, Maleah," she said as if her disappointment in her daughter couldn't sink any lower. "Rebecca Shoemaker called and said Lori from the bakery department at the grocery store had quite the story to tell her about you. Are you telling me Rebecca is lying? She's been a friend since we moved to Three Peaks. Just because your father and I retired to Hawaii doesn't mean we don't still have connections in town."

"Mom?" Maleah interrupted again. "I'm going to say this one time. There's nothing going on between me and Ben Erickson. If you call his mother, so help me God, I will never speak to you again."

Silence fell over the line, and Maleah wondered if she'd gone too far, or if Jona had already called Mrs. Erickson. But seriously? What in the world was happening? The absurdity of small-town gossip was too much for her at the moment.

"Well, then I should tell you that I don't need to call Mrs. Erickson because Rebecca already did. And I don't appreciate the tone, Maleah. I was excited to hear about your new relationship, and a little worried you were keeping good news from me," Jona said with a touch of concern that Maleah wasn't falling for.

She groaned, then settled her rankled nerves before starting over. "My only news is that I wasn't able to spend more than five minutes with Aunt Kiki. I'll go back first thing in the morning, but she didn't look good. Sorry. I wish I had better news. It's been a tough couple of days, Mom."

"Oh goodness. Okay. I'll let you go. I didn't mean to upset you."

"You didn't."

"I did," she argued.

"You didn't. Everything is fine," Maleah said, trying to end the call before her head exploded.

"It's not fine."

Arguing with her mother felt similar to beating her head against a mattress. It was pointless and didn't accomplish anything, but was still repetitively annoying. "I need to go now. I'll call tomorrow from the hospital."

"Okay. Keep me updated. I apologize for overreacting. You know how I get when it comes to your love life. I want grandbabies more than anything else. Your children will be adorable and beautiful."

Maleah cut her off before getting sucked into another wormhole of agonizing parental torture. "I'll keep it in mind. Bye. Love you too." She disconnected. Maleah blinked at the phone and wondered if death by ant bite would be more enjoyable.

"Hey," Ben said from somewhere behind her.

Maleah turned and they stepped outside together to stand beneath the dim glow of a streetlight in the alley. She was speechless after the weirdest call of her life. Someone called her mother in Hawaii to tell on her. What in the ever-lovin' this-is-no-one's-business-but-her-own kind of town was this? Ben didn't question her diminishing sanity as she stood there unable to talk.

"While you were on the phone, I checked with the electrician. He was here earlier today and didn't have the right part to make the repair. He'll be back tomorrow and should have the electricity on sometime in the afternoon."

"No electricity," she repeated, disbelieving, and then mumbled to herself more than to Ben, "Which means no lights, no cooking, freezer thawing, and probably no water either."

"You have hot water. The tank is heated with gas."

"Good, because even if I have to use candlelight, I need a shower."

"But..." Ben added knowingly and slowly. "The water pump is electric."

Kill me now. The vision of sleeping in the dark cold building or in the chair beside Aunt Kiki's bed at the hospital were fast becoming Maleah's best options. Paying for a hotel room wasn't in her non-existent budget.

After the extremely long day and too many things weighing heavily on her mind, defeat threatened to consume her.

"What now? Do you want to go inside and look around? We can use flashlights. The building is a work in progress, but it's great."

Maleah shook her head and stared at Ben's truck. "I hate to ask, but would you mind driving me to the hospital?"

"Why?" Ben asked.

"I don't have anywhere else to go." She felt embarrassed to say it, but without forewarning or an invitation, she didn't feel comfortable asking old friends, either hers or her parents', for a place to sleep. "I can't stay here and I need to be with Aunt Kiki."

"Err," Ben said. "I, uh," he stalled.

"I can't ask you and Kinsey to let me crash at your place. Thanks, though, but I really couldn't. Kinsey and I were never friends. It would be weird. And awkward. And weird. Did I already say it would be uncomfortable? It would be."

Ben lowered his gaze down and to the left. His jaw hardened just long enough for Maleah to notice, and then he stared toward his truck.

She didn't know if he would give her another ride, but she could hitchhike if necessary. If no one picked her up, she would walk. It wouldn't take too long, and the way her day had been going, a long, cold walk was what the universe probably had planned for her.

He said, "I wasn't going to offer you a room at the house."

Embarrassment and humiliation were simply icing on the cake. She stammered, "I'm such a goof. And I'm tired. I'm sorry for jumping ahead. I do that sometimes." Maleah walked over to the back door of the building. "Can you lock up? There's supposed to be a key around here, but with my luck it was swallowed by an alligator, and I probably will be too if I go searching for it."

"Maleah." Ben stepped in her path and held his ground. "I was going to offer you a place to sleep, but not in my old house. I've been staying in the camper." He tipped his head in the general direction of the fifth-wheel behemoth.

"What about Kinsey?"

Kinsey Robson and Ben were married the summer after graduation. When Maleah was growing up, Kinsey treated her like an outcast. Over many years, Kinsey made fun of her clothes, her honor roll status, and anything to make Maleah feel less than the pretty and popular blonde. Maleah learned to avoid Kinsey and her group of friends at all costs. Their maliciousness wasn't worth her time or energy. Maleah wasn't about to walk in on her and Ben's life now.

"Kinsey is not staying in the camper," Ben said. "It's sort of my office and my home at the jobsites. Come on. You can take a look inside, and if you want the spare room for the night, it's yours. There's even a shower with hot water."

The mention of a hot shower had her aching, stinging legs begging for relief, but she hesitated. Staying in Ben's camper didn't seem right. What did she know about Ben Erickson? Just because they grew up together didn't guarantee he wasn't a closet-gorilla-porn-watching-hot-dog-eating-contest-champion. *Is this what delirium is?*

"If I could take a load off for a few minutes and regroup, that would be nice. Thanks," Maleah said and mentally patted herself on the back for sounding like a reasonable, functioning adult for two seconds.

"Good idea." Ben entered the Columbine Building, then returned with Maleah's bags. He locked up and said, "Come with me."

A tornado had definitely hit an office supply store, made a run through a hardware store, whirled through the sporting goods, and then landed inside Ben's camper. Maleah stood at the door and wondered if she should leave her bags outside. There wasn't any other place to put them.

"Excuse the mess." His gaze seemed to move over the heaps and mounds cluttering the table and counter space before he turned an apologetic eye on her. "I'm in transition. This isn't normal." Ben opened the door at the front of the trailer. She watched his back and listened as he shuffled things around in what she presumed to be the spare bedroom. He returned a minute later. "It's good in there. I swear." He ran a hand over his short honey-colored hair. Ben picked up her suitcase and placed it inside the bedroom before she could object. Then he set about cleaning off the kitchen table, his movements hurried and disorganized.

"Please. You don't have to clean up for me."

"I know, but we need space to work on my leg."

"Oh! That's right. You're bleeding."

He shrugged dismissively as he stacked a laptop, notebooks, blueprints, piles of receipts, and computer paper into another heap. Maleah set her travel bag down in the small bedroom then took the shopping bag with the ointments to the decluttered table.

"Do you have paper towels or a clean washcloth?"

"Maybe," he said, opening one of the kitchen cabinets.

"Sit down," she ordered and gestured to the bench at the table.

Ben held a paper towel under the faucet and then turned to Maleah. "I think I can handle this on my own."

She shook her head and gave her most stern face. "No. I want to look. It's my fault you cut yourself. I want to see if you need stitches. She stared at his ripped pant leg but didn't see much blood. That was a good sign.

Ben sat, crossed one leg over the other to lift his cut ankle and calf, and began rolling up the remains of his torn pant leg. Maleah set the bottles and tubes of medicines on the table and picked up the wet towel. She stood over Ben's lower leg and stared.

"I've had worse damage," he said as he picked dead grass and a string from his ripped sock out of the scabby mess. Removing the debris from his cut caused blood to start leaking again. Ben glanced at the bottle of disinfectant. "Towel?"

Maleah reached out to either place the paper towel on the gash or hand it to Ben, but the bright red blood oozing from the cut and running over his ankle made her feel lightheaded. *Oh no.* She'd experienced this before. The sight of blood made her pass out. *No. Hold it together, girl.* Maleah tried to breathe, but the air was too shallow, too thin. There wasn't enough of it. The lights were going out, and Maleah couldn't stop the darkness from closing in on her.

"Maleah! Crap! Maleah!"

Before she opened her eyes, she listened to Ben panic. "What is going on? Maleah! Woman, wake up. Jesus! Should I call nine-one-one?"

"No," she said, the lightheadedness fading slowly but steadily. "The sight of blood makes me pass out."

"Shit! Don't do that! That's messed up." He raked both hands through his hair, leaving wild tufts sticking out in different directions. "Why didn't you tell me that *before* trying to help?!"

A tiny smile lifted the corners of her mouth at his emphasis on the word "before."

Lying down felt nice. *How did I get on the floor?* She must have fallen. Maleah mentally performed a quick body check to make sure nothing hurt. Everything checked out, and her gaze landed on Ben. The years had aged him but in a good way. Maturity looked great on Ben Erickson, and his day job obviously increased muscle tone, or he worked out... a lot. But she didn't think so. He didn't have the air of a gym monkey. His muscle tone had the quality of endurance *and* strength. The three-day beard wasn't scruffy or unkempt, but trimmed and neat. Maleah blinked and realized they'd both been staring at each other. Although she didn't have the stress lines creasing her brows like he did.

"I forgot." She pushed herself into a sitting position.

"You forgot that you black out when you see blood?" His tone indicated a level of disbelief and or irritation.

"Oops." She shrugged before picking herself up.

"That isn't something that's easily forgettable," he continued.

Maleah reached for the edge of the countertop and held on to something in case her body decided to betray her again. "I don't see fresh blood often... or ever. Normally, if I get woozy, I sit down before passing out. I was distracted. My entire day has been distracting."

"Mm-hmm." Ben made an exasperated sound and sat back down to inspect his injury.

"I'll step into the other room and take care of my ant bites and you do the same out here, mmm-kay?"

"Great idea," he said, still sounding irritable.

She grabbed the ointment and disappeared into the other room.

Five

THEY MET BACK IN THE MIDDLE of his trailer, a.k.a. his office and living space. Maleah appeared to have freshened up... and she was gorgeous. In the span of a few magical moments, she'd done something with her hair and clothes. *Yep,* she'd changed her outfit again. Ben took an appreciative look at Maleah Hale. *Foxy much?* Dang, he couldn't remember having such an instant response to someone before. And now it'd happened twice in the same day. He didn't possess the words to describe the consuming mental and physical reaction. Struck dumb was the closest explanation.

Ben had also stepped into his room and changed into clean, untorn clothes after attending to the cut on his leg. He wasn't concerned about the injury. It would heal and wasn't deep. The story about how he'd attained the scratches far outweighed the damages. And he was starving and in need of that beer he'd wanted hours earlier.

"You want to walk over to The Jackalope with me?"

Maleah glanced away, then up at the ceiling as if she might be uncomfortable.

He rubbed his suddenly sweaty palms on the front of his jeans. "Sorry about my temper. I've never dealt with someone falling to the floor before. You took me by surprise, and it freaked me out."

She nodded with the tiniest lift of her chin, acknowledging she'd heard him. Ben watched Maleah chew her lower lip. The way she stood, or the look on her face, brought back a memory of her as an awkward, skinny, and tall tween-aged girl. His heart warmed a little with the nostalgia. He suddenly recalled how sensitive and gentle Maleah had been when they were kids.

Ben stepped forward, moving closer to the door. "Can I buy you dinner? I haven't eaten and could use a drink. I usually walk over to The Jackalope after work and grab something."

"What is The Jackalope?" she asked.

"The brewery. They have a decent menu. How long's it been since you were in town? The brewery opened over two years ago."

"It's been about two years. My parents retired to Hawaii, and Aunt Kiki is my last relative in town. She and I flew to visit them last year, and I haven't been back to Three Peaks. I guess I've been too busy."

"Time flies, yeah? Come to the brewery and fill me in on the rest of what you've been up to all these years."

She still looked hesitant, so Ben opened the door and said, "I bet you need something to eat as much as I do." At the grocery store, he'd noticed she was careful not to spend too much and wondered if she were struggling with her finances. He said, "I'm buying, so why not? You don't even have to sit with me if you don't want to."

She laughed. "Really? You don't care if I sit and read on my phone, in my own booth, and you'll pay?"

"Whatever suits your disposition is all right by me." Ben walked outside but held the door.

She followed and stopped in front of him. "I appreciate it, Ben. I'll even sit with you. But I won't bore you with stories about work or the years I spent at school. I want to hear about you and your life since high school."

"Err... there's not much to tell."

"I doubt that. Even if your life seems boring to you, I want to hear everything."

Ben shut the door and thought about how he could make his existence of being a teenaged parent while taking college courses and building a construction company over the last nine years sound interesting. He couldn't. Had his life been that uneventful? His twenties were coming to an end, and he had a new start-up business and a camper to show for it. *Nah*. Maleah didn't need to hear any of that noise. "Everything about me since high school can be summed up in one famous Groucho Marx quote: 'Man is not in control of his own fate. The women in his life do that for him.'"

She fell into step next to him and laughed. "My father used to always say that we should go through life like a duck: 'Majestic on top, but kicking like hell underneath.'"

Ben let that sink in for a second. He'd been paddling nonstop for months, years. "Yeah," he said, giving the short reply.

They headed down the alley between the Columbine and Aspen buildings toward Main Street.

"So, where's this new brewery?"

* * *

The sparse Tuesday night crowd gathered at the bar or occupied a few tables inside The Jackalope. Summer was coming to a close, and school had resumed, which meant the number of tourists in town was at a minimum. They had about a month before the leafers returned to the mountains for the annual turning of the aspen leaves. Ben was glad to be in the off season and not have to wait for a table as he led Maleah to a booth. He gave Dana, The Jack's Tuesday night waitress, a wave as they crossed the dining room.

Dana's hands were busy with a tray full of pint glasses, but she called over, "I'll be right with you."

Ben and Maleah slid into the booth.

"What's good?" she asked.

"The Jackalope stout. If you want a lighter brew, try the summer wheat. The pale ale is strong and hoppy, but if you like the bitterness with some pine and citrus flavors, the Continental Divide IPA is the best in the county."

"I meant the food, but drinking our dinner is another option to consider."

"And a choice I can stand behind." Ben winked and then added, "But not tonight. Real food is a must. Everything is good. What are you in the mood for?"

"Anything."

"A girl with an open mind. I like that."

"And I'm so hungry I could eat a plate of grubs and be happy," she said.

Dana stepped up to the table and handed over some menus. "Grubs aren't on the menu this week, but the salmon salad is top-notch. If you're looking for something a little more local and exotic, try the Rocky Mountain oysters. What can I bring you to drink, loves?"

Ben looked at Maleah. "Do you want to sample what The Jackalope has to offer in the ever-expanding craft brew biz?"

"I do," she said with a bright smile.

Ben refocused on Dana, a difficult task, since he was drawn to Maleah's face and captivating mouth. "We'll share a flight, and can you bring some water?"

"You got it." Dana jotted down the drink order.

"Would you like anything else?" Ben asked Maleah.

"No, thank you."

After Dana shimmied away toward the bar, Ben and Maleah opened their menus.

She said, "Grilled salmon on salad sounds perfect. I'm not so sure about eating Rocky Mountain oysters. Have you ever had them?"

Ben's eyebrows stretched toward his hairline. Did Maleah know what Rocky Mountain oysters were? Her inquisitive expression suggested she didn't know they were deep-fried bull testicles. Ben licked his lips, kept a straight face, and said, "I have a nut allergy."

That broke her and she giggled. Maleah turned her head and lowered her lashes against rosy cheeks as her shoulders shook with laughter.

Apparently, she does know.

"I too have suddenly developed a nut allergy. Although I met a certain bull today who deserves such a fate."

Ben grinned at her sharp wit and appreciation of his humor. "Harsh."

She shrugged impishly as Dana returned with the sampler tray of seven different beers crafted at The Jackalope brewery. She took their food order, left the table, and Maleah's phone started buzzing.

"It's my cousin, Brielle. I need to answer. It's about Aunt Kiki." Maleah gave an apologetic look.

"Go ahead. It's no problem."

Maleah slid out of the booth and took the call outside. Ben drank half a glass of water before picking up one of the four-ounce beers from the taster tray.

As the light-bodied cream ale met its end, satisfying Ben's thirst for beer, Gilbert Cantwell and William Johansson slid into the booth, sitting across from him.

"The two of you combined aren't half as nice looking as Maleah, so get out," he said, half joking but mostly serious. He'd known these two clowns most of his life, but that didn't mean he had to put up with them. And seeing how Gilbert had already told half the town what he thought he saw on the side of the road, he knew a slaying was about to befall him.

"That's hurtful," William said. "Especially coming from a naked mole rat such as yourself."

"Nice. I'll take your naked mole rat, raise you a blobfish, and tell you two to beat it," Ben threw back.

"That's what she's for." Gilbert picked up a beer from the flight on the table.

Ben watched Gilbert help himself to his beer and said, "No. It's not. She's here visiting her aunt."

Gilbert chugged the lager, nodding to himself, and then said, "I saw everything. Kiki had some kind of episode. I had just left the brewery when the ambulance arrived. She didn't look too good to me. I hope she's all right. Have you heard any news? It'd suck if she kicked the bucket. You'd lose all that work she's hired you to do."

William elbowed Gilbert in the ribs. "You were so wasted, man. I don't know how you remembered anything from the other night. I had to drive your sorry ass home."

Ben waited patiently and was glad the conversation had turned to other gossip that didn't include himself or Maleah. "I was out at the ranch all weekend and today. I don't know a thing about what happened."

"You best find out if your employer is alive and kickin', dude," Gilbert said.

"Thanks for your concern," Ben said with little patience for Gilbert's lack of consideration and tact for the situation. He'd grown close to Kiki Brookhart, and she meant more to him than a steady paycheck.

"And I'm concerned about your new relationship status."

William placed his meaty forearms on the table, interlaced his fingers, and shook his head in agreement.

Gilbert continued, "You and Maleah Hale, huh? I couldn't believe it when I saw you two. So explain it to me, dude. How the heck did you get Maleah Hale to come back to this backwater Podunk nothing of a town? I thought she fled the coop and would never look back."

Ben inhaled a steadying breath. He'd already said why Maleah was in town.

"I wanted to marry that girl," William said. "She even went with me to homecoming one year. Afterward, she told me she thought of me as more of a brother."

"Ripped poor Will's heart out and ground it into the dirt with her heel, she did," Gilbert said and picked up another beer.

"Save some beer for Maleah," Ben said with a pointed look.

Gilbert lowered the glass and put it back on the tray. Maleah returned, phone in hand. She made eye contact with Ben and then said hello to the boys.

"Little Maleah Hale is all grown up. Damn, it's good to see you, lady," Gilbert said.

He should have stopped there, but Gilbert being Gilbert, added, "I can't believe you're seeing this doofus. How did Ben nail you down? Tell me his secrets so I can find someone as pretty as you."

William elbowed his friend again. Then he looked up at Maleah. "Gilbert hasn't learned the art of silence. Once an idiot, always a moron. How've you been? Is your great-aunt doing okay?"

Maleah made a pained expression. "I'm not sure yet. I need to go back and visit her again tomorrow morning. Thanks for asking about Aunt Kiki, Will. That's thoughtful of you."

Ben watched the exchange between William and Maleah and wondered if a girl like her would consider dating William. Back in the day, he'd known Will had a crush on Maleah and that she never took his advances seriously. William never married, and as far as Ben knew, he almost never dated. Could he still be burning a torch for Maleah after all these years? He supposed so. *Look at her.* Why hadn't Ben seen it before? Oh right, Kinsey had eclipsed his world. What an ignorant teenaged fool he'd been. Well, that was never going to happen to him again. He'd sworn to it.

Gilbert was never one to be ignored for long and said, "Ben told me not to drink your beer. Which one do you like the best and I'll order pints for everyone."

Maleah stood at the end of the table, since the boys had commandeered her seat. She chose a beer from the taster tray and took her first drink. "Which one is this?"

"The Arête Amber Ale," Ben said.

"This is tasty." She took another drink.

"I'll buy the next round," Gilbert offered and picked up the stout.

William chimed in again, taking everyone off guard. "So, are you dating our Ben here, or is Gilbert spreading horrible rumors?"

The color in her cheeks rose. God bless her porcelain skin, Ben thought with a snicker. He was coming up with the proper sarcastic response to William's untimely inquiry, but his tongue was busy swallowing the IPA.

Unfortunately, Maleah appeared to choke after hearing the question. She sputtered once, then sprayed beer on the glass and on her hand. Beer dribbled down her chin, and she went to wipe it away but smacked herself in the face with the glass. Flinching caused more spilled beer and now her shirt was wet. Three men fixated on the fascinating new "Maleah Show." Ben tore his gaze away and reached for the napkins. He offered them to her. She dabbed away the mess, then surprised Ben by sliding onto the seat next to him. Maleah planted a kiss on his cheek, then turned to face Gil and Will. She flashed her perfectly straight, orthodontically enhanced smile that was camera worthy.

"Ben's my savior. Truly, and we couldn't be more thrilled about reconnecting after so many years. I'm a lucky girl to have found him. If you don't mind, we're having a small, private celebration dinner."

Maleah squeezed Ben's leg beneath the table in a gesture that he thought she wanted him to go along with this contrived malarkey more than copping a feel of his thigh. Although the placement of her hand was acutely acknowledged by his bat and man Rocky Mountain oysters.

Ben cleared his throat. "You heard her, boys. The lady would appreciate a little privacy."

"I knew it!" Gilbert said. "You two look like a couple. I said to myself after seeing you two gettin' it on, 'Good for them.' I always liked you, Maleah. You're a sweetheart, and Ben needs that after the whole Kinsey mess."

Ben may or may not have accidentally thrust his steel-toed work boot into Gilbert's shin, but the effect was as desired. Gilbert shut his trap about Kinsey.

"Ouch!" Gilbert glared at Ben for a second then turned to Will. "Come on, pal." He slid over, pushing his way out of the booth. "I need a beer and I promised the happy couple I'd buy the next round."

William resembled a sad puppy as he and Gilbert found their feet. Ben wasn't about to rub salt in William's wounded heart, even if there was no relationship and Maleah was lying through her pretty white teeth. *What is she up to?*

Gilbert headed to the bar, but William lingered for another minute. "It's really good to see you, Maleah. I'm online all the time. You should friend request me so we can stay in touch. Or maybe you're not on social media? I live in town too. Ben knows where I live. We should have a cookout or something."

"Yeah. That'd be all right. Aunt Kiki needs me, but I'll check my schedule. Have a good night."

William looked reluctant, but he turned and joined Gil at the bar. Maleah moved back to her seat and didn't speak as she drank another beer.

Ben leaned forward and lowered his voice. "Does this mean we're officially dating?" he teased.

She placed her forearms on the table, meeting him halfway, and deflected the question like a pro. "Are you and Kinsey no longer together? When did that happen? And I'm sorry to hear it."

He did not want to talk about his ex. *Repeat that. No ex at the dinner table.* Ben scrunched up his face for a second and then tried to relax his jaw so he could speak.

Ben returned to the previous subject. "You may have crushed poor Will's soul. Gilbert said you stole his heart back in high school, and it appears you still own it."

She whispered conspiratorially, "It's in a jar in my mother's basement. Don't mess with me or you could suffer even worse consequences."

Ben sat back and saluted her. "Duly noted."

Their food arrived and Maleah shared the story about how William wouldn't stop asking her out when they were in the ninth grade. She refused to go out with him again after the homecoming dance, and he began leaving notes on her locker and giving her little gifts. Although he was a nice guy, she would never feel the same way about him as he did her. She didn't want to go through that again, which was why she lied about dating Ben.

"Since I'm only in town until I find out more about Aunt Kiki's condition, or until my cousin Brielle arrives, do you mind if Gilbert and William think we're seeing each other?" She took a bite of her salad, swallowed, and then apologized. "Sorry to put you on the spot without asking first, but I reacted badly, and now it's done."

"It's no problem on my end. I'll be working all week in the Aspen Building. I doubt I'll even be seeing you much after tonight," Ben said.

"Thanks." She let out a deep breath. "I appreciate it. I have a lot on my plate right now, and I don't need William distracting me too."

They finished eating, shared some laughs over school memories, and caught up on some mutual acquaintances. Time seemed to disappear as he talked with her, and then before he knew it, they had returned to the camper.

"You're still welcome to use the spare room if I passed the stranger-danger test."

"I wasn't testing you," she said. "Okay, maybe I was a little concerned at first about staying here. It has been over a decade since we've talked."

"I don't blame you for being wary. I would expect it, honestly. But I take it I passed with flying colors." He grinned, then unlocked the door and held it for her to enter first.

"You passed," she admitted. "And somehow I'll repay your kindness. I'm not sure how, but I'll make it up to you."

"You don't owe me a thing," he said as they settled in.

Ben found clean towels—thank God he'd remembered to do laundry last week before heading out to the ranch—and they stood in the central living/dining area, making sounds about going to bed and tomorrow's busy schedule.

"There's Wi-Fi if you need it. The password is longduckdong16, all one word," he said, wondering if she had any idea where the movie reference came from.

"What's happening, hot stuff?" she said with an incredibly bad Asian accent and not missing a beat. "Why do you have a *Sixteen Candles* password?"

"I have no idea. My brain holds onto the weirdest information."

"It's easy to memorize at least. I loved that movie. I used to have rom-com movie marathons when I needed some downtime."

"I don't know if I've ever seen the whole thing," he admitted.

"You know who Long Duck Dong is, but you haven't seen the movie?"

"Maybe?" he said as a question.

She nodded but wore a look of supreme uncertainty that made him smile. Maleah pushed her long dark hair back and hit her elbow on the corner of the wall.

"Ooh! I hit my funny bone." She flinched with the pain, then cradled her elbow in her other hand. Maleah turned and somehow collided with the bathroom door. She jumped back and managed to go perfectly still. Except for her breathing. Her chest rose and fell in fast, short breaths.

Ben watched the newest episode of Maleah Failing at Life and said, "Maleah, can I ask you something?"

She squinted at him as she rubbed her elbow. "If you really want to. But I'm an honest girl, so let that be your warning."

"Are you always such a train wreck?"

She didn't dignify his question with an answer at first and settled with giving him a haughty glare.

Finally, she said, "I don't think it's in my best interest to divulge my secrets to someone like you."

"Someone like me, huh?" He gave her a slow grin. "You were always the smartest one in our class. I wouldn't share secrets with me either. My villainous side has been known to sneak up on me when I least expect it. Then I get into trouble."

"Says the guy who buys me dinner and lets me sleep inside his trailer for no other reason than being nice."

"Don't be too sure I don't have ulterior motives."

The way he looked at her indicated that he definitely did.

"I guess I'll take my chances."

"She plays with fire and dances naked on ant hills. I always thought of you as more reserved and kind of shy."

They stood across from each other in the camper, Ben leaning against the kitchen counter and Maleah against the closed bathroom door. She tucked her hands behind her back.

"I guess I've grown up some since I lived here."

Should I make a move? She was too damned cute and sexy to boot. A cute sexy train wreck. Exactly what he didn't need. Ben didn't know how to do this. He'd only ever been with Kinsey, and he barely remembered anything about dating. Before Kinsey, he had been playing in the kiddie league. *Do you want to come over and play my Xbox?* didn't feel like an appropriate pick-up line at this age.

"Good night, Maleah. Make yourself at home. Hope you don't mind stuffed animals and a lot of purple. My daughter sleeps in that room when she stays here on the weekends."

Maleah glanced into the spare room then said, "I like stuffies, and purple."

Ben nodded, turned, and walked to the bedroom on the other end of the fifth wheel camper, closing the door behind him.

Six

WHEN BEN WOKE UP he sported an impressive stiffy. *Great. Freaking wonderful.* The gorgeous babe thirty feet away had absolutely nothing to do with his hard-on. *Nope, not a thing.* His current condition surely couldn't be related to the vivid images of her naked ass bouncing up and down alongside the road, which were now permanently stamped on his memory. Or her sultry laugh at dinner that felt like silk stroking his eardrums. *Stroking.* His thoughts were making things exponentially worse.

One important life lesson Ben learned when he was thirteen years old was that no matter how much you believed you had privacy in your own bedroom, anyone, especially parental figures, could and would come barging in at the most inopportune moment. Ben opted for a cold shower instead of taking care of things with a more hands-on approach.

After showering, Ben dressed and readied himself for the work day. Maleah's door remained closed, and he didn't want to disturb her. His schedule for the day was packed, but he could spare an hour to drive out to the hospital. Kiki was currently his most important client, due to the extensive amount of work she'd hired him to complete on her buildings. He felt he owed her a lot for hiring him to act as her general contractor, but besides the business aspects of their relationship, Ben had a soft spot for the elderly woman. Since her husband had passed away and she'd moved downtown, Kiki Brookhart had become like a grandmother to him. At least in some ways. He saw her nearly every day, and she always wanted to know if he'd eaten and she never forgot to ask about Skyla. If his daughter was with him, she would give her treats or small presents. Sometimes, Kiki would even give his daughter money for candy or ice cream. Kiki may be a little eccentric, but she was selfless, thoughtful, and had the energy of a woman half her age. Ben liked her a lot. Since his paternal grandmother had passed away when he was a teen, he didn't mind being fussed over by someone who had decades of life experience and owned too many flowery knickknacks and teacups.

His grandfather was a resident at the assisted-living facility, which was part of the Mount Tenderfoot Medical Complex. Ben needed to stop in and drop off the hot wings Grandpa Joe liked. He would be a day earlier than his usual weekly visit, but his grandpa wouldn't mind. Ben wasn't sure if Grandpa ever knew what day of the week it was anymore. Dementia hadn't been kind to the old man.

Ben grabbed a bottled sports drink out of the fridge and a protein bar from the cabinet and left the trailer as quietly as possible. A real breakfast would have to wait until later. If he saw Maleah, he'd offer to buy her a coffee at Mad Mountain Roasters. Prudence's Perk Place was closer, but Kinsey had claimed their favorite coffee and breakfast café as belonging to her during the divorce. Ben attempted to eat there one time since splitting up with Kinsey, and his order had been "accidentally" forgotten. When he finally received a cup of coffee to go, it wasn't what he ordered. Based on the icy glares from the girls behind the counter, Ben decided Prudence's was permanently closed to him. It didn't matter that he'd been a customer since the day they opened. What Kinsey must have told them was beyond his comprehension, but he knew where he wasn't wanted.

Ben pulled his keys out of his pocket to open up the Aspen Building. The electrician would be back to finish the job inside the Columbine Building, and then Phil of Phil's Electric was supposed to move on to the Aspen Building. Ben's subcontracted plumbers were currently replacing the fifty-year-old water and sewage lines. The plumbers were a great group of guys he'd worked with for years. Greg, the owner, had no problem sticking with him after the divorce debacle. Phil's Electric, on the other hand, were based over in Kebler, and Ben hadn't worked with him before. So far, Ben thought Phil's electrical skills were on par, but the man was hit and miss in the reliability department. Whether or not he showed up to work was completely dependent on the season. Skiing season led directly into fishing season, and Ben understood better than most that in Colorado, archery season was almost here and took precedence over most day jobs.

While he wagered the odds of Phil finishing the electrical job before hunting season started, Ben unlocked the deadbolt. The sound of an approaching vehicle caught his attention and he glanced down the alley. He half expected to see Greg, the plumber, but instead he stared at the familiar front end of his ex-wife's SUV.

Ben didn't know exactly what time it was, but if his daughter was in the car, he wanted to say good morning. That was the only reason he waited for Kinsey to park.

She shut off the motor but didn't get out. Ben could see her staring at her phone, and he suppressed the urge to roll his eyes. The back windows of the SUV were tinted dark enough that he couldn't see if Skyla was inside or not. Standing around trying to be patient wasn't one of Ben's strongest personality traits. He walked up to the car and Kinsey continued to ignore him. He opened the bottle of cherry flavored electrolytes and drank half of it before she opened the door.

"Where's Skyla?"

"At school."

"It's early, isn't it?" Ben said.

"She likes to eat breakfast with her friends before the morning bell." Kinsey lifted her chin and wore her customary look of being ready for an argument based solely on the way Ben was breathing that morning.

This was news to Ben, and was one more jab at the open wound inside his chest that was labeled "Horrible Parent." What else was new with his daughter that he didn't know about? He would have to wait until this weekend's visitation to find out. "I have work to do. Did you need something?" he asked. The faster he could get to the point, the better.

"I need to talk to you. Can we go inside?"

"No. Say your piece out here," Ben said. He didn't want to get comfortable with Kinsey. They were not friends. Nor would they ever be again. She'd lied in court to make him look bad. She'd accused him of doing things that she was guilty of. If she didn't start talking soon, he was walking away.

"I'm moving and Skyla is coming with me."

"The hell she is," Ben said as alarm bells rang inside each and every one of his blood cells.

"Mario is being transferred to Anchorage. The job is too good to pass up. He asked me to go with him."

"You should go. You should move as far away from Three Peaks as possible," Ben said with so much calm certainty that Kinsey should have known it was time to climb back inside the car—the car Ben had bought and paid for—and driven away before things got ugly. "But you will not be taking my daughter to fucking Alaska." He kept his voice steady, but his nerves were already on edge due to the topic of discussion.

When it came to fighting, Kinsey could never walk away and come back when the two of them had calmed down. And Ben had learned everything he knew about bickering and backstabbing from her.

"I'll do whatever the hell I want. You should be thanking me for telling you in person. My lawyer thought I should send a letter."

"What? How long have you been planning to take Skyla?"

Her gaze shifted, and she suddenly wouldn't look at him. *Oooh.* Anger hummed close to the surface, but Ben held himself in check... for now. She was too easy to read. Kinsey had been planning this for a while. She'd spoken to her lawyer about this and who knew what else.

"I'm closing on the house in three weeks."

"You sold our house!"

"My house," she said, lips tightening as she threw him the defiant, bitch-with-her-broom-stuck-up-her-ass look once again.

Ben was about to walk away. He needed to call his lawyer, but Kinsey wasn't finished. She never was.

"I sold my half of the construction company last month to Dick. You remember Dick, don't you? The same man you sold everything you owned to, which was practically nothing after our divorce. He was more than happy to buy me out. Although he was pretty mad that I made him pay double what he paid you. How could you give away your business like that?" she asked as if there was something seriously wrong with him and she wasn't the cause.

Ben wanted to scream that he'd done everything in his power to get away from her as quickly as possible, but instead he said nothing. Kinsey would have her say no matter what Ben said or did. He held onto the image of his girl. For Skyla, he wouldn't act on impulse and do something regrettable.

"You're just going to stand there? What is the matter with you? I'm so glad I met Mario. He is the man you will never be." She was trying her best to make Ben respond, but he didn't want to fall into her trap. He'd been in this same situation one too many times. Kinsey wanted him to react badly so she could blow her retelling out of proportion and make him look bad. The last thing Ben needed was fresh waves of gossip flooding through town.

"Do you even care that Skyla is moving away with me?" she asked.

"I already told you she isn't moving. Our visitation agreement is in writing and court ordered."

"The court won't do anything to me. I am her mother. We're moving in less than a month. You have a couple more weekends with Skyla and then we're out of here. After we get settled, I'll text you our new address."

If Ben had his way, she would spontaneously combust on the spot. He held his ground and his tongue. His silence infuriated her.

As much as he tried to hold in the rage, she must have seen the impact of her words on his face. She narrowed her gaze, but there was pleasure in the tight-lipped smile she delivered before adding, "Don't fuck with me over this, Ben, or I'll take our daughter to the Alaskan wilderness and you'll never see or hear from her again. Got it? You should be grateful I'm willing to stay in contact with you at all."

Ben lowered his gaze and looked away from the hatred that oozed out of her icy blue eyes. How had he let things get so far with Kinsey? Her level of hatred for him was beyond anything he'd ever known before. They'd fallen so hard for one another as teenagers, but they'd grown exponentially farther apart.

"My lawyer will be in touch with yours. If you go against the visitation schedule again, I'll have you arrested," he said, feeling sad and weary for a life he never wanted but was now living.

Her palm met his cheek. She screeched, "How dare you threaten me? You would rather see me in jail than give me one ounce of happiness. I'm moving to Anchorage with my fiancé and you can't stop me!" She hit him again and it stung.

Ben grabbed her wrist, twisted, and lowered her arm. He had tried to remain calm, but now she was attacking him. He wasn't going to take another slap and decided to be rid of Kinsey for the remainder of the morning. Ben moved them closer to her car. But Kinsey was now receiving exactly what she wanted and she fought back. He had to use more of his strength to protect himself. She kicked and scratched and then began screaming for help. Ben got a hold of both arms and he forced her small body to the car. He released one hand to open the door and she managed to rip her nails over his forearm before he stuffed her inside and closed the door.

Kinsey continued to yell and curse. "I hate you! Skyla wants Mario to be her dad now instead of you!"

Ben held the door closed so she couldn't come after him again.

She lowered the window and tried to claw his face, but Ben stuck his boot against the door and leaned back. Kinsey's reach was pathetically short. Greg's truck pulled into the alley and Kinsey must have heard or seen the oncoming vehicle. She stopped fighting and started the engine. Witnesses to her rage wars were not in Kinsey's best interest and she was malicious enough to know it. The transmission ground into reverse and then the tires protested against the pavement as she gunned the gas pedal. He wished she would have run over the short guard rail separating the alley from the grassy river bank. Wrecking the SUV in the river would have made his morning, but she stopped with an inch to spare of the railing, shifted again, and sped away.

By the time Greg opened his door, Ben was already inside the Aspen Building.

* * *

Maleah woke with Ben in her thoughts. The night before, he'd wanted to know if she was always such a train wreck. The truth was she hadn't thought of herself as a walking, talking accident-prone disaster at all. Responsible, focused, and hardworking were more her MO. Sometimes she was a little distractible, but she was always reliable. That is until... Maleah had to think about how long it'd been since she felt normal. Had it only been two days since her life started falling apart?

Today was a new day, she told herself. That meant she could start with a clean slate and take each moment as it came. No more hot mess. She needed normalcy again. Not that Maleah could control her lack of employment or even lack of electricity inside the building she was supposed to be staying in. But she could control how she responded to these inconveniences. *Right?* The theory was sound. Her unpredictable responses to these new external stresses were something else entirely. Like why had she kissed Ben's cheek instead of telling William the truth? Why had she yanked off her skirt on the side of the road and thrown it instead of doing something more rational?

Maleah didn't know the rational response to being attacked by biting insects, but losing her clothes and hopping around like a madwoman wasn't normal. *Is it?* Then at dinner, she'd gone temporarily insane again. Ben was charming, but moody, witty and funny, but also sarcastic and cynical. *Who was I last night?* Maleah had never flirted with someone so easily. Or not in a long time. Even with Holden she'd never felt so at ease to say whatever came to mind. And when had she become so serious all the time? In college? It felt so good to laugh and relax with Ben last night.

The reminder of Holden made her pick up her phone. Before falling asleep, she'd silenced her alerts. She had missed an email from him.

Maleah,

When you have time, will you forward me your list of contacts, spreadsheet, and emails etc. regarding investors and grants. Is there a time you can come in? I know you would be volunteering, and I am sorry for that, but I do a lot better in person when it comes to computer files and someone else's organizational systems. Let me know. Thank you, Holden McNutt, CEO True Green Bioplastics.

Maleah slapped her palm to her forehead. In her moment of self-pitying, drinking, mourning the loss of her career, plus driving across the state to take care of family, she'd forgotten to email Holden. She dug out her laptop from her bag and powered it up. There was one file that would be of interest to Holden. The other files were in the desktop computer at work. She had intended on returning to True Green to take care of her desk and the important files yesterday and had promptly forgotten. How had she forgotten to go to work? It was so unlike her, and yet similar to everything else that had happened recently. The hangover may have had something to do with her absentmindedness, but that wasn't an excuse she wanted to tell her boss. *Umm, former boss.*

She replied to the email and explained she was out of town on a family emergency. Keeping the message succinct, she ended the email by telling Holden he could call her at his convenience if he needed access to her work computer immediately or that she would return to Boulder as soon as possible. Maleah attached a copy of the file to the email and hit send.

There was also a phone message from an unknown number that she promptly ignored. Maleah needed to get on with her day. Her short visit with Aunt Kiki the day before had been disturbing, and she was anxious to return to the hospital.

Maleah opened the bedroom door to peer into the camper. Ben's door on the opposite end of the trailer was open and the RV was quiet. She stepped into the restroom and that's when she heard the arguing. The low timbre of a male voice could be heard but no distinct words stood out. The woman's scream brought Maleah to the window and she peered through the blinds.

Maleah's heart skipped a few beats and her breath caught in her throat as she watched Ben manhandle Kinsey and force her into a black SUV. Kinsey was near hysterical, her words hard to understand, but Maleah heard her say that Ben was hurting her. The viciousness of Kinsey's defense against Ben was terrible to see, but the blank unfeeling look on Ben's face as he forced Kinsey inside the car was frightening. Maleah stopped watching, panic fueling her reactions. She stuffed her few belongings back in her bags, zipped them up, and headed to the door. She had enough sense to look outside before opening the door. After what she'd witnessed, she wanted to avoid Ben. Kinsey and her SUV were gone, and she couldn't see Ben anywhere. A truck with a sign on the door that read "Rocky Mountain Plumbing" sat in the parking lot, and the driver had his back to her as he fiddled with something in one of the large tool boxes.

Maleah hauled herself and her bags outside and straight to the back door of the Columbine Building. Daylight made finding the flowerpot where her aunt hid a key to the building a lot easier and Maleah was inside a minute later.

The main level of the Columbine Building still had a lot of work to be done, but the front of the building looked like it would someday be retail space. Maleah gave herself a quick tour of the large open floorspace. She looked over the antique built-in counter along the north wall with an appreciative eye and then noticed the wood floors needed to be refinished. There was damage to some of the plaster on the walls, but the main level was in pretty good shape. There were two restrooms on the first floor, and the tilework and plumbing appeared to be new. Her mind went in five directions at once as she pictured fresh coats of paint, electric sanders, varnish, wainscoting, and finally, accessories.

Her parents had a life-long hobby of fixing and flipping properties. After her father retired from the army, her parents became even more serious about remodeling. Growing up, Maleah had moved from house to house. On more than one occasion, Maleah wished and begged her parents to stay in one home, but they lived on the profits of their labor. Jona and Albert Hale chose Three Peaks because there were a lot of dilapidated and historical homes and a booming real estate market. Maleah knew her way around a construction site, and she had more experience than some at renovating. Her parents didn't believe in idle hands and had taught Maleah everything about remodeling.

The second and third floors of the Columbine Building looked as if they were intended to be apartments. The third floor needed more work than the second, but Maleah didn't take much time to investigate. She needed to figure out how she was going to get to Mount Tenderfoot Medical Complex when her car was on Route 9 with a flat tire. The answer sat on Aunt Kiki's cluttered dining table. Maleah recognized the keychain and the keys to her aunt's old Land Cruiser. The thrill of discovering her aunt still drove the classic four-by-four and a solution to her transportation problem eased the knot of tension in her belly. Ben and Kinsey's blowup was not her problem, and she didn't want to be involved. Maleah hung onto her earlier thoughts of needing normalcy today as she jogged down the stairs to find her aunt's Land Cruiser outside. She'd worry about her car later.

She headed down the hallway but stopped when she heard men talking inside the utility room by the back door.

"No. That is not going to work for me at all," Ben said.

"I'm dead in the water here, Ben. I'm not going to be able to finish without the right panelboard."

"You said last night you'd have it today. So where is it?"

Ben sounded angry now. There was a pause in the conversation, and Maleah wondered if she should sneak out now, but she'd have to pass the open door, and she hesitated.

The electrician hmmed then coughed. "I thought I'd drop in here first and make sure I, uh, wasn't forgetting anything before I drive to Gunnison. It's a long drive and I don't want to make it twice. These old systems need parts I don't have in my van. I'm being thorough."

"Or maybe you were lying to me last night on the phone. You were supposed to be done in here two weeks ago. Now I come in after being away for a few days, and it looks worse than anything I've ever seen before."

"Are you accusing me of something, Ben?"

"Such as doing a half-ass job? Or showing up whenever you feel like it, which is hardly ever?" Ben offered back.

"I don't have to take this. I have more than enough work to get me by. I'm done here."

"Great! Collect your crap and get out!" Ben said.

There was some commotion from inside the room, and then a middle-aged man with graying hair walked out of the utility room. Maleah turned and stepped lightly, going down the hallway in the opposite direction.

Something slammed against the wall or the door behind her with a bang. She swallowed and wished she had the ability to make herself invisible.

"Damn it!" Ben cursed and she walked faster. "Freaking wonderful," Ben said from behind her. "I just lost my electrician, but I'm guessing you already heard that."

Maleah turned around and composed her face. Innocent? Unsuspecting? Judgement-free zone? This was what she was going for, but her face probably looked more constipated. "I heard something, yeah."

"And?" Ben sounded irate and argumentative.

"And what?" she asked, confused.

Ben responded like his detonation button had been pushed. "You think I shouldn't have let Phil go. I don't know when the electric will be back on. Shit!"

Maleah shrank back, but the exit was behind Ben. "Maybe you could apologize. I'm sure he's still outside."

"Apologize? Phil's shown up for work roughly one day out of every seven. Screw that. He's out of here!"

"And so are you. You are out of line, Ben. Please move. I have places I need to be."

He must not have expected her terse reply, or her demand. But there was a fighter in him and her as well.

Maleah stood her ground. "Please leave the building."

"Leave? I think you should leave. I have work to do and you're in my way," he said, matching her tone and the stiffness in her back and shoulders exactly.

"I mean it, Ben Erickson. Go. You need to cool off."

"Cool off now, is it? I am a fucking iceberg. Cool off," he scoffed but still didn't move.

She wondered if she should walk out the front door, but she wanted to lock up the building, and without Ben inside of it. Besides, he needed to know that the way he spoke to her wasn't acceptable. Not even a little. He may be able to bully Kinsey and the electrician, but not her. If there was one thing Maleah wouldn't tolerate, it was a bully. She'd dealt with plenty of bullying growing up, and it was vital she stand up for herself. She'd teach him.

"Leave my aunt's building right now and take a day off, or do whatever you need to clear your head. Maybe you should try finding a reputable electrician," she said with more attitude than she would normally speak to someone with. Ben seemed to bring out an assertiveness in her she rarely ever exuded.

"Find a new electrician? As if it's that easy," he said, still in argumentative mode. "You have no clue how difficult it is to find reliable contractors. Here, in the middle of nowhere. In case you didn't notice, we're not exactly in a highly populated area where you simply call someone else and they'll be right over."

"Ben," she said, her nostrils flaring but her voice calm, "I'm not arguing anymore. Go outside right now or you're fired and banned from my aunt's building."

He actually laughed at her. A loud single, "Ha! That's hilarious."

"I'm not joking. I saw your temper earlier. You're not listening to me, and I want you out of here. You're fired until I speak with my aunt."

He raised his brows as if surprised and as if he finally heard her. Ben rocked back on his heels, stuck his tongue in his cheek, and stared at the wall behind her and above her head. Finally, he turned and headed for the door. "We'll see what Kiki has to say." Ben slammed the door behind him and Maleah jumped.

"Good riddance," she said, relieved to be away from him but suddenly awash with a sense of loss and regret. She'd had fun with him yesterday. Some guys were cute on the outside but awful ogres on the inside. It made her sad.

Maleah inhaled a steadying breath. Wasn't she better off seeing Ben's ugly side now? Still, the loss of a new friendship hovered for a moment in the periphery of future hopes and dreams, then extinguished like a snuffed-out candle.

Seven

AFTER FINDING THE CLASSIC FJ40 Land Cruiser parked on the street, Maleah hopped inside and sent up a silent prayer that the engine started. The motor turned over but didn't catch. She pumped the gas pedal once, just like her father taught her when she was a kid. She tried the prayer thing again. Who had her mother been evoking the other day? Wakea? Maleah asked Wakea for assistance with the FJ, and then felt foolish for doing so. *Wakea's in Hawaii, duh. Did the Ute people pray to gods for help with combustible engines? Great Spirit? Manitou? Loki, Pan, Babi? Some help would be appreciated over here.* She was throwing out names willy-nilly, and that might be another mistake. Summoning a gang of vengeful gods or demons wasn't in her day planner. It wasn't in her life planner, and besides she didn't have her survival kit. *Just ignore my previous requests for help, k? Thanks.*

But Maleah wasn't above begging a hunk of steel and some lubricant to do her bidding. *Man, that could've been interpreted in a totally different way*, she thought to herself with an amused smile. Unfortunately, her dirty mind wasn't going to get the Land Cruiser running. She kept it simple and said, "Come on. Please start." Maleah cranked the key again and the engine turned over and rumbled awake.

As she drove to the hospital, she called her parents.

"Hi, Mom," she said.

"It's early, Maleah. Is everything all right?"

"Sorry. Did I wake you?"

Jona yawned and said, "No. We're just starting our day. You didn't answer my question. Are you okay? How's Auntie?"

"I'm on my way to see her now. Hey, can I talk to Dad?"

"Why? What are you doing?" Jona asked, her curiosity thriving even at five-thirty in the morning, Hawaii time.

"I want to check on him and see how he's feeling, and I have a question for him. I'm going to be out of cell range soon. You know how it is in the mountains. Can you give him the phone?"

"Hold on," her mother said, and Maleah heard movement in the background.

Her dad came on the line. "How's my girl doing?"

"Living the dream," she said before asking about his foot and if his wrist felt any better. Knowing her father, he delivered the expected condensed version about his injuries and she was grateful for brevity. Maleah moved on to the other reason she wanted to speak with him. She gave her own short story about the lack of electricity in Aunt Kiki's building and asked if Uncle Raymond stilled lived in the area.

Her father was a true hero. He didn't need or want any more chitchat or explanations.

He said, "I haven't talked to Ray Trujillo in a coon's age. I'll give him a call and see if he can take a look at the problem you're having downtown. How's it looking, anyway? Everything was booming when your mother and I decided to leave the mountains for a warmer climate."

"Still booming, I think," Maleah said.

"I sure don't miss it. And you can keep your snow too. I definitely don't miss shoveling out the drive."

"Still sounds better than being attacked with coconuts while trimming trees."

"Well... There's always a trade-off, isn't there? I'll call your uncle Ray and see if he can help out."

"Thanks, Dad. Love you. Hope you heal fast."

Uncle Raymond was not her real uncle, but he had served with her father in the army and had moved to the mountains because of Albert and Jona. Blessedly, he was also a retired electrician. It would be good to see him, and it would be even better if he could fix the electrical problem in the Columbine Building.

Maleah reached the Mount Tenderfoot Medical Complex where Kiki was in the hospital about ten minutes later and parked the Land Cruiser. The medical facility had expanded since the last time she'd been in town, and there were new buildings, including a rehab center and an assisted-living apartment complex. The growth in town had not only boomed, as she'd told her father, it had exploded. The little mountain hospital from a couple years earlier had quadrupled into an entire medical complex. As she crossed the parking lot, her phone rang. She checked the caller ID and didn't recognize the number. Being harassed by scammers and telemarketers was the scourge of cell phone users everywhere, and Maleah stuffed her phone back into her bag. If it was important, they'd leave a message.

Inside the lobby, she checked in at the reception desk, and the smell of roasted coffee and the gurgle of an espresso machine overtook her senses. Realizing she hadn't eaten, she followed her nose to the coffee cart and bought a cup of house brew, an apple, and a croissant. Spending the money hurt a little, but she had to eat. After doctoring her coffee with cream and sugar, while stuffing the croissant into her mouth, Maleah found Aunt Kiki's room.

Her aunt sat in the hospital bed, looking older than Maleah had ever thought of her before. It was unnerving, since Aunt Kiki had never seemed like an "old" person in her mind. Kiki's drab hospital gown, bandages, IV, lack of makeup, and the bruises added up and the results were depressing.

"Hi, Auntie," Maleah said as she went straight to the bed, sat on the side, and leaned in for a gentle hug. "I'm so glad you're awake. I was here yesterday. Do you remember?"

"Goodness, no. The medications they gave me sent my blood pressure through the roof. I thought I was going to die. Maybe I did. It felt like I died. I was so out of it." Her eyes widened and she said, "I saw the light." Then Aunt Kiki winked and Maleah's discomfort over her great-aunt's health eased a little. Kiki squeezed Maleah's hand tight in her own. "Thank you for coming, sweet girl. It's a relief having someone here to help make sense of all the gobbledygook they keep telling me. No one will listen. They all think they know what is best for me, but if they had been paying attention to what I said, they wouldn't have sent me into those seizures yesterday. It's terrible, I tell you. Doctors don't know shit. I'm pretty sure they tried to kill me last night."

Maleah nearly snorted at Aunt Kiki's last pronouncement. "I'm sorry I couldn't get here sooner." She leaned in for one more careful hug.

"I know. Everyone is busy. My own daughter is not here, so what does that say, hmm?"

"But Brielle will be here soon, and then you'll have both of us to help you."

"You spoke with my granddaughter? I would like to see her very much." Kiki's eyelids closed in a slow blink as if she were tired.

"Yep. She's on her way from Ireland. That is why it is taking her a little longer to get here. What happened, Auntie? Why are you here?"

Aunt Kiki leaned forward and took both of Maleah's hands in her own. Then she settled back against her pillows again. "This is important, Maleah. I need you to find my turtle. It's inside the dumpster behind my apartment."

Kiki's expression was so grave that Maleah had no choice other than to take this seriously.

"What turtle?" Maleah pictured a poor box turtle or possibly a red-eared slider or some other pet that would now sadly be DOA after cold nights inside a metal dumpster.

"I was trying to get Ricky out when this ridiculous accident happened. Getting old is not for the birds. My darn ribs cracked when I was leaning over the side of the dumpster, trying to get the box out where Ricky must have fallen in." As if mentioning her cracked ribs renewed her discomfort, Kiki winced and placed a hand on her ribcage.

Maleah's confusion bobbed around her brain like a lost rubber ducky as she tried to process Kiki's account of Ricky the turtle. She tried to sort out the facts. "Did you just say you broke your ribs dumpster diving for Ricky? Then what happened?"

"Oh, Maleah. It hurt so bad. I tell you. As soon as I felt my chest give, I backed off the dumpster and then mis-stepped. I'm not sure of everything after that. They say I hit my head. There are stitches to prove it, but I don't remember. It was late at night. I know that much. I'm awake all hours," she explained. "Not sleeping well happens when you get old, I guess. I didn't notice Ricky missing until late that night. Then I remembered how I was cleaning out the storage rooms and closets earlier in the day and how I threw a bunch of boxes of old garbage into the dumpster. After searching the storage rooms and the hallways, I knew my necklace must be inside one of the boxes."

A lightbulb went off like a floodlight inside Maleah's head. "What does Ricky look like, Aunt Kiki?"

"Oh, you've seen him. I never take Ricky off. Your uncle gave me my turtle when I was twenty-six years old. Ricky's shell is black and white diamonds and his setting is all white gold. The chain is missing too. That turtle means everything to me." She touched the base of her throat where her most beloved piece of jewelry should be. "I hate to ask, Maleah, but the trash company comes on Thursday mornings. I need someone to pull those boxes out and look for my Ricky. I don't want anyone to get hurt, but can you find someone to do this for me? I may break out of here today and look myself." She frowned. "Broken ribs? This is the most ridiculous thing that has ever happened to me," she scoffed at her own injury.

"Yeah, of course I'll look. I'll do it later today."

Aunt Kiki released her hands. "You go on then. I can't relax until I know he's been found."

Really? Maleah thought. Great-aunt Kiki was booting her out the door to go dumpster diving. "Don't you want me to stay here with you a little longer?"

"Sure, sure. Be bored with me. This place is a real laugh a minute. We can watch courtroom drama or talk shows together. Bring some peach or blackberry brandy too. That would be extra helpful."

God love her. Maleah wondered if she would be able to speak her mind so freely when she reached her eighties. "I'll go look for Ricky, but can I talk to your nurses or your doctor before I head back into town?"

"Yep. Turn on your bullshit meter, though. They think I hit my head a lot harder than I did."

Maleah nodded and tried to keep an open mind to both her aunt and the doctors. "Auntie, I need to ask you something else."

The stress lines on her aunt's face had noticeably decreased with the knowledge that someone was finally listening to her about her turtle. Kiki looked exhausted, but she wore a tender smile as she waited for Maleah to go on.

"I fired Ben Erickson today and kicked him out of the Columbine Building. He made me nervous after I overheard him arguing with an electrician." Maleah refrained from mentioning the fight between Ben and Kinsey.

"Ben's such a nice boy. Are you sure you heard correctly? He has been a real lifesaver this year. You should see what he's done inside the Aspen Building."

Maleah's shoulders crept toward her ears as she remembered the tense morning. "Yes, I'm sure. Is it okay if I keep him out of the Columbine Building while I am here?"

Kiki had to think about her answer for a moment, but then she said, "Of course. He has plenty of work next door. I don't want you to feel uncomfortable while you are in town helping me."

Maleah leaned over and kissed her aunt on the cheek. "I'm sorry if this is horribly inconvenient for your remodel, but I can do whatever you were doing before you cracked your ribs. Give me a list of what you need done and I'll take care of it. I'd love to help." The idea blossomed all golden and shiny in her mind. Maleah wanted to help Aunt Kiki any way she could. Since it was her fault for kicking Ben out, she'd make up for it. That is, until she needed to return to Boulder, or found a new job, or fell inside a dumpster and was carted off to the hospital. *There are so many possibilities for a better tomorrow.*

"There is a three-ring binder on my dining table with my plans for Columbine. Next time you come, bring it, and we will go over everything. Ben knows what is to be done, but I can show you too. And I trust you. If you think Ben needed to be taught a lesson, then I believe you." Aunt Kiki pressed her lips together and smiled again. "Bring my handbag with you too. I need my lipstick."

"Of course. Also, I'm driving your FJ. I got a flat tire on my car."

"Enjoy it. Uncle always said, never sell the Land Cruiser. Before he passed on, he made me promise the Toyota would stay in the family. That means you or Brielle will inherit the mountain beast anyway. It needs driven. They don't do well sitting around unused. Kind of like me, you know."

Maleah slid off the side of the bed. "I'll be back with the renovation plans and your purse as soon as I find Ricky."

* * *

The purple rubber gloves provided minimal protection against Maleah's imagination of what germs and other disgusting things were inside the dumpster behind Aunt Kiki's building. Although the contents inside the dumpster were mostly cardboard boxes and construction materials, she couldn't stop her inner germaphobe from taking the helm and steering her mental ship. The importance of finding the turtle necklace kept Maleah pulling out boxes, scraps of wood, old wiring, heaps of crumbling drywall, bags of garbage, and bags of body parts. Okay, there were no body parts... then again, she didn't look inside the bulky black trash bags, so who knows. It was possible. There was no blood or guts, though, so she was fairly certain lé dumpster was corpse free.

Shortly after noticing Ben eyeballing her from behind the Aspen building, she ignored him and returned to the tedious task of exploring the dumpster. That was when the bottom of a large box fell out. The contents exploded in a cloud of murky gray powder that smelled of mildew and acid. Maleah blinked away the dust and refused to look over at Ben. She could have imagined it, just like she was imagining she was already infected with anthrax or the plague, but she was fairly certain she heard a laugh. That was also the moment she decided she must have a dust mask.

Maleah left her task and went inside the Columbine Building to wash up. Then she remembered there was no running water. She peeled off the gloves and wasn't sure what to do next. Fortunately, someone knocked on the back door and provided a distraction.

Uncle Raymond greeted Maleah with a huge smile. "Look who's all grown up."

"I'm pretending I'm an adult. Don't let my height fool you," she said. "And I'd give you a hug, but Aunt Kiki had me digging through the trash. I could use a shower like you wouldn't believe."

She held the door open and stood aside to let him in.

"Let me guess. You can't wash until the water heater is back on."

"You got it. You really know your business, don't you?" she teased.

"Maybe, but don't get your hopes up quite yet," he said, playing along. "I make no guarantees, especially since I haven't seen what the problem is."

"I'll show you where the breaker box is," she said as they entered the hall and she gestured to the utility room. "It's great to see you, Uncle Ray. I can't thank you enough for helping. I know you retired some years ago, but me and Aunt Kiki are in a pinch."

"Well, I haven't done anything yet, but let me have a look." He pulled a flashlight off his tool belt and shined it into the room.

Maleah assisted Raymond, and she felt like she was ten years old again but with new and slightly more mature stories to share when he asked about her current life.

The power came back on about fifteen minutes later and she cheered, actually cheered out loud for its return.

"This is a temporary fix," he said.

Her smile fell as she instantly wondered if her hopes of a hot shower were about to be crushed.

"Don't look too sad, Maleah. This is temporary until I come back tomorrow with the parts I need. That said, the whole system needs upgraded. I don't have a crew working for me anymore, but I can recommend someone."

"His name isn't Phil, is it?" she asked.

"No," he said and pulled a business card out of his wallet. "Tell Guillaume I told you to call. He'll take good care of this place. It's good to see your aunt is making an effort to keep these old buildings going. By the way, how is she doing?"

"She's going to be okay. And Brielle will be here tomorrow."

"Good, good," Uncle Ray said as they walked toward the back door. The hallway glowed with beautiful electrical lighting. Not that Maleah didn't appreciate the natural light coming through the old leaded windows, because she did. But at night, electricity was definitely an industrialized step up from candles and lanterns.

She thanked Raymond again and told him to come back whenever it was convenient for him, and that she would call the number on the business card he'd given her. Maleah also sent her well-wishes to his wife.

With the pressing need for a shower driving her every step, Maleah went upstairs and started looking for her aunt's stash of clean towels. Waiting on the water heater tested her endurance levels for wearing garbage filth, but a full tank of hot water was worth her patience. She washed her hands and forearms at the sink and then looked for a snack in the cabinets of her aunt's kitchenette. The apartment was huge, but it appeared to never have been used as living quarters before. Everything needed renovation. The construction on the apartments on the third floor didn't seem to extend to her aunt's living quarters. She couldn't wait to dig into the plans and see what was in the works for the space. But that would have to wait.

The food choices were minimal, and since Maleah didn't want shots of brandy, she slathered peanut butter and strawberry jelly on crackers. Her stomach appreciated every bite. Maleah was going to have to go to the store if she didn't want to starve.

But first, a shower.

The bathroom was set up for handicapped accessibility and she wondered if her aunt had added the safety railing or if the room was equipped that way when she'd purchased the building. She hoped Aunt Kiki wasn't in need of safety bars and handrails quite yet. Although her auntie had a petite frame, she always seemed strong and unbreakable. Remembering how Kiki looked in the hospital bed saddened Maleah again. Getting old wasn't for wimps, but she knew Kiki would come out of this on top.

Maleah set her bag of toiletries on the sink and draped a clean towel on a towel bar. She turned to face the shower tub combo. The faded tilework looked to be a remnant from the sixties. Turquoise and rust-colored stains marred the porcelain tub near the drain and the sliding glass doors were less than appealing. A faint musty smell hung in the air. Like the rest of the apartment, everything needed to be updated or repaired. She opened the Flemish textured window to let in some fresh air. The size of the bathroom had awesome potential, and she wondered what Kiki had planned for this room. She peeled off her grimy clothes and stared at the old window. That was the one thing in the bathroom that should be saved.

Maleah placed her shampoo, conditioner, razor, and bodywash inside the tub and then turned on the water. She waited until the faucet ran hot before pulling the lever to switch to the overhead nozzle. Gratitude for being clean literally washed over her.

All was right in the world again as the suds washed away all traces of dumpster diving. It was a shame she hadn't found the turtle necklace, but she couldn't keep looking without a full hazmat suit or something comparable. Could she find one at the hardware store? And she was running out of time. The trash company was supposed to be there in the morning. Could she tell her aunt she'd tried her best but failed?

As usual, her mind was full. She finished shaving one leg and then raised her other leg and propped her heel on the shower's handrail. Maleah reached for the bottle of bodywash so she could lather up before running the razor over her skin. Her heel slipped toward the wall and she hopped to keep her balance. The foot on the safety bar slipped to the side and wedged between the railing and the wall.

"Ouch!" she said as the bar pressed against her ankle bones.

Maleah pulled her foot back up, but it didn't budge. She shifted, twisted slightly, and tried again with the same result. After sliding her ankle along the narrow space and pulling again in a different spot against the wall, she began to panic. Her foot would not come out.

Maleah stood balancing on one leg while her other foot was stuck between the safety rail and the wall.

"Oh. My. God." All the deities in the world were not going to save her now.

The water grew colder as Maleah tried to contain her panic and methodically work through her problem. But no matter what she did, add soap, turn her ankle, yank maniacally, cry like a baby, or try to break the bar off the wall, nothing made a difference.

She resorted to going numb to the situation and facing her death. *So, this is how it ends.* Her moment of morbidity lasted all of about thirty seconds. Calling for help seemed like the next reasonable solution. And of course, singing, because she was fairly certain singing in the shower would solve all the problems in the world.

Eight

"SON OF A BITCH," Ben muttered to himself when he watched Raymond Trujillo step out of a red pickup truck and knock on the back door of the Columbine Building.

Maleah found an electrician. Ben was well acquainted with Mr. Trujillo and knew the man retired four years ago. With a shake of his head, Ben locked the door of the Aspen Building and climbed into his truck. Ben had to deal with other things, and if the electricity was being taken care of next door, then it was one thing he could cross off his list.

Ben's brother, Jeremiah, sat on the passenger seat.

"You sure you should be doing this?" Jeremiah asked.

"I think so," Ben said.

"You don't sound real confident about it."

Ben ran a hand over the scruff on his jaw. "I had a rough morning. This is the least I can do."

"You said she fired you," Jeremiah noted.

Ben had already filled his brother in with some of the details. He didn't give all the specifics, but enough to know that Maleah Hale had returned to town, Gilbert and William were spreading false rumors about the two of them seeing each other, and how Kinsey was trying to screw him over once again. After Ben took a drive over to the senior village and stopped in at the hospital, his brother arrived at the Aspen Building to lend him a hand. Ben appreciated the favor.

"She did, but I visited with Kiki and told her what's up. Kiki isn't taking things too seriously, and thinks her great-niece probably needs to learn a lesson. She suggested I give Maleah some space and a little time and let things play out. I trust my employer more than her irrational and uninformed niece," Ben said.

"Irrational and uninformed," Jeremiah parroted with too much emphasis on three simple words. "You're not projecting a little of Kinsey on Maleah, are you?"

"No," Ben said adamantly. "Maleah didn't know what was going on this morning and jumped to every wrong conclusion. I was in a hell of a bad mood and she caught me in the middle of it. I'll explain later. That is, if she'll speak to me again. In the meantime, let's take care of this errand, all right?" Ben said, already done rehashing his crappy morning.

He drove along Park Street, turned onto Chipeta Way, then made a right on Main to head out of town.

Jeremiah needed more answers. "What are you going to do about Skyla?"

"Grandpa Joe suggested I dig a deep hole and throw Kinsey in it."

"Leave it to Gramps to come up with a quick solution. Did you see him today too?"

"I did. Since I went to visit Kiki over at the hospital, I stopped in and brought Grandpa's weekly beer and wings."

"You're a day early."

"It's all right. I'll visit him tomorrow too, so his schedule isn't upset," Ben said. "It's good to check on Mrs. Brookhart. She doesn't have any family in town anymore."

Jeremiah nodded in agreement. "Except for Maleah."

"Yeah," Ben muttered under his breath.

Grandpa Joe did a lot better with a regular and consistent schedule. Between Jeremiah, himself, and their parents, Grandpa had someone to check on him at least every other day.

As they drove away from town, Jeremiah said, "So, tell me again about the bull, the bare ass, and the ants. I need a better mental picture of what I'm volunteering to assist you with." Jeremiah's grin stretched from ear to ear.

Ben's smile matched his brother's as he retold the abridged version of Maleah's bad day.

Jeremiah chuckled before saying, "She's hot, right? You wouldn't be helping her out if she wasn't. If I'm wrong, I'll buy you a six pack."

Ben inhaled a slow breath and kept his eyes on the road. *Oh yeah, Maleah is hot.* He said, "You're wrong. I don't care what she looks like. And that isn't why I helped her out. In case you've forgotten, I'm not a giant prick like you and your pals."

"And you're a terrible liar," his brother said. "You confessed she was in a field of pretty flowers, on her knees, right in front of your junk, and with your pants hanging open. You don't even know it, but she owns your sorry ass. You're totally suckin' up to her now, and hoping for a repeat performance of the best accident that's ever happened to you."

Ben rolled his eyes. "Wrong again. That's all you. You'd try and play her, but not me. My motives are nothing but innocent."

"Utter bullshit," Jeremiah said as a knowing smirk played at the corners of his mouth.

Ben admitted nothing. He slowed the truck and pulled onto the berm, then into the grass.

"You can shut your trap now. We're here."

They finished Ben's errand and returned to town. Jeremiah did not buy that promised six-pack of beer, but Ben didn't bring it up again. His brother said he needed to get back to the ranch. Ben thanked him for helping out, and they parted company behind the Aspen Building.

Normally, if Ben had been away from a jobsite for the day, he liked to do a walk-through and see what progress had been made while he was away. He appreciated the quiet time and lack of distractions so he could make notes or erase things off his mental checklist. Since he was "fired" from working on the Columbine Building, he could still inspect the Aspen Building.

As he approached the back door, the sound of faint singing caught his attention. A female's voice seemed to be coming from the alley between the two buildings and somewhere up high. He turned and stepped into the alley, trying to pinpoint the location. Ben stopped again to listen.

At first, the song sounded like a sorrowful lament, but as he neared the open window on the second floor, the words became clearer and he heard a familiar folk song rhythm but with odd lyrics.

"In the bathtub, I'll meet my maker. She died while shaving. When she should have been misbehaving. Gone too soon. It wasn't even a blood moon. Oh, sorrow of sorrows, her life was cut short. The tragedy of tragedies. Someone help me."

Ben stood there listening for too long... *but what the hell?*

"Hello!" he called. When the singer didn't reply, he yelled, "Hey! Is there a problem up there?" Ben was fairly certain that the window was located in Kiki's living quarters. *Maleah?* He couldn't be certain, but who else would be inside.

"Help! Please!"

Ben didn't waste another second, and he darted for the door and then up the stairs. Her voice was hoarse and ragged, but he was sure it was Maleah and the panic had been obvious.

He threw open the bathroom door and saw her standing inside the shower naked. "What's wrong?"

"No! Get out!" she yelled and slapped her hands over her private parts.

He slammed the door then stood there and blinked at the wood panels, wondering what the fuck just happened.

"Come back! Don't leave!"

After being yelled at for barging in, Ben stared at the doorknob and questioned whether or not he was more likely to be figuratively castrated for opening the door or for leaving it closed.

"Ben! Is that you? Are you there?"

"I'm here," he called back.

"Don't go! I'm stuck," she said.

The glimpse of her happened so fast, but he thought he saw Maleah in a rather compromising position. *Or is my brain making shit up? Those legs, though.* He wasn't making that part up. Ben had plenty of time to memorize her legs yesterday, and a second viewing wouldn't go unappreciated.

"Do you need help or what?" he asked.

"Yes! My foot is stuck in the shower. Can you bring a drill or a sledge hammer or something? Bring anything."

Her voice had calmed and she was no longer yelling, but he still didn't fully understand.

"Maleah? I need to come in and see the problem before I grab my tools."

"Okay," she mumbled.

Ben scrubbed a hand over his head in preparation then turned the knob. Out of respect, he kept his eyes on the tiled floor.

Even so, she said, "Don't look. Toss me the towel. Then you can look at my stupid, ridiculous, horrible predicament."

Ben pressed the side of his hand up to his face to use as a blinder as he glanced toward the sink and vanity. He caught a glimpse of Maleah's head in the mirror, but quickly focused on the towel. He picked it up then walked backward a couple steps. He tossed the towel in her direction then looked over his shoulder.

"You looked," she accused as she caught the towel.

He averted his gaze and tried not to laugh. "Did not," he lied.

"You totally looked," she repeated but didn't sound too mad.

"Hey," he said in his defense. "It's a reflex to look where you're throwing." Before she could argue some more, he asked, "Are you decently covered now?"

"Yeah," Maleah said, and Ben turned.

"Well, that's a fine pickle you've got yourself in." He rubbed at his jaw and tried his hardest to not ogle her slim, toned, and forever—from here to Tijuana—long legs. *What is her deal? Who actually has legs like that?*

"Ben? Today would be helpful," she said as he contemplated the problem.

"Right," he said slowly, but his brain snapped out of what was quickly becoming known as the "Maleah Effect." It's where drool collected in his mouth, dribbled down his chin, and he appeared to go catatonic due to her apparent need to be without clothes and in compromising situations right in front of him. *Is she some kind of damn test of my morality? Would going to hell over petting her legs—with my tongue—be worth it?* Despite the angry red bug bites and the consequential look of being mildly diseased, the answer was yes. *Oh yeah.* Eternity in hell for a minute of those legs wrapped around his hips would be acceptable. Damn, how long had it been since he'd slept with a woman? *Too long.*

"Hang tight," he said and strode out of the room.

With a hefty bite of sarcasm, she called to his back, "Do I really have any other option?"

Ben grinned at her reply. He returned a few minutes later with his socket wrench set.

"Where's the drill, Mr. General Contractor? Or a hammer?"

She wore the bath towel in a way that reminded Ben of a full body diaper. She held the corners of the towel in one hand near her shoulder, keeping herself relatively well covered. The terry cloth wasn't as appealing as what she'd worn the night before, but given the circumstances, she looked great. *You know, partially naked and bug bitten, but totally great.* He needed mental help. *Stay focused, dipshit.*

"Let me try removing the bar first, and if that doesn't work, then I'll go with your blunt force method," he said as he began test fitting sockets over the bolt heads holding the safety railing to the wall.

The handrail must have been installed decades ago, because no one in the right mind nowadays would allow for such a wide gap between the bar and the wall. Plus, the corrosion and hard water stains were terrible. The rail needed to go. Today was a good day to say *adios* to outdated hardware. Ben wrenched the bolts loose and Maleah was free from her prison.

She lowered her leg and made a sound of distress. Ben had turned to set the wrench in its case, but at the sound of her pain, he spun back around and reached for her.

"I'm okay," she said quickly, but her face wore a mask of discomfort.

Ben dropped his hand, and she tried to step out of the bathtub. He could tell she wasn't yet steady on her feet.

"I can't feel my leg," she said as she tripped over the edge of the tub.

Ben attempted to offer assistance, but nothing in the next few seconds went right. She landed on him, and her forehead banged against his cheekbone. Ben flinched and pulled his head out of the way as she tried her best to stand while gripping onto his shirt, arms, chest, or anything to help steady herself.

Likewise, Ben fumbled against her panic-driven flailing, and they danced a couple steps, twirled, and he stepped on her foot.

"Yow! My toes," she cried.

Conscious of how heavy his work boots were, he tried to get his feet and legs away from hers, but it was impossible as they were already a tangled mess of limbs.

The tumble was both fast and in slow motion. Ben's protective reflexes kicked in and he rolled to ensure she was safe and unharmed. The end result landed Maleah on top of him... naked. Her breasts pressed against his chest, and he had his arms protectively around her... with one hand firmly gripping her ass. *A great ass it is too*, he thought.

"Are you okay?" he asked, his breath rushing in and out of his lungs.

Maleah blinked rapidly, their faces mere inches apart. "I... I'm not sure."

Her entire body shivered against his.

"Did I break your toes?"

"No. I think they're okay."

"Your leg coming back to life yet?" he asked.

"Slowly. Yeah. I don't know. Maybe."

"You're freezing," he said as she continued to shake.

"I was stuck in there for so long." Emotion rose close to the surface of her incredible gray eyes.

They were more silver than gray and flecked with bits of gold. Her eyes were the most exotic thing he'd ever seen.

"I thought I was going to die." Maleah closed her eyes, her eyelids shaking with emotion. Tiny amounts of moisture collected at the corners.

Ben held her tighter. *Death?* Maleah felt cold, but he didn't think she would have died. The building was heated after all, and she had water. This was not the time to voice his skepticism. But he wasn't totally oblivious to the need for comfort in scary moments. He was a dad, after all.

"You're okay now. I swear you wouldn't have died. Someone would have found you if I hadn't. You're fine now, Maleah. I promise. Do I need to take a look at your piggies? Are they going to market? Personally, I think we should save them, but sometimes we have to have our bacon."

She stilled before opening her eyes and meeting his gaze again. "My piggies are not going to market. What? Why would you suggest that? That's awful."

He cracked a grin. "It was awful, but suggesting your toes should be butchered has taken your mind off the other things."

Her gaze shifted to one side then the other, and a sense of awkwardness slid into the room. Maleah rolled off his chest and sat with her back to him, knees pulled up high and tucked against her chest. She swiped her fists over her eyes.

"I should probably get dressed." She leaned across the floor and snatched up the fallen towel.

"Probably?" Ben had to say it. "You sure?"

"Get out," she said, but he saw the humor playing on her lips.

Ben picked himself up from the floor. "What if your leg or ankle gives out on you again? I can be your crash mat one more time if you need me. But I'll need to up my life insurance before the third time. Rule of threes and whatnot."

"I assure you I can handle it from here."

He stepped closer to the door, but then backtracked a few feet, keeping his eyes off Maleah.

"The door is the other way," she said.

"I know." He didn't stop his mission and grabbed her clothes off the counter and dropped them by her side.

"Thank you."

He closed the window, effectively shutting out the chilly evening air. "All in a day's work," he said casually then remembered he no longer worked there. *Details, details.* "Oh, right. I don't work here anymore."

Ben crossed the room and shut the bathroom door behind him.

Nine

MALEAH CLIMBED OFF THE floor carefully and tested her weight on her goofy leg and ankle before trying to walk. The numbness had subsided and she was once again steady on her feet.

Since humiliation and embarrassment seemed to be her two new besties, Maleah accepted her reality and left the bathroom to thank Ben again for his help and possibly hug him and never let go. Having her foot caught in the shower had to be one of the worst things that had ever happened to her, and she wanted Ben to know how much she appreciated his coming to her rescue. She opened the door, humbled, and ready to deliver a speech, but he wasn't there.

"Ben?" she said tentatively and limped farther into her aunt's apartment.

He'd left. No goodbye. No courteous exchange of words. Maleah wasn't sure if she should be grateful her embarrassment was over, or put out by his abrupt departure. She sat at the dining table in front of her purse and car keys and picked up her phone. It felt wonderful to be off her feet after standing in the freezing cold shower for so long. She needed food and she should find a blanket, or a cocoon of blankets to wrap herself with, but in the moment, she needed to sit and contemplate what she'd just experienced. Was the building haunted? The Columbine Building had taken out her aunt and then targeted Maleah next? Had she prayed too hard for help from gods she didn't believe in and they were teaching her a lesson? The logic behind this kind of thinking didn't get far. A simple answer would be so easy, but Maleah knew there were no ghosts or gods involved.

Pressure began building inside her chest and lodged in her throat. Maleah swallowed and stuffed her hurt feelings back where they weren't pestering her any longer. Losing her job, her father and her aunt getting injured, a flat tire, attacked by creepy-crawlies, and now trying to kill herself from a shaving mishap were nothing. Inconsequential. The inconveniences wouldn't control her emotions. In the grand scope of life, they were insignificant. Maleah tried to picture her future and everything she had to look forward to, but the loss of her dream job was a glaring red light she couldn't see around.

She sniffled and tapped the button on her phone to check her messages. Stewing over her problems wouldn't fix them. Action and staying busy were the key, and focusing on a new goal would help everything. Even a temporary distraction was welcome. Too bad the distractions were so uncomfortable.

Three messages waited for her, and one was from Holden. The harsh red light of her squashed future dimmed and went all soft pink with the thought of Holden. She listened to her voicemails.

"Hi, Maleah. I hope your aunt is feeling better." He paused, and she wondered for a second if the line had dropped. "This is tough. I'm not used to asking for help in this manner. Maleah, I could use you here. I'm sorry. I know you're with family right now, so maybe when you are back in town, give me a call? Okay, thanks. I'll talk to you later, and don't worry about me if you can't get back to town. I just... I miss seeing you this week."

Maleah replayed the message. He missed her. Was he finally realizing how much she meant to him? She missed him too. Oh, God, did she miss him. Loneliness crept in and took up residence alongside the humiliation of her recent shower and ant problems. As she took some small comfort from hearing Holden's voice, she realized that the next message in her voicemail was halfway finished.

Someone's voice, whom she vaguely recognized, was in the middle of saying, "...please call me back as soon as you get this message. It's extremely important you are not in your apartment when the exterminators are here and for four hours immediately after the fumigation. Thank you, Ms. Hale. Call me to let me know you received this message."

As the message came to an end, she realized she was listening to Kyle Jurgis, the property manager of her fourplex apartment building. What he said was only beginning to sink in when his voice returned to give even more bad news on the next message.

"Hi, Ms. Hale, this is Kyle Jurgis again. I apologize for the short notice, but did you receive my previous message about fumigating the building? I know this is not news anyone wants to hear, but we have to take cases of bedbugs seriously. Since I couldn't get ahold of you, after I tried to call multiple times, I allowed your apartment to be inspected. Good news! The infestation from 1A has not affected your apartment. The licensed exterminator found no signs of bedbugs or any other problems in your unit. Thank goodness, right?" Her property manager chuckled into the phone and Maleah glared at the screen as if he were a complete moron. *Infestation!*

She continued listening. "The extermination company had a last-minute cancelation for a whole structure tent fumigation. We want to take advantage of their schedule opening and the exterminators will be tenting the fourplex on Thursday. Are you out of town by chance? That could be for the best. You will need to stay out of the apartment overnight. I apologize for the inconvenience, but at least your apartment and your belongings are bedbug free. That cannot be said for 1A and 2A. We need to get a handle on this immediately, Ms. Hale. Call me."

Bedbugs.

Even though Mr. Jurgis said her apartment was pest-free, her skin started to itch and she eyed her luggage. *Tent fumigation?* Every paranoid thought she'd ever had about cancer-causing chemicals and neurotoxins invaded her head. All her clothes, personal belongings, her bed, and the few other pieces of furniture were about to be blasted with some kind of agent orange, DNA manipulating, mutant gene toxic gas bomb.

Was she overreacting? *Yes.* Did she care? *No.* Maleah didn't know what type of gas would be used on her apartment, but she'd heard the word Thursday and knew she didn't have time to do the proper research. Maleah stood, turned, and banged her knee on the table leg. Her bruised and sore knee. She cried out in pain and hobbled away from the table.

"I have to save my stuff! And Holden needs me!"

"Do what?"

"Ahh!" Maleah jumped at the sound of the voice behind her. When she saw who stood by the door, arms weighed down with two suitcases and shoulder bag, she cried out again. "You made it! Yay for perfect timing!"

Her cousin Brielle unloaded her burden by the door, straightened her back, and yawned. "You would not believe what it took to get here from Ireland this fast."

"And you wouldn't believe the amount of ludicrous fuckery I've been dealing with this week."

"Sounds like we should toast the moment with some of my grandma's brandy."

"I'll give a hearty 'yes, ma'am' to that."

They exchanged a long overdue hug. Brielle opened a cupboard and set glasses on the counter. She filled one with water from the tap and drank an entire glassful in a long chug.

"Traveling is dehydrating. Now where's Granny's liquor?"

"Cabinet to the right of the sink," Maleah said. "I don't think I'm staying here tonight."

Brielle's hand rested on the open cabinet door as she stared at Maleah.

"I have to empty out my apartment tonight. If I don't, I'm going to worry about growing a brain tumor for the rest of my life." Maleah grimaced at the thought but knew there was some truth to her paranoia of chemical insecticides.

"Maleah, tell me you haven't gone totally mental like so many of the other women in our family. Please. I need one sane relative to commiserate with." Brielle took the bottle of blackberry brandy from the shelf, opened it, and drank as she stared hard at her cousin. She lowered the amber bottle and said, "Why do you have to drive to Boulder tonight? And how is that connected to your imaginary brain tumor?" She waved a fluttery hand toward Maleah's head.

"My landlord is going to tent fumigate the entire building for bedbugs. I just found out, and since you're here, I'm going to go rescue my stuff. Afterward, I might throw myself at my old boss because I desperately need to get laid. The cows, haunted shower, and the stupidly sexy general contractor living in the parking lot can stuff it where the sun doesn't shine," Maleah said in a rambling word vomit that didn't make much sense to her own ears, let alone to her cousin's.

"Whatever you need to do." Brielle accepted the nonsensical as fact before swallowing more brandy. "I'll be here, holding down the castle and bringing Granny Kiki bento boxes, rice balls, and mochi."

"You don't have any mochi, do you?" Maleah lifted her nose and her eyebrows inquisitively.

Brielle recapped the bottle and placed it on the counter. She walked over to her bags and bent down. "Wouldn't you like to know?"

"You brought Kiki her favorite dessert? You're such a good granddaughter." Maleah watched her cousin unpack Japanese and other assorted Asian goodies from a plastic shopping bag.

"I had to get something to eat after leaving the airport. I found an Asian food market before leaving the city. I thought I'd grab a few things. Grandma would do the same thing for me." She turned her warm amber eyes on Maleah.

They had almost nothing in common when it came to looks. Brielle's physical traits resembled her father's side of the family. Maleah had a few vague recollections of her uncle, but he had divorced Brie's mother when she was young and then he basically disappeared. Brielle was shorter than Maleah and paler. Which was a definite feat considering Maleah had spent the better part of the last year inside True Green Bioplastics and had been faithfully chained to her computer. Acquiring healthy amounts of sunshine had somehow dropped off her priority list. The same looked to be true for her cousin.

"Are you feeling okay?" Maleah asked Brielle. "You look a little pale. If you're sick or something, I won't leave."

"Pale? Ha!" Brielle huffed out a small laugh. "My pasty complexion is the direct result of sitting inside castles and libraries for the last year. It doesn't bother me. Well, it didn't until you pointed out that I look ill. It is what it is. I don't go outside much."

"Okay, you're going to have to explain that later. I need to get going before I don't have time to save my clothes from the dreaded fumigation."

"And you're going to have to explain everything about the hot guy in the parking lot, the haunted shower, and whatever else later."

Maleah circled her ankle gingerly. "I will. Do me and yourself a huge favor and skip shaving in Kiki's shower until I fill you in."

"No problem. I didn't even pack a razor."

"Lucky you." Maleah hesitated then added, "Hot guy has a temper, so avoid him at all costs." She gathered her bags to make her retreat to the city and back to her normal life.

"You are coming back, aren't you? I just got here." Brielle glanced around at the makeshift apartment.

"I think so. I'm sorry to bail but"—she tapped the side of her head—"avoiding a brain tumor is a good course of action."

"And you need to get laid." Brielle rolled her eyes and then grinned.

"It'd help a lot," she said with a sigh. Would Holden even be interested? "At this point, I could just use a hug. The last couple days have been the strangest and most painful in my life."

"I think you meant to say that you need to hug his penis with your vagina."

"Ew," Maleah said even though she laughed. "I swear, I'm not even sure if there is anything going on between Holden and me. He did ask me to call him and come see him as soon as I was back in Boulder, so…"

"Go get 'em, tiger." Brielle gave a half-hearted fist pump into the air.

"Rawr." Maleah shouldered her bag and grabbed her keys off the table.

* * *

Maleah hauled her luggage outside and to her car. *Wait. Hold up.* The moment struck her like a flash of brilliant white light directly into the corneas. *My car.* How had it gotten here? She peered at the tires and saw the flat had been repaired. Her gaze fell on the nearby camper trailer. Ben's kitchen light glowed softly from behind the closed blinds. She chewed her lower lip for a moment. Did he fix her tire? Without asking? And how had he gotten her keys? They had magically appeared on the table in the apartment. But where were her keys before that? She couldn't recall their location to save her life.

Maleah set her bags on the seat inside the car and pulled out a notebook from her laptop bag.

Dear Ben,

She hesitated after writing, "dear," changed her mind about using such a personal greeting, flipped to a fresh page, and started writing a new note.

Hi, Ben,

You didn't have to fix my car, but I am so grateful. And that goes doubly so for the shower incident. I am in your debt.

She paused, not wanting to be in Ben's debt, but she was. She owed him a lot. Maleah already wrote the words, and starting over for a third time was wasting paper and time. Time she didn't have. She scribbled more words.

That said, I unfortunately cannot rehire you to complete the work on the Columbine Building due to what I saw happen between you and Kinsey. Kiki approved these changes in her plans for the building.

Please send me a bill for your time and the tire repairs. I will pay you as soon as I get my next paycheck. Please leave the invoice at the apartment.

Thanks. And sorry. I hope you can understand the position you've put me in. (Kiki says you are still her General Contractor for the projects on the other buildings.)

Maleah H.

She hurried over to Ben's truck and tucked the note under the windshield wiper.

Watching Three Peaks grow smaller in her rearview mirror was a relief and a regret, but she had to take care of things at home, and so Maleah went forward.

When she was within an hour of Boulder, she called Holden to let him know she was on her way back.

"That's an unexpected surprise. Your aunt is doing much better then?" he asked.

"My cousin arrived in town and is taking over for me while I take care of a problem at my apartment," she said, loving how he sounded happy to hear from her.

"Problem? Is there anything I can do to help?" he asked.

Maleah inhaled a calming breath. She didn't want to involve anyone with her problems, but she wasn't sure how she was going to deal with a middle of the night move by herself.

"I need to clean out my apartment... tonight." She choked back the rising anxiety and the accompanying tears and tried to keep things brief.

"What's going on?"

Since he asked, she told him about the bedbug scare and tent fumigation. "I can't believe this is happening. I am probably overreacting, but I don't want to live there any longer." The words were out of her mouth before she realized what she'd said. And it was true. She couldn't stomach the thought of sleeping in her awful, damp basement pit of an apartment. Now that there was confirmed bedbugs in the building, she didn't think she'd ever be able to rest or relax there again.

"That's terrible. I'm sorry, Maleah. Do you have a plan? How can I help?"

His words perked her up, but she wasn't sure what to say. "I don't know. I'm not sure what I'm going to do other than throw my clothes into bags and load my car up with anything that will fit."

Holden paused then said, "There's a twenty-four-seven trailer rental place on Broadway. Do you have a hitch on your car?"

"You're a genius! Yes, I do," she said, loving that he came up with an instant solution to her problem.

"I'll meet you at your place later and help. Text me, and I'll drive over when you're ready."

"Really?" she asked, feeling another push of emotions clogging her throat. She swallowed the lump.

"Sure. It's the least I can do. Do you need help with the trailer? I can meet you on Broadway instead."

"I'll get the trailer. Don't worry about that. Are you sure, Holden? I'll need you in the middle of the night." *Oh, God.* She held her breath, wondering if he'd read more into those last few words than she intended... except she actually wanted him to take the words literally.

"I'm happy to help, Maleah."

His voice had a seductive and low timbre that purred through the line. She squeezed her thighs together and wished she wasn't so hormonal. Jeez, it's been too long since she'd had a boyfriend... or a date.

"I'll text you when I get to my apartment."

"See you soon," he said and ended the call.

Self-service trailer rental by moonlight was probably one of the oddest and sketchiest things she'd ever done.

Maleah added the moment to her ever-growing list of the weird and unusual experiences this week.

It took her three tries to align the hitch on her car with the front of the trailer, but she felt a small boost of accomplishment when she did it correctly. It took watching a YouTube video and a healthy dose of frustration, but it was done, and she drove to her apartment without hitting anything or losing the trailer.

Holden arrived shortly after and he brought a dozen empty cardboard boxes. She was beyond grateful. Time disappeared into a blur of activity as they spent the next few hours packing and loading the small box trailer. Holden made all the difference in her attitude and somehow kept her dire situation from feeling like the end of the world.

"You can stay at my place tonight. Today," he corrected, since the sun would be up in another hour.

Maleah stared at him, longing to wrap her arms around his incredible, muscular body and... fall asleep. She was exhausted. "Thank you," was all she could manage to say.

Her eyelids barely stayed open on the drive to Holden's house. She parked, grabbed her overnight bag from the back seat, and followed him inside.

I'm inside Holden's house. Wow. Would he share his bed with her? Maleah suddenly found herself feeling more awake. She'd chug a six pack of energy drinks if it meant Holden was up for some getting-to-know-each-other-more-personally time.

She glanced around the open living room, dining room, and kitchen area. His house looked nothing like she had imagined. In fact, his house looked nothing like anyone's home she'd ever been inside of. *Does he even live here?*

It could have been the shocked look on her face or her silence, but he said, "I'm a minimalist."

"Oh?" she squeaked out the reply.

"I don't like clutter. It distracts me." He walked into the kitchen and washed his hands at the sink. "You can have the spare bedroom. There are towels in the cabinet. Make yourself at home, Maleah. I'm going for a run, and then I'll be at the lab."

She swallowed as she absorbed Holden's homelife and lack of... everything. The kitchen had one barstool at the breakfast bar. The living room contained a sleek contemporary leather couch, a tiny square end table, and a TV on the wall. He owned no rugs or decorations. The windows had simple white blinds that could have come with the house. The kitchen was modern and beautiful with its marble countertops and high-end appliances, but there was absolutely nothing on the countertops or the walls. Not a dish or piece of silverware was to be seen.

Holden opened the cabinet beneath the sink and tore off a paper towel from the roll to dry his hands. The soiled paper towel was deposited in a bin inside another cabinet.

He smiled. "I don't have a lot to eat, but you're welcome to anything. There are some eggs and plenty of protein bars. It's what I eat," he explained. "If you want, I can blend up a shake. I usually have one after a run."

She returned the smile and hoped her look of perplexed bewilderment was thoroughly masked. "Don't fuss over me. I'm fine. A shower would be great. I might try to sleep for a little while. Then I'll join you at the office. You need help with my filing system, right?"

"I do. The guest room is down the hall and on the left. See you later?"

"Yep," she said and took her bag to see what other surprises waited for her in his minimalist house.

There were plenty. *People live this way?* She had no idea. At least there was a futon, but there was nothing else in his guest room. In the bathroom, she found one bath towel, one washcloth, and one hand towel. There was no bath mat or soap or décor. Even the walls and the trim were one color, eggshell white. What did Holden think of her apartment? She wasn't messy, but she loved different fabrics, textures, and colors. Her few pieces of furniture were mismatched and eclectic. And she loved art and things she could hang on the walls.

Maleah heard him leave the house to go on a run. She knew he trained every day for his Iron Man competitions, but she didn't know he also went without sleep. After a shower, she lay under the one thin blanket on his guest futon. She was too tired to think about Holden's unusual lifestyle anymore, and she passed out.

* * *

With the moving trailer in tow—Maleah wasn't about to unhitch the thing just to hook it back up again when she figured out where she was going—she arrived at True Green Bioplastics shortly after lunch. It was weird walking into the place when she wasn't officially employed there any longer. Her former coworkers talked to her and acted like nothing had changed, but everything felt different to Maleah. She was already an outsider after missing a few days of work.

Holden met her at her desk and pulled up a chair. She showed him her organizational system and copied all important documents and emails into an external drive.

"I guess I need to clean out my cubicle," she said with a nervous laugh. "This week has flown by."

"You can stay if you want to," he said with a look of genuine distress. "But there's no money. I am working on it, though."

"I received my final paycheck today. That will get me by for a little while." *Sadly, not for very long*, she thought to herself.

Holden nodded. "Would you like to stay at my house again tonight? You can. I, uh," he stumbled on his words, and it was so unlike him that her heart gave a shout of triumph.

He may be a minimalist, somewhat rigid and controlling, and a health nut, but he cares about me.

He raised his chin an inch, straightened his spine, and started over. "Would you like to have dinner? I'm buying, and then if you need a place to stay, you're welcome to come back to the house. You know, until you figure out the situation with your apartment."

"That's very thoughtful and I'd love to."

"I'll be ready in an hour," he said and rolled his chair into the empty cubicle behind hers.

"That will give me time to box up the rest of my things."

"Sounds like a plan."

They had a date! She was beyond thrilled, and the lightness in her chest eased the hard task of having to say goodbye to her dream job all over again.

Then Davis slid into her cubicle, parked his butt on the edge of her desk, and crossed his ankles.

"Hey, you're back."

"Not really. I had a few things to show Holden. Now I'm packing up."

"Too bad."

"Says the guy who stole my job," she said without looking up from her task of cleaning out the bottom side drawer.

"You would have had a job if the grant wasn't axed."

She slid him the side-eye. *Is Davis being nice to me?* A half smile almost gave him the appearance of being a decent person. Maleah returned to organizing and sorting.

"Thanks, but having a job in a parallel universe doesn't help the current situation I'm in. See the problem?"

"That's what I like about you, Maleah. You are one of the few chicks I've ever met who will throw out a random quantum mechanics reference. Science girls are awesome."

"Uh-huh," she mumbled.

Davis wasn't going to ruin the moment. She had a date with Holden. She'd lost her job to get it, but she was having dinner with a dreamy scientist... and minimalist, her brain reminded her. But it was still a date. Their dinner would give her a chance to find out more about his decision to live simply. She could respect someone who was against overconsumption.

"Want to hang out after work? Now that we're no longer working together every day, we should date. We could go somewhere and grab a bite to eat. Or there's always my place."

"Ow!" Surprised by his invite, Maleah accidentally pinched her finger as she closed the cabinet. She turned and stared at Davis like he'd suddenly sprouted an alien head. Did Mr. Job Stealer just ask her out? Maybe she was the one who'd grown an extra head... or maybe she *had* been transported to that alternate universe.

Instead of asking if he was feeling okay, or had freaking lost his mind, Maleah said, "I have plans with Holden tonight."

Davis crossed his arms over his chest, looking smug. Her desire to poke him in the eye made her throbbing finger twitch.

"Holden?" he asked with a twinge of surprise and something that resembled cruel humor in those dark chocolate eyes. "Call me after you figure out it will never go anywhere with him."

"Rude." She picked up the box she'd filled with her personal effects.

"I'm not being rude. I'm being honest. We had a similar conversation before, remember? I'm blunt but not rude. You flipping me the bird on Monday was rude, but I didn't take it that way. I think you look pretty cute when you're angry."

"I'm leaving now." She glanced at her desk and the small space where she'd spent countless hours focused on helping make True Green's dream of a better planet come true. She wished Davis wasn't blocking her final view, but nothing about this week or her job had gone the way she'd expected.

"Good luck with Holden." Davis half snorted and half laughed, then sauntered down the hallway and turned left to enter the lab.

Whatever his intentions were with the huff and the snark, it wasn't nice. Maleah sighed as she took one final look at her lost dream of working full-time for True Green Bioplastics. The idea that additional funding or another grant could be acquired sat like a small glowing lovebug in the far recesses of her hopes and ambitions, and she let it live there. She could get her job back, right? One day. Maybe soon.

* * *

Holden asked if Maleah would prefer going out or if she was all right with takeout and eating at his house. She liked the idea of having him to herself and staying in, and said so. They ordered dinner from India Garden and ate at Holden's breakfast bar. He stood up and ate because he owned one barstool.

"I don't mind. I eat right here every day." He smiled then drank his alkali water.

Holden didn't have alcohol in the house. He told Maleah he would buy her anything she wanted, but he wouldn't be joining her if she wanted wine or beer.

"When I'm training hard, I don't drink alcohol. It's a personal preference. Alcohol is dehydrating, and drinking can affect my motivation. I want any extra edge I can get when I am close to competition time."

"Oh, yeah. Right," she agreed and sipped her glass of alkali water that tasted exactly like... plain water. "How many Iron Man competitions have you competed in?"

"Five, but I also race in marathons and different cycling events. Would you like to move to the couch and watch something?"

"Do you have a movie in mind?" she asked.

"Let's find something we both like. There are quite a few documentaries in my queue I've been meaning to get to."

"Sounds good." Maleah slipped off the barstool and brought her empty plate to the sink.

"Don't worry about cleaning up. I'll take care of it later." Holden waited until she walked out of the kitchen and they entered the living room together.

He pulled the remote out of a small drawer in the end table and pointed it at the television on the wall.

"Everything in your house is..." She paused then started again. "It's so sparse and clean. Clutter free but to an extreme I've never seen before."

"Do you think it's weird?" he asked and sounded interested in her opinion, but not offended.

She sat down and he filled the other half of the small couch.

"No. Maybe. I don't know. It's different but not in a bad way. Have you always lived like this?"

"No. Not at all. I read this book about getting rid of clutter, but it wasn't only about decluttering your home. It was also about clearing mental space and being more productive. The ideas and concepts stayed with me. I kept researching minimalism and then adopted some of the practices. I noticed quickly how much clearer my mind was, and that led to being more focused on my goals. This"—he gestured to the room at large—"works for me on so many levels. It's okay if you think it's strange. I know it is compared to the way most people live."

"But you have everything you need and want, right?"

"I do," he said and looked pleased with her observation. "When I am not distracted with a lot of physical stuff, then I can direct more attention to my health, fitness, and most importantly my company. I may not always live minimally, but for now, it's okay."

"I think it's amazing that you know yourself so well."

Holden shifted so he was facing her. He set the remote to the side, the documentary forgotten. "I do. My focus on work and competing has left other areas of my life kind of empty and shallow, especially in the area of relationships." He took Maleah's hand in his.

Is this it? Would he confess his feelings for her? Should she?

"Holden, I..." She sucked in a breath and held it.

"You've been an amazing intern at True Green. I think I've told you that before. And you're incredibly attractive. This isn't easy for me to say. I don't open up to people often. It's difficult for me." He swallowed and smiled softly at her again.

"I like you too, Holden. Working at True Green has been the most incredible experience, but mostly it's because I was able to work with you." *Oh, God.* She wanted this. She wanted him to whisk her off the couch and take her to his bed. Single pillow, single blanket and all. Those things didn't matter. She wanted to feel his nakedness against hers. To run her hands over every muscle of his taut and delicious body. She leaned in.

"Maleah." Holden brushed a lock of hair off her brow. "I enjoyed working with you too. Now that you're no longer my employee we can become better acquainted."

"Yes," she breathed out. "I'd like that."

"But you need to know that I don't date women. I mean, I don't date men either." His brows pinched and he suddenly looked distressed. "I'm asexual."

She blinked, but the shock of being stunned with more bad news wouldn't be blinked away. She became temporarily frozen.

His distress lightened slightly, and he looked at her with a kind of longing she didn't recognize.

"I enjoy friendships and being around people. You are always so positive and easy to be with. I appreciate that about you so much, but I don't have those other feelings."

"Like, sexual feelings?" she said to clarify.

"It's rare for me to want someone in that way."

The taste of curry rose in the back of her throat, and she had to force it back down. "That is so interesting," she said with a flare of enthusiasm that was more forced than not. "You're incredible. The competing, your company, your dedication. I am in awe of your strength." She leaned in and gave him a hug. Maleah held on to Holden, closed her eyes, and silently prayed for some kind of mental fortitude or a bloody freaking miracle to get her through yet another situation she had no experience with. "Thank you for trusting me enough to tell me."

"It doesn't bother you?"

"No," she lied. "Can I ask you more about it? Or would you rather not talk about yourself?"

"Ask me anything you want. I know you won't judge me harshly. That's one of your greatest assets. You're open-minded and so kind. Do you want to take this conversation to the hot tub? I could use a soak. It's part of my self-care regimen."

"Hot tub?" The ability to maintain equanimity over freaking out and losing her mental-emotional shit was becoming more difficult by the second. *Now he wants to get almost naked with me, but sex is apparently not going to happen... ever?*

"The hot tub is on the patio out back. How about joining me? You have no idea what a relief it is knowing we can be good friends without the pressure of you needing me to take my pants off. You're such a treasure. Thank you for being exactly who you are." He rose from the couch and rolled his shoulders, twisted his trunk, and turned to look down at her.

"You're welcome," she said numbly. "I... I think my swimsuit is buried in the trailer. I doubt I could find it."

"That's okay. You can wear a pair of my shorts and a tank top. Or nothing. It's not as if seeing you naked will affect me."

"Umm..." She stood and tried to come up with the proper response.

"I'm kidding. Not about borrowing my shorts but about skinny dipping. Although, if that's your thing, it doesn't bother me. I have a biological viewpoint on the human form. No more, no less."

"I'll borrow some shorts and a tank top if you don't mind."

Ten

THERE WAS A NOTE jammed beneath the windshield wiper on his truck. Ben read it twice.

She can't rehire me after what she thinks *she saw between me and Kinsey. And she wants me to bill her for my time. Maleah Hale cannot afford the price of my time.* In Ben's opinion, time was more valuable than any other commodity. He'd given of his time freely because it was the right thing to do. He'd rescued her from the shower because it was the right thing to do. Thanking him in person would have been the right thing to do, too. But no, Maleah had written a terse note, which reinforced her decision to take away a large portion of a substantial contract he had with Kiki. And told him to leave a bill for *her* to pay at *her* convenience.

Things obviously needed to be cleared up between them. Ben would make time to set her straight on the situation between him and his ex and what she thought she saw. He turned to face the Columbine Building, intent on taking care of this right away. Then he stopped himself. Did he really have to prove anything or defend himself? The straight-up answer was no. Ben had learned over and over with Kinsey that whenever he thought he was right, his arguments would backfire. He'd be the one left standing there regretting ever opening his dumb mouth. Holding his tongue, letting things go, or choosing his words carefully, after the heat of the moment had long cooled were hard lessons learned, but he'd learned.

Plan strategically and don't take anything too seriously—unless death is on the line. After the years of stress and constant battling in fights that never had a winner, futility had become a drain on his life he no longer needed or wanted to participate in. Having a little fun was something else entirely. He'd wait. And he'd come up with something to let Maleah find out exactly how much he didn't appreciate her note.

* * *

Maleah blew into the coffee shop much like the gusty fall winds barreling down Main Street. Dust, debris, and fallen leaves swirled around the front doors of Mad Mountain Coffee Roasters before seeking the open spaces between cars and buildings and then rocketing off through town. She closed the front door against the atmospheric assault and smoothed her wild, dark hair with an impatient hand. Maleah missed a fluff of hair and it was left sticking out on the left side of her head. Her shirt collar was askew on the right side and the disheveled look indicated how ruffled Maleah was. With his invoice clutched in her hand and the hard line of her mouth, Ben anticipated he was in for a treat.

"You billed me eleven thousand dollars! A tire repair and the removal of a safety bar. You have to be kidding." She slapped the bill on the table.

Ben sobered his expression. "I assure you I am not kidding. Have a seat and let's discuss this."

She yanked the chair out from under the table and slid onto it. "But... what the hell, Ben? Please explain."

"The note you so thoughtfully left on my truck asked me to send you a bill for my time and services."

"I was imagining maybe a hundred dollars. Did you accidentally add a few zeros?"

"Nope."

She waved the paper at his face. "This is ridiculous. Absurd! You're a scammer."

"Am I?" His eyebrow ticked and he took a drink of coffee. "Should we discuss my payment options?"

She lowered her hand to the table, raised her chin, and set her jaw. "I'm not paying you eleven thousand dollars."

"I have your note as evidence to use in small claims court. I also have my brother to testify to the work completed on your car. Let's not make this more complicated than it needs to be. I will let you pay me off on a schedule that best fits your budget."

She blinked and her nostrils flared, but what Ben adored above all the rest of her signs of frustration and rising anger was the rosy blush coloring her cheeks. Damn, she had the prettiest complexion he'd ever seen. And the messy hair... yeah, he'd enjoy seeing her with mussed hair in a more intimate setting.

"Pay you off! I'm about two seconds from telling you to—to—" She glanced around the coffee shop. Two women with a toddler sat at a nearby table. The muscles of her jaw flexed and she said through clenched teeth, "To fork off and stuff this bill up your bung hole. You should be ashamed of yourself."

"Fork off? Is that similar to forking?" He couldn't help himself.

Her anger flared and she clearly didn't appreciate the wisecrack.

She leaned forward and lowered her voice. "Did you take advantage of Kinsey in a similar way? Is that why she was confronting you the other day? Did you screw her over too? Is this your dirty little secret, Ben? Taking advantage of women who need a helping hand? Do you pretend to be a nice guy and then rape them with outrageous fees for minimal work? What are you charging my aunt?"

He was glad she finally got to the crux of this meeting. Although the direction her mind went concerning Kinsey and his business ethics wasn't where he would have preferred, they could now move on to the reason he really wanted her here.

"Maleah, calm down." He'd always wanted to tell an irate woman that and watch them implode. Then he would reap the rewards when they figured out he was right after all was said and done.

"Calm down?" She kept her voice low enough to not be overheard by the other patrons in the shop—mostly. "Are you seriously out of your mind? I will not calm down. You are trying to take advantage of me when I was in a vulnerable position. Listen here, buddy, I am not some helpless female, and I certainly won't let you put your paws on me the way you did to your wife." She huffed, sucked in a breath, and was about to keep expounding, but Ben interjected.

"First of all, if you'll let me explain the bill, maybe you could try and see things from a contractor's perspective."

Her nostrils flared again, but she remained silent.

Ben continued. "What you thought you witnessed has cost me one-third of my contract with Kiki."

She interrupted, "You can't bill me for that!"

"I wouldn't have, but since you asked me to with your oh-so-pleasant note, I felt obligated."

"My note, but I thought..."

"You thought you should thank me for saving your butt... twice... but then couldn't get over yourself enough to ask me about Kinsey. Assuming the worst about me is what drove you to cancel everything Kiki and I have worked on for months. To find the right subcontractors, rental equipment, hours of meetings, phone calls, plans, and inspections are now all *finito* because of what you thought you saw or heard. Well, sweetheart, my time is more valuable than your assumptions and the eleven thousand dollars doesn't even cover all of my losses."

Her face paled and Ben watched as she stopped breathing. Would she faint? *What's happening?*

Maleah's lips barely moved as she said, "But you shoved her into the car. It was terrible, and I heard you yelling at that poor electrician. I don't want you working in the building if you are a danger to me or my family. My aunt agrees with me."

Ben's conflict with Kinsey had been scary but not in a way he was willing to discuss with Maleah in a coffee shop. He was scared because his ex had proved in the past she would do anything, say anything, and use his daughter to get what she wanted, no matter the cost to Ben's livelihood, sanity, or heart. No, this wasn't the place to talk about his personal problems.

"I, uh, I'm sorry," she said, stumbling over her words. "I'm not sorry for excusing you from your contract with my aunt. But I am sorry for getting myself worked up over your outrageous invoice. I see we have reached an impasse." She straightened her shoulders and blinked twice before continuing. "I cannot afford to pay this off in one payment. I will have to make some adjustments and then I will get back to you. I might speak to an attorney first."

Ben cracked a slow grin. "Now that I have your attention, let me clear something up." He placed his hands flat on the table. "First, I wrote out that bill to get you as worked up as I felt after reading your note. Kinsey assaulted me, among other issues, and I was protecting myself. You can choose to believe that or not. I can't make you change your mind about what you saw and heard. Second of all, the electrician deserved to be fired. He is a worthless, lazy jackass. If I was slightly more agitated and forceful with him the other morning than I normally would have been, it is because of what happened between me and Kinsey. I'm not going into the details about the conversation and demands Kinsey laid on me, but I was upset. I admit it. No, I don't expect you to pay me eleven grand. I don't even want a single penny from you. Understanding I am not the monster you have somehow made me out to be is the sole purpose for this meeting." He picked up the false invoice and ripped it in half.

"But... you. You wanted me to meet you here because of what?"

She was clearly confused, and Ben didn't want to deliver the whole speech again. "Darlin', I just like teasing you. And they serve a good cup of coffee in here."

She stood and stepped out from behind the table. Maleah delivered her slow blinking stare again. He was growing used to the contemptuous glare she could deliver with a blink of her expressive eyes framed with those gorgeous long lashes.

"You like the coffee here?" she asked, and the tone of her voice sent a shiver over his arms.

"I'll buy you a cup for your trouble," he offered. "And you can confirm with at least half the folks in town that I'm not some kind of hustler, and that I would never lay a hand on Kinsey or any woman for that matter."

She tipped her head to the side and narrowed her pretty almond-shaped eyes. "I suppose if I were to ask Kinsey or her friends, I might get another story."

"Possibly. As I said, I can't make you change your mind about what you saw. I might have some bruises and scratches from what she did to me. I can show you later if you want."

Maleah's head jerked in a nod... or a twitch. She leaned over the table and jabbed her finger at the ripped invoice. "And you made up this bill just to get me down here so I could make a fool of myself?"

The urge to laugh had Ben sticking his tongue in his cheek. She wasn't playing, and he was walking a razor thin line. He shrugged. "You should have come and talked to me. Your note was equally frustrating."

"Frustrating? You have no idea what I've been dealing with, Ben Erickson." She sounded an awful lot like his mother after he'd done something exceptionally disappointing.

The thought made him smirk to himself. *Why am I like this?*

"Would you care to sit down and talk about it over coffee?" he offered again, but she wasn't anywhere near ready to settle down.

"Over coffee? Sure." She calmly picked up his cup and took a drink. He couldn't take his eyes off her slender hand wrapped around the coffee mug and the way the rim of the cup touched her shapely pink lips. She lowered the mug and smiled, but it wasn't kind or caring like the way she'd smiled at him over dinner at The Jackalope.

As he stared, trying to figure out what had morphed her expression, she dumped the coffee over his head. "You've just started a war, pal."

* * *

After an eye-opening night at Holden's, Maleah found herself more emotionally unsettled than before returning to Boulder. Brielle texted her constantly, and Maleah didn't have all the answers. What she figured out within hours of waking up in Holden's guest room was that she couldn't stay in his empty house, and she was still needed in Three Peaks. Also, she didn't want to continue paying rent for the moving trailer or rent a storage unit for her belongings. By late morning, she was at the gas station once again refilling the tank on her car and ready to make the return drive to her home town.

She'd found Ben's fake invoice that evening and nearly had a coronary. Brielle settled her down and told her to wait for their meeting at the coffee shop.

The nerve of him. Maleah didn't know how she was going to get back at Ben for making a fool of her, but she swore she would figure something out. Currently, she had too much on her plate to give Ben a lot of thought. Too bad he was constantly invading her head anyway.

The following morning after the disastrous meeting with Ben at Mad Mountain Coffee, Maleah and Brielle went to check up on Kiki. The three of them sat in the hospital room discussing the renovations laid out inside Kiki's three-ring binder.

"The thing is, I don't need a contractor's license to do most of the remaining work on the Columbine Building. Thankfully, the exterior work is finished," Maleah said. "Uncle Raymond has hooked us up with a new electrician. Drywall and texture can be hired out, and so can the trim work. I can lay tile, paint, and refinish the floors. These are all the things I did with my parents growing up. The building is larger than the houses we worked on, but I can do this. And I will do it better than Ben Erickson." Maleah was talking herself into taking on the massive project just as much as trying to convince her aunt and cousin.

"Are you sure this is what you want, Maleah? What if you get a job offer in the middle of retiling the bathrooms? Will I have to beg Ben to come back and clean up after you?" Aunt Kiki asked.

"No. I won't do that to you." She hesitated and stared up at the ceiling, thinking and considering all the possibilities.

Brielle said, "I'm here for the foreseeable future, Grandma. If Maleah leaves because she's offered the job of a lifetime, I'll take over. We decided to do this together if you let us live in the building."

"Of course you have to stay in the apartment for me. Who knows when they will let me out of this joint," Kiki said with a heavy sigh laden with a dose of frustration.

Maleah laid her hand on Kiki. "You have to heal a little while longer, but you'll have your mobility back soon, I promise."

"Getting old is the pits, girls. The alternative isn't great either. I'm stuck here for now, and I think you will both do a wonderful job managing the remodel of my building. It makes me happy knowing I can count on you. But I want you to promise me something."

Brielle said, "Anything."

Maleah said, "What can we do?"

"Don't take yourselves so seriously. You're young and you need to enjoy the process. Before you know it, life is flying by at warp speed and miseries are landing in your lap faster than you can blink at. Work at a job that's fun. If you enjoy working on the Columbine Building, I am happy for you. If it stinks, then fire yourselves and move on. If you don't enjoy your work or get some satisfaction from it, you'll regret those lost years. Okay? That is what I need from both of you. And I need you to keep an eye out for my turtle."

Maleah had broken the news about not finding Ricky in the dumpster, but Aunt Kiki had not given up hope of finding her diamond and gold turtle necklace.

"I'll keep looking, Auntie," Maleah said.

"I don't have any experience with remodeling, Grandma, but if Maleah is set on doing this, then I want to help. And I have a plan to make this venture suit my skills as well. Being back in Three Peaks is going to be great for all of us." Brielle's smile held a hint of mischief.

"What are you talking about, Brie?" Maleah asked.

"I'll tell you everything later. I have some details to work out before discussing it with you."

"I don't like the face you're making," Maleah said.

"Same to you." Brielle's grin grew wider.

They had always acted more like sisters than cousins. It'd been too long since they'd spent time together. While Maleah had been so focused on building her career, she hadn't realized how much she missed her family. Even though she had lost so much in the last week, having their support was holding her up and keeping her sane and grounded.

Maleah tried again to wheedle Brielle's plans out of her. "You're up to something," she accused.

"Yep, and I'm not ready to talk about it." Brielle focused on her grandmother. "You'll know everything when I do. I need to let the ideas stew longer."

"Take as long as you need. I'm not going anywhere. The doctors are monitoring me for everything. I tell you, at this rate, I should move in here permanently. But at least you girls can have the apartment to yourselves."

Maleah and Brielle exchanged a look.

"No. You're going to be able to go home soon," Maleah said, even though the doctors had been vague about Aunt Kiki's release from their care."

"They want to sort out my blood pressure problems, my bone density, and my real hair color. Soon, they're going to be asking if I'm a republican or a democrat and whether or not the moon is made of cheese. This place is ridiculous."

Maleah nodded in agreement and was glad Kiki's gumption was intact.

"We'll have a meeting with your doctor. All of us. Together," Brielle said.

"I will set something up before we leave today," Maleah added.

"You two are angels. Thank you for being here," Aunt Kiki said. "I think I'll take a nap now. I get tired so easily."

Maleah kissed her aunt's cheek. "You're still healing. Take this time to rest as much as you can."

They stood and said their goodbyes. With the binder in her hands, Maleah was now ready to take on all the projects that needed to be finished.

She and Brielle scheduled a face-to-face meeting with Kiki and her doctor for the following day. While Maleah waited for Brielle to use the restroom, Ben walked into the main lobby.

"Look who it is," he said and then continued when she experienced instantaneous mental comatose trying to come up with an appropriate greeting to her new arch nemesis. "I enjoyed my coffee bath. That was a memorable touch to our meeting," he said with that teasing lilt that simultaneously put Maleah on guard and secretly made her crave for more.

"What are you doing here?" she asked. *So smooth,* she thought and wished she had another cup of coffee.

"Visiting my grandfather," he said without a blink.

Maleah was expecting him to say something about Kiki and was surprised by his answer. Her sympathy kicked in before she could stop herself. "Oh. I'm sorry. Is he okay?" Her soft spot—she had many—for the sick or injured couldn't be tempered.

"He's doing okay, thanks." Ben's tone softened after she asked with genuine concern. "He lives in the assisted living apartments, but he had a minor episode this morning. They moved him to a hospital room for twenty-four-hour observation as a precaution. We're keeping our fingers crossed that he'll be back in his apartment by tomorrow."

"Let me know if there is anything I can do." She said the words automatically and then regretted it. She forced a sympathetic smile and reined in her empathy. No, she didn't want to do anything for Ben, no matter how cute he was or endearing those dimples were. Maleah was still upset about his prank at the coffee shop.

As if reading her mind, Ben said, "I see you have Kiki's portfolio. Did you decide it's too big of a job for you after all?" The teasing smirk was back.

"Umm… no," she said, letting her annoyance be heard. "Not even close. I'm starting the plaster repair today." She was stretching the truth, but she was going to start researching the cost of supplies.

"That's great. It'd be fun to see you on a pair of stilts. Can I come over and watch? Or I could lend a hand. Maybe give you a lesson."

"No," she said again. "What part of you don't work there anymore is hard to understand?"

He shrugged. "Just thought I could offer some expert advice. I'll be on the job site next door after I finish up here. You can fetch me when you're in need of an extra hand. I'm very handy."

"You're unbelievable," she corrected.

"Right back at you, babe."

"Don't call me that." She narrowed her eyes, staring at him like the insignificant spec he was turning out to be. A sexy, muscled spec that needed to be wiped away and forgotten.

His teasing grin lingered, and for a brief second, she thought he knew she was thinking about the bulging biceps and sculpted pecs beneath his flannel shirt.

Ben stepped in closer and lowered his voice. "My apologies, ma'am. I have some bad habits that are hard to break."

"Invading someone's personal space must be another one of them."

"You didn't mind when you were naked in the shower, though, did you?"

She swallowed. "That was an unfortunate situation that I won't put myself in again, thank you very much."

"Hmm..." He made a thoughtful sound as he lowered his face an inch closer to hers.

Is he smelling me? She wouldn't back down. She couldn't let herself look weak or intimidated. *But he smells amazing.*

"I just thought of something you could do for Grandpa Joe."

Dang it. Why had she opened her mouth? *Stupid. Stupid. Where is Brielle?* "What's that?" She breathed out the words as regret filled the spaces between them. Maleah was too responsible to take her offer to help back... and it was for an injured old man not Ben. She waited.

Ben drew out the pause, then said, "Never mind. We don't need more of your drama in our lives right now."

She was so surprised by his reply, which sounded an awful lot like a judgmental assessment of her character, that she temporarily forgot how to speak.

Ben laughed and backed up.

Maleah shoved his shoulder. "You are… just…" She was so worked up that her words came out in a disjointed mess.

Ben completed her sentence. "…never going to let Ben Erickson tease you again," he said slowly and laughed as he started to walk toward the doors that led to the patient care wing.

"Yeah, that," she said lamely.

He turned around, walked backward, and smiled a most satisfied and glorious grin. "You make it so easy, Maleah. By the way"—he placed his hand on his chest—"I can't wait for retaliation. Bring it on, babe. Bring it on. Oops, I used the forbidden word again. Sorry," he said and didn't look the least bit sorry. He spun back around in time to reach for the door.

"Fork you, Ben Erickson!" she called and watched his shoulders shake with another hearty laugh.

"You're yelling. Inside a hospital."

Maleah startled at the sound. She unclenched her fists when she found Brielle staring at her. "Ben! Ooh," she growled. "He makes me so—"

"So flustered and adorable."

"Shut up. I am not adorable." Maleah rolled her eyes and stalked off toward the exit.

Brielle caught up with her and they left the hospital. "I bet he thinks you are. Why else would he keep getting in your face and triggering you?"

"How much did you see?" Maleah made a beeline for the Land Cruiser and tried to ignore Brielle.

"Enough to know why you call him 'Hot Guy.' He's super cute."

"Yeah, you think so?" she said with as much snark as she could muster. "Good, because you can have him. But don't say I didn't warn you."

They climbed inside the vintage four-by-four and Maleah set the binder on the floor behind her seat. She cranked the key and gave the engine a minute to warm up.

"He is nice to look at," Brielle said conversationally. "Rugged but not too rough. He has an appealing body shape and a nice face. You can't go wrong there, but he's not my type." She shook her head and looked adamant about her statement.

Maleah laughed, releasing a healthy amount of the wire-taut tension in her body. "He's cute, so you know he's not your type? Explain," she said as she drove out of the parking lot.

"I appreciate nerdy types. I know how ridiculous that sounds, but that's what I always go for. There's something sexy about weird, awkward guys that seriously turns me on."

Maleah laughed again. "It's because likes attract."

"Yeah, probably." Brielle turned wide, accusing eyes on Maleah. "You just called me nerdy and awkward, didn't you?"

"Yep," Maleah said unapologetically.

"Yeah, I know. The more I want to be popular or cool or pretty, the weirder I realize I am. It's okay. I'll stick to my computers, research, and books. They're better company than most of the people I meet."

"What are you always doing on your computer anyway?" Maleah tried to understand what her cousin did to make money when she'd said she'd been in libraries in Ireland, but she'd ended up spacing out after about a minute of Brielle's explanation.

"Besides gaming, I'm mostly digital archiving. I acquire, arrange, describe, and preserve regional history and cultural materials. I determine the appropriate intellectual organization and digital storage structure for the materials I'm assigned to work with. There is intellectual content and historical research involved and then the preparation of metadata descriptions. In Ireland I was digital archiving as a subcontractor for the head librarians to work on specific small collections. They paid me per finished collection. I could have stayed and worked on a new project, but Grandma needs me here. So, now I'm here. Honestly, it was probably time for a break. I get so wrapped up in the job that I forget there is a life outside of books, documents, files, and organizing and creating."

"Uh-huh," Maleah mumbled because she'd zoned out again about halfway through what Brielle said. Something about the words digital archiving sent Maleah's thoughts in any alternative direction. Her first project inside the Columbine Building excited her, but the way Ben smelled when he stepped into her personal bubble was all-consuming. His cologne reminded her of amber and sandalwood but with a woodsy undertone.

Oh, she could bury her nose against his neck, feel the soft scratch of his jaw against her skin, and breathe him in until she narrowed down if she was smelling fresh cut lumber or his sweat.

She refocused on her cousin. "Oh, right. I get that. I've been buried in the science of sustainable, biodegradable plastics. I don't even know who I am anymore," she admitted half to herself and half to her cousin. Apparently, she'd heard enough of Brielle's explanation to add her sympathies.

"Since we're both out of our comfort zone, I say we embrace the changes that have befallen us."

Befallen? Maleah let her cousin's word choice slide and asked, "How are we going to do that?"

"We're doing it right now by living in a construction site and doing things we've never done before."

"You've never done them before. I was forced to help my parents remodel, renovate, clean, scrub, paint, and build just about everything."

"Okay, new to me," she conceded. "I'll be your apprentice."

"And I think I will be on the phone quite a lot with my dad," Maleah said, thinking about everything she didn't know about construction.

"I can learn anything on YouTube," Brielle said with a snort.

"Great. And I'll probably be watching over your shoulder," Maleah said. Her confidence in being able to do everything that was needed on the building wasn't nearly as high as she wanted it to be.

They shared another laugh as Maleah pulled into the hardware store parking lot.

* * *

Over the next few days, Maleah discovered that subcontractors were extremely unreliable. If Maleah wanted to stay anywhere near Aunt Kiki's renovating schedule, she was going to have to do what she could, when she could, around whichever workers decided to show up.

Luck continued to be on her side when it came to the electricians. Her uncle's referral came through, and Guillaume arrived with a crew of men on the day they said they would. The electricians were going to rewire and update the entire building. Late in the afternoon, Maleah walked outside to dump the old bathroom tiles in the dumpster and noticed Guillaume speaking with Ben. They walked past the Aspen Building and entered the Cinquefoil Building together. She wondered if Ben still needed a reliable electrician. If she was on better speaking terms with him, and not contemplating her revenge, she might have joined them and taken a tour of her aunt's third building. She chose to stay out of it. Ben could hire anyone he chose as long as he didn't steal the contractors working on her building.

Guillaume confirmed the following day that Ben asked him if he was available to do a similar job on the Cinquefoil Building as what he was currently doing for Columbine.

Maleah nodded graciously. "I'm happy to hear you will be able to complete the work on my aunt's block."

"Why are you working separately? Ms. Kiki owns the whole block, does she not? Why am I working for you, here, and Ben over there?" He gestured vaguely in the direction of the Cinquefoil Building. "This is more paperwork for everyone, yeah? I enjoy working on these historical places, but this make no sense to me." His accent created somewhat stilted sentences, but Maleah loved the sound and cadence.

She worked her lips back and forth as she attempted to come up with a PC answer that wouldn't embarrass her or anyone else.

Perhaps he noticed her sudden discomfort, because Guillaume waved a dismissive hand and said, "I only curious, but tis no matter. This is a truly wonderful building. Me and my guys will finish in about a week. I get back to work now." He nodded to himself and turned for the stairs.

The electricians were wiring all the apartments on the third floor while Maleah was laying tile in the new bathrooms or retiling the old bathrooms. The first-floor restrooms were finished, but that left a lot of work for her to do on the second and third floors. Brielle helped, but they quickly discovered Maleah had to do all the tile cutting. Brielle couldn't seem to get the hang of it, but she was good at laying the tiles and grouting. They worked well together, save for Brielle's need to take extended breaks and video record everything. Maleah rolled her eyes at the requested video lessons, but Brie insisted that it helped her learn how to do the tile work. She wanted to watch the videos instead of continually asking Maleah to show her again.

At night, they watched tutorials or scoured the internet for design ideas in an attempt to educate themselves for their upcoming projects. Somehow, after countless days, they had finished one bathroom and started on the second one.

In the midst of the bathroom remodeling, Maleah called the drywall company to confirm their start date.

"We should be able to start on Monday. I'll let you know if something comes up, but at the latest Tuesday or Wednesday."

Her father had warned her of how likely it was to run into these guys who would keep stringing you along, and she was prepared for it, but she'd also give the drywallers the benefit of the doubt and wait until Wednesday before panicking.

She and Brielle ran out of the glass accent tiles on a Wednesday afternoon. They returned to the supplier for two more boxes, which should be enough to finish the project, and were informed there were no more in stock. The tile had to be ordered and would arrive by the middle of next week. End of the week at the latest.

They walked away from the customer service counter and Maleah said, "I'm going to start patching the walls and then painting what I can. I can't do nothing for an entire week."

"Floors after paint, right?" Brie asked.

"I think that is for the best. If we refinish the floors first, then I'll be super paranoid about getting paint on the pretty new floors."

"And paint before the trim work, yes?" Brielle said as they walked toward the drywall, plaster, and joint compound section of the store.

"Wherever we can. Again, it will save us work later."

"I have to tell you. I have never been so sore and tired in my entire life. No wonder Hot Guy has such huge muscles. Ugh. This kind of work is so hard."

"Because you're not used to it," Maleah said.

They put drywall mud, tape, screws, and a broad knife in their shopping cart.

Brielle whined some more. "Exactly. I'm not used to it. I suck at manual labor."

"But we're embracing the changes in our life, remember? This is good for us," Maleah said, even though she was also sore and tired. But the difference between her and Brielle was that she found the work incredibly satisfying. She liked puzzling the bathroom tiles together, seeing each piece fit against one another, and how the bathroom was transforming into a beautiful space. Her muscles ached and the skin on her hands was raw, but she didn't mind.

"Whatever. I need the weekend off. And I need a hot tub, a heating pad, and a bottle of tequila."

"Don't forget the limes. Should we stop at the store before heading back then?"

"Yes! Let's pick up a pizza, breadsticks, and some salad. Then we should treat ourselves to margaritas. Next week, I am working with a pitcher of sangria by my side and taking shots of laudanum as necessary."

"Really?" Maleah asked, giving her cousin the side-eye.

"No, not really." Brielle sighed and her shoulders drooped. "I'm too responsible to become a druggie. Too bad."

Maleah laughed quietly to herself. "I feel ya. But taking the weekend off is a good idea. Also, I'm on a ramen diet. So, unless you're buying the alcohol and takeout, consider me not pitching in. I'm jobless and broke, remember?"

They set their items on the checkout counter.

"I am buying. That's not up for debate. I totally need my comfort food and comfort bed, pillows, blankies, cozy socks, and a soak in the tub. I need to veg out with my laptop for a solid forty-eight hours. I'm all about comfort. I don't know why you aren't."

"I'm too poor."

"Too motivated and strict is more like it," Brielle said.

"Probably," Maleah said.

They paid with Kiki's business credit card and headed back to the Land Cruiser. Maleah had been living on such a tight budget for so long that it had become normal for her to constantly scrimp. Brielle acted as if money was an endless supply. Maleah didn't know what that was like. Aunt Kiki insisted on paying Maleah an hourly wage for her work, but Maleah was adamant about a two-week pay schedule, documenting all her hours in a spreadsheet, and she wanted rent taken off her wages. To her, it was fair. Brielle agreed to the same deal, but acted like they had been paid four times over when they hadn't received their first checks yet. Maleah was curious as to how much money her cousin had saved from her work as an archivist, but she didn't ask. It was none of her business, but she was curious about her cousin's spending habits.

After shopping, they were so tired and hungry that making margaritas was too much effort. Maleah drank one sparkling wine cooler with her pizza and salad and then fell asleep.

For the next two days Maleah dove into drywall repairs and cleaning. Brielle insisted on videoing everything Maleah did and didn't actually do much work. As planned, they would take the weekend off and celebrate their accomplishments for the week with a margarita party on Friday night.

Margaritas of the traditional variety tasted exceptional, but Brielle wanted to try frozen strawberry and peach flavored margaritas as well. They drank and then drank some more. Maleah couldn't recall the last time she'd been so blitzed. Then she remembered her night spent with the bottle of Marsala and her stomach churned.

"I'm going to go eat jalapeno poppers and that giant cheesy pretzel thing they serve over at The Jackalope. Do you want to come with me?"

"No," Maleah said as she stared at the hazy yellow light streaming in through the large apartment windows facing Main Street. Reflective streaks of white, blue, and amber light blended together and made her think of Christmas. Would she be in Three Peaks at Christmas? Would she still be working on the building? Should she be looking for a new job? What would happen when she was finished working on Columbine? Would she be homeless again? Would she have to start waiting tables or working as a cashier at the store? Drunken worrying had set in, and she didn't want to go to a public place in her current mood. "You can't keep buying me expensive food and drinks. I'm not a mooch. I'm going to eat toast and contemplate the meaning of my dry-toast filled life."

"You are not a fun drunk."

"No. I'm not. This is why I don't drink. Too often," she amended. "Life is hard, Brielle. How did I wind up here, working for my great-aunt in the town I grew up in? I'm pathetic. My life is broken."

"I'm walking out now," Brielle called from somewhere by the door. "Don't dwell on things that make you unhappy. Come eat salty, fatty bar food with me. I think The Jackalope has live music on Friday nights."

"No. I'm not a moocher. Stop tempting me. I want toast. Plain, boring, and cheap toast. And I want to be sober."

"You're such a drag. See ya," Brielle said.

Maleah heard the apartment door close and she was grateful to be alone.

Then she wasn't. Her mind was stuck on all the things that had gone wrong in her young life. Feeling bad for herself wasn't who she was. She needed to focus on the positive. A distraction was exactly what she needed to get out of the funk she'd put herself in.

Maleah hefted herself off the couch and into the kitchen. First things first, she needed food. Toast still sounded good. Bread would help soak up the alcohol and help clear her head. Then she would feel better and stop brooding over the things in her life she couldn't control.

She saw a package of tortillas and decided a bean burrito went better with margaritas. She filled a tortilla with canned refried beans, cheese, and hot sauce, threw it in the microwave, and chowed down. Then she made another one.

If you're going to do something, go all in. She'd learned that from her dad. With thoughts of her father, she picked up her phone and called. Drunk calling her parents was acceptable, wasn't it? How was he doing? Was her mother going stir-crazy having to nurse him every day?

Am I going stir-crazy? Driving back and forth to the hospital had become another one of her new jobs. Her mind was beginning to circle back to her plight when she realized she'd listened to her mother's entire voicemail message. They weren't home. Maleah said something about nothing and then ended the call.

Brie was right, Maleah was not a fun drunk.

But she was motivated. Earlier in the day, she'd finished the drywall repairs in two bathrooms and the entire first floor hallway. The rooms she'd worked on were ready for paint. The idea struck her that if she could see some color on the walls it would feel like she'd made a giant step toward finishing at least one part of the building.

Maleah stuffed a handful of tortilla chips in her mouth, chewed, then washed everything down with a glass of water. She felt slightly more sober. At least enough to start working again. Work kept her busy and kept her mind off her problems.

Eleven

GRANDPA JOE WAS UNABLE to return to his apartment after slipping and falling on the bathroom floor in his hospital room. He sprained his wrist and hit his head. His nurses and doctor insisted on further observation and tests to be sure he didn't fall because of an underlying issue that could possibly be related to his dementia.

Ben accepted the news much the same way he'd dealt with all of Grandpa's health problems. It was difficult to watch one of the strongest and most sound men he'd ever known deteriorate, but Ben remained grateful that his grandfather was still with them. Whatever hand Grandpa Joe was dealt, whatever he needed, the Ericksons were there for him.

But when Ben pushed the door to Grandpa's room open and found a woman in bed with him, he backpedaled so quickly he nearly took out some poor nursing assistant in the hallway.

"Whoa there! Sorry." Ben stumbled, turned, and said, "My apologies, ma'am."

She gave him a disapproving look and went back to studying the chart in her hands as she continued down the hall. Another staff member approached and placed her hand on the door, ready to go in.

The warning was out of his mouth before thinking of the repercussions. "Joe may be indisposed at the moment."

She gave him a questioning look. "That's all right. I'm his nurse. There isn't much I haven't seen."

She pushed the door open before Ben could explain further... Then again, he didn't want to. He didn't want to speak of what he witnessed ever again. Yet, as he stood there, his mind couldn't stop reliving and thinking about what was transpiring on the other side of the door.

Holy hell on wheels. Grandpa has a woman in his bed. That dog. But how? Why? And who? Ben had not taken the time to see who she was. How was Joe handling the situation? Over the last couple years, his grandfather's mind had turned into an enigma that could not be defined. The dementia wasn't terrible most of the time, but some serious incidents had been concerning enough to Joe and all the family members that moving into the assisted living complex was justifiable and necessary. Could someone who couldn't always remember where he lived or to turn off the water have a girlfriend? How would that work?

He contemplated leaving and coming back later, but he heard voices from inside the room. Ben knocked before entering this time. One thing he knew for certain was that it was important for Grandpa to have an advocate or an extra set of ears in the room.

Kiki Brookhart stood next to Grandpa's bed as the nurse delivered a speech about hospital policies and patient protocol regarding personal and private visits. Ben's mouth and throat went dry and he slapped a hand over his eyes to hide from the truth. *Kiki? They are probably close to the same age but...*

"You're his grandson, aren't you? You should hear this as well," she said and then continued, "Who is Mr. Erickson's official guardian?"

Ben massaged his forehead then dropped his hand. "My parents," he said.

"I will be contacting them immediately to discuss what has happened today. Then we will move forward with disciplinary steps."

"Whoa, there. Discipline? Wait up a minute—" Ben said but was interrupted by his grandfather.

"Stop talking to me like I am a child," Joe said with enough authority to make the nurse pull back. "I've heard enough. Go on and excuse yourself, Nurse Ratched. You're dismissed." He motioned to the door.

"I will not be dismissed. You are the patient here, Mr. Erickson," Nurse Ratched said.

Ben wondered what her real name was, but for the time being, Nurse Ratched was equally hilarious and completely fitting.

Grandpa pulled the sheet back and began to swing his legs off the bed. "If you won't leave, then me and my gal will."

Since his gown was pushed up around his waist, everyone in the room got the Full Monty view of Grampa's junk. Ben turned his head, blinked, and poured imaginary bleach into his eyes.

"It's okay, Joe. I need to get back to my room. We'll work this out later with Nurse Jenny. She's a sweetie and will listen to us better than this lady." Kiki placed a hand on Joe's shoulder, holding him back from leaving the bed. "Don't get up. I'll see myself out." Joe leaned back and looked at Kiki. Ben noticed how his grandfather instantly settled down and how Kiki held his full attention. He and the nurse were forgotten. Kiki bent down and kissed Grandpa's cheek. "See you later, cutie."

"You better come back and see me," Joe said. "I ain't no piece of meat to be used at your discretion. Or maybe I am."

Kiki giggled and patted the side of her head where her hair was in more disarray than Ben had ever seen before.

She walked around the bed and smiled up at Ben. He closed his mouth, which apparently had been hanging open.

"We'll talk later, okay? Is everything all right on my Garden Block? No exploding gas lines or dumpster fires?" Kiki asked, her head tilted inquiringly.

"All is well," he managed to say.

"Good, good." She didn't look at all embarrassed, although Ben suspected she was.

The woman must have had years of practice at putting on a good façade when needed. Ben considered himself fairly adequate at covering his true emotions with diversion or a joke, and he recognized the tactic now in Kiki.

She let herself out, and Ben returned his attention to his grandfather and the nurse.

"She's still here," Grandpa grumbled. "Ask her to leave. Apparently, I am nothing but a child to be scolded."

Ben shifted his gaze to the nurse.

"I don't appreciate your attitude, Mr. Erickson. We have rules and regulations in place to protect our patients."

Grandpa shook his head and lines of discontent and impatience deepened on his weathered, wrinkled face.

Ben intervened before Grandpa decided to try and leave again or personally escort the uptight witch from the room.

He faced Nurse Ratched. "Would you mind giving us a minute alone, please? I'll speak with him about the situation, and you can contact the family if you think it's necessary."

Her mouth tightened, and she didn't look pleased, but she left.

The humor of the moment began to sink in and Ben closed his eyes before turning back around. *Why me?* Ben found himself questioning his reality often but had learned to accept whatever the present moment delivered. What else could he do?

"I don't want to hear it, young man. Your grandmother and I have been married for over half a century. It's our business and no one else's what goes on in the bedroom. Not to mention that I enjoy the female body. Don't you?"

Grandmother? That set off alarm bells. "You mean Ms. Brookhart, right?"

"Of course. Who else would I be talking about? Do you think I'm some kind of man slut? Never have been. I've always been faithful. I never even looked at other women when I was married to Helen."

Ben let his grandfather's slip of the tongue go for now. With the dementia, it was increasingly difficult to know when Grandpa mixed up words or memories.

"So, have you had a girlfriend for long?" he asked as casually as possible and took a seat in the visitor's chair by the bed.

Ben's tone seemed to ease Joe's tension over being caught doing the deed in his hospital room.

"Ms. Brookhart and I have known one another for years. I never thought of her as a girlfriend until the other day when she stopped by to see how I'm holdin' up. She's a good gal, isn't she? Cutest little piece of ass this side of our eighties."

Ben started to laugh at his grandfather's choice of words but covered it up by clearing his throat. "She's been easy to work with, and she's an excellent cook. She loves Skyla."

"What more could you ask for?" Grandpa winked and slapped his thigh. "I think I'll keep her."

Ben nodded as his grandfather's announcement sank in. "As long as you're both happy, right?"

"Damn straight. Did you bring my wings and beer? I sure could use them after my time with Ms. Brookhart."

Ben's discomfort peaked. He stuck his tongue in his cheek before telling his grandfather he'd bring the hot wings next time, and didn't mention the missing beer. Something that wasn't allowed in the hospital room.

Ben stopped by his parents' house on the way home to forewarn them about Joe's new relationship and offer his side of the story versus what the nurse might have said. He didn't want to rehash the story, but they shared a laugh, and then his mom offered to feed Ben dinner. He couldn't tell her no, and truthfully, he didn't want to return to his trailer either.

He was supposed to have Skyla for the night, but his daughter had called and begged to go to a birthday sleepover at her friend's house. Since Kinsey was still threatening to take Skyla to Alaska and away from all her friends, he couldn't tell her no. Ben was alone on a Friday night... again. Dinner at his parents' filled his stomach but didn't relieve the loneliness of being without his own family, namely his daughter... or his dog. Yep, Kinsey had the dog too.

After visiting with his parents, Ben returned to town, but instead of sitting in his trailer watching TV or working on miscellaneous business matters, he hiked across the street and stepped inside The Jackalope.

By the time he got there, the Friday night band was taking a break between sets. He planted himself on a barstool and waited for Riley, the bartender, to take his order.

"What're you drinking?"

"Pint of stout," he said.

Riley pumped the beer from the brass tap and set the glass in front of him. The bartender asked the woman next to Ben, "You doing all right? Ready for a refill?"

She said, "I'm fine for now."

Ben noticed her for the first time. She sat two barstools over and he wasn't sure how in the world he'd missed an entire human being, especially a nice looking one, but he had. Then he realized it was Brielle, Kiki's granddaughter. He'd seen her going in and out of the Columbine Building.

He spun the barstool a few degrees in her direction. "How's it going? I'm Ben. Your neighbor."

She had been in the middle of taking a drink. The glass clunked against the bar top as she set it down in a rush to reply. "Hey. Yeah, I've seen you around." Her shoulders curled forward and she leaned closer to the bar and stared at her glass.

Ben downed about a third of his pint and wondered about Brielle. On the outside she was rather cute, but if he was reading her posture correctly, he was making her nervous or... something.

He'd try one more time to be friendly. "How's everything going at your place? I'd like to thank you and Maleah for finding a new electrician. Guillaume seems like a great guy and a hard worker."

"He's been all right, I guess," she said with a measured dose of awkwardness. Ben was going to let it go and leave Brielle alone, but she kept talking. "Maleah is better at hiring the contractors. I'm just her slave."

A grin spread across Ben's face. "She's a slave driver, eh? I wouldn't have guessed."

"She's terrible. She's always on me about doing some new thing, or hauling supplies and equipment from one side of the building to the other. Up and down the elevator, all day long. And she's always cleaning something and trying to make me help her. I'm not cut out for this kind of abuse."

Ben nodded, enjoying Brielle's story a little too much. "Is your cousin here?" He glanced around, hoping to get a glimpse of the pretty, but apparently demanding, Maleah Hale.

"I couldn't talk her into coming with me. I needed a change of scenery. You must know how it feels to live and work in the same place all the time. It's dreadful. How do you do it? I have plans to make this renovation thing more... um... exciting. Don't tell my cousin, though. I'm working out some details." She took a drink and bumped her lip. Brielle grabbed a bar napkin and cleaned her face. "Oops. This drinking thing is a messy business."

Ben then realized he may be conversing with a rather drunk young woman. "Exciting how?"

She placed her forearms on the bar and leaned his way. With a lowered voice she said, "I can't tell you. I want to, but I don't believe in revealing my secrets to any Joe Schmo."

"I understand. Do you need someone to walk you home?"

Brielle inched forward. Ben feared she might slip off her barstool.

"I don't sleep with men I just met. Even when they're cute. Maleah calls you the Hot Guy. I probably shouldn't have told you that, but look at you. She's not wrong, but she also calls you the obtuse jackass, so there's also that."

Ben swallowed a laugh. "I was offering to walk you home to make sure you get there safely and nothing more. I promise. I think your grandmother would appreciate you being taken care of seeing how you're having difficulty sitting up."

"Oh!" she said, surprised, and threw herself upright. "I am having trouble. Is it that obvious?" Her brows drew together and she frowned. "I should not drink this much in one night. Did I tell you my body hurts? I am an archivist not a construction worker. I should go to bed."

She slipped off the stool and almost fell. Brielle grabbed the chair to steady herself. "Wow. That was fun."

Ben wanted to be embarrassed for her, but she was entertaining him too much. He stood, pulled some money from his wallet, and set it on the bar. The bartender saw him and they exchanged nods.

"Come on," Ben said to Brielle.

He didn't take her arm but stood close enough to be able to catch her if she were to trip again.

Brielle babbled on about something, but Ben didn't hear anything clearly until they were on the other side of the street and cutting through the alley toward the back entrance to the Columbine Building. "My grandmother likes you a lot."

"I like her too."

"She thinks what is happening between you and Maleah is all some big joke. She told me lots of things about you when Maleah wasn't around."

"I don't know if I need to know this," Ben said as he steered Brielle toward the wide-open back door. "Why is the building open?"

"No idea," she said. "Let's find out." Brielle picked up the pace but stumbled over the entrance.

Ben caught her arm. "Watch your step, okay?"

"I would, but when I look down and back up again, everything starts to spin."

"Right," Ben said unenthusiastically. "I'll take you upstairs. Are you staying in Kiki's apartment too?"

"Well, duh. It's the only living quarters in this place. If you can call it that. I can't wait for the apartments to be finished. If I'm staying. I'm probably not staying, but Maleah might. Then again, maybe not. It rains a lot in Ireland. Did you know that? That's where I was living until I came back to Colorado. It's so much sunnier here than Ireland. She's a scientist. What is a scientist going to do in Three Peaks? Nothing, absolutely nothing. Tiling a bathroom and repairing old walls. Her talents are being wasted."

Speaking of talents, Ben heard music playing from the front of the building and he thought he detected Maleah's voice above the other sounds. Since Brielle wouldn't stop talking, it was difficult to hear.

They rode the elevator to the second floor. Ben seriously doubted Brielle could handle the staircase in her condition.

"My grandma was right about you. You're a gentleman. Thank you for seeing me safely home. I will put in a good word for you with my granny... and my cousin. She needs someone like you, Ben."

He stood inside the door as Brielle shambled over to the kitchen sink. She filled a glass with water and drank the whole thing.

"Who needs me? Your grandmother or your cousin?"

Brielle's eyes focused on the ceiling, or the top of her skull. He wasn't sure where she was looking as she considered her answer.

She held up a finger and then said, "My cousin. She's in desperate need of a good guy. After the whole hermaphrodite problem with the last guy, who could blame her?"

Did he hear that right? Ben decidedly chose to skip that can of worms. "All right. Well, you have a nice night."

She refilled her water and called over her shoulder, "You too, Hot Guy."

Ben closed the door and headed for the stairs, smiling to himself over drunk girls calling him hot. Yeah, he could get used to living next door to Brielle, even though she was a little quirky. He could do quirky, but he also wouldn't be living in the parking lot for much longer. The situation wasn't ideal and had presented itself out of convenience. Ben could park his RV on the ranch, or he could buy his own piece of land, but Kiki suggested parking the camper in her lot and he'd taken her up on the offer. Free rent, electricity, and water. Who could say no? Plus, he was on the jobsite. Since Maleah, and now Brielle, had entered the scene, he began to consider what his current lifestyle might look like to single women. It wasn't the most appealing. He didn't even want to think about the long-term ramifications on his daughter regarding her father living in an RV. Ben needed to remedy his living situation, but not tonight.

He stepped onto the landing at the bottom of the stairs and heard the music again. And this time he definitely heard Maleah—singing along with the recording. And she wasn't singing her death song either.

Her voice was good, melodic, and so pleasing to the ear that a sensation like a cool mist brushing over his arms and shimmying down his back raised the fine hairs all over his body. The memory of Maleah singing in their high school madrigals choir came to him suddenly. Back then, he'd never paid much attention to choir or anyone who sang in it, but maybe he should have. Her voice was beautiful, especially when she wasn't lamenting over her funeral in the bathtub.

As summer was nearly at its end, the mountain air carried a crispness that hinted at the coming of autumn. A light breeze moved down the hallway and with it, the smell of paint. Instead of walking out the back door, Ben followed his nose and the lit hallway toward the front of the Columbine Building. The music, lights, and her singing were too much to pass up without a quick peek. He also thought he should tell Maleah about Brielle being drunk as a skunk upstairs, and about Kiki and Joe. That was his excuse to see what she was doing. And since it was Maleah, he wasn't disappointed in what he found.

She must be a nudist. This was the third time he'd found her naked or partially naked. Maleah stood at the top of an eight-foot ladder rolling painter's tape along the trim work of the main room. Her dark hair was pulled back and tied up with a band, and most of her upper body was exposed since she was wearing a sports bra. Her jeans were tight, ripped in various places, and spattered with what appeared to be a little of everything from spackling, paint, and possibly spilled drinks.

The song ended and Maleah stopped singing.

"You're making a hell of a mess of that," he said.

She twisted around to look down at him. "It probably has something to do with all the margaritas." Maleah was still half-turned and looking at him as she stepped one foot on a lower ladder rung. "I suppose you—" she started to say and slipped. "Ah!" she shrieked.

Maleah slipped. Her weight wasn't centered and the ladder tipped to the left. Instead of righting herself, Maleah panicked. Ben leaped forward, arms out, and ready to be her hero—again.

Why did she always need to be saved?

What he didn't anticipate was his boot catching on the drop cloth, causing him to stumble, or kicking the paint can in his haste to keep her from crashing to the floor.

Ben held out his arms as he tripped and reached for her at the same time. A whoosh of air blasted out from his lungs as her one hundred and thirty pounds crashed against his chest. Momentum and gravity joined forces as Ben twirled, his feet, legs, and their bodies tangling with the drop cloth, the paint can, and the other paint paraphernalia. Although he tried his best to remain upright, no good deed went unpunished in his world. He landed backward with Maleah on top of him. He closed his eyes and thanked God the ladder hadn't crashed on top of them.

"Ben," she said.

He was still conducting an internal and silent survey of the potential damages when she spoke. "Yeah?"

"I'm beginning to think you're doing this on purpose."

He opened his eyes and found her silver gaze on him. Their legs were tangled in the drop cloth. The ladder lay on its side near the wall. He was pretty sure he'd hit his head, but not badly.

"What purpose would that be?" he asked.

"Secret motives you aren't allowed to share with the female species."

"You're on to me, Maleah. Now I'm going to have to distract you from discovering anything else you're not supposed to know," he said, keeping a straight face.

"You're definitely distracting. Look what you did." She reached up and pinched his chest. "I was fine making an ugly mess out of that wall, and then you come strutting in and make me fall off the ladder."

Ben reached up and scratched his head. "I think you meant to say thank you for saving you."

She let out a huff, but made no attempt to remove herself from his chest. "Thank you? For making me fall off the ladder? No. I'm not thanking you. You're going to have to try a different distraction because making me worship all this..." Maleah waved a hand toward his arm and shoulder while trying to look annoyed. "Muscles and beefiness. Your manly superpowers aren't going to work on me. I'm immune to you, Ben," she declared as amusement played with the corners of her lips.

At that moment Ben knew she wasn't injured in their tumble to the floor. So why was she continuing to lie on top of him? Not that it bothered him. He liked when she was on top of him. Once again, he was reminded about how long it'd been since he'd slept with a woman. And it was an embarrassingly long time. To put it frankly, monks got more action than he did.

His chest rose and fell beneath her weight as he chuckled. "Immune? That's awesome. And, just so you know, I'm also immune to your wily feminine charms. And the nakedness has no effect whatsoever." Ben rolled his eyes and tried to look disgusted. "My God, Maleah, why are you half naked again?"

"Naked? I'm not naked!" she said defensively.

He ran a hand over the exposed skin on her low back. "Are you sure about that?"

She squirmed beneath his tickling. "This is a sport tank."

"A bra," he corrected. "And you didn't answer my question."

"I didn't want to get paint on my shirt. I like that shirt. There's spackling and dirt on my jeans, but my shirt was clean when I decided to start fixing the walls. I was too lazy to go back upstairs for a paint shirt." She picked at his own shirt as she explained, then traced a fingertip over his chest.

"Too drunk sounds more likely." Her exploring fingers and the press of her incredibly soft breasts against him were sending all the wrong signals to the region below his belt. Ben waited another second to let her make a move or to remove herself from his chest.

"I must be the only straight bastard, ignorant, son of a bitch in this county who wouldn't already have made a move on you. Why are we still lying on the floor?" he finally asked.

Instead of rolling off, Maleah snuggled in closer. Her cheek lay near his collar and her hair tickled his neck. "You're comfortable," she said with a sigh. "And it's nice that you aren't immediately trying to get me out of my pants."

"Because I'm an idiot," he mumbled. And then louder, "I've seen you out of your pants multiple times."

"Yeah. That was unfortunate. I'm also an idiot. We're like a club—with two members."

"Do you want to have another club meeting tomorrow? I can teach you some tricks of the trade for covering the water stains and protecting the old woodwork and plaster."

"Maybe," she said noncommittally. "I have questions first."

"Of course you do," he said. She was nothing if not thorough and curious. He made the offer to show her some things without thinking it through first. Maybe he was only being nice, or maybe he wanted to spend more time with Maleah. Either way, she was now about to grill him, and regret hovered nearby as he waited for the inquisition.

"Is it me? Why don't sexy men want to be with me?"

Ben lifted his head and he stared at her. *She's kidding, right?* "Hey," he said, trying to get her to look up at him. When she did and their eyes met, he said, "Did you not hear me say what an idiot I am?"

Maleah lowered her lashes. Her non-response was a response.

Ben secured one hand on her low back and the other against her head, bracing her body against his. He rolled over and then lowered himself until they were face to face.

"Make no mistake about it. I want you." Ben placed his lips against hers, hesitating for a fraction of a second to see if she would pull away. When she didn't and her hands gripped the back of his shoulders, he let the full force of his need take charge.

Lust, desire, and frustration fueled his movement, overpowered his mind, and drove him wild. He took her mouth like a starved man, hungry for connection yet yearning to fulfill a primal and instinctive need.

She met him with equal urgency, and her tongue slid against his, circling, plunging, savoring. She tasted of sweetness and tequila. If the world suddenly came crashing down around him, Ben wouldn't stop tasting and exploring her unbelievably inviting mouth. Maleah clung to his back as he shifted his weight to his right arm and cupped her breast in his hand and savored the soft weight and female perfection. He'd seen her naked but hadn't allowed himself to think too much about her curves, her rosy nipples, taut and tantalizing when she'd been so cold from the shower. Now those hard little peaks pressed against the sports bra and yearned to be toyed with. Ben ground his pelvis against hers and a deep-seated groan rose from low in his throat. Yes, he definitely wanted her. More than he thought humanly possible.

Maleah wrapped a leg around his waist and thrust her hips against his rock-hard cock. Holy hell, he was going to shoot his load if she kept that up. Ben rode the wave for three more seconds and then he pulled back. He hovered above her, taking in the look of her long lashes lying against pink flushed cheeks, and her breaths rushing in and out of lips slightly parted.

He brushed a light kiss to one closed eyelid and then the other, and then Ben found himself backing away and on his knees a couple feet away. He took a long, steadying breath that did nothing to slow the pounding of his heart or cool the heated blood pumping through his veins.

Her eyes opened and she looked surprised by the sudden space between them. She also looked slightly dazed. And God, she was the most beautiful woman he'd ever seen.

It'd be so easy to unbutton his jeans, then hers.

She peered up at him, wearing a small smile of pleasure and happiness. But he also saw something akin to innocence and vulnerability. Ben reached out a hand and she took it.

He pulled her up and said, "Come on. If the paint dries on the floor, we'll both regret it."

She glanced around at the mess. "Oh no!"

"Exactly," he said as he released her hand and began folding the drop cloth over itself to contain some of the spilled stain-blocking paint she'd been using.

Maleah hurried toward a pile of rags and a roll of shop towels and began wiping up the splatters. Ben picked up a rag and then jogged down the hall to the storage closet. He found the mineral spirits and then dampened the rags in the bathroom sink. He returned to the front room and cleaned any remaining spots from the old hardwood floor. He righted the ladder as Maleah tossed the soiled paper towels into a trash bin.

She turned to Ben. He saw it again, her innocence, a hint of shyness within her sweet and funny personality.

"Tequila doesn't mix well with renovating."

"You should tell that to some of my workers. They show up hungover or still drunk more often than they should."

"Good to know." She took a step closer.

Ben hesitated for a brief second. Damn, he wanted her so bad. But he couldn't do it. He couldn't take advantage of her vulnerabilities. He wouldn't do that to her. She was too sweet and he was an asshole.

Ben ran a hand over his head and moved toward the hallway. "Tomorrow then? How about around seven?"

A look of confusion crossed her face. "For a painting lesson?"

"Yeah. Sure. You up for it? Club members only." A sly smile lifted one side of his mouth.

She dropped her gaze, then met his eyes and leaned forward slightly, lowering her voice. "Is our club clothing optional?"

He shook his head at her response and then laughed a little. "It definitely is in your case."

She shrugged. "I'll have to think about it then."

Ben stood at the threshold between the front room and the back hallway. "Same," he agreed and wondered if she was thinking about all the same things he was worried about. "If the door is unlocked, then I'll be here at seven. Good night, Maleah."

She bit her lower lip and stared at her feet. She was beautiful, kind, smart, funny, and too good for him. *I'm so screwed*, he thought and left the building.

Twelve

"HE DOESN'T WANT ME," Maleah said and eyed the remaining tequila in the bottle on the counter. "What is wrong with me? I'm a pariah, a swamp creature, a crone. Do I smell?"

"Yeah," Brielle said. "You definitely smell."

"I knew it! Ugh. I'm going to die alone. Every guy I'm interested in thinks I am a smelly, uninteresting weirdo who won't stop talking about saving the planet with biodegradable plastics made from mushrooms."

"You know, you currently smell like pity and whine. Whining kind of whine, not wine made from grapes. There's nothing wrong with you. The men you like are strange. It's not you." Brielle hesitated and then added before Maleah had a chance to speak again, "Oh, you might smell like a construction site, but so do I. It could be worse."

"Drywall mud and paint fumes? I opened the windows and the door. What else am I supposed to do? We *live* in the middle of the construction." Maleah was trying to not let last night's complete and utter failure at getting laid get her down, but rejection was a spiny and uncomfortable pill to swallow, and it was currently stuck in her gullet.

"Chill out. I'm kidding, and besides, Mr. Hot GC also smells like construction. He wouldn't notice. He probably gets off on it," Brielle said.

"Exactly! And he left. I couldn't have been more willing to roll around on the floor with him buck naked, but he slunk away like I'm a leper or a hippo. A hippo with leprosy. That is what I am." She had officially acted as slutty as she had ever attempted with both Holden and then, admittedly and shamefully, with Ben, and she'd failed—both times.

"I'd ride that." Brielle grinned at her own stupid joke.

Maleah stared at her cousin and wasn't amused. "Hippos don't get leprosy. I'm saying there is something horribly wrong with me and I need you to help me figure out what it is. I've slept with three guys. One of them doesn't even count, so it's more like two. Am I a pariah? Be honest. You can tell me. I can take it."

"What do you mean, one doesn't count? If you bumped uglies with a man, it counts." Brielle was now eyeballing Maleah much the same way Maleah had just been looking at her.

"I, uh. The story isn't worth sharing. But, believe me, it wasn't good. He, umm, he had a problem. All I'll say is, he finished... quickly. Like, you know, he was done before we really started."

"Ohhh..." She drew out the sound and then said, "The one-pump chump. Got it." Brielle gagged then cleared her throat.

Maleah scrunched up her face in distaste at remembering the unfortunate experience with Desmond. At the exact same time, their gazes met, and they both said, "Ew."

Maleah looked away. "He never called again, so maybe he was more embarrassed about it than I was. Nice guy, though. And smart." She sighed. "It really is me."

"It's not you," Brielle reiterated. "It's them."

"You say it's not me, but I'm the common denominator. And I'm fairly certain math doesn't lie. Something is wrong with me." Maleah began pacing. The conversation was uncomfortable, and now that she'd narrowed down the problem to being her fault, she needed to get up and move.

"There's nothing wrong with you, except for being attracted to the wrong guys. But since you've convinced yourself you're the problem. What are you going to do about it?"

Maleah fiddled with her fingers as she walked up and down the length of the living room. "Keep going. Keep moving forward. Try to learn from the experience. Don't let it get me down."

"Boring! That's what I would do. That's also what your dad would tell you to do. We are so dull. I need to find a library and move in. Books never complain about their boring life or their guy problems." Brielle rolled her eyes.

Maleah stopped and faced her cousin. She took a deep breath and then another. "You're absolutely right. I am going to keep going through life as the boring, predictable person I am. And if I don't change my dull and tedious ways, then I will be doomed to keep finding men who are unavailable to me in the way I need them. What the hell, Brie?" She waved her hands in the air with her sudden exasperation. "How did I get this way?"

Brielle tapped her chin. "Let's see now. You were in madrigals, you studied science for like an eternity, then you hid out in some science lab fawning over some dude who doesn't like sex. Couldn't see this coming at all, could we?"

Maleah let out a huff. In other words, she'd done this to herself... over a very long period of time.

"So, once again, I'll ask. What are you going to do about it?"

The answer she would never have thought of before came to her in a flash of brilliance. "I'm not going to be depressed any longer. He can't kiss me like that and walk out. What an ass. I'm going to get even. I owe him twice over for making me feel foolish."

Brielle's shoulders shook with a laugh. "Now you're starting to use that enormous brain of yours. Good for you!"

* * *

Jeremiah dug inside his wallet and pulled out a condom wrapper. Then another one... and another. He tore one off the row and tossed the condom into Ben's lap. He put the remaining two back and stuffed the wallet inside his pocket.

He and Ben sat on the edge of the deck, legs hanging over the side, and taking a breather. Ben chugged the last of the water in his bottle and felt the satisfaction of completing a solid nine hours of work at his family's historic Copper Valley Cattle Ranch. After a long day of redoing the log chinking on the old bunkhouse and beginning construction of the new front porch, he felt like the old cabin was finally coming together. The structure was over a hundred years old, and he and his brother agreed that the bunkhouse was worth saving. It was an investment, but Jeremiah had plans to turn the log bunkhouse into rental income. From the deck of the main house, they had a good view of the bunkhouse to the east by the aspen grove and the barn. In Ben's mind he could picture the finished cabin and the future of the ranch.

Throughout the day, his brother had somehow wheedled information about Maleah out of him, and the consequences of opening his mouth resulted in condoms being thrown at him.

Ben tossed the condom back at his brother. "I don't need this but... three? Really?"

"Unlike you, I don't want to father children anytime soon." Jeremiah eyed the wrapper, which landed on the deck near his leg.

"I meant the quantity not the purpose," Ben said and recapped his water bottle.

"The rest of the box is in the glovebox of my truck. There's more inside the house. Take 'em if you need 'em. I gave you one because I figured it was more than enough."

"Shut the hell up," Ben said. "I don't need my brother giving me condoms. Thanks, but no, thanks." Ben climbed to his feet and looked out across the yard and into the distance where the sun was approaching the western range of mountains overlooking the entire Copper River Valley.

"Oh, that's right. My brother is an idiot who turned down the only offer he's gotten for sex in a year. I don't get it. Maleah was half naked—again—drunk, willing, and hot." Jeremiah followed Ben's lead and stood up. "What was the problem again?"

Ben shook his head as he walked toward the partially finished steps. They were rebuilding the decks on the main house as well. The improvements to the house and bunkhouse were going to add functional space and esthetic, but also increase the property value. Ben was glad Jeremiah was investing so much into the family ranch.

"You're running away. Look at you go," Jeremiah taunted as he followed Ben off the deck.

"I'm not running anywhere. I need to pick up Skyla. That's why I had to finish by five, remember?"

"Yep, and you are blowing off the babe because of the kid. The babe could be blowing you, but you're an idiot." Jeremiah spelled it out for him again, as if Ben weren't already beating himself up for the mistake he made by telling Maleah he would be back at the Columbine Building around seven.

"I'm going to apologize and reschedule. Maleah knows I'm a fuck up. She thinks my temper is out of control and I can't be trusted. I can't make things worse than they already are." Ben opened the door of his truck and hesitated before climbing in.

Why couldn't Ben be a little more like his older brother? Date whoever came along. Sleep with beautiful women and send them home the next morning with no regrets and no promises. Ben shook off the unwanted comparisons. The reasons were plain. He wasn't like Jeremiah when it came to women, and he'd never been.

Last year, when Jeremiah hooked him up with a blind date, a hairstylist named Christy, Ben totally blew it. She was gorgeous, great tits, fun, and energetic. She'd convinced him to get a room at the Hilton after a concert in Denver, and he'd wholeheartedly agreed. But when she'd slipped off her leather boots, turned, and asked him to unzip her dress, he'd chickened out. Ben made up some excuse, left the hotel, and texted her he was sorry. Yeah, he had problems. Maybe it had been her feet. She'd worn those tall, sexy boots all night without socks. Who did that? Maybe it had been her hair color. He'd noticed immediately how close her hair color was to Kinsey's. Either way, he'd been put off and chosen to drive all the way back to Three Peaks instead of screwing his brains out—something he desperately needed.

Ben slid onto the truck seat and slammed the door shut. He rested an arm on the windowsill and turned the key to start the motor.

"Except you are making it worse. Good luck with that. One day soon, Ben, you gotta get Kinsey out of your fucking head."

Ben gave a curt nod. "Yeah. Maybe." Even though he hadn't said anything about Kinsey all day, Jeremiah understood that his ex was still messing with him in ways that were hard to understand and never going to be articulated.

Jeremiah stepped up to the door as Ben gripped the wheel and reached for the gear shifter. "You know what would help you move on?"

"Don't say it," Ben said.

"Getting laid."

He said it.

Jeremiah tossed the condom wrapper into the cab where it landed on the dash. "I'm not making this up. Getting laid helps. It's similar to getting a new puppy after losing your dog."

"No one died, and she's not a puppy." Ben pushed the gas pedal and left Jeremiah talking to himself in the driveway.

Jeremiah yelled, "Get back on the horse, you sorry asswipe! I believe in you, Ben!"

Ben tossed his hand out the window and waved his middle finger. In the rearview mirror, Jeremiah wore a huge smile as he returned the matching farewell gesture.

* * *

"They are the prettiest cats in the whole wide world, and Mrs. Thornton said I can have one if it's okay with you. All the kittens need a new home. This one is Sir Mittens, and he loves me." Skyla held the kitten up to her face and buried her nose against the fluffball's cream-colored coat.

Ben eyeballed the kitten in his daughter's hands and then the rest of the litter. The mother cat looked like a Siamese but with longer hair and the kittens were similar in color. And they were old enough to cause plenty of trouble. His daughter's friend sat on the blanket playing with the other kittens. Mrs. Thornton had stepped into the other room to take a phone call and left him alone with his extremely persuasive daughter.

Ben's mind was made up about cat ownership, but explaining adult reasoning to his kid, who was already clearly attached to the small predator, was going to be difficult.

He tried to go easy. "We can't have a cat right now, Skyla. I think you know why."

"Yes, we can. Mom won't allow it, but you can keep Sir Mittens in the trailer. You'll love him. Look how sweet he is." She lifted the small creature so Ben could see its face. With the blue eyes set in the dark chocolate face, Ben understood why his daughter wanted to take it home.

Ben held firm and tried again. "Skyla, the answer is no. When I have my own house again, we will talk about getting a puppy or a kitten. Okay? But not today."

She lowered Sir Mittens and held him protectively against her chest. "You're being mean and Mom won't ever let me have one. Please, Daddy. He's perfect and I love him."

Ben inhaled and let it out slow. He didn't need or want to take care of a kitten. With work and the upcoming battle with Kinsey over her move to Alaska, he didn't have the energy or desire to be responsible for one more thing.

"Please put the cat down."

Skyla accepted the resolve in his voice, and he watched the tears well up in her eyes before placing the cat back with its litter mates.

"Maybe my mom will let me keep Sir Mittens and then you can play with him whenever you come to visit," Angie, Skyla's friend, said.

Ben stepped back and let his daughter have a minute to say goodbye.

She stroked the kitten's fur and said, "But I'm not coming back for a long time. My mom said we'll be in Alaska before the end of the month."

"I'll send you pictures," Angie said and smiled kindly at his daughter.

Parenting continually brought new levels of difficulty, but this evening's challenge was almost more than he could bear.

"Okay," Skyla said, sadness muffling her voice as she gave Sir Mittens one last cuddle.

Ben couldn't take it any longer. "Skyla, say thank you to Angie and Mrs. Thornton for having you over and let's get going. I'll meet you in the truck."

"Okay, Dad," she said and Ben walked out.

Skyla opened the back door on the truck and took her seat. She set her bag on the floor between her feet and wouldn't meet his eyes.

"Buckle up," he said, and she reached for the belt without comment. Ben stared ahead and suddenly remembered the condom wrapper on the dashboard. As nonchalantly and quickly as possible, he stuffed it into his wallet.

As they pulled out of the driveway, he tried to sound upbeat and as if he hadn't just run over her dreams, ground them up, and spat them out. "You hungry? You get to choose tonight. How about pizza?" That was her favorite and something she never turned down.

"I guess," she said, not looking at Ben. "Can we take it back to your house? I don't feel like eating in a restaurant."

"Sure," he said and checked the time on the dash. Six-fifteen. "We can have it delivered. How does that sound?"

"Okay, I guess."

Her melancholy sat like a brick wall between them and wasn't going away any time soon, but Ben knew he'd done the right thing. A kitten, no matter how cute, wasn't a good move to make right now. On the drive across town, he called in an order to the only pizza place in town that offered delivery and told them to throw in some breadsticks and a giant chocolate chip cookie. Skyla would enjoy the dessert even if she was still upset about the kitten.

When they arrived at the trailer, Skyla hopped out of the truck and went straight to her room. He'd already spent most of the day feeling like a jackass for what happened the night before with Maleah. Now with Skyla giving him the cold shoulder, he may as well take up a drinking problem. Not that he would. He should, but he wouldn't, because Ben was too responsible and cared about screwing up his daughter's life, unlike say a certain blond mother he knew. Did he have any beer in the fridge? As he contemplated the answer to the necessity of beer, Ben kept his ears directed at the bedroom door.

His lawyer told him they were in for another battle. Since Kinsey would be acting against the court-ordered visitation schedule, one option was to wait until after Kinsey broke the agreement and then go after her for contempt of court. This path was the vilest, but so was Kinsey's assumption that she could take Skyla away from him without discussing it first. Ben learned long ago, his ex couldn't be trusted. He grabbed a beer out of the refrigerator. More than anything, Ben wanted this feud with Kinsey to end and stop hurting their daughter, but there wasn't a snowball's chance in hell that he wasn't going to fight for his rights over this move to Alaska. And since Kinsey was set on stealing Skyla away, he would see Kinsey in jail or at the very least in court.

With the cold beer nestled in his hand, he called out, "Sky? The pizza should be here soon. You should wash up."

She didn't answer and he didn't open the beer. Ben usually didn't drink alcohol when he had his daughter. It wasn't because he would get drunk, not even close, but the thought of having beer breath around her didn't sit well with him. What if they had to go out? What if the guardian ad litem came knocking while Ben was trying to relax after work? Yep, they'd been assigned a guardian ad litem after Kinsey's false claims about Ben's supposed abuse and neglect toward his daughter. In the end, there was no proof that Ben had been anything but a stable, loving, and providing father, but the judge believed Kinsey's lies and granted her full custody. And when Ben's attorney called her out as a lying, manipulative witch, a guardian had been assigned to their case. It was all total bullshit, because Kinsey was hurt and emotionally unstable during and after their breakup.

The guardian hadn't called or checked in on him in a year, but Ben put the beer back anyway. He could drink it tomorrow, along with the rest of the six pack, after dropping Skyla off at home.

Knocking on the bedroom door, he said, "Sky? Did you hear me? Come out and wash your hands before dinner."

"The pizza isn't even here yet."

"It will be. Come out of there and talk with your dad. It's been over a week. We need to catch up," he said, trying once again to play the good guy.

A knock clattered against the screen door and Ben spoke to the closed bedroom door. "The pizza is here.

Open your door now or I'm going to," he said more sternly. *So much for being the nice guy.*

He waited until he heard her move behind the door, and then went to pay the delivery guy. Ben stepped outside rather than have the delivery dude climb the steps to enter the trailer. He held the door open as he fished out the necessary bills. As they exchanged the cash for boxes of takeout, his daughter appeared in the doorway behind him, bent over, and chasing a putty-colored furball.

"Crap," Ben muttered.

"Sir Mittens! No! Come back here!"

The kitten dashed between the legs of the delivery dude. His kid went streaking out of the trailer and across the parking area after her escaping contraband.

"Keep the change," Ben said as he hugged the boxes tight against his body and followed in pursuit of the runaways.

"Skyla!" he started, but then didn't know how to follow up. Yelling at her wouldn't solve anything.

The kitten had a good lead and Skyla was unable to get ahold of him. Ben couldn't blame Sir Mittens for wanting to get away from the overenthusiastic, smothering ten-year-old. What he could blame the traitorous kitten for was running straight toward the soft glowing light coming from inside the back door of the Columbine Building.

"Stop!" he yelled at the back of his daughter's head, but it was too late.

By the time he caught up with them, they were in the large front room where Maleah stood, looking surprised as she cradled a purring Sir Mittens against her perfect, round breasts. *Lucky bastard*, Ben thought as his mouth filled with saliva. The drool had nothing to do with the pizza boxes and everything to do with the cleavage, long legs, and bare midriff.

What the hell is she wearing? was his first... and only thought, but was quickly followed with, *Why is she talking to Skyla dressed like that?*

Ben hurried forward but hesitated to interrupt as he listened to their exchange.

"He is the cutest! Is he a Balinese or a Siamese?" Maleah asked.

"Balinese. How did you know?" Skyla asked as she reached out to pet the kitten in Maleah's arms.

"I always wanted a Siamese cat until I learned the difference between the two breeds. The long hair is so pretty with their color, don't you think?"

"I do! And I'm not supposed to have him." Skyla dropped her chin and looked appropriately shamed.

It killed Ben more to see her remorse, even though she was now in more trouble than he could ever remember her being in before.

"Is Sir Mittens not your cat?" Maleah looked from Skyla to Ben and then at the kitten. "Is he a stray?"

"I took him home, but I wasn't supposed to."

"No, she wasn't," Ben agreed, wearing the appropriate disapproving dad face even though he could feel himself caving with every passing second.

"Once, when I was ten, I brought home this gigantic Samoyed that I found at the park. He was so huge and white and the fluffiest dog I had ever seen. He loved me and I adopted him. He followed me home, so I knew he was my dog." Maleah scrunched up her face and then continued the story. "My mom was so mad at me. By the time my parents realized I had a new dog, I had made him his own bed from the blankets in the closet and I used my mom's kitchen bowls for water and food dishes." Maleah dropped her chin to her chest with the same look of shame and embarrassment Skyla had been wearing. "The dog belonged to someone who lived by the park. They had been out looking for him and I accidentally stole him. My parents kept apologizing to the people. I got into a lot of trouble."

Skyla's face brightened as she said, "I'm ten years old too. This kitten needs a good home, but my dad doesn't want a cat right now and my mom hates cats."

"I understand," Maleah said. "I was never allowed to have a cat growing up either. My mom is allergic and my dad said we moved too often. I always had a dog, though."

"I have a dog. His name is Digger. He's getting kind of old, though. I guess that's good because he doesn't dig as many holes in the yard like he used to."

"Digger is a cute name and very clever," Maleah said as she handed Sir Mittens over to Skyla.

Since his daughter and Maleah were apparently best friends now, Ben was left standing there like an intruder. He interrupted. "I'm going to break this up now. I'm sorry, Maleah. I forgot it was Saturday when I told you I would give you the painting tips and tricks. I have Skyla tonight." He scratched his head. "And it looks like you—" He cut himself off and eyed her clothing for the briefest of seconds. "That you're ready for a hoedown?"

Maleah dropped her gaze to her outfit and then met his questioning glance. Her eyes went wide and her cheeks flushed a deep crimson.

"I, uh, I was practicing for a play," she said, obviously making up the answer on the fly. "This costume is so silly. I don't think I'm going to use it after all. I need to change. Excuse me for one minute," Maleah said, keeping her composure while managing to sound like the sweetest of angels even though she was dressed like a stripper catering to rodeo cowboys.

Ben raised an eyebrow. Now there was a thought. Maleah stripping. Pole dancing would be a high form of entertainment. His cock stirred and he immediately shut down all imaginings.

"Your top is cute, but your shorts are a little too short. If I wore those to school, I would definitely be sent home."

Holy fudge, Ben thought. *There it is.* His daughter was a tween going on twenty-something. She sounded exactly like every teenaged girl he ever dreaded being around. *Clothes, hair, boys, sex, gossip.* When he was a tween and teen, he'd avoided the girls who talked trash at all costs. Apparently, fate decided he shouldn't skip that part of growing up and he would suffer through it via a daughter.

"Do you live upstairs with Kiki?" Skyla asked.

"I do live here," Maleah said. "Kiki is my mother's aunt, which makes her my great-aunt."

Her blush extended to her cleavage and Ben swallowed the pool of liquid that had filled his mouth. She moved toward the stairs, muttering something about finding a sweatshirt.

"Can she share the pizza with us, Daddy? Please. Are you friends? How come I've never met her before? She's beautiful. Is she a model?"

Ben stared at his daughter, still holding the now subdued kitten in her arms. He made the mistake of glancing at Maleah, and Christ, her shorts were short. The curve of her ass hung below the hemline of her cutoffs. He'd seen bikinis on women that covered more flesh. He held in the smile at her excuse of practicing for a play. *Play my ass.* What had she been up to when they walked in?

"I don't think she's a model, Sky. She's a scientist." He watched his daughter's face for her reaction. "And I guess, she's also an actress. She's also a pretty good singer," he added as an afterthought.

"Really? I'm going to join the choir in middle school. I hope there's a choir in my new school. Dad"—Skyla paused, her mouth turning down—"I don't want to move to Alaska. I like my school here."

This wasn't the right place or time for this conversation, but with a ten-year-old, Ben thought he better address the issue while she was thinking about it.

"I don't want you to move either, sweetheart. Did you tell your mother you don't want to go?"

"Yes, but I don't want to leave Mom either."

Ben tried not to take it personally that his daughter hadn't mentioned she didn't want to leave him either, but it stung. He set the pizza boxes down and knelt in front of Skyla.

"I understand why you wouldn't want to live without your mom or leave your school. Moving can be really hard for a lot of reasons. You know you can move in with me anytime you want, right? If you wanted to stay with me here and not switch schools, I'll find a real house right away. All you have to do is say so."

Skyla petted the kitten, who had fallen asleep in her arms. "Mom said I have to go with her. She said you wouldn't want me to move in with you and the court wouldn't allow me to stay here with you."

The strength it took Ben not to cuss out loud or curse his ex to the depths of hell for eternity resided in an unnamable, unfathomable place inside himself, but he managed to hold it in by focusing on Skyla.

He placed his hands on her shoulders. "I will fight in court for you with every breath in my body. You matter more than anyone else in my life, Skyla. I have a good lawyer and I will do everything it takes if you don't want to move to Alaska. You also need to understand that I will follow the rules set by the judge. Sometimes it takes a long time to work everything out, but your mom decided we have to do everything in court and that is the way it has to be for now."

"Which means I have to stay with Mom until the judge changes his mind and makes new papers for you and Mom to sign."

He squeezed her shoulders lightly. It was awful that a ten-year-old understood the justice of injustice at such a young age. "That's right. I wish none of this were the way it is, but for now, we have to do it Mom's way."

"She's not very flexible, Dad. Mom is so stubborn, and she listens to me about as well as she listens to you. She's not going to let me stay in Three Peaks with you." Skyla lowered her voice as tears filled her eyes. "I don't know if I could live without Mom either," she confessed.

The sadness in his daughter's eyes reached out and stabbed him right in the heart. He would give anything, pay anything, sacrifice his soul to take his daughter's pain away. And with the acknowledgement of doing absolutely anything for his daughter, he said, "It's okay if you want to live with your mom too, Skyla. She loves you as much as I do, but the choice is yours, not hers. You are ten now, and you're still a kid, but you are intelligent. I know you know what is best for you. You can stay here or you can go and see what you think about Alaska. Just because you go there doesn't mean you are stuck there. I will fly to Alaska and check things out with you if that would help you make your decision. I will stand by your side as you tell Kinsey what you want. Anything you need, I've got your back. Understand?"

She nodded and the pain in her eyes lightened. Ben felt mildly better as well because everything he'd said was true, and having voiced the truth helped solidify a plan for the future.

Skyla swallowed, raised her eyebrows in a look of hopefulness, and asked, "When you say you've got my back, does that mean I can keep Sir Mittens? He's the best cat, and Mom will never let me have a cat. You know how she is." Skyla rolled her eyes with exasperation at Kinsey's hard and fast rule about no cats.

Ben just got bamboozled and he knew it. He ran his tongue over his teeth and tried not to let his daughter see how well-played her hand had been. "You know, I could use some male company in the trailer. I suppose I'd be willing to give Sir Mittens a trial run. But you, missy"— Ben tried to sound like his own father. He probably missed by a long shot, but he kept it up anyway—"you are going to help me raise, train, and take care of this little hell cat, got it? He better learn to sit, stay, get down, and there's no shedding on my clothes either."

Skyla giggled. "Dad," she whined. "You can't train a cat. They're not like dogs. Duh."

Ben winked at his kid and then stood up. *Jesus H. Christ*, he now owned a cat.

Thirteen

MALEAH HEARD TOO MUCH, but she couldn't not listen to Ben with his daughter. She was afraid if she moved and retreated back up the stairs, he would know she'd been listening. She swiped a tear away and then walked into the front room.

With a huge smile on her face, she looked at Ben's daughter and asked, "Do you know what a janitor says after jumping out of the closet?"

Skyla shook her head.

Maleah held out the small pet kennel she'd been holding behind her back and said, "Supplies!" They shared a giggle over the silly joke and then Maleah said, "I found the kennel in Aunt Kiki's stuff upstairs. You can borrow this if you need it. They're useful when you take Sir Mittens to the vet for his checkup and shots."

"I get to keep him! Dad just said it was okay."

"Ooh," Maleah cooed. She couldn't help it. The kitten was possibly the cutest thing she'd ever seen, and so was Skyla... and so was Ben. Her ovaries twinkled and then shimmied. She nearly gasped. Her ovaries had literally never crossed her mind before, and now she was pretty sure she'd just ovulated and released a gazillion pheromones into the atmosphere. *Holy crap.*

"That's so sweet. I'm happy for you," she said, and meant it.

Her inner child wanted to snuggle with Sir Mittens. She had to extinguish the urge to beg for the phone number of the people who owned the rest of the litter. Maleah placed the travel kennel on the floor near Skyla. The girl knelt down and opened the door and gingerly placed the kitten inside.

Turning her attention to Ben proved to be nearly impossible. How could she look him in the eyes now? It wasn't because she'd been eavesdropping either. Maleah had planned to seduce him and then drop him like a dead rat when he tried to kiss her again. Getting even with him was proving to be impossible.

Earlier in the day, she'd gone to the second-hand store and found the ridiculous and slutty halter top made out of red and blue paisley bandanas. Then she'd cut a pair of skin-tight jeans into the shortest pair of booty shorts she could stand to put on and topped off the outfit with cowboy boots. Styling her hair and putting on makeup had all been for the express purpose of taunting Ben and then dumping him. She even had a backup plan in case he stood her up—which was to work on the walls again. The drop cloths were laid out and her tools and supplies were ready to go. When all else fails, get productive.

Getting to work was exactly what she planned to do when she headed back downstairs after throwing on her old DU sweatshirt and the stained and ripped jeans she'd worn the night before. Instead, she found herself wanting to play with a kitten and get to know Ben's daughter better. She was adorable, well-spoken, and totally endearing.

After making sure Sir Mittens was okay inside the kennel and the door was securely latched, Skyla stood back up. "Thanks. He's going to be the world's best cat. You can visit him anytime you want. Since I only get to spend the weekends with my dad, Sir Mittens will need another friend. My dad works a lot too. You can be my kitten babysitter." She paused, looked thoughtful, and added, "If you want to."

"I'd like that. Thank you, Skyla. I don't think we were properly introduced. If I'm going to babysit your new baby, then you need to know who I am. My name is Maleah, and I'm staying upstairs with my cousin, Brielle. We're here while Aunt Kiki is recovering from her accident."

"Nice to meet you, Maleah. Can I meet your cousin?"

"Sure. She's not here right now, but I'm sure she'd love to meet you too."

"Cool," Skyla said and then asked her father, "Can we eat dinner now?"

"Yep," Ben said and then to Maleah, "Sorry to intrude. We'll head back to my place and get out of your hair." He edged toward the takeout boxes sitting on the counter where he'd left them.

Skyla asked, "Would you like to eat pizza with us? My parents always tell me not to be rude. Not inviting someone when they are standing right in front of you is rude, right, Dad?"

Ben cleared his throat and then flashed his pearly whites in a forced smile. "That's correct, dove. How about joining us, Maleah? We ordered more than enough."

Maleah didn't want to continue intruding on Ben's visitation time with Skyla. She hemmed and floundered to come up with an excuse. "I'm supposed to be..."

"Working on the walls, yeah?" Ben said. "It's my fault we're not making progress." He picked up the boxes, walked over to the clean drop cloth, and said, "How about we have ourselves an indoor picnic?"

"Yay!" Skyla called out and carried the pet crate over to the spot where Ben was setting out dinner. "Come on, Maleah. This will be fun. I love picnics!"

Maleah couldn't say no to Skyla. She grabbed the box of shop towels and joined them on the floor. "We can use these as napkins... or plates."

"Perfect." Ben accepted a heavy-duty paper towel as she passed them out.

The impromptu dinner date with Ben and his daughter turned out to be a thousand times better than her previous intentions of seducing him and then kicking him to the curb. At one point, Ben's silly jokes had her and Skyla in tears. The pepperoni pizza and breadsticks were uncomplicated but unbelievably delicious. Maleah had a new favorite pizza place in town, and she couldn't wait to eat there again.

After they ate, Skyla asked, "What do you like to sing? Daddy said you're an actress and a singer."

"I'm not much of an actress," Maleah admitted, even though she had fibbed about rehearsing for a play. "But I can sort of sing. I used to sing a lot when I was in school."

"Sort of?" Ben said. "I've heard you belting out pop songs, country, and choir music."

"Can you sing any Taylor Swift?" Skyla asked.

"Maybe," Maleah said as Ben flinched and shook his head in disfavor. Maleah asked Skyla, "Do you know 'The Meatball Song'? It's way better than Taylor."

"Teach it to me."

Maleah lowered her chin to her chest, composed her face, and swallowed. After dredging up the lyrics from the basement of her memory, she looked back up and said, "This is a serious addition to your future singing career. I can tell you are a fast learner. Are you ready?"

"Yeah! I am," she added.

Maleah took a breath and began singing, "On Top of Spaghetti."

Ben joined in and they harmonized the next lines. Skyla groaned and covered her mouth to hold in the laughs. Maleah continued the old camp song and sang about the meatball rolling off the table and onto the floor. Ben bowed out by the third verse. Maleah finished the song and then winked at Skyla.

"You ready to try? I'll sing it with you, but remember, this is serious. There's no smiling or laughing when you sing about lost meatballs."

"That was terrible, Maleah. I'm not a baby," Skyla said.

"And yet, you want to sing it with me, don't you?" Maleah nodded and tried to look convincing. "We could always try 'Little Bunny Foo Foo' instead."

Ben watched the two of them and didn't interrupt. Maleah ignored him, or tried to, and enjoyed spending time with a kid. She honestly couldn't remember the last time she'd had fun hanging out with a child, and Skyla was a total doll.

"Ready?" she asked. "We'll go slow so you can learn the words."

Skyla giggled and agreed. They sang the spaghetti and meatball song no less than one hundred times before Ben said his ears were bleeding. It wasn't a hundred times, but Maleah was definitely done with the nursery rhyme by the time Ben spoke up. He'd cleaned up the dinner boxes and paper towels and looked ready to call it a night.

"Sky, take Sir Mittens to the trailer, please. I'll be right there. I need to speak with Maleah about some work stuff."

The girl looked at each of them then said, "Umm, okay." She took the cat carrier with her down the hallway.

Ben peered after his daughter and waited until she was close to the trailer before turning his attention to Maleah.

"She's amazing," Maleah said. "You're really lucky."

"I am," Ben said. "Thanks for not getting pissed about my scheduling mistake. I honestly forgot it was the weekend."

"Things were a little distracting yesterday." The shame and embarrassment returned with the mention of what happened the night before. She stared at the wall. The wall with the water stains.

"How's tomorrow night, about eight p.m.? I have to drop off Skyla at seven-thirty and then I can come back here to show you a few things."

"I don't think so. Brielle and I can finish the walls. Then we're going to start painting the bathrooms." The thought of what she'd planned to do tonight now made her feel ill. She wasn't that kind of person. There wasn't a vindictive or manipulative bone in her body. Even though she wanted to start a war with Ben, she really wasn't cut out for it. But she didn't want rejection again either.

Ben took three long strides and stepped into her personal space. "Are you sure? I don't know what kind of shirt is made out of a couple bandanas, but I wouldn't mind taking a closer look, or doing some painting with you in those daisy dukes."

Was the room suddenly warmer? Had the furnace kicked on? "I don't know if that was a shirt or more of a horrible error in style and poor judgment."

"If you say so."

"I do." She hesitated and felt more confused than ever. "I don't think tomorrow is going to work for me."

"Okay," he said quietly and moved back.

"Good night, Ben."

* * *

"The nurses didn't have to call you," Aunt Kiki said with an air of impatience. "Since you're here anyway, I wanted to let you know about the plans I've made with Joe."

Brielle and Maleah exchanged a glance.

Brielle asked what Maleah was also thinking. "Joe who?"

"Joe Erickson, Ben's grandfather. He and I are..." Kiki sat up taller, folded her hands in her lap, and said, "We're courting. He's my new beau, and we've decided to move in together."

"What?!" they said together.

Kiki's bags were packed and Maleah had been under the impression that her great-aunt would be going home with them today. She and Brielle had been discussing and preparing for Kiki's homecare, rehab, and therapy schedule.

"Don't get your panties in a twist, girls," Kiki said.

Maleah tried not to choke as she held in the laugh at her elderly aunt's word choice.

"Joe and I have come up with a wonderful solution that will help us both out. His memory is shot, see? Mine is perfect, but I also need a nurse. As wonderful and helpful as the two of you are, I won't be a burden on either of you. Or more than I have been already."

"You're not a burden to either of us, Aunt Kiki. Don't say that. I want to be here for you."

Aunt Kiki smiled and gave her niece an appreciative nod. "I know, I know. But—"

"No buts. We're here for you, Grandma. Don't shack up with some random guy just because."

"Because of what?" Kiki asked, defensive and slightly put out.

"Nothing," Brielle corrected quickly. "Tell us what you're thinking."

"As I was saying. Joe lives here in one of the assisted living apartments. He's asked me to move in with him. I spoke with the director and everything is being set up. A nurse will come check on me twice a day while I need her. Joe's daily routine will stay virtually the same, but I will be there if anything happens to him. Plus, my appointments for therapy are right here at the Mount Tenderfoot Medical Complex. Everything is falling into place and I couldn't be happier."

"Wait, you can't move in with someone you just met. That's crazy, Grandma."

"Is it? I've known him for decades, Brielle. He's a wonderful man. We're both widowed and we're lonely. This is a good move for us."

Maleah couldn't argue against that, but she had concerns. "How bad is his memory, Auntie? Are you sure this is wise? What if he forgets who you are or something terrible like that?"

"Come here and sit closer to me for a minute." Aunt Kiki patted the bed, and she and Brie sat along the side of their tiny relative. "Joe and I are old. Bad things happen all the time, especially when it comes to our health. We have to accept it and move on. I'm recovering from my unfortunate run-in with the dumpster, but I'll heal. Joe's mind will most likely not recover. I know that. But if we have one month together, isn't that better than none? He makes me happy. And he's so handsome and funny. I'll cross whatever bridge when I get to it. And if we cross these bridges together, then that's better than doing it alone."

Kiki's explanation eased most of Maleah's worries. She leaned over and wrapped her arm around her aunt's shoulders. "If you're happy, then so am I. What can we do to help you get settled?"

"I'm going to need some of my things from the apartment. And I will need you or someone to keep an eye on my buildings. Once I can start driving again, I'll be able to do it, but for now, I think I'm going to enjoy having caregivers and a place to live that isn't so drafty and always under construction. Most of all, I'm going to like having a man to take care of again. Oh, there is one snafu. None of this is going to happen unless Joe's guardians give us approval. It shouldn't be a problem, but some of the staff here are against us. You'll take our side, won't you, girls?"

Maleah and Brielle shared another look. They agreed, and Maleah wondered what would come next.

* * *

Brielle, Kiki, and Maleah left the hospital room a couple hours later. Kiki was officially discharged and they set off to find Joe's apartment. The day shone bright, and the temperature was warm enough to wheel Kiki across the complex in a wheelchair.

When they arrived, Grandpa Joseph wasn't alone. His son and daughter-in-law, a.k.a. Ben's parents, were there along with the director of the assisted living community. As it turned out, Joe Erickson wasn't about to be told who he could or couldn't invite into his life. If his mind was a little feeble, Maleah couldn't tell. The Ericksons must have dominant genes, Maleah thought. The resemblance between the Erickson men were obvious to the extreme.

Pauline Erickson, Ben's mom, remembered Maleah instantly. The inquiries about Maleah's parents and reminiscing about elementary school parties and the annual Christmas program followed immediately after the decision to let Joe and Kiki live together.

While Maleah was trying to wrap her head around the morning's activity and announcement, and what that might mean in the near and distant future, she overheard Joe say, "Well damn, son, we aren't getting married anytime soon. I'm in my eighties in case you've forgotten. I've committed enough sins to go to hell ten times over. Living with a woman without being wed first isn't going to send me down there."

"Oh, Joe," Kiki said and smiled at her new boyfriend.

"Alrighty then," Garrett Erickson said with a heavy dose of resolve. "It's your choice."

"Garrett, I think they'll be okay," Pauline said. "And it's nice to have Mrs. Brookhart here to watch out for your dad."

"I suppose so," Garrett mumbled.

Brielle made a list on her phone of items Kiki wanted from her apartment and from the store. Maleah, Brie, and Kiki were gathered in Joe's bedroom, planning and organizing the newly shared dresser and closet space.

Joe told Kiki to do whatever she wanted with the place, and Kiki was happy to add her personal touches. In Maleah's opinion, the apartment décor resembled a hotel suite, and she wondered if the space had come furnished.

As they peered into the bathroom, Kiki asked, "How's Ben doing? I haven't seen him since he walked in on me and Joe the other day."

Brielle looked at her grandmother. "Walked in on you and Joe? Where were you?"

"I thought he would have told you. It was quite embarrassing, which means I thought the whole town would have heard about our scandalous tryst in Joe's bed."

"Okay, I don't need to hear any more." Brielle covered her ears and backed out of the doorway to let Kiki enter the bathroom.

Aunt Kiki smiled to herself as she opened drawers and cabinets looking for empty spaces to put her toiletries.

"I think Brie and I have been out of the loop when it comes to town gossip," Maleah said.

"Count your blessings," Kiki said. "Doubtless Joe and I will get away with remaining anonymous about moving in together, but I'm prepared for the onslaught of rumors."

"I think everyone will be happy for the two of you," Maleah said with optimism.

Kiki made a small doubtful sound and turned around. "This will do. This is a nice room with plenty of space. The tub is large enough for two."

Brielle groaned and purposely averted her gaze away from the oversized bathtub.

Kiki returned to her previous question. "And how is Ben? I thought I might see him today. Have you?"

Brie said, "This is definitely a question for Maleah. She had dinner with him and his daughter last night."

Maleah didn't like being put on the spot, but since the cat was out of the bag, or in the kennel as it turned out, she said, "He's borrowing your cat kennel. I hope you don't mind. I found the cage in your closet. Did you use to have a cat, Aunt Kiki?"

"Don't change the subject. Tell me about my general contractor. Isn't he a dear? Dinner with Ben and Skyla is one of my favorite things to do on a boring evening. We should get together as a group for dinner sometime next week. I'll ask Joe if he'd like that." Kiki left the bathroom and unzipped her travel bag.

"Ben's complicated," Maleah said. "But yes, he is nice."

Kiki sorted the clothes from the bag and placed them on the bed. "He's not complicated. He's good at masking his problems. There's a difference. Any sign of Ricky yet?" Kiki asked.

She'd brought up the missing turtle necklace every time they visited, but the answer was still the same.

"Not yet." Maleah couldn't help but think the necklace was in some landfill far away.

Brielle said, "No. I haven't stopped looking, though. We're not giving up on finding him. I've been working on something that may help."

"Thank you, girls. I appreciate it even though I'm starting to believe he's gone forever. Maybe it's a sign to move on." She sighed. "So many changes in life right now. We must accept what we cannot change. But there's always the possibility of better things to come." Kiki picked up a pile of dirty clothes and headed out of the bedroom.

Maleah appreciated her aunt's positivity and wondered if that was who she'd gotten it from.

They followed Kiki out of the bedroom and Maleah elbowed her cousin. "Still being cryptic, are we?"

"It's not that. Well, kind of," Brielle admitted. "It's been a secret project, but only because I wasn't sure if it would pay off. I'll show you what I've been doing when we get home. And I found something you'll want to see."

They said goodbye after making promises to return the following day with Kiki's things from the apartment. As they headed back to the parking lot by the hospital, they ran into Mr. and Mrs. Erickson.

"We had to complete some paperwork in the director's office," Pauline said. "Being the guardian of a parent isn't how you picture spending your own retirement, but we're handling it." She sounded tired.

"It is what it is," Garrett Erickson said. "Dad's discomforts are worse than our own."

"That's true," Pauline agreed and then said to Maleah, "It's wonderful seeing you again. How do you like being back in Three Peaks?"

She considered her answer before speaking. With everything going on, Maleah hadn't given any thoughts to how she was faring or if she liked being back in the mountains. In all honesty, survival had been her single motivation. Remodeling the Columbine Building distracted her from dwelling on her lost life back in Boulder.

"It's different than I thought. The town has grown a lot, and I have too. I'm settling in slowly."

"Does that mean you're going to stay? I think Ben would enjoy that," Pauline said.

"Really?"

Pauline wore a close-lipped smile and didn't add any additional insights about Ben's opinion on whether or not Maleah remained in town.

Maleah continued. "I doubt I'll be staying permanently. I've been looking for a new job in my field, and it's only a matter of time before I find something."

"I heard you took over Ben's job at the Columbine Building. Will that hold you over for the time being?"

Pauline said it without any accusations or hurtfulness, so Maleah kept her tone light and sincere.

"I've been enjoying the renovations. More than I thought I would. And I didn't mean to steal Ben's job. I hope there are no hard feelings about the situation."

She placed a gentle hand on Maleah's forearm. "Whatever transpired between the two of you, I'm sure it happened for a reason, and I'm glad for it. Ben's had a hard time over the last couple years, and you arriving in town has brought something out in him we haven't seen in a long time. Isn't that right, Garrett?"

Mr. Erickson gave a brief nod and then kept walking, eyes on the parking lot ahead.

"I don't know if you know anything about his past, but his wife hung him out to dry. She even had him arrested for no reason. He's weary on the inside, but he'll come around in good time. Seeing him smile again over the last couple weeks has been a nice change."

They must not know about Skyla's move to Alaska, Maleah thought and felt the wrench in her gut over what she'd heard the night before.

"Umm, I didn't know anything about his ex. I'm sorry to say this, but I doubt I have anything to do with Ben's change in attitude. I'm pretty sure I only cause him new headaches."

Pauline's eyebrows lifted in question. "Ben may not realize it, but he enjoys a challenge. You keep giving him a hard time. If not for his benefit, then for ours."

The Ericksons glanced at one another. The look of humor and understanding that passed between them spoke volumes that could only be understood by a couple who had spent decades together.

They stopped next to Maleah's car and Pauline said, "I look forward to seeing the two of you around town. Take care now."

Garrett tipped his hat at her and Brielle and then took Pauline's hand in his. As Maleah and Brie opened the car doors, she glanced over and saw the Ericksons climb into a silver, heavy-duty pickup truck.

"I think you just got inducted into the Erickson clan."

"You too. Kiki's your grandmother," Maleah said.

"Yeah, but I'm not the one their son is interested in," Brie said.

Maleah started the engine and contemplated what she'd learned about Ben. "Brie?"

"What's up?"

"I think I may have made a terrible assumption and then acted on it without knowing all the facts." She tapped her fingers on the steering wheel and chewed on her bottom lip.

"About Ben?"

"Mm-hmm," Maleah said.

"You're really going to hate yourself when I show you the video."

Fourteen

"THERE ARE SECURITY CAMERAS in the building?" Maleah asked.

She and Brielle sat on the couch, looking at Brielle's laptop computer.

"A couple downstairs, on the exits, and one out back. How have you not noticed?" Brielle asked.

"I don't know," she said. "I think I noticed at some point. I assumed they were dummy cameras or not hooked up. How long have you been looking at the footage?"

"Not long. Okay, maybe a while," she amended. "I asked Grandma about the cameras and she said she asked Ben to take care of security right after she moved in. Since I didn't want to ask Ben for help, I thought I would try to figure it out on my own. Grandma gave me the password to her computer, and I've been messing around with the program and the files. I've been combing through the images of Grandma and trying to pinpoint exactly when she may have lost her necklace. I copied a bunch of the files to my laptop and wanted to show you something."

"I'm impressed... and surprised you didn't mention this to me until now," Maleah said.

Brielle continued to explain what she'd been up to. "The cameras are good quality and have uninterruptible power supply, which means they have a battery backup if the power goes out. Plus, I'm able to zoom in on the images. The hard part is getting the right angles to see if she's wearing a necklace or not. Here, let me show you what I found." Brielle opened a file with a set of images of Kiki. All the images had a time stamp. When Brie zoomed in on two different pictures, it became fairly clear that Kiki had the necklace on in one, and it wasn't there in the other. "Grams was not wearing Ricky when she hauled all that trash out of the building."

"Why didn't you tell her this?"

"I don't always have the right words. I prefer to work alone and do things on my own time without having to explain everything. If it turned out to be nothing, I didn't want to get her hopes up. Her necklace is still missing. I'm telling you now because of what else I found." Brielle twisted on the couch to look her cousin in the eye before adding, "And because you need to see what Kinsey did to Ben. Watch this." She clicked the play button on a video file.

Maleah's eyes went wide and she forgot how to blink as she watched the replay of Ben and Kinsey in the parking lot the morning after she'd returned to Three Peaks.

"I should have believed him. It happened so fast, and the way Ben grabbed her and shoved her into her car. It was so awful."

"I wasn't there, but yeah, you suck."

Maleah gave Brielle a pointed look. "You know, you're awfully opinionated and judgmental for an introverted librarian."

"I'm an archivist... and I'm an introvert. But I'm comfortable around you, which means you get the full

Brielle experience. There's an ample supply of judging, sarcasm, inappropriate humor, and weird fandoms. Consider yourself one of the chosen."

"I'm so honored," she said with her own dose of sarcasm. "Who else are the chosen few? I need someone to commiserate with when your Brielle-ness is peaking."

"Like... there is no one else. I have a couple of friends in Ireland, but you don't know them."

"I can always Face Time with them to talk about you."

Brielle looked over her shoulder and said, "Not going to happen. They're pretty much exactly like me, introverted and avoiding people at all cost."

"You are a special breed of human, aren't you?" Maleah asked.

Brielle nodded and turned back to her screen. As she tapped away at the keyboard, she said, "I'm going to keep looking for clues about Grandma's necklace. What are you going to do about Ben? Hire him back?"

Maleah lowered her shoulders from around her ears and took a deep breath. Firing Ben had been a terrible mistake. "I'm going to work on the walls and hope a hammer falls on my head."

"While you're at it, you should start anticipating the taste of crow."

Maleah rose from the couch and opened the door of the only closet in their so-called apartment. She wanted to change back into her painting clothes. "Since you're trying to make this situation easier on me, you could come downstairs and help."

"It's Sunday. I'm going to work on admin stuff."

"Admin stuff? For us or for your other job? You're being vague again." Maleah pulled off her T-shirt and changed into the paint stained one.

Brielle didn't look up as she said, "I'm working now, so I can no longer hear you." Her fingers rattled against the keyboard and then went quiet as she lowered her face closer to the screen.

Maleah shook her head and accepted that she and Brie had wildly different definitions of work. If she were being honest, she needed time alone to figure out what to do about Ben. She hadn't forgotten the so-called business meeting at the coffee shop. He'd defended himself and said she shouldn't make assumptions. And instead of giving her specific details, he'd played with her head. He should have told her what happened that morning with Kinsey. Worst of all, when she should have been angry with him, she found herself more attracted to him than before. Her confusion was unsettling, to say the least, but the crow she was about to eat was going to be bitter and extremely hard to swallow.

* * *

Maleah turned up the stereo and sang to herself as she covered water stains, taped off trim, and rolled on new coats of paint. Singing helped ease Maleah's melancholy and remorse, but mixed emotions and formal apologies continued to carve circles around the inside of her head and heart over what she'd done to Ben and his business. She'd made an honest mistake, but it was still difficult to forgive herself. As she processed the situation, Maleah plowed forward and continued to bring the Columbine Building one small step closer to full restoration.

When she spotted the two-inch paintbrush she used for cutting in around the windows or other areas she didn't want to tape off, she remembered something her father used to let her do when she was a kid.

Without thinking too hard about it, she painted the first words that needed to get out of her head. Her word dump started with "sorry" and "I'm not perfect." That was the crux of her misery. She strived for perfection in all areas of her life, and messing up this badly was incredibly difficult to accept. She sighed and stared at the wall.

But her father had given her one rule about painting on the walls.

He said, "Maleah, if you're going to leave your writing on the wall, make your mark something positive. Nobody needs subliminal messages that aren't kind or uplifting."

Maleah used the paint roller to cover her first words. She picked up the brush and began painting words of hope to herself. They flowed onto the wall in a decorative style of loops and spirals. She finished, stepped back, and looked at her handiwork.

It might be corny and clichéd, but the words helped straighten out her mind. She planned to paint over it before she was done for the night. No one else would ever see the message.

Gratitude for her life and dreams of a brighter future kept her painting and repairing until the west and south walls of the front room of the Columbine Building were finished.

She painted over her words of encouragement last and then cleaned up. After hours of internalizing the problem and letting her subconscious work through it, Maleah knew what she needed to do for Ben.

But she also hated confrontation and was more than a little bit of a coward. Maleah went upstairs and found a piece of paper and a pen to write him a letter. She licked and sealed the envelope and headed downstairs before she changed her mind. Maleah had no intention of facing Ben tonight and said a silent prayer he wasn't home. When she walked outside, she was thrilled to see his truck wasn't parked by the trailer. Once again, she found herself thinking of deities and gods she didn't know much about. *Thank you, Wakea.* Hawaiian gods were better than none, right?

She approached the camper trailer. Muted light shone from behind the closed window shades, but she heard nothing. She opened the screen door and tucked the letter into the door seal and a dog woofed from inside.

When did Ben get a dog? The door opened right after she had finally gotten the envelope wedged into the crack.

"Ben!"

The letter fell to the floor of the camper and landed on his bare toes. They reached for it at the same time, but Ben was faster. An enormous silver and white Husky dog barked once and lunged at her. Ben was once again faster and grabbed the dog's collar before it could run out of the open door.

"Digger, wait."

"You have your dog," she said lamely.

"Yep," he said as he stared down at her.

Maleah looked into a pair of hazel eyes that were red-rimmed and full of pain. There were streaks on his cheeks and tears clung to his lashes. Ben had been crying.

"I'm... I'm sorry. I didn't mean to intrude." She took a step back.

He held up the envelope. "What's this?"

Digger squirmed, twisted, and tried to get free of Ben's grip.

"Nothing," she said too quickly and corrected with, "Open it later."

He arched a brow and asked, "How about I open it now?" Ben let go of Digger to tear the envelope.

The dog took advantage of his freedom and jumped down the steps and right into Maleah.

"Shit," Ben cursed and moved to go after Digger, but he stumbled against the doorframe and stepped backward. The screen door slammed closed.

Maleah pushed the dog off her chest and grabbed his collar to hold him steady. "Ben, are you okay?" she called out.

"I am freaking fantastic," he said and with the volume that often accompanied drunkenness.

"I have my dog back, right? That makes up for losing my daughter, doesn't it? It's a tradeoff I never asked for. You know, I fought for custody of this dumb dog two years ago, and I lost anyway. Now here he is. And I also get Sir Mittens to keep me company while I fight to get Skyla back." Behind the screen door, Ben teetered out of her line of sight.

Maleah wasn't sure what to do next but standing outside holding on to a large and strong dog wasn't helping anyone. She opened the door, guided Digger inside, and climbed the steps.

Sir Mittens meowed from behind the closed bedroom door on the right, while Ben slouched over the dining table. He held a bottle of Jägermeister in his hand. Her envelope lay beside a collection of beer bottles. Some of the beers were open but most were capped and full.

"I'm sorry, Ben," she apologized again.

Even though she'd released Digger, his interest in her didn't waver. The dog sniffed at Maleah's shoes and pants with keen interest. The cat yowled from the other room, and she heard scratching on the door.

"No, I'm the one sorry. It's a zoo in here. Would you like a drink? It helps ease the tension."

She eyed the table but was more focused on getting the envelope back. In his current state of intoxication, she was starting to regret writing the letter. Maleah stepped closer to the table. "Sure."

Ben held out the liquor bottle and simultaneously reached for the envelope with his other hand.

"Didn't we try passing messages once before? I didn't think that turned out so well last time." He stared at the envelope in his hand, then slid her the side-eye.

She caught the sparkle of amusement in his hazel irises before he turned his attention back to the letter.

"I've never had the opportunity and desire to pour hot coffee on someone before," she admitted.

Maleah sniffed the licorice-flavored liqueur. It'd been years since she'd drunk the stuff and thought, why the hell not? She sipped and the alcohol coated her tongue. The sweet and unique taste wasn't exactly pleasant, but it brought back a lot of memories of being younger and terribly naïve. She took another, larger drink, and Ben's eyes followed her movements this time.

He gave the envelope a little wave. With a lopsided smirk, he asked, "Do I detect another Maleah hate note inside?"

"Umm." She bit her lip, unable to admit the truth of the letter. She set the bottle on the table and looked at the beer. She could use something to wash the shot of Jaeger down.

Ben turned and slid onto the bench seat, facing her. He tapped the edge of the envelope on the table and then laid it down and covered it with his hand.

She frowned and reached for the open beer bottle that looked mostly full. "Do you mind if I share your beer? That shot was a little strong."

"Go for it. Drink them all."

Maleah wasn't in the mood to get completely blitzed, but Ben was right about taking the edge off the tension. And a beer back went well with the shot. She gulped the stout beer and Digger decided he'd had enough of sniffing her feet and knees and went right for her gooseberry.

The force and strength, not to mention the surprise intrusion of the dog's nose to her backside had her lurching forward, spewing beer in an impressive spray while also dribbling it down her chin.

"Ack! No! Get off!" She plunked the beer down and bumped the table hard enough to knock over a couple other bottles. Ben righted the bottles as Maleah spun around to get Digger away from her crotch. She pushed him aside with her leg, and the dog decided her action was an invitation to either A) start a family with her or B) dominate the crap out of her. Maleah kept pushing Digger off, but he had his forelegs wrapped so tight around her that her efforts were useless. Digger's humper moved with impressive stamina and robustness. She tried backing away, but there was nowhere for her to go other than into the table again.

"A little help here," she said over her shoulder to Ben.

He held a beer in his hand and casually took a drink before saying, "Attaboy."

"I meant help *me*! Not your dog." Maleah moved down the length of the table, but Digger wouldn't let go. His dew claws were latched into her jeans.

"He is helping me." Ben held it in, but she could see the quiet laughter playing with the corners of his mouth. When she shot daggers at Ben with her eyes, he said, "Digger, off."

The dog released his hold and stood in the middle of the floor, looking mildly ashamed... and spent. Maleah blinked and wondered if she should stop invoking Wakea.

Ben said, "Go lie down." Digger went to Ben's bedroom and disappeared inside. "Sorry," he murmured but didn't look repentant about his dog's lack of manners.

She narrowed her gaze at Ben and was ready to take her leave, but before she could say anything, Ben rose from the seat, reached over his head, and pulled his T-shirt off in one smooth move that exposed his tight six-pack and hard chest in a slow motion reel that emptied all but the most basic human needs from her mind, body, and soul.

Maleah snapped out of the instant trance and slapped her jaw shut. "What are you doing?"

"Someone, I'm not naming names or anything, but she gave me a beer shower. Although I like stout, I generally don't wear it. You want to join me? Your shirt is a little wet too."

She dropped her chin to her chest and stared at the spill marks and paint splatters. When she looked back up at Ben, he was also staring at her chest. Her nipples went instantly hard and she had to resist the urge to cross her arms to cover herself and her tell-all breasts.

His gaze moved as slow as a dawning sun, rising over her body and eventually meeting her eyes. "I've seen you naked before, and I know you're not shy about taking your shirt off."

"You're drunk," she accused but didn't move to the door.

"Getting more sober by the minute if it makes any difference."

"I'm still standing here because I'm worried about you, not because you're ogling me."

"I think you enjoy being on the receiving end of my ogling as much as you like staring at my bare chest."

She let out a small huff. "Do not," she lied.

He laughed. "Come on, Maleah. You liked kissing me the other night as much as I did. Admit it."

"I will not." She paused, and it was obvious he knew as well as she did that their chemistry was out of this world and beyond anything she'd ever imagined. Maleah lifted her chin. "Why did you walk out on me the way you did?"

His gaze dropped to the floor for the briefest of seconds and then back to her face. "It's complicated. I'm—" He shook his head and didn't go on.

"You're what? Sexually confused? Gay? You can tell me." Her emotions rose as all of her frustrations soared and took flight in a near rant that she could no longer hold in. "I've fallen for a premature ejaculator and an asexual iron man. What's your problem, Ben? Go ahead and spit it out. Let's get this mystery out of the way. I find all the wrong guys and it's ridiculous."

He snorted.

She was about to cry. The bottle of Jaeger looked ever more appealing. She reached for it, but Ben stopped her. He moved off the bench and stepped in front of her in a swift move she wasn't ready for. Ben anchored his hands on her waist and pulled her into him. The front of his jeans pushed into her belly, and Ben lowered his mouth to hers.

He didn't ask before claiming a kiss. And Maleah held nothing back. The crush of his mouth and the sweeps of his tongue sent her to a wonderland of dizzying need and desire. Weightless, floating, tingling. Every luxurious sensation sparkled and danced in her blood and she was utterly lost in his kiss.

"Maleah," he said after pulling a mere half inch back from her lips. "There's nothing wrong with my cock. It's my damn head that's the problem."

"Does that mean you're going to kiss me and then walk out again?" she asked through shallow, fast breaths. She had to know. She had to be better prepared this time.

"If you tell me to stop, I will." His hands roved over her ass and along her back. His lips moved to her neck and he sucked at her pulse point, and Maleah didn't push him away.

The battle between doing what was right and doing what felt right was an inner war. Her feelings won as she said, "Don't stop, Ben."

He groaned against her flesh and nibbled a path down her neck and to her collarbone. Then he was cupping her breast in his palm, pushing up, and massaging with firm, deliberate pressure. He pulled his lips away from her neck and planted them against her taut nipple. He bit lightly and Maleah gasped. She raked her fingers through his hair and squeezed a handful by the roots as he began to toy with her hardened bud through her shirt. Maleah arched her back and a moan of pleasure escaped from her lips as he toyed with her breast.

"Holy hell," he breathed out. "You're going to undo me."

"Yes. It's the same for me too."

Ben's cock pressed hard and tantalizing against her pelvis. He raised his head to look at her. "Are you sure about this, Maleah?"

The serious look took her by surprise. His sincerity smoldered with a mixture of lust, longing, and a wildness she'd never seen in someone's eyes before.

The connection between them in that second left her speechless, and all she could do was nod. Yes, she definitely wanted this.

Maleah ran her hand over the deliciously hard planes of his ribcage, over his hip, and gripped his firm butt.

Ben brushed his fingers along the side of her cheek with a delicate and careful touch. "I can't promise you I won't regret this tomorrow."

"I have similar hesitations," she admitted.

"Then we're on the same page?" he asked.

"I think so," she said as a tiny twinge of doubt seeped into her brain about what she was doing and why.

"But that doesn't change the fact that I want you more than I've ever wanted anyone. I need to take you to my bed and make you come so hard you see stars."

She let out a deep sigh of relief at hearing his admission. "I want you exactly like that too."

With that, Ben scooped her off her feet and carried her to his bed.

"Digger, get out," he ordered and kicked the door closed behind the dog.

Ben placed Maleah on her feet and pulled her shirt over her head.

* * *

He was completely and totally consumed by her. Within seconds of taking her in his arms, Ben turned into something wild and intangible. But one thing had become clear. Pleasuring Maleah held a priority that had never occurred to his simple mind before. In the moment, his cock ruled the world, but she was the driving force behind his kisses, his strokes, his toying and teasing.

When she whimpered, he kept lapping his tongue or sucking her satin-smooth skin. When she ripped her fingers across his back or dug her nails into his shoulders, he continued tasting and savoring the delicate and sensitive parts of her, head to toes, and with a feverish need that couldn't be fulfilled. Maleah gasped and purred beneath him. Her moans for more sent shivers of desire over his flesh and through every nerve in his body. And Ben gave it to her. More of everything, more of himself than he knew he had in him to give.

Her breaths came harder, her chest rising and falling, panting. Her thighs tightened around his ears. His close-cropped beard brushed the silky skin of her legs. Ben worked his crooked fingers against her inner walls and licked at her swollen pearl. She squeezed her legs tighter together, but he held her open.

"Let go, Maleah. Come for me." He plunged his tongue deep into the well of her center and tasted her shuddering and pulsing release.

He eased back and rose above her. Ben wiped the back of his hand over his mouth and then lowered his face to kiss her. He wondered if she would let him after what he'd just been doing, but she opened her mouth and accepted his tongue as if she was starved for more of him.

Ben let himself get lost in the waves of sensation as he kissed and stroked up and down her beautiful body again, but his cock wouldn't be ignored for much longer. As if reading each other's minds, her hand glided down his torso and wrapped around his shaft, where she stroked up, down, and with the perfect amount of pressure.

As he fumbled for his wallet, and the condom thoughtfully donated by his brother, Maleah said, "Ben, please. I can't wait any longer. I need you inside of me."

He rolled to the side, ripped open the package, and suddenly felt like an amateur. Putting on the damn condom took him out of the moment, but Maleah was quick to bring him back and distract him as she worked her lips over his chest and along his stomach. The ripples of torturous pleasure caused by her mouth, tongue, and teeth were driving him crazy. Once he had the condom rolled on, he let his lizard brain take full control.

She lay on her back a moment later. Ben moved between her thighs, gripped his cock in his fist, and pressed the head to her opening. He grabbed the back of her leg and held her up and open to him as he pushed into her.

The sound she made when he filled her was surreal, not of this world. He joined her, not only with a groan of satisfaction, but in a way that had no words to explain their connection. The following rhythm and movements were contained in the three-dimensional world, but he was lost in a dimension he'd never known existed. He was lost in Maleah, lost in her scent, her softness, her pleasure.

As Maleah crested then reached the peak once more, Ben's release came swift and absolute. The rush, the pounding of his heart, the finale wrapped him in a heated fog that was the emphasis and oblivion of pure animal fucking. But coming with her also blindsided him with the fortification of a relationship he was not prepared to be a part of.

* * *

Even though the intensity of what they'd done left him uncertain, Maleah felt too good, too perfect against his body to let her sense his wavering emotions.

Ben held her close and refused to think as their heartbeats gradually returned to normal. He lowered his face to the side of her neck and kissed the sweetest-smelling skin he'd ever known. Maleah's hand moved up and down the length of his body, and neither one spoke for endless minutes. Ben felt more relaxed than he had in… possibly ever before.

She broke the silence first. "Ben?"

He held her breast in his hand and thought about bringing his lips back to her tantalizing nipple for yet another taste. "Yeah?" he murmured.

"Sir Mittens is still meowing."

"I'm ignoring him. You're a much more important distraction."

"Is he okay?"

"He has everything he needs. I checked on him before you stopped by."

She nodded and went quiet for a minute. "Should we bring him in here? Maybe he's lonely."

"Does that mean you're going to stay all night?" Ben wanted the decision to be hers. If he started thinking about the implications of what he'd just done with Maleah, it was going to get complicated fast. He wasn't ready for that. Ben wanted more time with Maleah, naked in his bed, but he didn't want anything to do with serious conversations or what the future might bring.

"I…" She sounded hesitant.

Ben raised his head and tried to read her expression or look for a reaction. The slant of muted gray light coming from behind the window shades didn't give him much to see by.

She tried again. "Do you want me to?"

"Yes." Letting his honest answer have a voice felt right, but he was too aware of his fears and how they manifested into bad things. "But only if you want to. No pressure, okay?"

"Mm-hmm." She made an agreeable but noncommittal sound, and Ben was okay with that.

Digger barked once from behind the closed bedroom door. Ben knew Digger's different alerts and he uttered a silent curse. The dog needed to go out.

Maleah pulled away from him and trailed her fingers over his chest and down the length of his torso. "Can I ask you something?"

"Sure. Anything," he said and instantly regretted the "anything" in his answer. He swallowed and waited.

"Was that..." she started. "I, umm..."

He watched her face again and saw her tuck her lower lip beneath her teeth. Her chest rose with a heavy breath.

She let the exhale out slowly and asked, "It's just that I haven't been with many guys before, but it's never been like that. I mean, it was good, don't get me wrong. But I didn't know sex could be so intimate. That sounds wrong. Of course it's intimate." Maleah hesitated again and then asked with way too much uncertainty, "Did you like it?"

Damn, she's so beautiful and adorable. How could she be so sexy and unsure at the same time? Why did her uncertainty turn him on even more?

He didn't want to say the wrong thing, and it caused him to stall. Ben found that he loved looking at her, watching her reactions, and he continued to do so as she waited for him to say something. He found himself needing to touch her and he raised his hand to her temple. Ben traced the outline of her face, then brushed her eyebrow and her cheekbone. His lips moved to hers without conscious thought and he memorized the way her mouth fit against his. He pulled back and looked into her eyes. The slight pinch creasing her brows made him realize he still hadn't answered.

With the tip of his index finger, he drew a line down the center of her forehead and over the bridge of her nose where he lightly bumped the cute round tip. Then he kissed the spot before pressing his lips to her forehead.

He gathered her in close and rested his cheek against her hair.

She stiffened ever so slightly. "Did you just boop my nose?"

He smiled because he had, even though he hadn't really meant to do so. Yeah, he had problems. It wasn't a secret.

"Maybe," he said, wondering if he'd royally fucked up. Again.

"What kind of answer is that?" She sounded both inquisitive and slightly perturbed.

He had to make things right... or at least better.

"I have no clue." Honesty wasn't one of his weaknesses, even if it meant he often came across as an imbecile with no filter.

"Was that a 'Hey, Maleah. Yep, I totally liked playing roll in the sack with you?'"

The laugh rose out of him and he couldn't hold it in. She pushed against his chest to escape him. She apparently thought he was laughing at her. Ben didn't loosen his hold. He held tight with one arm and used his other arm to push himself up and roll her onto her back.

Ben caged her in, pinning her to the mattress. She didn't fight him but kept her face neutral.

"I'm not laughing at you. But you make me laugh, Maleah. You make me smile. And I should have given you a clearer answer. I'm sorry if I made you feel unsure." With her beneath him, naked and hot, his cock stiffened and was ready to go again. He pressed his hips forward, letting her feel his hardened length.

"Did I like it?" he asked, repeating her question. He hovered, dipped low, licked her sumptuous nipple once, and then raised himself up to see her amazing almond-shaped eyes. "I can't even begin to describe how unreal, surreal…" He kissed her like a man starved and then said against her lips, "Unbelievable that was. I didn't know being with someone could be like that either."

"Are you saying that so I don't knee you in the balls?"

His hips lifted reflexively away from her body, but he didn't release her. "Ouch. No. I can't lie about this stuff." He paused and tried to decide if he should tell her something that might help her believe him. *Shit.* Honesty was getting the best of him tonight. "I've been with two women, so maybe I don't have a fucking clue about what just happened between us, but damn, I felt like God when you came. I don't think there's any other way to describe it." He held his breath and waited to see if she believed him.

Her eyes rolled up, breaking their gaze and appearing to think about something. The look lasted a second before her body let go of the tension she'd been holding. She softened all over, not only physically, but the look in her eyes. A smile touched her lips and he let go of his breath.

"Want to try again? Could be a one-time fluke." She gave a tiny shrug.

He ground his hard-on against her mound. "Yeah, I want to try again. But I know it wasn't a fluke." Ben sealed the deal with another long, promising kiss.

She whimpered into his mouth and met his grinding hips with her own.

"Maleah," he said. "I don't have another condom." It was a hard truth to speak aloud, but he never did this kind of thing and wasn't prepared.

"I'm clean and I'm on birth control. If you're worried, pull out before you finish. I'm okay with that."

He should have been more worried, but Ben somehow trusted Maleah completely.

* * *

Digger and Sir Dictator, a.k.a. Mittens, were not going to let him rest. Had he grown too used to living alone? Seeing to Skyla's needs on the weekends was one thing, but the demands of a dog and a kitten were something else entirely.

Digger howled, a lengthy wavering guttural sound that was more like talking, from outside the door. In the moment, Ben would sacrifice his left nut for a dog door and a fenced yard. Maybe not his nut, considering how valuable they were to him in the last couple hours. How about his right brain? Yeah, that could go. He needed to stop thinking so much anyway.

The door handle rattled against the catch. *What the?* Would Digger let himself in?

Ben wasn't willing to let go of Maleah, but he had no choice. He didn't think she was asleep yet, and whispered, "Sorry. The animals need me."

She said softly, "It's all right. I understand."

He heard the smile in her voice, and a hint of roughness in her throat. The thought that he'd been the cause of her scratchy throat from all the moaning and calling his name stroked his ego in the best possible way.

Maleah rolled onto her side and watched him as he picked up his jeans off the floor. "Anything I can do to help?"

He zipped up and leaned over the side of the bed. *Beautiful, sweet, thoughtful.*

Ben nudged Maleah's shoulder, pushing her onto her back. She moved willingly and, *fuck*, if he didn't want to have her again for a third time. Two-plus years of abstinence must have caused a buildup of pressure and a need for release of epic proportions. Ben found his place on top of her, his knees on either side of her hips. He kissed as if it was their first and last kiss of all time.

He wondered if she was sore, her lips but other body parts as well. If so, it mattered not, because she kissed him back with equal need and intensity.

"You've already done more than enough. I'll be quick. Make yourself comfortable. If you need anything, it's yours." He brushed the tip of his nose against hers and bounced off the bed with a surprising amount of energy considering his entire body was more relaxed than a noodle. Ben landed on his feet and slipped out the door, careful not to let Digger push his way in.

Fifteen

MALEAH HEARD THE DOG'S nails click against the vinyl floor of the camper. Ben ordered Digger to hold still so he could put on the leash. The door opened and closed, and the cat had stopped meowing. The need to slip into an after-sex blissful coma for the next eight hours was a heavy seductive blanket she couldn't resist. She tucked a hand beneath Ben's pillow, breathed in his scent, and burrowed into the bedclothes.

Sleeping with Ben was possibly the best thing she'd ever experienced with another human being. Her mind wanted to argue against the revelation, but she honestly couldn't remember anything that could top what it felt like when they'd orgasmed. *Heaven on earth.* Even if this turned out to be a horrible mistake, or if he was just drunk and out of his mind, Maleah would never regret it. Her mind had been blown and she was probably ruined for all other men, but now there was no going back.

Maleah drifted in a haze, caught somewhere in the realm of half sleep, when she heard Ben return. She thought the shower was running, but she must have fallen asleep again. A minute or two later, Ben slid into the bed... and he was freezing. He pulled her in tight against him and she shrieked and tried to squirm out of his arms.

"Is it snowing outside? Let go!" Her words sounded garbled as she was half asleep and brain fogged.

"No. Digger decided he needed to chase something. I made the mistake of stumbling into the river."

"No, you didn't," she said as his refreshing coolness made her ten times more alert.

"Yep, I did. The shower was hot but not hot enough. Damn dog. He might have seen a cat, but in the dark, who knows."

"You took him to the park?"

Ben's body temperature was rapidly warming against Maleah's heated skin.

"That's the best place to walk him. You're a great heater." His whole body, from feet to shoulders, tangled with hers in the bed. "Thanks." He snuggled in even tighter.

"You're not welcome." She smiled as she said it and then inhaled the smell of soapy clean maleness.

"I'm exhausted. Thanks for that too," he murmured.

The feel of his hard, muscular body was intoxicating and she reveled in the simple luxury of being in the bed with him. She'd wanted, dreamed of, this moment with Holden for so long, and now here she was doing exactly what she'd fantasized about but with someone else... and it was good. Better than good. She was amazed and happy.

Maleah fell into a dreamless, weightless sleep and woke up to sunshine and without a care in the world. Oh, how she wanted to hang onto that feeling forever, but it was a new day, and she would have to return to reality. *Darn*, she thought.

The bedroom door was shut and muffled the small domestic sounds coming from the other side. The necessities of the body also accompanied reality. Maleah dressed, combed her fingers through her hair, and peeked out the door.

Ben sat at the table with a laptop computer open. He glanced up and smiled. Digger rose from the floor and trotted over to say good morning, but Ben caught him by the collar and said, "Digger, sit. Stay." The dog obeyed but whined at his owner.

There was no morning-after shame, but Maleah's lack of experience left her feeling a bit self-conscious.

"Morning, beautiful."

"Hi?" She sounded so unsure, she wondered if it was possible to literally screw your brains out... or more like her brains had been strapped to a rocket and sent to the moon.

"Were you hoping I'd be at work by now?" he asked, a questioning uncertainty tingeing his own voice.

She moved closer but didn't join him at the table. "No?" Her answer wasn't supposed to be a question. It was that she didn't have any expectations. Maleah leaned against the kitchen cabinets across from the table and tucked her hands behind her back. "I'm glad you're here. Is it late? I don't usually sleep in."

He was dressed, boots laced, and appeared ready for the day.

"I'm glad I didn't wake you. I was trying to be quiet. I picked up coffee and breakfast. Help yourself." Ben gestured to a to-go cup and a pastry box on the table in front of him. "It's a vanilla latte."

"Thanks. I need to step into the restroom before breakfast."

He nodded and said, "There's a clean towel by the sink if you want to shower."

Ben returned his gaze to the monitor as she went to freshen up. Since she didn't have anything except her clothes, she chose to wait until she was in her apartment to take a shower. But before leaving, she found a bottle of water in the fridge and then joined Ben at the table.

She drank the entire bottle of water before drinking the coffee and eating a cherry cream cheese Danish from the box. Ben ate a blueberry scone, and they talked like friends instead of enemies, frenemies, first time lovers, or anything else that came with a title. Just friends having coffee together.

"Your parents flipped houses when you were growing up, right?" he asked.

"Yeah. We renovated a house every year or two. Which means we moved a lot."

Ben tapped the keys on the keyboard. "Take a look at this." He scooted over on the bench and she joined him on his side of the table.

"You're looking at houses this morning?" she asked.

"I have to do something about my living arrangement. I've been thinking about investing in a new property for some time. I've been on the fence about building my own house, or renovating an older home. My current situation with Skyla, and now with Digger and the cat, I need to get out of this camper." He looked around the tight space and then at Maleah. "This was always a temporary solution. Kiki's been great, and I think she liked having me close by for security but also for company. But her situation has also changed recently."

"Yes. A big change. I guess you've heard the news about her and your grandpa."

One side of Ben's mouth lifted into a strained smile. "My mom called yesterday to see how I was doing after dropping off Skyla. She shared the news about Grandpa and Kiki while I was drinking with my brother."

"Is that where your truck is? At your brother's?"

"Yeah. I need to pick it up sometime today."

"I can give you a ride if you want," she offered and then instantly wondered if she'd made a mistake. Was it too soon to offer to hang out? Did they need time apart after sleeping together? She didn't have the answers. Maleah swallowed. She wanted to talk to Brielle. Did Brie notice she was gone all night? And was Brie a good person to consult? Brie didn't have much experience with men either.

"You're not busy today?" he asked, his face unreadable.

Was he feeling her out?

"Busy? Maybe? You know how much there is to do next door."

Where is the letter? she thought with a small jolt of panic, then calmed herself down. Nothing she'd written in her letter needed to be changed. After seeing him drunk, she'd had a moment of regret, but now she didn't. "I make my own schedule these days, so I can take you to your truck if you want. It's no big deal. I'd like to be here today to talk with the drywallers. That is, if they show up. You know how wishy-washy and unreliable the subs can be."

"Yep. Did Brendon say he'd be here today? If he said Monday, then he'll be here. He's one of the better contractors in the county."

"Good to know. And yeah, I think so. I should probably look at my calendar," she said and added that to her growing to-do list.

"After you check in with Brendon, do you want to go get my truck, or maybe take a look at a few of the houses around town with me?"

Maleah turned on the seat to face him. Their legs were touching and every centimeter connected with him felt as if there were actual electric currents passing between them. Here she had been wondering if it was too soon after spending the night together to offer to give him a ride, and he just asked if she wanted to look at houses with him.

She swallowed as she stared at his incredibly handsome face.

Ben lowered his head so their lips were almost touching. His eyelids fell closed and he placed a kiss on her lips. "If you're busy, or you want to run away from my dumpster-fire life, it's okay with me, Maleah. But I like hanging out with you. I also think it would be all right to have a second set of experienced eyes on some of these properties."

"I'd love to go look at houses. But first, I need to shower, change, and look at my schedule."

"Good, because I need to check on a few things in the Aspen Building. Meet you over there whenever you're ready to go?"

"Okay," she said and gave Digger a good scratch around his neck and ears before standing up. "Are you ever going to let the kitten out to play?"

Ben's jaw tightened as he tried to control his grin. "I almost asked you the same thing last night."

The tell-all heat flushing her skin, and the space between her legs, sent warm shivers through her bloodstream. "I'm pretty sure you did ask, Benjamin."

His smile broke through and she didn't hold hers back either.

He tapped at the keyboard and without looking up, said, "I'm glad you said yes."

* * *

They met up two hours later inside the Aspen Building. A lot of changes had taken place since the last time she'd been inside. Namely, that the entire first and second floor were nearly complete. The office space was modern, high-tech, and looked totally, well almost totally, out of place in the quaint mountain town.

"Who is leasing this space?" she asked.

She and Ben stood by the picture windows in the largest office on the second floor overlooking downtown.

"Do you remember Zebulon Cruz from high school? He's a year older than us," Ben said.

She thought about it for a minute. "I think so. Kind of a quiet kid, right? He was in the chess club and a total gamer."

"That's him. He's a good friend of mine, and he's decided to move his business into the Aspen Building. He wants to live in the mountains again, and I don't blame him."

"When is he moving in?" Maleah asked while looking at the details of the oversized office.

The built-ins along the north wall and the huge storage closet were top of the line. No expense had been spared. The wide-plank wood floors were rustic and masculine and went nicely with the exposed brick of the south wall. The wiring and type of electrical outlets were like nothing she'd seen before.

"In about a month. He wants to be settled in before the snow gets deep. So far, we're on schedule. The desks and office equipment are supposed to arrive next week," Ben said as he peered down at the street below.

Maleah glanced in the same direction and they watched a little girl with strawberry-blond pigtails playing with a helium filled balloon. The delight on her face as she spun in a circle and yanked the string over and over to make the balloon bob up and down made Maleah smile. Then she realized Ben was probably thinking of Skyla.

She had so many questions about Zebulon's company moving into her aunt's building, but it could wait. The pressing matter of Ben's homelessness came first.

"You ready to find a house?" she asked.

He turned his attention from the activity on the sidewalk and looked at Maleah. She definitely saw the stress and concern in his green and amber eyes.

"Let's do it."

* * *

They decided to pick up Ben's truck after looking at houses. Maleah suggested taking the Land Cruiser since it was roomy and could handle rough driveways if needed. And she liked driving the old beast.

"If we can stop by the top five properties on my list, that will be a good place to start. For Skyla, I'd prefer to stay in or close to town."

"Does that mean she's coming back soon?"

"I hope so," he said. "It's going to be another court battle, but Kinsey is breaking the law. She's not going to get away with it this time."

Maleah kept her eyes on the road. She was familiar with four of the five addresses on Ben's list. She said, "I think you're an amazing father. I don't say that lightly. The way you listen to your daughter and respond to her reminds me of my own dad. He's stern but fun. He always gave me consistent and fair boundaries, so I knew what my parents expected from me. You're the same type of parent."

Ben didn't reply at first, but then he said, "I try to be a stable parent, but Skyla's mother is another story altogether."

"And you can't do anything to change that," Maleah said, her sympathy soaring. "But you will continue to be the strong parent, because she needs you, and you care. Finding a house is part of being responsible, so good job."

"Right," he agreed with a heavy dose of sarcasm. "Totally making this being a dad thing up as I go, but thanks."

Maleah switched back to the subject of house hunting. "If you find a house you want, do you have a real estate agent, or are you doing this on your own?"

"I know a few agents. Who doesn't?" he asked.

"Around here, they're a dime a dozen."

"I thought I would scout on my own and narrow down the properties to my top two or three. Then I'll call an agent. Unfortunately, with property values exploding and so many people moving to Colorado who either work from home or are retiring, there aren't many houses to choose from," Ben said as they turned onto Elbert Ave. "New builds are in high demand, but there's limited space in town because of the obvious geographical restrictions."

Maleah glanced at the nearly vertical mountains bordering the northwest side of town. "Which makes Aunt Kiki's investment in the Garden Block even more valuable."

"That it does. The ranching community continues to feel pressured to sell off parcels of land. And I don't blame a single family who sells out. The profit on land versus running cattle is out of this world. The McCarthys sold their three thousand acres and bought a smaller place in Montana and in the Grenadine islands. They bought another house for their kids in Arizona and will never have to work another day in their lives."

"Is your family's ranch at risk?" she asked.

"Yeah, but my brother won't sell. He's too damn stubborn. Plus, he's attached to these mountains. Even more than I am. If he ever has kids, which I seriously doubt, then the pressure will fall onto their shoulders. It will be decades before that happens, if at all."

"What about you? Would you sell the land for millions of dollars and bug out for a beach lifestyle? A high-rise condo in downtown Denver, Vancouver, or Tampa?"

Ben stared straight ahead. "I've been thinking of what's best for Skyla for so long, I don't know what I'd do. What about you?"

"It's similar for me except without a kid. My career has been my only focus. Even in the boyfriend department I fell for my—" Maleah cut herself off. Telling Ben about her obsession with Holden probably wasn't a good idea.

"Who? Your boss?" he said, his eyes twinkling as if he already knew.

Maleah parked the Land Cruiser in front of house number eight-thirty-one, their first stop of the day. She didn't want to lie, but admitting her fantasy about a happily-ever-after with Holden was difficult. Giving up those long-held dreams was even more difficult. Losing her job was one thing, but admitting how foolish and naïve she'd been about her boss was an entirely different level of hell and humiliation.

Ben had opened up to her about Skyla, so Maleah swallowed a lump of pride. She scrunched up her face and nodded without looking at her co-driver.

"His name is Holden," she said.

"Holden who? I did some work for someone named Holden about three years ago."

She didn't want to say. Ben waited patiently for her to answer. Maleah sucked in a breath. Holden's name was mildly unfortunate, but they were adults, right?

"What?" The look of confusion brought Ben's shapely brows together and he licked the corner of his mouth. It was an unconscious gesture, but Maleah was all too mindful of her awareness of his tongue doing anything.

"Cat got your tongue, sweetheart?" Ben's tone lightened considerably and she was conscious of the shift in his mood now that she'd put herself on the spot.

Get it over with, she told herself. "His name is Holden McNutt. I doubt you know him."

A loaded pause sat inside the cab with them. She could all but feel what was cooking inside that handsome head of his. She didn't have to wait long.

"Holden McNutts," he repeated incorrectly. "Let me guess, his business partner is Jack Goff."

"You're not funny."

"But wait." The corner of his lips twitched. "There's more. How's Mike Hunt doing these days?"

She shook her head and sighed. "Don't know him, but probably feeling neglected." Maleah tried not to laugh as she thought about how neglected her own Mike Hunt had been until last night. She busied herself by unbuckling her seat belt then adjusting the scarf she'd thrown on before leaving the apartment and conveniently avoiding making eye contact with Ben.

Ben obviously couldn't stop himself now. "What about the senior execs, Dick Pound and Chris Peacock? How are they holding up without your perky influence around the office? Oh, and we can't forget about the HR ladies, Rose Bush and Barb Dwyer. You know I can do this all day."

She made the mistake of glancing over. He looked so entertained and full of himself. Maleah hadn't thought about Ben's nickname since middle school and she accidentally, on purpose, let it slip from her lips. It was too juicy and begging for verbalization. "The staff at True Green, who weren't laid off, are all doing well. Thanks for your concern, Ben... Dover of Erickson," she said, challenging him with a comeback.

"Ah, my favorite insult from seventh grade. Thanks for that." He gave her a scornful look yet winked at her. Ben laid his hand over his chest. "It warms my heart you remembered and can still drive the nail home right where it hurts the worst. Did you also remember my middle name is Gareth not Dover?"

She thought of something unrelated and asked, "Your middle name is Gareth, but your dad's name is Garrett. That's not confusing at all."

"Being bad at naming things is an inherited family trait. Did you meet my pets, Digger and Sir Mittens?" Ben popped the door open as they shared a laugh.

Maleah stepped onto the road and zipped up her jacket against the cool mountain air. "I like your cat's and dog's names," she said and hoped they'd moved on from talking about Holden.

"You would," he said, teasing.

She smacked his torso with the back of her hand for the snarky comment.

"You know," he said conversationally as they walked past the For Sale sign in the yard and onto the driveway of the vacant home. "Being Mrs. McNutts doesn't suit you in the slightest."

"It's McNutt, singular not plural," she corrected. Ugh. He hadn't moved on from the Holden topic.

"Please tell me you're not serious about a guy with a singular nut," he said, and then continued after she shot him another unamused glare. "The name doesn't go well with Maleah," Ben said as he began to inspect the front of the garage. "Maleah McNutts." He tried out the name and continued to say Holden's last name incorrectly. "I mean, Holden McNutts? How could you ever take a guy seriously with a name like that?"

"Be quiet." She peered into the large living room windows of the eighties ranch-style home.

"This is the same Holden the Hermaphrodite you're talking about? I don't know anything about that condition, but you've got to be better off without him, her, whatever the single nut is. Just sayin'." Ben followed her across the front of the house to continue peeking inside the windows.

With his question, Maleah tripped over something unseen in the yard, or over nothing. Her own feet? She coughed then choked on spittle before she could find the words. She turned and Ben nearly ran her over.

"Holden isn't a—He's not deformed. Not even close. Why would you say that, like that?" She had to know where he'd gotten this tidbit of false information. Last night, she accidentally ranted about her poor choice in men, and without naming him, Holden being asexual, not a hermaphrodite.

"Your cousin was drunk off her ass the night I walked her home from the pub. She was also chatty. I was wondering if she was a mute before I spoke to her at The Jackalope."

Maleah rubbed her temples and thought back to that night. "She probably told you a lot of things that weren't true." Brielle's tendency to run her mouth after ingesting alcohol was downright scary and scarily predictable.

Ben shrugged. "She made me laugh."

Maleah nodded slowly and looked up in search of answers she never could have imagined herself saying, but found them anyway. "Holden has some personal issues, but I know for a fact being a hermaphrodite isn't one of them." Okay, she'd never actually seen the man's bits and pieces, but she was ninety-nine percent sure. She had seen him in his swim trunks. That was close enough. In her book, Holden rated a nine on the scale of hot guys. Okay, maybe eight point five after seeing Ben naked, but still, absolutely nothing wrong with his man parts... other than that he never used them the way most men did. Maleah was so conflicted.

Ben shrugged, humor tugging at the corners of his lips. He raised his hands in surrender. "You might want to set Brielle straight on this subject. The rumors she's spreading will set this town on fire, if they haven't already."

Maleah pressed her lips into a tight line. Brielle probably got the facts wrong on purpose just to start something with Ben. Brielle could be a quiet and timid person, but there was way more going on behind the curtain than almost anyone ever saw.

She inhaled, turned, and started walking again. "Thanks for letting me know. I'll talk to her."

"So, what's his problem? Why didn't he jump if you were so into him?"

"It's, err..." She wasn't sure how to answer. Nothing had changed on Holden's end. They were friends. He'd confided in her. He said he felt close to Maleah and trusted her enough to tell her about himself and his asexual lifestyle. She stopped and turned back around again.

The look on Ben's face fell just enough to dim the light in his eyes. He gave a half smile, but she felt the shift in his emotions. "Are you still seeing this guy?"

"No," she said clearly and plainly. "He doesn't date. He's more or less committed to the company and his physical training."

"In other words, you would be seeing him if he was available."

"It's not like that either, Ben. It's complicated."

Ben walked around Maleah and opened the gate to the backyard. "Yeah, my life is complicated right now too. I get it," he muttered.

They walked around the property, and to Maleah's relief, the rest of their conversation was focused on the house.

She said, "This house doesn't have a lot of character, but it does have everything else on your wish list. The backyard is a great size, especially for a lot in town. The six-foot privacy fence is a major bonus since you own a Husky."

"Digger's a malamute," Ben said.

"Oh... that's why he's so big," she said with more enthusiasm than she felt, but as the mental lightbulb brightened and alleviated one little detail of her ignorance, her words came out all gushy. Maleah's keen interest in insignificant matters sometimes came out with way too much perkiness. She embarrassed herself all too often, but when something excited her, she would catch herself doing it again.

Ben typed into his phone, didn't look up, and said in his normal insert-a-joke-here voice—a voice she was quickly growing accustomed to and looking forward to hearing— "Yeah, that's what she said."

Her self-inflicted embarrassment and his jokes apparently went hand in hand. Maleah stopped overthinking, laughed, and they finished looking at the house.

The next two homes were definitely an improvement over the ranch-style house.

They moved on and Maleah parked in front of a white, two-story Victorian home. "I loved this house when I was a kid." She pointed at the small house across the street and three houses down. "We lived in the yellow cottage down the street when I was in fifth grade, but I wanted my parents to buy this one and fix it up. It wasn't for sale."

"The current owners still live here, so we can't look inside the windows this time. There are good pictures on the website of the interior. I needed to see the lot, proximity to the neighbors, and overall curb appeal in person. I don't think I'm a fan of the small rooms, but this house could be a sound investment."

"Would you have to get a permit from the city for historical preservation reasons?" she asked.

"Probably. I'll make sure and ask the agent if I am serious about this one. If you liked it as a kid, then Skyla probably would too. That matters to me."

"It's a very fairy-tale, storybook-looking house, so yes, it appeals to little girls," Maleah said.

"But the heating, thin walls, and getting the approval of some historical committee may not appeal to her father."

"That's understandable. It is a beautiful home, though," Maleah said, feeling wistful and nostalgic over her childhood dream of living in a Victorian home. "Are you ready to see the next house?"

"Sure," Ben said.

They drove across town and into a neighborhood Maleah wasn't as familiar with. She couldn't remember ever having been on that particular street. Finding someplace new within the old gave her a little thrill. The mature evergreens and aspen trees in the yards of the well-kept older homes gave the street a homey and stable feeling. She loved everything about it before even finding the house that was for sale.

"Number seven-thirteen." Ben made a motion with his hand to a house coming up on their right.

Maleah parked and jumped out without speaking. She'd already embarrassed herself once by being over-enthusiastic. This time, she would play it cool. Otherwise, she was going to gush and squee over how much she adored everything about Craftsman homes.

The home sat empty and they decided to have a closer look. It needed to be painted. The roof didn't appear to be in great shape either, but Maleah could picture this neglected house as being a real home someday. With a warm fire in the hearth, sit-down dinners, Christmas lights on the spruce tree in the yard and on the shrubs bordering the porch, she could visualize every detail with so much clarity. Her mind whirled with possibilities and ideas for decorating before even seeing the inside. If she were buying a home, she'd make an offer on this one today.

They climbed the steps and stood beneath the covered front porch. She peered out over the front yard, the street, and the gorgeous neighboring homes and sighed. What was her dream? Did she want this? A house, a family? Did those things mean anything to her? Deep down, she'd always thought that someday she would find the perfect guy, marry him, and have kids, but she also wanted a career. And focusing on her career had taken over every other part of her life. How had that happened? How did she forget that there was more to life than saving the planet? Her confusion and loss of direction weren't fun. She wouldn't call herself depressed, but the loss of a major part of her identity was slightly terrifying.

"No thoughts?" Ben asked.

"Too many." She turned around to look inside the wide front windows. "This is the house I would choose. I wouldn't even look at any more."

"Yeah?"

She tucked a loose strand of hair behind her ear and nodded. Maleah buried her hands inside her jacket pockets. "Sometimes, you have a good feeling and you know it's the one. I have that feeling here. It's silly, I know, but this is an amazing property."

Ben watched her face closely and she felt embarrassment warm her cheeks. A small and endearing smile curved his lips, and she wanted to kiss him and congratulate him for finding his house. But he hadn't said anything about even liking the Craftsman-style home. She kept her lips to herself.

"It's a new listing. And it needs a lot of work. I'll add this one to my list for a showing with the agent. Come on," he said and took her hand in his.

He led her off the porch and around the side of the house but didn't open the gate to the backyard this time. They crossed back in front of the house to peer at the other side of the home. Ben took a minute to look at the detached garage, then he said he was finished for the day. He held her hand in his until they returned to the Land Cruiser.

Maleah drove back into the business district, and as they rolled by the Garden Block, Ben said, "My brother must have come into town and he brought my truck."

Ben's pickup was parked in a space in front of the Aspen Building.

"Nice. I guess I have to get back to work then if we're not driving out to the ranch."

"Yeah, me too," he said.

Maleah pulled into the parking space that she'd come to thinking as belonging to the Land Cruiser and cut the engine.

"I'm going to suck at this," Ben said before she even had a chance to make their goodbye awkward. His fingers drummed against the armrest and then he went still.

She was instantly grateful for his admission but also worried because she didn't know how to do this either. "Today was fun. Thanks for letting me tag along." She paused, wrinkled her nose, and said, "That sounded lame. I liked looking at houses today. It gives me a lot of inspiration for all the work I'm doing here."

"I'm glad you came. Do you want to see me again?" He sounded as unsure as she felt.

"Do you want to see me again?" she asked in return.

His eyebrows jerked up toward his hairline. "It's special the way you always manage to turn my bullshit around on me."

"And you make me laugh," she said with a bright smile.

"Okay, then let's keep doing this then. See you around?"

"Mm-hmm." She nodded and felt a little shy at the way he was staring into her eyes.

"But not too soon, right? I don't want to scare you off right away."

"Same," she agreed. "You might figure out that I burst into song at the most random times. People can only handle limited doses of that, I think."

"I already knew that about you," he whispered, leaning in as if it was a secret.

They shared a grin and Ben opened his door. She met him near the front of the hood and they walked side by side down the alley until they reached the back door of the Columbine Building.

Ben said, "I'm headed over to the realty office."

"You're ready for a showing?"

"I think so."

"I'm happy for you, Ben."

"I haven't bought anything yet."

"But you're taking steps toward your future. That's worth celebrating," she said.

"Thanks," he said with that softness in his eyes and on his lips he rarely exposed.

She was about to say "See you later" and pull the back door open, but he was faster. In a swift and fluid motion, Ben stepped in close and bent down to kiss her. She wasn't expecting it, even if she was hoping to kiss him again, and she sucked in a small gasp before relaxing into the kiss and melting on the spot.

When he backed away, she noticed that a seriousness had replaced the warmth in his eyes, but she was weak-kneed and lost in a dreamy daze as she reached for the door handle. Maleah walked away before leading Ben back to his camper and his bed.

Sixteen

"NOT TOO SOON" turned out to be a twenty-seven-hour break. Not that she'd been counting. But yeah, every hour without seeing him had been an eternity.

After a long day of painting and then sanding wood floors, Maleah stepped outside to get rid of a bag of trash just as Ben stepped out of the trailer with Digger on a leash.

Self-conscious didn't even begin to describe her awareness of her dust-covered and stained work clothes. She found that wearing her hair pulled up and wrapped in a bandana kept most of the paint, spackle, sawdust, cobwebs, tape, and anything else she'd encountered out of her long hair.

He grinned when he saw her, and she couldn't help but think he was inwardly laughing at her state of disarray. Maleah threw the bag into the dumpster and then slid the bandana off as she spun around.

"Want to take a walk with us? We're going to the park," Ben said.

Then she noticed that Ben was also dusty and in his work clothes. So maybe he hadn't been inwardly making a joke at her expense.

Her gaze dropped to inspect how bad her clothes were. It was bad.

"No one at the park cares if you're not dressed up," he said, easily reading her hesitations.

"True. Okay," she agreed. "It'll be good to stretch my legs and get some fresh air after being cooped up all day."

"I see that you speak dog fluently." He gave Digger a pat and rub on his huge head.

"Pardon?" she asked, confused.

"You just said exactly the same thing Digger tried to tell me when I went inside to get him out of the trailer."

They fell into step and began walking toward the foot bridge that led over the river and into the park behind the Garden Block.

"Yep. Me and your dog are exchanging secret messages. He asked me to relay to you in human that he could use approximately six walks a day."

"Is that so?" Ben asked.

"He's a sled dog, so he probably needs a daily marathon."

"Can you tell him he needs a bath because he's making my place smell like dirty dog?"

She said, as if it were a no-brainer, "Ben, you know Digger can hear you? He's literally right here. And I think you hurt his feelings."

Ben didn't fall for her shenanigans. "I hope I did. He's disgusting. Maybe I should let him jump in the river again."

"I also feel pretty disgusting. Are you going to throw me in the river?"

"If you want," he replied without hesitation. He sidestepped and moved behind her. Before she could react, he grabbed her upper arms and started to push her toward the water.

Maleah slipped out of his grasp and stuck her tongue out at him.

"Do you have a death wish? You wouldn't dare." She narrowed her gaze at him.

"Try me," he challenged.

"No, thanks." She moved farther from his reach.

The aspen trees in the park had started to turn colors and the lime and golden leaves shimmied in the evening light. It was a lovely evening to take a lap around the park. Ben picked up a stick from beneath a towering ponderosa pine.

"Digger," he said, getting the dog's attention. "Fetch!"

Digger tore across the lawn, leash flapping behind him, and Ben rejoined Maleah on the path.

"I don't recommend the river for bathing. It works in a pinch, or when your dog drags you in, but there are better ways to get clean."

"I plan on taking advantage of more modern methods as soon as we head back across the alley."

He looked her up and down, taking his time and causing her skin to tingle.

"Why are you staring at me that way?" she asked. "Stop it."

A slow grin spread from one cheek to the other. "You really want me to stop? Or do you want me to make sure you don't have another unfortunate shower accident? I can monitor the situation in person if you want. And I'm also feeling a little dusty. This could be a win-win for both of us."

Her gaze slid left then right, anywhere but at his face, because the moment he saw her eyes, he'd know how much she wanted him. She swallowed the mammoth-sized lump of desire lodged in her throat. "I could definitely use some monitoring. We both know I'm a walking disaster in the construction site I live in."

"You got it," he said and then called to Digger. "Let's go!" Ben took her hand and immediately started hiking toward the bridge that led back across the river. He no longer seemed concerned about Digger. Maleah glanced over her shoulder, making sure the dog was with them. He was, his tail high, ears forward, and carrying the stick in his mouth. She peered up at Ben and found his dimples winking at her.

"I don't know about you, but I'm suddenly feeling very dirty." He picked up his pace.

* * *

Sir Mittens meowed at him from the top of the dining table. "Not now, cat."

His new kitten responded by pushing a pen off the table and onto the floor. Ben made sure the door was closed before releasing Digger from the leash. He scooped up the kitten as he passed the table and stroked his back. "You stay off the table. I don't care how precious everyone thinks you are, you're not allowed on the table or the counters." Ben entered his room and opened the closet.

Sir Mittens answered by rubbing his tiny jawline along Ben's fingers, and then promptly sank his tiny fangs into him. Ben's uber fast reflexes saved him from bloodshed, and Sir Mittens found himself flying through the air and landing on the bed a half second later. Ben stared at the little predator and saw right through all the supposed cuteness.

"Keep that up and you'll be living the hard life of an alley cat," he warned.

Mittens sat, spread his legs, and started licking his crotch.

"Ungrateful little..." Ben didn't finish the curse.

Maleah was waiting for him as he put Digger away and grabbed clean clothes. There was no way he would shower with her and then put dirty work clothes back on. He ditched his animal menagerie and met Maleah outside.

They entered the apartment and found Brielle sitting on the couch, head down, and fixated on her laptop. Ben glanced from Brie to Maleah and didn't speak.

"I'll be with you in a second," Maleah said in a low voice and pointed to the bathroom.

Ben glanced at Brielle again. She didn't look up or even give any indication that she was aware of them entering the apartment. He nodded and Maleah went to the large closet and storage space at the end of the kitchen.

As Ben entered the bathroom, he heard Brielle ask, "Where'd you go? I thought you were taking the trash out."

Maleah said, "I took a quick walk in the park. I really need a shower."

"Yeah, I already cleaned up. Today was messy. You won't believe what I've done online. I'll show you later, and you're either going to kill me or thank me," Brielle said.

"Okay, show me later. Shower first."

Maleah entered the bathroom carrying her own change of clean clothes. She locked the door and turned around to face him.

Ben had stripped off his shirt, boots, and socks. She stared at him for a brief second, looked at his chest, then dropped her gaze to the floor. Embarrassed or shy, he couldn't tell.

"Do you want help with your clothes? As a general contractor, I feel it's important to have multiple skills. I could definitely use some practice in this department."

"Is that so?" She unbuttoned her jeans and licked her lips.

He stepped closer but didn't touch her. Ben's need to be with her was intense, but only if it was what she wanted. "Yeah. This isn't my area of expertise, but I'd like to remedy that."

She lowered her gaze.

"Have you changed your mind? I can always stand guard outside the shower if you want. My cock will hate me for the rest of my life, but I can restrain myself if need be."

"I don't think we should disappoint your penis." Maleah met his gaze with her silvery stare.

He tried not to laugh, but he couldn't hold back the grin. She sounded and looked so serious. His shoulders shook with silent laughter. "He would be devastated."

"We definitely can't have that." Maleah reached for the hem of her shirt, lifted slowly, and exposed her smooth porcelain stomach and then her black satin bra.

She emerged with a smile on her face. Ben unbuttoned his pants and lowered the zipper. Side-stepping away from her before he forgot why they were shut in the bathroom. He opened the glass door of the newly enclosed shower.

"Do you like what we've done? This room looks completely different than the last time you were in here."

"I'm impressed. You must have talked Kiki out of the royal blue and cream-colored tiles," he said as she stepped up behind him to take a closer look at the new shower stall.

"Brie and I were adamant about not putting blue tile in here. Then Brie found an awesome deal on these tiles. We laid the tiles, but it was your plumber who installed the new shower heads... and the new safety bars."

"Safety is our top priority. I see the spacing between the bar and the wall won't let someone get their foot caught in it."

"Yeah... that's a huge upgrade." She playfully rolled her eyes. "I even tested it to make sure no body parts could get trapped."

"Good thinking. Although, you should have called me over before running such tests. I have the right tools in case something should go wrong again."

"I'm ready for another test." She reached inside and turned on the dual shower heads.

"Do I hear a little of your inner science nerd coming out, Ms. Hale? Do we need our own experiment?"

"Uh-huh." She nodded and pushed her pants over her hips. They dropped to the floor. Her bra and thong joined them. Maleah stepped beneath the rain shower head. Water poured over her naked body and Ben went temporarily brain dead and mute.

"I love experiments. What should we test first?" she asked.

Ben had never exploded out of his pants before—but he just might do so as his hard-on was instant and rather frightening. Suppressing the Hulk urge, he regained an ounce of sanity and moved on to living out the ultimate sex fantasy with a girl he never could have dreamed of.

"I got it." He stepped into the shower and was struck with a moment of brilliance. "We should test how many times I can make you orgasm."

The hot water was already making her skin flush, but her cheeks bloomed with an even deeper shade of rose. He placed his hands on her hips, his erection pressing against her belly, and leaned down to taste her mouth.

After a kiss hotter and wetter than the water pouring over them, she said, "I thought we were getting clean in here."

"You want soap? I can help you with that *and* count how many times you come." He grabbed a bottle of body wash from the shelf and squeezed some onto his palm. After circling his palms and lathering up, he placed his hand on her back and began to spread the slick suds over her entire body.

"What about you?" she asked as she let him massage every inch of her.

"What about me?" He circled her breasts and stroked along the side of her ribcage.

"I want to conduct my own experiment on you."

"If you want to, but orgasms aren't the same kind of science for guys. They're more like rocket science."

She laughed as the visual struck them at the same time.

"Okay, then my experiment will be to see how long it takes for launch." Her palm wrapped around his throbbing cock and she stroked him up and down.

"Oh," he groaned, enticed, equally enthralled, and a little scared at the upcoming torturous pleasure of her test. "I might fail spectacularly at this experiment. Especially if you keep that up."

"I think you meant to say, if you keep it up you won't fail."

God, he adored her comebacks. "Then before I lose—"

"This isn't a bet, because we're obviously both going to win, but it is a test."

"Since I'm clearly at a disadvantage, I get to go first." He picked her up, catching her off guard, which conveniently removed her coaxing hand. Her long legs wrapped around his waist and she clung to his neck and shoulders. Ben spun, placed her back against the wall, and kissed her until the need for breath separated them.

Maleah's slick body slid down his front until she was back on her feet.

"You're going to need to hang onto the safety rail, Maleah."

Her eyes widened. "Really?" she questioned.

Ben winked. "Trust me." Leaning in, he captured her lips for one more quick taste, his hands roving, exploring, savoring every inch of Maleah's naked body. He lowered his mouth to one pebbled nipple, teased the taut bud, then lavished the other with swirls of his tongue. Ben caressed her back and torso, then his hands slid over her sides and around her hips to palm her perfectly smooth, round backside.

Ben lowered himself until he was on his knees. He gently lifted one long, flawless leg and guided it over his shoulder. She was open to him, and he couldn't believe how lucky he was. She was gorgeous, pink, delicate, and he was near desperation level to taste her sweetness and make her come apart against his mouth.

He found her slick heat with the tip of his tongue, circled her pulsing bud, and went in deeper, lapping and stroking from all angles. Hot water from the shower ran over their bodies, but she was wet from desire and pleasure. Maleah threaded her fingers into his hair and her moans increased. Ben glanced up to see her face and found her watching him. He grinned, then noticed that she indeed needed to grip the railing. Her white knuckles proved how tight she was holding on to the shiny stainless steel.

Ben found himself responding to every subtle and not-so-subtle whimper and moan, the way she stroked his head, or shifted her pelvis against his mouth. He read her every movement, every sound as if she were giving clear instructions, except without words. Everything that passed between them was pure instinct, sensitivity, and responsiveness. But he knew, he knew to the depth of his core, how much she liked her clit being tongued as she rode his fingers. He sensed when to pull back, ease the sensations, then build her release to a new and higher peak. He continued until she was fucking dripping wet and out of control with a need to come. And he obliged, brought her to the edge, and sent her flying.

Maleah's womanhood throbbed and he continued to taste and savor the most glorious moment he'd ever given to a woman.

Maleah slid her leg off his shoulder and shifted slightly away from his lips. "I'm too sensitive," she said, breathless. "Give me a second."

Ben rose to his feet, kissing a path along her stomach, her breast, and neck. "Sensitive, eh? We should try to get you off again while you're so sensitive."

He saw her swallow and her mouth popped open, making a little O shape. The devil must be guiding him now, because he'd never been so bold with his needs before. He had to have Maleah while her inner walls still pulsed. Ben stared into her eyes, waiting for her to tell him to wait another moment, but she didn't. He took hold of her waist, spun her around, and tugged her ass toward his waiting member.

When she arched her lower back to meet him, he didn't hesitate. Guiding the head of his cock to her slit, Ben angled then thrust, sinking into her heat until he could go no deeper.

He paused, buried to the hilt, and felt the rhythm of her inner muscles throbbing. "You okay?" he breathed next to her ear.

"Oh my God."

Being called God was good enough for him, but they were new at this. He leaned over her back. Maleah held the wall and the safety rail. He circled his hips. "Is that good or bad?"

"Good God, don't stop. I need it, more..." she moaned. "Of you."

She was beyond sexy. Maybe a little crazy with lust, wild eyed and bewildered at what was happening to her body, and Ben couldn't get enough either. Maleah wiggled her ass against his cock, then rocked her hips, ready to set her own pace, since he was still grinning over her shoulder and delaying for as long as he could stand.

"Do you want the motion of the ocean?" He demonstrated by circling his hips again while pulling out then pushing back inside her heat. "Or pure, unadulterated manpower?"

"Both! Ben," she gasped out as he found a rhythm that suddenly and unexpectedly melted his mind and stole away his ability to speak.

The water, the shower, the building, this planet, all of reality slipped away as he lost himself with her. How could fucking, loving, screwing his brains out be this stunningly profound? Being inside Maleah was unreal. Her body spoke to him as he moved with her, met her every thrust as she met his. They peaked together and their release was in perfect harmony. *Unreal*, his brain told him again.

At some point, he floated back to reality and reluctantly slid out of her warmth and comfort. Hot water cascaded over them and he turned her in his arms and searched her face. Her eyelids drifted closed, but a small smile remained on her tender lips. He couldn't hold back the kiss. She was too tempting, too sweet to pass up. Ben took his time, lingered and appreciated every second of their connection. If burying his cock in Maleah was the most insanely perfect thing he'd ever done, kissing her was a close second.

"Thanks," he finally whispered against her lips.

She smiled and a small laugh rose from her chest and out of her mouth. "Are you thanking me for including you in my science experiment?"

"Yeah," he said. "Was the rocket launch satisfactory?"

Her smile widened. The glaze over her eyes and her pouty, swollen lips were possibly the most beautiful thing he'd ever seen. He'd never forget this day, this moment.

"It was. But we're going to have to compare today's results to future launches."

"I'll add rocket launches to my schedule. What are you doing tomorrow? Better yet, tonight?"

Maleah skimmed her fingernails across his stomach and she looked down at his cock. "I might be free tonight, but first, I think we should quit taking advantage of the instant hot water."

"Unlimited hot water might be my new all-time favorite invention ever," he said.

"Two shower heads are pretty great too."

"They are. My new house will definitely have something similar to this." Ben picked up the bottle of shampoo and opened the cap. "Do you need this? I do."

He had no idea women with as much hair as Maleah used so much shampoo. He needed a nickel-sized spot to wash his entire head. But she taught him, and Ben massaged her scalp and watched as the suds rinsed out of her long raven-colored hair.

After more soap, suds, conditioner, and learning that she truly was, at least in Ben's mind, the perfect specimen of the female body, they eventually stopped taking the world's longest shower. God bless instant hot water.

After dressing, Ben said, "I have to tell you something." He stood behind and to the right of Maleah. She cleared away the fog on the bathroom mirror with the corner of the towel and their eyes met in the reflection.

"This sounds serious. That's so unlike you. Should I be worried?"

"No. Yes, maybe a little." He hated seeing her face darken. Ben lifted his hand to her jaw and smoothed the tension and concern away by stroking his thumb over her cheek. He softened his own expression. "You're not supposed to be living in here. If the city building inspector comes by, you need to make it appear as if you and Brielle aren't living in the apartment."

"What? Seriously? I thought you might tell me your cat died or, worse, your grandpa got run over in the driveway. I think I just mixed those two things up." She smiled, flashing her straight white teeth.

Ben bent down and nibbled the side of her neck, which caused small whimpering sounds to escape from her lips. "I'm serious. The inspector and the ladies who run the office at the building department have been lenient and have turned a convenient blind eye because they are friends with your aunt Kiki. The Columbine and Aspen buildings have not received their final certificates of occupancy, which means the inspector can deal you a hefty fine if they decide you and your cousin shouldn't be in here."

"That's why the apartment looks the way it does, isn't it? And why my aunt has everything inside the closet."

"I can't answer for her, but probably. She knows the rules well enough. Kiki insisted on living on site during the construction. She's a persuasive woman when she wants to be. I think she could talk herself out of a Mexican prison by feeding them her yakitori or udon noodle bowls. But I don't know if the building department will treat you similarly because you're related," Ben said.

"You're telling me and Brie that we need to keep our personal stuff to a minimum inside the apartment, and if the inspector shows up, stuff everything into the boxes inside the closet?"

"That should do it, and don't admit that you've been sleeping here."

"Got it." Maleah flashed him another one of her gorgeous smiles.

"Can I buy you dinner?" he asked, feeling famished after the day's work and the extracurricular activities of the past hour. Plus, refilling his tank would go a long way toward giving him enough energy to pull another all-nighter with Maleah in his bed.

"How about I buy you dinner?"

"You're paying for my services now?" he taunted. "Have I been manipulated into becoming your personal male escort?"

"Tell yourself whatever you like, stud, but no," she said flatly. "I thought I would pay this time since you've bought the last couple times."

"Aww… fairness and equality. Whatever the lady wants, the lady gets. But I don't mind if you want to pay for my stud services. I need a good backup plan in case I lose my business again. You can be my first client."

Maleah shook her head, rolled her eyes, and tried to hold in the laugh.

Ben took her hand in his and led her out of the bathroom. "What are we eating?" He brought his mouth close to her ear in case Brielle was somewhere nearby. "Besides you, later, after dinner and in my bed. I didn't get my fill of you in the shower." He caught her earlobe between his teeth, licked the silken edge, and hummed with pleasure as the sweet taste of her skin tantalized his taste buds. Satisfied by her small whimper, Ben backed away and led them out the door.

She cleared her throat and asked, "How is the Asian fusion restaurant in town?"

"Awesome. Let's do it. I'm starved."

* * *

Over the next week, Maleah hung out with Ben during her lunch breaks. They ate takeout from the brew pub, deli, and the pizza place. After eating together, they walked Digger around the park and talked about work, goals, the future, the past, hobbies, dislikes, and likes. Their conversations flowed from everything to nothing, but always left Maleah laughing or lost in thought as she returned to painting, staining, or working on the floors. At the end of the work day, they met up again and ate dinner together, then spent the night in Ben's camper.

The days flew by and Maleah found that she quit obsessing over her emails, or lack of emails about finding a new job. There seemed to be no paying positions available in her areas of expertise, or she didn't have enough experience. Starting a new internship felt like taking ten steps backward. All the internships that interested her were non-paying positions. If she wasn't going to get paid to work, she would be at True Green. As much as she missed being a part of the incredible advancements in new types of biodegradable plastics, she couldn't afford to live in Boulder, or anywhere near it, without an income. Which led her right back to where she was—living and working in the town she'd grown up in.

Reconnecting with old acquaintances, learning how to maneuver and survive the ancient practice of small-town gossip, and thriving in her new role as a general contractor brought exciting challenges almost daily. While she never could have guessed she would be living in a hundred-twenty-year-old building while it was under construction, and with her cousin, Ben was the most surprising change in her life.

He was sexy, funny, caring, and even though he joked a lot, he was incredibly thoughtful. When she'd point out or thank him for thinking of her, he'd make a joke about it. His diversions didn't always sit well, but the laughs they shared made up for it. The way they connected in bed was indescribable. He possessed her mind, body, and soul. That was the best description Maleah could come up with. The intensity was otherworldly. Often, as she started to come down from unimaginable heights of climaxing with him, they would stare into each other's eyes, and she swore they were the only beings in existence. For her, those moments were the most intimate experience she'd ever had with someone. In bed, he was one hundred percent present with her and completely unguarded.

They slept together every night for a week, but in the morning it was back to work and back to being friends. Their relationship was good, great in fact, but neither of them spoke of commitment or claimed the B or G words. That is, being boyfriend and girlfriend. Since Maleah had no plans to stay in Three Peaks, and Ben's future was cemented there, it seemed to be for the best.

On Saturday morning, Ben stepped out of bed and stood in front of the closet. It was early, earlier than normal for starting the day. As daylight approached, the small room was slowly transforming from charcoal black to shades of gray. Maleah lay on her side, eyelids and limbs heavy with the need for more sleep, but Ben's bare chest and shoulders were too gorgeous to look away from. As she watched him dress, her memory refreshed and she lay there mentally reliving some of the finer moments from their night together.

As if picking up on her vibe, Ben glanced over his shoulder, caught her eye, and then raked his gaze over her body.

"You have no idea how hard it is to leave you in bed when you look like that."

"Like what?" she asked, thinking her cavewoman appeal couldn't be that hot. Could it?

Ben stopped buttoning his flannel shirt and returned to the bed. He knelt on the edge and Maleah rolled onto her back to look up at him.

"Sleepy, naked," he said slowly. "Needing woken up by my willing... hands and other parts of me who would enjoy participating."

"Did you just refer to your penis as a separate identity?"

"Possibly," Ben said, a sparkle of challenge in his eyes.

"And does he have his own identity and a separate name?" she asked.

"Possibly, but I can't tell you."

"You can, but you won't," she said and then added, "Besides, he'll tell me when he's ready. Although, I'm trying not to take this denial too personally, considering how well acquainted we are."

"He's shy. If you keep speaking to him directly, he'll probably let you into his circle of trust." Ben crawled farther onto the bed and closer to Maleah.

"Does 'speaking to him directly' mean he wants me to whisper in his ear, like super close up? Maybe with my lips against his head?"

Surprise widened Ben's eyes, and one side of his mouth lifted in a lopsided smile as he straddled Maleah. "He's telling me that would be an excellent start."

"A start? If I'm remembering correctly, I was even closer to him than that last night." She paused, trying to keep a straight face. "But I might be willing to try again. Maybe by the time you return from Alaska, I'll have some new techniques to coax his real name out of your little friend."

"Little?" Ben asked, faking being insulted. "Now he's never going to confide in you."

Maleah wouldn't fall for the ploy. "That's okay. I have my own name picked out for our highly sensitive, easily offended appendage."

"Do tell, Ms. Hale."

"*Ginormous strongus giganitcus*. That's his scientific name," she explained. "In case he's not familiar with zoological nomenclature."

"A perfect name, but zoological? Was that necessary?" Ben asked, snugging his knees in close to her body and pinning her tighter beneath the blanket.

"Definitely. You should hear yourself when, umm, you know."

"When I what?" he asked, leaning down and rubbing his nose against hers in an Eskimo kiss.

"When you... I'm not going to say it."

"What if I make you say it?"

"You can't make me. I'm withholding my comment until you tell me the name of your cock."

"Cock? I like when you say that even more than when you call my penis Ginormous gigantic strong man."

"You totally butchered his scientific name," she pointed out.

"Don't care. Now tell me what I'm doing when I make sounds that justify you calling me a zoological creature. I'm going to torture you until you spill it."

"Ooooh... we've moved on to threats."

"I gave you plenty of opportunity, and now you have earned your punishment." Ben kept her pinned between his legs as he brought his lips to the side of her neck and began sucking like a vampire.

A whimper of need rose from her throat. He knew the exact right spot and amount of pressure to make her instantly desperate to have him.

"Your torture technique is awful. Oh, God, stop," she said with every ounce of flat sarcasm she could muster. Even though warm heat pooled in her lower belly and went straight to her sex, she wanted to make fun of him for his terrible effort at making her uncomfortable.

"Mm-hmm," he hummed against her pulse. Then his hand moved to her breast and he massaged and tickled her sensitive chest.

Within a few seconds, Maleah began to squirm in earnest. He was increasing her arousal with speed and skill, and she couldn't do anything but lie there and take it. Her arms and hands wanted the freedom to give back to Ben what he was delivering, but she couldn't move under the blanket and sheet. Ben lowered his hips and pressed them against her pelvis. He began rocking against her, and she met his thrusts the best she could.

His lips moved along her neck and across her jaw, alternating ticklish kisses and nibbling bites. When his mouth met hers, she opened to him and their tongues danced and circled as he applied gentle suction.

When she was certain that time had stopped and they could go on kissing for the rest of the morning, his hand moved to her ribcage and he began a new form of torture. Tickling. Pure, unrestrained, wiggling, and torturous fingertips against her ribs.

Maleah tensed, then fought to get out from under him. She wasn't a little ticklish, she was extremely ticklish. Something he'd figured out the third time she'd stayed the night. She squirmed enough that the covers managed to slip down between them, allowing Ben access to her bare skin. Panicking was quickly becoming her only option as the nerve endings in her skin were equally oversensitive and eliciting fight or flight mode.

"I sound like a zoo animal when I do what?" he asked again, his hands now on the inside of her hip, a spot even more ticklish than her ribs.

"I, uh…" she babbled between laughter, whooping, and screeching.

"Who sounds like a monkey now?" he teased.

She couldn't get out from under him. He kept moving his hands to different places on her body, which fooled her nervous system into thinking she was free of the torment, but then a couple seconds later, he was on a different spot. Oh, he's good... too good at this.

"Come on, Maleah. Tell me when I sound like a sex-crazed grizzly?"

"Grizzly? No, no. Not that." She'd say anything at this point and blurted out, "You sound like an animal when you... when..." She couldn't say "come." She didn't know why, but she wouldn't admit it aloud. What if she told him and he said she sounded like a dying air siren when she orgasmed? She would die. She'd never be able to face him again. "When you shoot your nail gun."

"Is that a euphemism or are you messing with me?"

"Yes! No. Stop tickling me! Please."

"Begging now? Do it again." He bent low and licked her incredibly taut nipple, circled the areola, and blew softly across her wet skin.

Instead of begging him to stop, she moaned. He captured her lips with his again, and his hands mercifully stopped tickling all her most sensitive spots.

When he pulled away, she asked, "Don't you have to be at the airport?"

"I do. I need to go."

"You should. You can't miss your flight."

"I guess I better make this quick then." He reached between them and worked at opening his jeans. "Do you mind if this is fast?"

"Fast and hard sounds perfect," she admitted as she worked her legs free of the sheets and helped push Ben's jeans over his hips.

It was fast. And hard. Maleah felt ruined and used in the best ways possible.

"God, you are fucking amazing," he breathed in her ear.

"And I won't be the reason you're late to the airport. Go. I'll be around when you come back."

"Promise?" he asked and she realized this was the first and only time he'd mentioned her in his future.

"Yeah. I have tons to do around here. You know that," she said and kissed his stubble-covered jaw.

"Thanks for taking care of Digger and the cat." His breaths were fast and heavy as he hovered over her.

"I love them. They're no problem at all."

"I—" Ben cut himself off, and she thought he was about to say that he loved her. *Wow. Whoa.* It was too soon. They hadn't known each other long enough for that, even though every time they slept together it was so much more than sleeping together. Her feelings were just as intense, and full of love, but they hadn't even admitted to each other that they wanted a relationship. She was grateful he hadn't let the L word slip.

"I'll let you know as soon as I know when I'll be back."

"Okay. But please take all the time you need. Skyla needs you, and I know you don't know exactly how things are going to play out with Kinsey in Alaska." Maleah held him tight and then released her hug. She wasn't sure what time it was, but his drive to the airport would take over three hours.

He moved off her and stood next to the bed. Ben adjusted his clothes, then bent down and placed one more kiss on her lips.

"Good luck. You're doing the right thing, Ben."

He nodded. "I hope so," he said and was out the door.

Maleah listened as he grabbed his packed bag and truck keys, said goodbye to Digger, and opened and closed the door of the trailer. After she heard the truck pull away, she drifted back to sleep. She never could have guessed that while Ben was out of town, her world was about to spin one-hundred-and-eighty degrees... again, for the second time that autumn.

Seventeen

WHEN DIGGER WASN'T HUMPING her leg like a teenaged sex fiend, Maleah adored Ben's dog. He was playful, animated, and the sweetest cuddler she'd ever met. Well, second sweetest cuddler. Ben was pretty good at it too. Sir Mittens was turning out to be a love bug as well. But Digger liked to talk in a mixture of howling and comical sounds when he wanted attention, and he loved to fetch, which Maleah enjoyed while Ben was out of town. With so much personality and an overload of cuteness, Digger's leg humping problem was easily forgiven, even if it was a bit incommodious. Maybe Digger would outgrow the impulse to make her leg his bitch... She could only hope.

Maleah's phone alerted with a new text as she tucked Digger's bag of dog food into the pantry closet in Ben's kitchen. While Digger munched his dinner, she checked the message.

Holden: *Hey, I have some good news. Do you have time to talk?*

Maleah: *Sure. What's up?*

She hadn't heard from Holden in weeks, and her heart skipped a beat. *Good news?* Could this be about her job? Their relationship? Admittedly, Maleah hadn't thought about him or her old job in a long time. Was that about the time she'd started seeing Ben? Did Ben have everything to do with the switch in her focus, or had she finally moved on? Her work on the Columbine Building had been all-consuming. There hadn't been much time to think about True Green. The realization that she had so easily moved on was startling.

Maleah realized she was standing inside the trailer, lost in thought, and her phone had gone silent. Digger finished wolfing down his dry dog food and was now lapping water from his water dish.

She said, "Be a good boy while I'm gone, and I'll be back later."

Maleah pocketed her phone and ran her hand over Sir Mitten's back. She picked the kitten up and set him on the upholstered bench. "You stay off the table."

Fat chance the kitten would obey her orders, but Ben was trying to train Sir Mittens to stay off the table and counters. Maleah wanted the kitten's training to be consistent while Ben was away. As she walked to the door, the cat jumped back onto the table. She retraced her steps, set the kitten on the floor, and sighed. "Stay off the table." Sir Mitten's tail twitched and then he disappeared beneath the table. Maleah left the trailer before Sir Mitten sucked her into playing a never-ending game called "Who's in Charge Here?"

Maleah walked inside the back entrance of her building and wondered if Brie was upstairs. Her cousin had begun disappearing on a regular basis. Brie said she liked working at the library or at Mad Mountain Coffee Roasters for a change in scenery, and Maleah didn't blame her. Even though her cousin was extremely introverted, it was still nice to get out of the apartment sometimes. Her phone pinged as she approached the stairs.

Holden: *Where are you? Can we talk now?*

Maleah: *I'm at the Columbine Building in Three Peaks. Yes, I'm free to talk.*

Holden: *Can you open the front door?*

What?! She froze. Maleah stepped back from the stairs, turned on her heel, and walked to the front room. Holden stood outside, the upper half of his body framed by the antique wood and glass front door. The ornate brass hinges creaked as she swung the door open. In the back of her mind, she added "oil the hinges" to her mental checklist.

She said, "Hi! This is a surprise."

His smile was wider and more beautiful than she ever remembered seeing before. More often than not, Holden walked around with a slight crease pinching his brows. He spent most of his time concentrating on work, and she'd grown used to the way he was always half-distracted and uber serious.

"This building is astounding," he said. "No wonder you enjoy fixing it up."

She closed the door to the chilly evening air, and Holden stood in the entry, looking at the vast open space of the front room and the punched-tin ceiling. Then he focused on Maleah, stepped forward, and wrapped his sinewy, strong arms around her shoulders.

"It's good to see you. I've missed you." He pulled back and stared at her face.

Taken by surprise, she simply stood there for a moment, then blinked. "It's good to see you too."

Holden took her hand in his. A completely shocking move on his part, as far as Maleah was concerned, but she let him have her hand and wondered if he could possibly have been targeted by Cupid.

"Is there someplace we can talk? I love the building, but I've been driving for over four hours and I can't wait to share my news with you. Will you give me a tour later?"

"Umm, yeah," she said uncertainly. "You're acting kind of different. Is everything okay?"

He laughed, actually laughed, and it was fantastic. She grinned back from his contagious joy. She'd only seen the lighter side of Holden a couple times. Now that she'd spent so much time laughing and giggling with Ben, Holden's generally serious demeanor stood out as being completely opposite. How had she found him so attractive when he rarely smiled and never joked around? But the answer was simple: Holden was hot and his intelligence made her swoon.

He led her farther inside, keeping her hand tucked inside his. "Everything is great. I had to tell you the news in person. Is your apartment upstairs?"

She was about to say yes, but he continued speaking before she had a chance.

"Doesn't matter." Holden stopped by the elevator and placed his hands on her hips. "I'm here to offer you your job back. The job comes with an annual salary and full benefits. Thanks to you, Maleah, and your incredible connections and organization, True Green has a new investor and they want us to continue our work for as long as it takes. They believe in me and our dreams for a better future and what True Green Bioplastics has to offer to make that happen."

He said "our dream." As in, his and mine? Maleah needed a moment to process and rearrange her thoughts to include True Green as being part of her future again. It'd taken what felt like forever to start thinking about her life without True Green—and without Holden—and now he was here, offering her life back to her.

"Who? And what do you mean by my incredible connections?"

"Your file of industry execs and businesses to follow up with," Holden said. "I contacted your leads, and it paid off. You're incredible. I should have never chosen Davis over you. He's a good chemist, but you have a way with people and keeping things running smoothly that I shouldn't have overlooked as being less valuable. True Green needs you. I need you."

Maleah dropped her gaze and let his words sink in. "I was only doing my job. You were the one who followed up."

He squeezed her hips a little tighter. "Yes, but everyone I spoke with remembered you. Maleah, I can't wait until you come back. I didn't realize how much your presence in the office made my day so much better. What do you say? Will you return to True Green?"

"I, umm..." Part of her wanted to jump up and down and break into song, but another part of her stood there and thought about how much she wanted to keep working on the Columbine Building. And what about her and Ben?

"You're hesitating." The excitement in his eyes and the smile on his lips dimmed. "Did you receive another job offer? I know I've not been the best about keeping in communication with you, but that's because I've been so busy trying to secure True Green's future."

"No. No, there's no other job offer," she assured him. She'd been watching her email for new prospects and any possible interviews, but there had been nothing.

Holden watched her expectantly.

She blurted out, "I gave up my old apartment. I'm going to need a place to live if I return to Boulder." Her savings was so minimal, she wondered how she could afford rent, the deposit, and getting her utilities turned on. She'd paid off her credit card with the money she made working for Kiki, which was great, but she would need another paycheck or two to afford moving expenses. Maleah hated asking her parents for a loan, but that might be the only way she could finance another move. The worries began piling up like a landslide. She should be ecstatic, but instead she was filled with concerns and logistics.

Holden must have caught on to her less than enthusiastic attitude. He tipped his head to the side, and she saw the concern in his eyes. "Can I buy you dinner? Let's go out. We can celebrate and talk things over."

"That's a good idea," she said.

He headed for the exit. "Any place in this town have a decent selection of organic food or vegetarian?"

Maleah blinked as she remembered how Holden was particular about what he put into his body.

"I think the Asian fusion place may be our best bet. It's probably not organic, though."

"I'll make do," he said. "Like you've been doing, right? Making the best out of a bad situation."

"Something like that." She led him toward the back door out of habit, plus she didn't have her keys with her. Maleah used the hidden key and locked the door behind them.

He took her hand in his again as they walked down the alley.

Holden said, "I bet you can't wait to get out of this dinky town and back to civilization. Three Peaks is rather isolated. Is there anything to do here other than drink beer and hang out with the cows and the trees?"

"Did you know I grew up here?" she said, feeling mildly defensive for a place she loved.

"You told me. And you also said you had the most boring childhood anyone could imagine. Now I see why. There's not a lot here, is there?"

Maleah straightened her spine and set her shoulders back an inch. "I think there's more to see than meets the eye in Three Peaks. And yes, as a girl, I was bored a lot, but now that I've grown up, I have a different perspective on small towns." She shrugged. "It's kind of eye-opening how our perceptions change over time."

"That couldn't be more true." He looked down at her and smiled that brilliant, heart-melting smile again.

They ate dinner and Maleah felt like a gluttonous pig for eating her entire plate of Japanese pan noodles with seared scallops compared to Holden's salad with a light drizzle of Asian vinaigrette and bowl of miso soup with extra tofu. He said he was losing a pound-and-a-half before his next race, which was a week away. Since he had such a low percentage of body fat, and meant to stay that way, he had to watch everything that went in his mouth. Maleah explained that after tiling bathrooms all day—the third-floor apartments were ready for tile—she was famished and could probably eat an entire second meal. He laughed and suggested she do just that. Maleah didn't order another plate, and refrained from eating dessert, even though she loved the green tea matcha cheesecake. She didn't think it would be polite to eat cheesecake in front of someone on a diet.

During dinner, Holden expressed his excitement for the future of True Green by sharing the details of finding his new investor, the meetings he'd been to, and the ideas for future expansion. He told her everything, and it was by far the best meeting, or date, they'd ever been on. As he talked, Maleah quickly shifted back into her scientist frame of mind. Ideas flowed like the gates of a dam had been thrown wide-open. It felt great to use her education and her mind and talk with someone who challenged her professionally.

They left the restaurant in good spirits. Her worries about leaving Three Peaks and returning to the job she loved were no longer weighing as heavily on her mind. In fact, she couldn't think of any reason why she would stay. If she and Ben were serious about one another, they could continue seeing each other on the weekends. It wasn't as if they were officially dating or anything. They'd avoided the subject of commitment or permanence as if it was a foul and rotten thing that should be shunned.

Maleah and Holden approached the back of her building and she asked, "Where are you staying? You're not driving back to Boulder tonight, are you?"

"I have a room at the Spruce Haven Lodge. I didn't know if I would even be able to get ahold of you today, so I rented the room."

"That's good. I would have offered to let you stay with Brie and me in the apartment, but it's not the best accommodations at the moment. I've been sleeping on the couch and Brie stays in the only bedroom. Once the building is done, the apartments will be amazing, but right now, it's kind of a disaster. I can give you a tour if you want."

"I think I'll say good night here. Seeing you tonight has been extraordinary. On the drive here, I started to regret my spontaneity and almost turned around, but now I'm convinced I made the right decision by coming in person."

"Oh? You're surprising me. I'm not sure I've seen this side of you before. And I always liked you, a lot, but this impulsiveness and your mood is kind of addicting. It's fantastic."

He laughed. "I like this side of me too. Most of the time, it's hard for me to relax. I admit it. But I feel good, and I think it has everything to do with you."

They stopped walking and stood in the amber glow of the security lights in the alley. She was about to say good night and ask if he'd like to meet up in the morning before he returned to the city, but Holden spoke first.

He lowered his voice and the small pinch between his brows—the serious look he so often wore—returned. "I thought of a solution to your problem."

"Which problem is that?" Maleah felt great and she smiled up at him. She didn't want to think about leaving the Columbine Building behind, telling Brielle and her aunt she would be moving back to Boulder, or nights without Ben. This last realization struck like a sledgehammer, but then she reminded herself that if they were serious about one another, they could make it work.

Her thoughts were completely derailed as Holden said, "You could move in with me. You've seen my place, so you know I have plenty of room."

He lightly laid his fingers against her jaw.

What's happening? she thought as her past dreams of being in a relationship with Holden crashed into her current life in a spectacular train wreck of confusion.

"We don't have to date, but I'd like to. You could move in as my girlfriend. I confided in you about my asexual nature and you didn't scorn me for it. You don't know how much that means to me, but I also care deeply for you. I would be willing to try and be the man you need in all ways, if that's what you want. And if it's not, I will be okay with whatever you choose. I think we could have something amazing. Working and living together. We'd be perfect."

Maleah stilled and she may have stopped breathing. Her mouth went dry.

She tried to come up with the right words, which were currently far, far away in a galaxy of turmoil and unrest... *No, wait, that's from* Star Wars.

Before words could form properly, Holden leaned in and placed a kiss on her lips.

She'd daydreamed of this moment so many times it was embarrassing, and now that it was finally happening, Maleah wasn't ready. Her mind screamed that this was all wrong. Her heart protested that he wasn't Ben.

But Holden's lips were soft and capable. His hands were strong and comforting, and clammy.

He removed his lips and immediately wrapped her in a tight hug. "I don't have much experience with relationships, but you mean a lot to me. I believe we could make this work and we could do great things together. You don't have to give me an answer tonight. I'll text you in the morning." Holden released his embrace and stepped back. "Good night."

"Night?" she said, sounding confused as she stumbled to the door. Then she remembered she needed the hide-a-key.

Holden waited until she was inside. She closed the door behind her and tried to breathe. Maleah drifted toward the staircase but couldn't go to bed without letting Digger outside one more time. She counted to sixty before walking back outside. Holden was nowhere to be seen and it was a relief. Maleah's life just pivoted and she needed a moment to find her balance.

* * *

"You know what?" Brielle asked without looking up from her laptop. "You can't control who walks into your life." She paused, fingers tapping away at the keyboard with the speed of a demon on meth. She glanced up and said, straight-faced, "But you can control which window you push them out of." Brielle cocked an eyebrow in a look that indicated she was both serious and not serious about Holden's offers of a job and an asexual boyfriend. She returned to focusing on the laptop monitor.

"So, you think I should take the job?"

"I didn't say that."

"You think I should commit extreme violence against my future employer by shoving him out of a window?" Maleah needed clarity and probably wasn't going to get it until Brie put the laptop aside.

"No, not exactly," Brie said as she continued to type.

"I'm having an existential crisis here. Can you focus on me for a second?"

Brielle stopped typing and looked up. "Existential denotes that you are questioning your existence. You know you exist. This is your quarter-life crisis, which is something else entirely," she said, clarifying Maleah's mixed terminology.

"Quarter-life crisis? Is that a thing? Did you make that up?"

"I'm serious. I had mine after my dad died. You're facing a turning point. A potentially life-changing twist in your life-map. I said to throw Holden out the window because he dropped this on you like a bag of hot steaming llama poo and look what happened. You're a walking, talking, indecisive disaster."

"Oh my God. Is this supposed to be helpful?"

"I don't know. You tell me." Brie smiled another devious yet persnickety grin. "And you're not helping my productivity either. I'm calling us even."

"What are you doing that tops my crisis?"

"Right now, my mental focus is on getting to level nineteen and upping my XP while monitoring our new YouTube channel."

This wasn't the answer Maleah was hoping for, and yet Brielle's description of being bombarded by a hot bag of steaming poo sounded about right. The job offer and Holden's return was messy and it stank.

As she contemplated what to do next, Brielle said, "Sorry. I get caught up in what I'm doing and forget there's real world issues to deal with. Let's start over. Consider how you felt after finding out your dream guy is a total weirdo. And don't forget that Holden chose Mr. Ass-wipey, Davis over you. Mostly, though, I think you like being here in Three Peaks. You're singing again, and you look forward to laboring on this old building." Brie shrugged. "I'm not inside your head, but from my perspective, you seemed pretty happy these last few weeks. Do you want to go back to Boulder? Were you happier and more fulfilled living in that horrible basement and working fifty to sixty hours a week as an over-educated office gopher?"

Defending Holden was an automatic response. "Holden apologized for choosing Davis instead of me, and he's not a total weirdo. Okay, maybe he is a little," Maleah corrected herself. "But aren't we all? Just because he doesn't own stuff and isn't the most sexually active person doesn't mean he deserves harsh criticism. And I was not a gopher. Not really, anyway. Only part of the time."

"Okay, okay," Brielle acquiesced. "We're all strange in our own ways. If your strange matches Holden's, then I say go for it. But if I have anything else to add that will help you make the decision, it's this: Do what is right for you. Follow your gut. It will not steer you wrong. And I know this isn't an easy decision. You went to school for a long time to work in environmental science, but not everyone works in the field they went to school for. It happens all the time. You're not the same person you were ten or fifteen years ago when you were determined to save the planet. It's okay to change your dreams and goals. It's also okay to follow them, whatever they are."

"You made this so much harder. And did you say, 'our YouTube channel'?"

"I did. Do you want to see it?"

Maleah hesitated, searched the inside of her brain, found that one more issue to deal with would make her head explode, and said, "No. Do not show me anything on YouTube that will tip me over the edge. I can't take another surprise in my life."

"'Kay," Brielle said with nonchalance. "You're going to want to see it, though, when you're ready to have your mind blown."

"Nope," Maleah denied with a shake of her head. "The only thing that matters right now is if I should return to True Green."

Brielle said, "I think you know deep down what you should do."

"I'm glad one of us is confident about my quarter-life crisis. Too bad it isn't me."

"Want to drink Grandma's brandy and watch a romantic comedy? Or you can join me in this server. I'll teach you how to play."

"I'll pass on the video games, and the brandy. I think we drank it all."

"Huh. I guess that's good, because we needed to empty out the cabinets anyway," Brie said, looking thoughtful. "I can't wait to get the new kitchen installed in here. It's going to be such a huge improvement."

"Yeah, it is." Maleah glanced around the makeshift apartment and was also excited about the transformation of what would become the best and largest apartment in the building. The third-floor loft apartments were nearly complete and their kitchen was the last to be installed. She and Brielle were supposed to start the demolition of the old makeshift kitchen on Monday.

"See, right there. If you move back to Boulder, you won't have drinking nights, and/or days, with your delightful cousin any longer. You won't be able to set your own hours or choose what you're working on next. And you won't have your best-ever fuck buddy every night either. To me, your answer about returning to Boulder is a no-brainer. But like I said, I'm not you and I'm not living in your head."

* * *

Without snooping—too much—Maleah kept glancing around Ben's trailer for the missing letter. She visited, fed, watered, and walked Digger and Sir Mittens a few times a day while Ben was in Alaska, anyway, so if her letter happened to be lying around, she would see if Ben had ever opened it. But, like Aunt Kiki's turtle necklace, the letter had disappeared.

After their first night together, Ben never mentioned the letter. They'd been equally busy working on their buildings during the day and getting to know each other better at night. Not once did either of them bring up the letter. Maleah wasn't good at confrontation. She dreaded it with a heart-stopping, sweat-inducing fear and decided she would let the issue go for as long as possible. But she'd whole-heartedly meant what she'd written and would have to face the music when Ben returned. Since her job situation was about to change again, maybe it was meant to be that they hadn't discussed Ben's return as general contractor for the Columbine Building until now. She was excited and apprehensive to discuss the situation with him, but it wasn't going to be for another week, because Ben was stuck in Alaska until the local authorities were able to take care of his case against Kinsey for removing their daughter from Colorado and going against the court-ordered visitation schedule.

He texted or called Maleah every night. When they spoke on the phone, she filled him in on renovation details for the day and updates about Digger and Sir Mittens. Digger couldn't seem to stay out of the river during their evening walks. After day three, she stopped battling the dog's need to splash and romp alongside the river bank and included toweling him off as one of her daily chores before putting him to bed. With the amount of stress Ben was under, Maleah chose not to bring up the topic of True Green Bioplastics or begging him to take his job back at the Columbine Building.

Each day of the week blurred into the next with as much activity as she could cram into twenty-four hours. Even Brielle took their final week working together on the apartment seriously and proved that she could be both muscle and a busy worker bee when she wanted. Maleah continued to catch her cousin videoing her at odd times, but for the most part she ignored the camera.

They ripped out the old cruddy kitchen, and the cabinet and countertop installers arrived on time. She and the contractors hustled to make the new kitchen a culinary dream. The plumber, who had been working on the third-floor apartments, came downstairs to install the sink and hardware. He connected the dishwasher and had the kitchen usable by the end of the day. There was still a lot to do, but they had running water and the electrician was supposed to be there the next day to wire the appliances and install the switches and light fixtures.

By the end of the week, Maleah had never been so sore and tired. But she was still excited for Ben to come home. He was supposed to arrive sometime in the middle of the night. Thanks to the video footage of Kinsey's attack on Ben, and Kinsey's blatant disregard of the custody agreement, Skyla was returning with him.

She and Brielle were invited to have dinner with Aunt Kiki and Joe. She, Brielle, and Aunt Kiki worked out the details of what was left to do inside the Columbine Building and who would take on which responsibilities after Maleah returned to Boulder.

"Ben should be part of this conversation," Aunt Kiki said.

"I agree," Maleah said. "Why don't you come by tomorrow or the next day and see the building? Then all of us can discuss this together?"

"I think I will do that. You will have to be patient with me. I'm not moving as quickly as I used to. These darn ribs are taking their sweet time to mend."

"You can move slower than a snail and I wouldn't mind, Auntie."

"Okay then," Kiki said. "But let's give Ben time to settle in and get back to work before throwing all this at him."

Maleah nodded and the trepidation of what needed to be said about everything he'd missed while trying to take care of his daughter sat heavy and dim in her chest. The conversation was bittersweet and left her emotionally drained.

On the drive back to town from Joe and Kiki's, she thought about how wonderful it would be to sleep in Ben's bed and wait for him, but she couldn't, since his daughter was also coming home. She returned to the couch in the apartment after dinner with her aunt and couldn't wait to see Ben.

As it was, Ben was nowhere to be seen for the next forty-eight hours.

When she'd woken up the following morning, his pickup had been parked in his usual spot. By the time she'd dressed and gone to say good morning, it was gone. Maleah went to work on tiling the kitchen backsplash. She hoped she could finish the job in one day. Ben sent a text message in the early afternoon.

Ben: *I'm stuck out at the ranch helping Jeremiah with the fall calves. Vet emergency with one of the heifers. Any chance you can let Digger out tonight?*

Maleah: *Of course. Hope everything is okay.*

Ben: *It should be. Thank you. I owe you.*

Maleah: *You owe me nothing. I'm happy to help.*

Eighteen

MALEAH PULLED HER COAT tighter and fastened the zipper until it reached her neck. Even though the calendar claimed it was still fall, the temperature and dormant plant life clearly proclaimed that winter was king of these mountains. Lazy snowflakes drifted from a bleached gray sky. The last of the season's golden aspen leaves clung to spindly branches and drooped under the weight of melting snow. Her boots sank into the layer of fallen aspen leaves providing a muffled cushion against the forest floor. The faintest sign of a trail could be detected among the leaf litter, but she continued forward through the aspen grove and farther onto old man Fred's property. The sting of cold bit at her cheeks and the tip of her nose, but Maleah breathed in deep lungsful of the crisp air and let it cleanse her muddied mind.

Emerging from the trees, Maleah followed a narrow game trail into a meadow of yellow grasses and brown shrubs already turned inward for the season. She scanned her surroundings and her gaze lifted to the horizon. With appreciation and more than a little awe, she watched the moisture-rich clouds roll over the high peaks before dipping low over the side of the mountains to blanket Copper Valley. She followed their path until her gaze landed on Ben. He stood with his back to her, facing Fred's stock pond. With his hands stuffed into the pockets of his Carhartt jacket, narrow waist, and long legs encased in his jeans and the wooded hillside on the opposite shore, she was tempted to take his picture.

Maleah captured the image with her mind and refrained from pulling out her phone to take a picture, even though he was stunningly handsome. "Hey there."

Ben turned, watched as she crossed another ten feet through the grass, then dropped his gaze and turned back to the water. Maleah joined him at the water's edge.

At first, neither one of them spoke, but then Ben asked, "What are you doing out here?"

"I saw your truck parked along the road and stopped. I took a chance and snuck through the fence, wondering if you were out here."

"You found me," he said with enough distance to feel like he was still speaking to her from Alaska.

"You've been avoiding me and I want to know why. I want to know why you moved your trailer and didn't tell me? I have news to share with you too."

"That you're moving back to Boulder? I already know."

"I've been waiting to tell you about my job offer so I could say it in person, but you've been unavailable. How did you find out?"

Ben wouldn't look at her, and the coldness was now coming from more than just the temperature outside. Maleah held her ground. She wasn't chasing him, but she felt she deserved five minutes of his time after everything they'd shared over the last couple months.

Ben's silence spoke volumes. Even though she was ninety percent ready to return to her life and job at True Green, the remaining ten percent was holding tight to an invisible thread connected to Three Peaks. He turned his head a few degrees and looked at her from the corner of his eye.

"I stopped by to see Grandpa and Kiki yesterday on my way back to town. She told me about your return to Boulder. She also let me know about an upcoming building inspection by the city. That's why I moved the trailer. It was time anyway."

"Time to move? Where did you move to?"

"I have a place," he said cryptically and without further details.

Maleah's curiosity fell from her lips without room for pause. "Did you buy a house?"

He shrugged as if it was inconsequential. "Are you moving in with McNutt?"

"Maybe. Temporarily. But it's not what you are thinking. Rent in Boulder is high and there aren't many places available."

He gave a curt nod in a way that was somehow also dismissive. "Maleah McNutt. It has a certain ring to it, doesn't it?"

"You're not being nice right now," she said, trying her best to keep her composure.

"Oh, my bad. I'm sorry. How about if I revert to Holden the hermaphrodite. The more I think about it, the more I'm sure you two will make a great couple."

"What are you talking about? Why would you assume I'm going to start dating Holden?"

"Start?" Ben leaned back on his heels and turned an icy glare on her. "I saw the surveillance video from when I was out of town. Seriously, Maleah? I'm gone for the week and you immediately have another man in your bed. I know I'm a stupid asshole, but at least I only date one woman at a time."

Her emotions rose, but she wouldn't back down. "Are we dating? I didn't know what we were calling this." She waved a frustrated hand between them. "You never wanted any exclusivity, and I didn't—" Maleah was going to say that she didn't invite Holden to kiss her behind the Columbine Building, but Ben cut her off.

"Damn it." Ben ran his hands over his head. "I don't know," he said, exasperated with himself, her, or the moment, she couldn't tell. "I don't know what the fuck I am doing most days." He paused, inhaled, and said, "I like you. Too much. I wasn't supposed to fall in love again. It's not a possibility for me. She broke me." He closed his eyes to the harsh truth, then opened them again and looked at her. "I can't do this with you, and take care of Skyla, and deal with Kinsey." He stepped away from the water. "I'm happy McNutt is back in the picture. He makes letting you go a hell of a lot easier."

A chill, both warming and freezing, raced along her spine and through her bloodstream. *Kinsey broke him but... Ben fell in love with me?* Her heart picked up its pace. She wanted him to take her in his arms, hold her, make promises about a happily ever after the likes of which only existed in fairy tales. But instead he was hurt, anguished, suffering, and telling her to leave.

"I wanted to talk to you about my job and how much you mean to me too. Maybe we can continue to see each other on the weekends. It could work. I won't be that far away."

"You don't get it, Maleah. I'm a ticking time bomb. I have too much on my plate right now. I will never have spare time to spend my weekends in Boulder. You should jump all over McNutt. If anyone can bring him out of his asexual asphyxiation, it's you. You sure as hell cured my celibacy."

In her mind, her palm met his cheek hard and fast. In reality, she was the one who felt slapped. Maleah froze. The sting of his cruelty hurt much worse than any physical blow.

She noticed the flash of remorse as it crossed his face. She watched the pinch of pain and regret in his hazel eyes, but he didn't take it back.

Maleah straightened her spine. "That was rough and uncalled for."

He tipped his head slightly and crossed his arms over his chest. "Well, we both know you like it a little rough." His lips quirked ever so slightly, and his smug, teasing look at the exact wrong moment broke her.

Taking the moral high ground, remaining optimistic, and always looking for the bright side no longer existed. "Screw you, Ben. You can't talk to me this way."

"Then why are you still standing here?" he asked, acting like more of an arrogant jerk than she'd ever heard before.

Affronted, she yelled, "I'm not!" She was, but only because it was difficult to move since she was stunned into immobility. Once Maleah realized her state of being, she was able to break free. Fight or flight? Well, she'd never been a fighter. With heels to the ground, she propelled herself around and back to the trail.

"Have a nice life," Ben called to her back.

She glanced over her shoulder and saw his brokenness. Or maybe he was only mirroring her heart.

Maleah could rant and rave and punch him in his stupid hot face, but she wasn't that kind of person.

She stopped walking away. "I never kissed him back," she said, finally able to spit out the words that had been stuck in her throat since he accused her of cheating. "I'm not Kinsey and it's hurtful and insulting that you could compare me to your ex." Maleah couldn't leave Ben behind, no matter how cruel he was to her, with the idea that she had been seeing Holden behind his back.

She turned to the trees and ran. Her life waited for her. Her dreams of working in a lab and making a difference in the world were a four-hour drive away. Hurting this much when she had everything she'd ever wanted waiting for her was a cruel way to begin again, but Maleah understood that when you're at your lowest and feeling the worst, things can only get better. It had to, right?

* * *

The weather forecast predicted clear skies for the next three days. Ben's window of opportunity to repair and replace the roof on the bunkhouse at the ranch had opened and he'd be a fool not to take advantage of the decent weather. Jeremiah was ready to get the work done, especially before the colder snowy days of winter arrived. The dry air and high-altitude sun had kindly melted the snow from the previous week, and the clock had begun ticking as soon as the sun rose that morning.

Maleah had been gone for five days, not that he'd been counting, except he had. But Ben had also been swamped with his ever-growing list of responsibilities. During the daylight hours, ignoring Maleah's absence was easy. He was too busy to think about her. But at night, after Skyla was in bed, after finishing his bookwork, going through messages and emails, taking care of the dog and the cat, and after he showered and lay down, that's when life became difficult. Exhausted from both laboring during the day and the mental stress, his body and mind should've disengaged and turned off the moment his head hit the pillow, but instead, thoughts of Maleah waited for him.

She was there, in his head, every night since he'd been a complete jackhole. Ben alternated between reliving their last run-in at Fred's pond and remembering every perfect moment they'd shared since he found her on the side of the road, half naked, gorgeous, and better than any X-rated fantasy.

Ben managed to fall asleep but then he'd dream about her. They shared a dinner date in some romantic restaurant, and then she'd joined him for the night, except it wasn't inside the trailer, but inside the house he'd recently signed the paperwork on. The dreams felt real. And after he made love with her, he'd brush her hair off her cheek and whisper how much he loved her and wished she'd been the one he'd married after high school. She'd stare up at him and smile as her fingers traced circles around his shoulder and along his side. Her lips parted as if to tell him she loved him back, but before she spoke, Ben woke up.

...To the sound of the dog puking.

He was out of bed and through the doorway in an instant. His foot landed on something cold, wet, and slippery. Ben spotted Digger heaving next to the front door of his new house. His foot slid on the wood floor and shot out from under him. Ben grabbed for anything to stop his fall and his knuckles smacked the doorframe. He hopped, stumbled, and cursed his way to the door, still hopeful of getting Digger outside before having another mess to clean up.

Ben flung the door open. "Get out!"

Digger didn't have to be told twice as he leapt across the porch and down the steps in a blur of gray and white fur. But the fun didn't stop there.

New to the neighborhood, Ben was slowly becoming aware of and acquainted with his neighbors, and so was Digger. Neither of them had met the orange tabby cat until that moment. Taken by surprise at Digger's appearance, the cat was either not quite right in the head or pre-loaded with excitement-triggered rocket boosters. In comparison, Sir Mittens had never once exhibited the ability to shoot straight upward, all four paws, and over three feet off the ground from a single look at Digger. The same could not be said for the orange cat as it flew into the air.

The cat landed in the driveway, and Digger, vomiting now long forgotten, gave chase. Ben was tempted to let the dog have his fun, but the stupid cat was too bouncy and yet not fast enough to evade Digger's jaws. A tuft of orange hair whipped up into the air and Ben wouldn't be responsible for the death of his neighbor's cat. The cat's yowl of pain raised the fine hairs on Ben's body as he pursued the potential murderer.

The tabby managed to escape Digger's mouth and darted into the overgrown junipers bordering his driveway. Ben almost caught up with Digger as the cat disappeared into the shrubbery. He *thought* that was the end of the drama, but Digger decided that he too fit inside the prickly bushes. With his tail held high and waving excitedly, Digger pushed farther into the junipers, which caused additional hissing and yowling.

"Digger, no!" Ben ordered, but his dog had suddenly gone totally reprimand-deaf. Funny how dogs have selective hearing, isn't it?

Barefoot and only wearing a T-shirt and briefs, Ben finished crossing the flagstones pavers of his driveway and grabbed Digger around the middle, securely holding him by the hips. Ben pulled the malamute backward, but his dog was beefy, strong, and determined to get another taste of the orange cat. Digger dug in, claws ripping the ground, and half of his body inside the spiny bushes. Ben wasn't certain where exactly the cat was, but by the sound of it, the tabby was halfway to the grave. If he were to save the cat, it was now or never, he thought and heaved and grunted against his hundred-and-fifteen-pound deaf and determined malamute. *Damn dog.*

As Digger's rump repeatedly rammed into Ben's front, he suddenly realized how ridiculous he must look.

"That's it, dog!" he barked as he stopped humping his dog and used more muscle to force Digger away from the junipers.

Digger backed away then turned his massive head and gave him a scathing look of insult for interrupting his morning romp. Ben kept his fingers tucked around Digger's collar and began a retreat to the house. Ben winced as he became aware of the juniper needles stabbing his feet. He adjusted his stance and felt another prickly needle in his other foot.

"Son of Satan!" he said as he stepped again and a needle found its way between his fourth and pinky toe. It stabbed his nerve ending and he bit back another curse.

Digger whined and looked up at Ben, this time without the insult and with a genuine crease of concern knitting his doggy eyebrows.

Ben released Digger's collar to remove the worst of the juniper needles. Ben was the biggest fool there was. The instant Digger was free, he was back in the shrubbery.

"The hell you won't!" Ben dove in after his dog.

Being stabbed with tiny needles was nothing to losing a battle of wills with a malamute. Ben accepted the pain and torture as he wrestled Digger out of the junipers for a second time.

"I will not murder my dog," he repeated to himself as they headed for the front door.

In his peripheral vision, something caught his eye, and he looked over at the neighbor's house. An older gentleman with salt and pepper hair and wrapped in his bathrobe stood on the porch. He raised his coffee mug in salute. Ben blinked and gave a half-hearted wave in return. The man chuckled as Ben let a silent string of curse words run through his head. He stuffed Digger in through the front door and went straight for the bathroom to remove the juniper needles with tweezers and take a hot shower. When he stepped out of the restroom, he opened the door and stepped in something warm and squishy.

As Ben's mind processed the situation and wondered if his dog had a death wish, Skyla looked over at him from the kitchen.

"Digger puked on the floor while you were in the shower." She stared at Ben's bare foot, planted in the dog vomit. "Is he sick? Does he need to go to the vet? I have to be at school early today. Sorry, I forgot to tell you last night. Oh, and I accidentally spilled my juice."

Ben noticed the dish rag on the counter. His face heated with rising frustration. Now he had two more messes to clean up.

But Skyla surprised him and said, "I found this letter stuck to the box on the counter when I was cleaning up the juice. Your name is on it." She held up the envelope.

Ben hobbled over and took it from her. The new house was a disaster. Everything from inside his RV had been placed wherever it happened to land. Mostly on the kitchen counters, since he didn't own any furniture. Ben stared at the letter Maleah had brought to him the night they first slept together. He'd been drunk when she arrived and then had gotten distracted with other things. When he remembered the letter, it was gone. He figured she'd taken it back and had her reasons for doing so. Being as sensitive as she was, coupled with the fallout from her first letter, he hadn't brought it up. No use in stirring the pot.

"Thanks. I was wondering what happened to this." He stuffed the letter into his pocket to read later when a certain pair of ten-year-old eyes weren't on him.

Skyla finished wiping up the spilled juice, and Ben cleaned Digger's messes from the floor.

The rush to get Skyla to school—early—then take care of miscellaneous responsibilities at the Aspen Building, and drive to the ranch, resulted in Ben arriving an hour later than he had told Jeremiah he'd be there.

His brother joined in unloading the roofing supplies from the construction trailer. Ben refrained from speaking and focused on the task at hand. After unloading, he needed to set up an area to measure and cut the metal roofing sheets. Then he wanted to see how far his brother had gotten on prepping the roof with the waterproof felt.

Jeremiah worked by his side for a few minutes without talking, but apparently, he needed to speak his mind. "Good thing I woke up early so I'd be done with the chores and ready to get started when you got here."

"Dude." Ben held up his gloved hand. "I don't need a lecture. It was out of my control."

"Really? So when did having a girlfriend in your bed give you a license to blow off your responsibilities?"

"Shut the hell up," Ben said as he carried the circular saw out of the trailer and set it down next to the rolled-up extension cord.

"You could have given me a heads-up. I could have replaced the water pump out at the tank, but I made myself head back here to meet up with you," Jeremiah complained.

"Sorry," Ben mumbled and stared up at the roof. Rehashing his morning wasn't worth his time. He didn't want to talk, and his brother didn't need the details.

"Yeah, I'll remember this next time," Jeremiah said with a sour note of revenge.

"Fine. Whatever. You got all the felt in place?"

"Yep."

"Did you measure?" Ben asked as he set his drill next to the saw.

"I did."

"I'll cut and drill the holes in the sheets if you want to get started on the flashing and the seals."

Jeremiah gave him the measurements and Ben wasted no more time. Talking was limited to the necessities of the job, and his brother never brought up Maleah or his personal life for the better part of the next three hours. Ben intended to work through lunch to give him the hour of daylight he'd lost that morning, but his mother arrived with sandwiches and thermoses of soup. Tempted to tell her he'd eat it later, Ben changed his mind and put down his drill when she called up to him that she was also there to help. He knew it meant a lot to her to help on the project and that she'd be insulted if he didn't eat her food.

The turkey and Swiss cheese sandwich hit the spot, and the broccoli cheddar soup reminded him of cold winter days as a kid, snowed in with his family, dipping fresh baked bread in his mother's homemade soup. The lunch filled his stomach and gave him a needed boost of energy, but he was still surly and avoiding all small talk.

After eating, Ben climbed the ladder and scurried up the newly covered roof to finish installing the base flashing around the stone chimney. It was the last section of the bunkhouse roof to work on that day, and he was pleased with their progress. He also had to be back in town to pick up Skyla after school. Then he discovered the measurements for cutting the flashing to fit the corner of the chimney were off by an inch and three quarters. He wasn't sure how it had happened, but as he nailed in the flashing, he spotted the error and cursed. Ben pulled the nails from the corner flashing and, unhappy about having to re-do his work, flung it off the side of the roof.

"Watch out!" Jeremiah yelled from somewhere below.

Ben scooted closer to the roof's edge and peered down.

"Damn it, Ben. You nearly took my head off." His brother glared up at him then bent down and picked up the piece of roofing metal. He dropped it in the construction site trash bin, which was where Ben had been more or less aiming.

"My bad. You should watch where you're walking. It could be dangerous."

"I was watching out, you dumb fuck," Jeremiah said, extra pissed at Ben's apathy.

"Want to bring me—" he started to ask, but then changed his mind and went to the ladder.

Ben needed to cut the piece of flashing, nail it in place, caulk and seal and be done with the chimney. He thought he had enough time to install the last sheets of roofing metal before leaving. Jeremiah could screw on the ridge cap.

His brother met him at the pile of remaining roofing materials. He eyed Ben as he drank from a water bottle, then said, "You're about as pleasant as a hot pile of cow shit today. Cut the crap or keep it to yourself."

"I thought I was keeping it to myself."

"Hardly," Jeremiah scoffed. "Did she break up with you or what?"

"Why do you think this has anything to do with Maleah?" Ben wanted to know.

"The only time I've seen you this moody is when a woman is involved."

"Could be about Skyla."

"When it's Skyla, you're a totally different kind of butthole."

Ben clamped his mouth shut and picked up a piece of the base flashing.

"Would you looky here? Hell finally froze over and my brother doesn't have a comeback." Jeremiah paused and scratched his jaw. "She really dumped your ass, didn't she? What the fuck did you do?"

Ben ignored Jeremiah's question and asked one of his own. "Where are the tin snips?"

"Mom needed them to fit the metal screen behind the attic vents."

The muscle in his jaw ticked. Jeremiah stepped in front of Ben.

"I'm not letting this go. What the hell happened to make your shorts wadded so far up your ass that your eyeballs are about to pop out of your head?"

"I said things I shouldn't have." Ben tried to step aside and move on with his task, but Jeremiah shifted with him.

"As you've always done when you're backed into a corner."

"She should've left me alone the moment I told her I'm a dumbass," Ben said.

"Agree again."

"I'm not cut out for dating. Letting my guard down and allowing myself to be with someone after Kinsey was a mistake. It's not Maleah's fault. I shouldn't have gotten involved in the first place." He looked his brother in the eye, a challenge to prove him wrong. Ben wasn't wrong about this. He was no good as a boyfriend, or friend with benefits, or whatever it was that he and Maleah had been. Kinsey ruined him, and he'd come to terms with his acquired relationship disability.

"One screwed-up chick is all it took? No." Jeremiah shook his head in denial and partial disgust. "You're using your ex as an excuse to not get hurt again. That's fucking bullshit. You can't stop living your life because of her. She's evil and she screwed you over. Don't get me wrong, Ben. We all know what a bitch Kinsey is, but that doesn't mean she gets to control you forever. Don't you get it, man? If you let her continue to mess with your life, then she wins. I can't let you do that to yourself anymore. One mistake made with the wrong person does not get to rule your life forever." Jeremiah poked Ben in the chest. "You hear me? You cannot let Kinsey dictate who you are, because we all know you're better than she is. You are better than her crazy, manipulating, lying, heartless, ice-queen bullshit."

Ben lowered his gaze to the ground.

Jeremiah dropped his hand. "I'm not like you when it comes to this one woman, one man crap. But I know it's how you are wired. If there's any chance Maleah may be the one, the girl who puts your world back in order, why the fuck aren't you begging Maleah to take you back instead of moping around here with your cock all tied up in knots?"

As much as Ben wanted to deny everything Jeremiah let loose on him, the denial and other arguments of bad timing and being too busy wouldn't resurface. Even telling his brother that Maleah was better off without him refused to be voiced. Because deep down, he didn't believe it, and if Ben had one fault, it was that he couldn't lie to his family. Lying to himself, sure, but to the people who cared about him most in the world, he couldn't do it. They'd see through him anyway.

Jeremiah asked, "Are you going to let Kinsey dictate the rest of your life? If you do, then you really are a dumbass." He walked around Ben and said nothing more about it.

Ben walked over to his truck and trailer in search of another cutting tool to finish the flashing for the chimney. As Ben searched inside his toolbox for another pair of snips, his mother appeared at his side.

Without hesitation, she cut straight to the point. "I overheard some of what your brother said."

"Were you eavesdropping? Haven't you always taught us how rude it is and how it's the road to starting false rumors?"

"Listen here. I don't need to be censured by you, young man," she scolded, but Ben knew his mother wasn't angry or as serious as her tone indicated. "You and your brother were discussing private matters in the open. If you don't want someone listening in, you should keep quiet until you have some privacy."

She lowered her hands from her hips and added, "With that said, Jeremiah's right. Maleah is the best thing that's happened to you in a long time. I had a good feeling about her from the moment I saw her bright and pretty face. She's not only worth pursuing but keeping close to your heart. I won't tell you what to do, but it's sure been nice seeing you happy again. You deserve some happiness in your life. I know you don't want to hear it, and I know talking about your girlfriend with your ma is uncomfortable. I'm sure you're thinking of a joke to make light of this situation, but, Ben, if you care for her, give the two of you a chance. You can't go through the rest of your life thinking every girl out there is like your ex. They're not. Granted, sometimes you get a worm in your apple, but Maleah isn't one." Pauline patted Ben's arm and gave an encouraging smile.

"Did you hear me say I already chased her away?"

"She comes across as the forgiving type. You can figure out a way to apologize."

"I'm not sure I can. I fu—" Ben choked on the curse word mid-sentence and adjusted with, "I fudged it up."

"I believe you and Maleah will work through this if it's meant to be. And speaking of fudge." Pauline pinpointed her gaze on Ben and gave her best stern look. "You and your brother are not too old or too big to have your mouths washed out with fudging soap. You watch your damn mouths. I raised you both better than that." She hardened her already tense stare and then handed over the tin snips and gave him a wink. "You looking for these?"

Ben wrapped his hand around the snips and tightened his grip on the handles. If he hadn't already been feeling about as big as a flea, being reprimanded by his mother would have put him in his place. *Long live the queen*, he thought, and wondered if he should bow next time his mom passed by.

As he finished his work on the roof, he remained quiet and focused. His family gave him the space he needed and didn't bring Maleah up again. This allowed his mind to turn circles over their comments. It galled him that Jeremiah had made a potent and compelling argument. Hating his ex had turned into a festering boil that controlled his life. His downturn had been inadvertent and subconscious, but he'd let it happen.

Ben drove back to town to pick up Skyla from school. As he sat in the pick-up line, he took another bullet and read Maleah's letter. He'd put it off all day, but since he was fighting inner demons already, why not throw another one at him?

Dear Ben,

I owe you the world's biggest apology and I'm too embarrassed and horrified by my mistakes to say I'm sorry in person. I witnessed what I thought was abusive behavior against Kinsey the morning after I arrived in Three Peaks. Then I overheard you arguing with the electrician. I should not have made assumptions based on partial conversations, but I was triggered and acted out in negative ways. I'm so sorry, Ben. You didn't deserve to have your contract ended with my aunt for the work on the Columbine Building. Everything will return to exactly the way it was before I butted in as soon as you say so. I have disturbed your business in ways I can't even imagine. I sincerely hope what I've done can be reversed. I am so terribly sorry. Let me know how I can fix this and I will do anything you need or want, even if that means stepping back and disappearing so I can't cause any more problems.

Maleah

Ben thought about the timing of Maleah's letter with their time spent together after she brought the letter. He put all the pieces together into a bigger picture. And one thing that stood out to him was how Kinsey never admitted her faults. His ex had never apologized to him. Everything had been Ben's fault from the moment Kinsey decided she wasn't happy. In his hand was written proof of exactly how Maleah was so entirely different than his ex. She was sweet and humble. Maleah was sexy on the outside, but so beautiful on the inside that her selflessness made Ben ache in places he didn't know could experience feelings.

From that moment on, he knew with every ounce of his soul, and with the determination of a bull with its ass on fire, that he would change his ways. But this time he would choose what kind of man he wanted to be and what he wanted for his future. How that might affect a relationship with Maleah, well, that remained to be seen.

Nineteen

MALEAH'S TO-DO LIST was longer than her arm. Literally. Okay, well, it would be if she put all the sticky notes together and then added the list from inside her phone. One of the top items to do was unpack.

Since moving her stuff into Holden's house, she had yet to put anything away. Holden had been an absolute gentleman in every regard. He offered his bed to her, with him in it, but Maleah said she needed some space as she settled into a new routine and decided what she wanted. He was fine with her decision and told her to pick any room she wanted in the house. He said he'd grown used to living a minimalist lifestyle but didn't expect her to live the same way. He wanted her to feel comfortable, and Maleah could place her belongings in any of the common areas. Holden admitted that clutter made him feel anxious, and when he was anxious, he wasn't as productive at work and training, but he had been serious about inviting Maleah into his life and he would adjust.

Maleah simply appreciated having a nice place to live and wouldn't make Holden uncomfortable. All of her boxes and furniture went straight into the large bedroom she now occupied or into the garage. Since Maleah had originally packed everything in a matter of a few hours, and then had hastily moved to Three Peaks, her stuff was disorganized and had been shuffled around multiple times. Her life felt more like a disaster now than it had when she was living out of suitcases and boxes in the Columbine Building.

Maybe Holden had it right and Maleah could continue living with the bare minimum. She'd been doing that since moving to Three Peaks. Almost everything she owned had remained in storage while working on the building. She eyed the stacks of boxes and bins in her bedroom and considered giving it all away. But she knew she wouldn't do it. She was too attached and adored her mismatched set of coffee mugs, favorite books, and collection of sweaters and jackets. Even so, Maleah had to decide to either be okay with the disarray until she figured out what she was going to do—stay at Holden's or start looking for her own place—or unpack. And sooner rather than later.

Until this weekend, she hadn't had time to do anything other than work. The few hours she'd had to herself since returning to True Green had been spent on the necessities of living. Nothing more than eating, laundry, and sleeping. Holden's stamina and drive to be the best and stay in top form were admirable, and he'd convinced her to start running with him before work and bought her a guest pass at his gym so they could work out together. The after-work gym visits had happened two times. Holden often stayed at True Green later than Maleah. She decided twelve hours at True Green were enough. If Holden wanted to work fourteen or sixteen hours and then hit the gym, that was his choice, but she needed to sleep if she was going to be mentally capable the next day.

Today was her first day off since moving back to Boulder. She had the entire weekend to herself and an empty house. Holden left the night before for a half iron-man competition in North Carolina. Around her, the house was perfectly quiet except for the occasional sound of a passing car or a neighborhood dog barking.

With time to herself and only her thoughts for company, she spent the morning drinking tea and doing nothing except thinking about everything. She missed Ben and wanted to call him, but didn't. The ache to hear his voice, or even drive all the way to Three Peaks to see him brought tears to her eyes. She hadn't been expecting the rise of emotion and realized she hadn't let herself think about him since leaving town. Now that she was alone, he was first and foremost on her mind. Maleah put her metaphorical heel down and did not call or text. Ben was no longer a part of her life and maybe he had never been. Just a short-lived fling and nothing more. Dwelling on the loss wouldn't solve her despair or heal the ache of longing for his company, so she headed to her room to deal with the boxes and the other corner of her life that was disorganized... but was something she could control.

Or that had been her intention. The first box she opened contained her favorite scarves, hats, and keepsakes from childhood to her college years. Maleah placed the royal purple suede hat on her head, wrapped a silk scarf around her neck, and parked herself on the floor. She leaned back against her bed and opened a journal from her middle school years. The handwritten notes, doodles, and stickers brought back a thousand memories, and Maleah was lost in the past until her phone rang.

"Hi, Mom," she said.

"Maleah? This is your father."

She'd expected her mother's energetic and familiar voice, and hearing her father was a nice surprise. "Oh, hi, Dad! How's it going? Everything okay?" He didn't call often, and Maleah suddenly wondered if something bad had happened. After her end of summer and fall disasters, Maleah was a little gun-shy over possible bad news and braced herself.

"We're fine. I thought I'd call and see how my little girl is doing. Your mother told me you moved back to Boulder and have your old job back. Is that what you really want, Maleah Keiko?"

"Yeah," she said, thinking that his question was kind of strange and to the point. "I think so. Why do you ask? I wouldn't be back in Boulder if I didn't want to be."

Albert Hale paused long enough that Maleah was about to ask if he was still on the line, but he said, "Oh, I don't know. I had the feeling you were settling in and staying in Three Peaks, possibly permanently. I liked the idea. My old buddy, Raymond Trujillo, thought you might stick around too."

"But I never planned to. I live in Boulder, and my job is—" Maleah hesitated. She was about to say her job was fantastic, perfect, everything she wanted, but the words wouldn't come out. The truth was, Maleah was mentally exhausted, but her body was antsy. She missed the freedom of making her own schedule and working on the renovations. Her father held the line, and she didn't want to keep stalling, so she said, "My job is challenging, but we're making incredible advances in biodegradable plastic products."

"Oh? That's good to hear." He paused, then added, "The last time we spoke, you sounded pretty happy about the work you were doing in Kiki's building. Were you able to finish up before leaving?"

"I did. Mostly. The remaining work will be handled by the general contractor. He'll do a great job. He's a talented carpenter and responsible. Aunt Kiki likes him too."

"Ben Erickson, right? Yes, I know his parents. Good family. It's too bad the two of you didn't work out."

"Dad," she said, shocked. "What are you talking about? How did you—"

"Don't act so surprised. Your mother and I may not live in Three Peaks anymore, but we hear everything, or your mom does. Then she tells me whether I want to hear it or not. From the sound of all the gossip, and your aunt Kiki filled me in with other news, I was sort of rooting for the Erickson kid. He sounds a lot better suited for you than this athletic scientist you're currently living with."

"I'm renting a room in Holden's house until I figure out what I'm going to do. That's all, Dad. He's not my boyfriend," she said, then wondered if that was totally true. Holden had invited her to move into his bedroom. He'd kissed her when he left Three Peaks. He had given her his itinerary for his trip, apologized for leaving her behind, and said she was welcome to go with him to the next race. Maleah made no personal commitments to Holden, but he was definitely treating her as more than a roommate and coworker. *Holy dingbat*, she thought and pushed aside the revelation. Now wasn't the time. She had to get through the conversation with her father first.

"Okay, then, if you say so, I believe you. Your mother thought you were serious about this Holden fellow, even though he sounds like a boring, driven egghead. I don't think you will be happy with someone who is so focused on work. You're a hard worker too, but you have a free spirit and always have. I'd hate to see you lock yourself into a situation that may seem good on the outside but isn't in your best interest in the long term."

Maleah felt instantly defensive of her choices, and of Holden, but before the rebuttal escaped her mouth, she settled down. Her father would never voice his concerns without having considered every angle of the situation. He was a thorough and thoughtful man. Her mother, on the other hand, was more spontaneous and apt to jump to conclusions without knowing all the details. Maleah liked to think her parents balanced each other out.

"I know you have my best interest at heart, and I appreciate you calling but..." There it was again. Maleah couldn't give him reassurances, because she had so much uncertainty still running amok in her brain and wreaking havoc on her emotions. "Dad." She sighed and pulled the hat off her head and tossed it into the box. "How can I tell if I've made the wrong decision? I thought I wanted to be back at True Green, but I'm not enjoying it anymore. We've been super busy and I'm not settled into my own place. I don't know if that's the problem or if it's something else."

"That's a good question. Here's what I can tell you. When you find your passion, the work no longer feels like a job. Sure, there's times when things get tough and you may be working harder than you ever have before, but every morning you wake up and you can't wait to start again. Do you feel like that at True Green?"

"I don't know." Maleah shifted, uncrossed her legs, and sat up taller. "I used to, but since I returned, it's like I'm on autopilot. And I'm not getting enough sleep. That could be part of the problem. But the pay raise is great and I believe in what we're doing."

"Believing in your work is important, and making money and taking good care of yourself is equally important, but if I've learned anything in my short life, it's that if you can do those things and also follow your passion, you'll never feel like you've worked a day in your life. This kind of fulfillment is something money can't buy and no one can take from you."

Maleah hesitated for a second and then she said, "Thanks, Dad. That helps a lot."

"About that boy..."

Maleah held her breath, waiting to see what he might say next. "Yeah?"

"Don't settle. You deserve the best."

"You're required to say things like that."

"Because it's true. You're entitled to make your own mistakes but try to avoid marrying the wrong man. I don't want to see you get hurt." He cleared his throat, and Maleah was about to thank him again for looking out for her, but Albert continued, "I haven't met this Ben fellow, but Kiki sure thinks highly of him. You sure things are over between the two of you?"

"Dad!"

He cleared his throat. "Well, I see I've stepped over the line. That's all right. I can tell you don't want to talk about Ben. It's always nice talking with my favorite daughter, but I better get off here. Let me know how things work out. And I'll be rooting for the blue-collar fella. He sounds all right."

Maleah smiled and shook her head. "Love you. Tell Mom I'm doing fine and all is well."

"Okay. I'll lie to her for you but only because you said to."

She laughed and they disconnected. Maleah leaned back against the side of the mattress and stared at the mess in her room. With a sense of enlightenment and the feeling of an enormous weight lifted off her shoulders, she knew exactly what she needed to do with all the boxes. Leave them packed.

* * *

Brielle cocked her head to one side. A thoughtful expression appeared to be frozen in place. Ben tried ignoring Maleah's cousin as he cleaned up the paints, stencils, and brushes, but she stood still like some judgmental statue, and he had to keep moving around her.

She finally spoke. "I've been trying to stay out of your and Maleah's business, but..." Her words trailed off and Brie didn't finish the sentence.

As much as Ben wanted to ignore the mention of Maleah, he heard her name and was curious about Brielle's take on their current situation. Brie continued to stand there, unmoving, and staring at Ben's work. He folded the drop cloth and she moved out of his way.

"Go ahead and share your opinion. Everyone else has. You're close with Maleah, so I'd actually appreciate hearing your thoughts."

Brie crossed an arm over her chest and rested her elbow in her other hand. Her pointer finger tapped against her chin as she said, "Maleah is going to love the mural, but I don't know if she's going to forgive you because you can paint pretty pictures on the wall. She's been a pathetic mess since moving back to Boulder. At this point, if you dropkicked Sir Mittens over Three Peaks, she'd probably be more likely to forgive you over telling her she's better off with McNutt. You screwed the pooch, Benjamin. How's Digger, by the way?"

Brielle's judgment of the situation let Ben know exactly how well-informed Maleah's cousin was. Their circles ran small in Three Peaks. His pride had taken multiple beatings since Maleah left town, and he didn't let Brie's candid response shut him down. Determination to make things right with Maleah kept him going and optimistic.

Ben stared at the wall he'd just finished painting and framing. "If she doesn't want to see me when she comes back to town, then I'll move on." It was that simple, yet equally complex. If, or more likely, when she rejected him, Ben was going to be a mess. He'd already experienced the disaster of letting her go. The dreams, the daydreaming, the complete shambles his life had turned into wasn't something he wanted to deal with for a second time, but he would. If anyone understood rejection, breakups, and losing your dream of a better tomorrow, it was Ben. He'd survived the ultimate destruction and fallout once before, and he would live through a breakup with Maleah.

"You should go ahead and buy a ring for Digger, maybe a condo in Durango. I think he'd like a nice retirement village as he gets older," Brie said, straight-faced, but Ben definitely detected the snark. "You and him are destined to be life-long bachelors."

Ben played along and tried to figure out how serious she was. "You must not know Digger too well. He's going to be running free and wild and howling until he keels over."

"If you say so."

Her expressive eyes and candor were hard to decipher.

"By the way, I would never kick a cat."

"I know. I used that as an example, because Maleah would never forgive someone who abused animals and your chances of getting her to trust you again are even less likely."

"Thanks. I appreciate your optimism and support," he said, letting the sarcasm roll.

She nodded and gave a hint of a smile that revealed her inner evil villain. "Sure, sport. Anytime."

Ben gestured vaguely at the wall in front of him. The inspiration behind the project had given him a lot more confidence about convincing Maleah he wasn't the troll-faced douche he'd acted like the last time he'd seen her. But Brielle was getting to him, and his ego could only take so much. "I'm okay with what I've accomplished here, but—" He stalled, looking for the right words. Brie's lack of support made him question his efforts. "I'm trying to redeem myself and..."

Brielle looked at his work again. "You might want to step up your game, that's all. Maleah's all cheery and sweet on the outside, but she's a tough nut to crack if you've wronged her. Once she's done with a guy, she's done. They no longer exist in her mind."

Ben didn't have that impression of Maleah at all, but Brielle was one of Maleah's closest confidantes. He blinked and the sinking feeling that started with Brie's scrutiny continued to plummet.

"Well, good talk," he said. "I think I might go hang myself with piano wire now."

Brielle laughed as she crossed the large open floor of the main level of the Columbine Building and headed for the stairs. "Benjamin, don't you think that's a bit extreme? I thought you said you'd accept whatever Maleah wanted."

Ben nodded. "It is what it is." He raised his arms overhead, tightened the imaginary noose around his neck, and jerked the invisible rope as if he were shoved off the gallows platform.

"Yep," Brie agreed. "Nice mimicry." She gave him two ironic thumbs-up before jogging up the staircase.

Putting the morbidity aside, Ben shrugged off Brielle's comments and finished cleaning up. Maleah was supposed to be back in town tomorrow and he was almost ready for her return.

* * *

"Ben left this for you earlier," Brielle said as she handed over an envelope Ben had left at the apartment.

Maleah looked at the lavender-colored envelope with her name on it. "Did he say anything about it?"

"Not really. Just to give it to you. I'm not his favorite person at the moment," Brie said and left her obscure statement open-ended.

"What does that mean?" Maleah watched her cousin's face. "What did you do?" It wasn't the words Brie said as much as the way she'd said them.

"I let him have it." A sly grin curled the corners of her mouth. "You know," she said, sounding suddenly thoughtful. "I kind of like Ben. I don't get to fuck with people too often in real life. Online, I'm pretty good at it. I think it means I'm comfortable around him. Otherwise, I wouldn't be able to pull off what I did without him catching on."

Maleah's eyes widened. She licked her lips in an attempt to moisten her suddenly dry mouth. "Tell me what you did."

Brielle laughed. "You should have seen his face."

Maleah's brows pinched together with growing concern.

"I think he might have cried in his beer while hugging a teddy bear after what I said."

Maleah put her fingers to her temples and squeezed. "Why, Brie? Why?"

Brielle flashed a pointed look at Maleah. "He screwed you, and not in the good way. I wanted to make his pathetic ass suffer. You're too nice to do that to him."

"I am not." Maleah defended, paused, then added, "Okay, yeah, maybe I am. But you don't know how much he's gone through. Besides, if Ben doesn't want to date me, I'm not going to make him feel worse about it."

"But I can and I did. He needed to learn that it's not all right to make everyone around him miserable just because he's in a mood."

Maleah sighed. "No, it wasn't okay. I told him he can't speak to me that way. He's apologized twice. Once in a text and once in a voicemail. And he asked to see me."

"When did that happen?" Brielle asked.

"Sometime last week. I was trying to finish up some commitments at True Green and get organized to move again. This time permanently. I told him I was moving to Three Peaks and he asked if he could apologize in person once I returned to town."

"You didn't tell me," Brie said.

"I'm telling you now. It's been hectic trying to get my life moved again. Would you have taken it easier on Ben if you'd known we are sort of speaking to each other?" Maleah wondered out loud.

Brielle considered the question, then shook her head. "Nope. I might have laid it on even thicker. He hurt your feelings, so I hurt his. That's what cousins are for. Besides, if his balls can't handle a minor bruising, then he's not tough enough for our family."

Maleah gave Brielle a doubtful look and was not going to join in on the subject of Ben's bruised balls. She lifted the envelope in her hand. "So, what is this?"

Brie shrugged. "No idea."

They stared at the envelope. Whatever was inside was thicker than a card.

"Open it. Ten bucks says the card is him groveling and begging you to take him back."

Maleah's doubt increased. Ben had already apologized via messaging. She wasn't sure if she'd fully

Jody A. Kessler

forgiven him. She hesitated. Her feelings for Ben ran deep in her blood, and she wasn't ready to expose how much his words meant to her in front of her cousin.

"I might have a clue about what's inside, but I told Ben I wouldn't tell you."

Maleah glanced up. "You're in on this?"

"Not really. I did screw with his head, but he's a good guy. If you get back together you can tell him I was lying."

"Now you're messing with my head. If and when I start talking to Ben, the only thing I'll tell him is how crazy you are and to beware."

"Fair enough." Brielle tapped her jaw and smirked. "The quiet ones are usually the scariest."

"You should get out more. You spend way too much time in your head and on your computer." Maleah took a deep breath, undecided about when she should read Ben's card.

"I definitely do. Which reminds me, I need to be online for a live chat. Also, I deposited two thousand seven hundred and forty-one dollars into your bank account yesterday." Brielle walked into the living area, sat on the couch, and opened her computer. "Have fun with Ben. And don't forget, if he starts giving you any crap, just fuck with his head. It's pretty easy since he's so vulnerable right now."

Maleah drifted toward the living room in pursuit of her cousin. The oversized two-bedroom apartment was exquisite. Since she'd left town, all the remodeling and finishing touches had been completed. There wasn't a lot of furniture, but she now had time to do whatever she and Brielle wanted with the space.

"Excuse me? Did you just say you put thousands of dollars in my account? Why?" She was close to being flabbergasted.

"Remember when I asked you if you wanted to see our new YouTube channel and you said no? Well, it's really taken off. You and Ben are freaking popular as an online couple. Your mini-tutorials are fantastic, but your bloopers and the singing are what the subscribers really want to watch. Of course, I make a decent co-host as long as I don't have to show my face too often. But... you and Ben are the stars. Your videos keep going viral and making us some great extra cash. Now that you're back, I can start uploading new content again."

Maleah blinked, coughed, blinked again. "You've being doing what now?" She refused to believe what she'd heard. But then she couldn't dismiss Brielle's confession either. "You made a YouTube channel out of me? Without telling me!"

"And I made us some decent extra money too," Brie said from the couch. "I knew you were low on funds, and you're adorable on camera, especially when you think you're only talking to me."

"Why didn't you show me the videos before posting them?"

"I knew you wouldn't want me to, or wouldn't let me. I work best alone, and I didn't want your external influence either. No offense or anything. And it turned out great. You should watch the episodes when you have time, okeydokey?"

"Not okeydokey. Crap, Brie. This is sort of a huge invasion of my privacy."

"It's not. Just watch the videos. I can always delete them if you don't like what I've done. But I know you can use the money," she taunted and smiled up at her cousin with false sweetness.

"Does Ben know about this channel?" Maleah asked.

"No. You can break the news to him after you guys hook back up. I don't think he should earn any of the money, but if he wants a cut I'll figure out what percentage he gets. And he might be waiting for you. I'd open that card before the last petal falls off the rose."

Maleah's jaw fell open. Did she just make a *Beauty and the Beast* reference? Maleah decided not to panic or overreact about being online... and apparently being popular. Brielle had been correct about needing the money. Since the videos were posted, and had been for months, she needed to take care of the envelope in her hand first. She returned to the kitchen to open the envelope in relative privacy.

Inside was a card with a picture of the Three Peaks for which the town was named, Mount Stargazer, Mount Massive, and Mount Tenderfoot. She opened the card and found three notes folded in half and numbered.

The card read:

To Maleah,
Open the notes in order and one at a time.
Ben
(I'm not good at this, but I'm trying not to mess up again.)

Maleah glanced over at her cousin, but Brielle's attention was fixed on her laptop.

She opened note #1 and read:

Step into the hall and follow the path of gifts. Everything you find is something that reminded me of you. Stop on the landing and open note #2.

Maleah left the apartment and immediately found something that looked familiar but was folded into a square and wrapped with a wide satin ribbon. As soon as she bent down to pick it up, she knew what it was. Ben had managed to get her skirt and sandals back. She untied the ribbon and unfolded the long fabric. The tears from the barbed wire fence had been mended with matching thread. The damages were only noticeable upon close inspection. She'd be able to wear her favorite long skirt again. Warmth filled her insides, and she smiled at the fabric in her hands. Then she glanced down the corridor and spotted something else sitting at the top of the staircase.

The next present was a stuffed animal. It was a bull wearing a little red skirt and with a red bow tied around his neck. The cross-dressing bull was so dang cute, Maleah wanted to kiss it. Instead, she draped the skirt over her arm and cuddled the stuffed bull close to her body as she started down the stairs.

The next gift waited on the landing. She wasn't sure if she should read note #2 first or open the box. She opted for the note first.

Maleah,
You've brought me back to myself and helped me focus on what is important. I have stopped hanging onto anger

and the past. I now appreciate every day no matter what it brings. The days I had the pleasure of spending with you have been unbelievable.

You're incredible. Without trying, you've made me want to be a better person, a better father, and a better man. I may have saved you from angry ants and a memorable shower incident, but you are the one who rescued me from a life of misery. Whether you forgive me for what I said and did, or not, you've already changed me. Thank you.

Her sentimental heart nearly burst when she untied the next ribbon and unfolded the white tissue paper and found an antique ornate picture frame with a photo of Ben, Skyla holding Sir Mittens, and Digger with a stick in his mouth. They sat on the steps of the Craftsman house over on Ouray Street. Ben didn't tell her he'd bought the house, and the revelation made her even more emotional. Happiness for him and Skyla filled her with joy.

She held back the tears and calmed the swells of emotion before heading down the rest of the stairs. Was Ben waiting for her? When was she supposed to open the next note? She wasn't sure, but she was already overwhelmed with his thoughtfulness, so she plunged forward and prayed she wouldn't dissolve into a gooey mess before thanking him.

Instructions weren't needed. She saw the next gift as soon as she entered the front room of the Columbine Building.

The words she'd painted on the wall, when she'd finished remodeling the room, were now repainted and framed. A vase of flowers sat on the floor at the corner of the frame.

Her eyes drifted from the vibrant multi-colored blooms back to her words on the wall.

Laugh More.
Live Every Day.
Love is Infinite.

Somehow Ben had found her words, repainted the message, and then built a giant wood frame around them. She'd needed the inspiration the night she'd painted on the wall, but the words continued to resonate with her beliefs to be positive and keep going no matter what life throws at you.

Maleah glanced around the room and down the hallway toward the back door, but Ben wasn't anywhere nearby. She was tempted to check her phone for messages, but she hadn't heard any new alerts.

There was one more note to read. It was folded over multiple times and something hard and chunky was inside. She set the picture frame, stuffed animal, sandals, and her skirt by the bouquet of flowers and unfolded the final note. Aunt Kiki's turtle necklace slid into her palm. She stared at it for a long second, wondering where he'd found it. The note read:

A job offer.
If you are in need of permanent employment in Three Peaks, you are hired immediately upon acceptance of this offer. I invite you to be my project manager for any and all construction jobs you choose to work on. You've proven

your abilities to handle the hiring and firing of subcontractors, scheduling, and time management. Your labor skills are aboveboard and you're a fast learner. I would be honored to have you on my team. I am offering you 15% higher than the average salary for a management position.

Maleah—if you don't want to work with me, I understand, and will not hold it against you. Please give Kiki her Ricky back next time you see her. I found her necklace in the storage room.

Love, Ben

Aunt Kiki would probably cry when she saw her beloved necklace. She called the turtle Ricky because that had been her pet name for her husband, Robert. He'd given her the necklace decades earlier. To Aunt Kiki, Ricky the necklace was the single most treasured item she owned from her deceased husband. Maleah sniffled as the tears rose up again and spilled down her cheeks.

"The job is yours if you want it." Ben's voice carried from the hallway. She turned as he approached. "I've been offered another large remodeling project. It's going to take at least eight months. Plus, I have your aunt's Cinquefoil Building to complete, and we've barely started."

Maleah stared at Ben. He wasn't wearing a suit, or polished shoes, and his hair was slightly mussed. His three-day scruff of beard looked neat and trim, and she yearned to feel the short hairs brush her face. He was so exactly opposite of Holden, and yet he was everything she wanted in a man. Just the sight of him settled the month-long tension that had been keeping her tied in knots.

She swiped away the wetness from her face. "Aunt Kiki hired me to be her building manager. Right here for the Columbine Building."

"Oh." He dropped his gaze for a second.

"It's only a part-time position, especially since we don't have any tenants yet," she said tentatively.

"Does that mean you'll consider my job offer?" He stepped a couple feet from Maleah and stuck his hands in his pockets.

"I might." She remembered Brie's advice to play with his head a little as payback for hurting her. "Does the job come with any benefits?"

"I could look for medical and dental insurance if I need to." He paused and she watched one side of his mouth quirk. "Wait." Ben rubbed the bridge of his nose, then said, "Were you asking about health insurance, or um, other kinds of *benefits*..." He lifted a brow to match the humor twinkling in his eyes.

His teasing was always contagious. "Is there a hint of lewd suggestion in that eyebrow tilt?" she asked.

"Do you want there to be?" Ben took a step closer.

She smelled his aftershave and his unique Ben smell of the Copper River Valley, fresh cut pine, and masculinity. She wanted to bury her face against his muscled chest and breathe him in forever, or the remainder of eternity. She wasn't sure which lasted longer.

Instead of immediately accepting his offer and telling him how much she loved his thoughtfulness and was dying to ask how he'd gotten her skirt back, she leaned back onto her heels and said, "I think a contract might be a wise decision before I can give you an answer."

Ben crossed his arms over his chest. "A contract would be wise. Should we discuss it over at The Jackalope? I'd be willing to buy you some dinner while we negotiate the terms of placing my balls on a platter and how to make my bank account cry over your salary."

Her gaze shifted left then right, as if she needed to consider the offer of a business meeting. She licked her lips and asked, "Are you sure? Didn't Kinsey help run your business before you separated?"

The laughter in his eyes dimmed slightly and he nodded. "She was our accountant and worked from home. I've given this a lot of thought, and I've consulted my grandpa, your aunt, my parents, and my brother, because I never want to put myself in the same situation I was in before. I don't have a lot of experience with relationships. You already know that. And I know that you are not Kinsey. You are nothing like her and never will be." He stepped forward again and dipped his head a little lower so they were eye to eye.

"Maleah, I'm serious about you. If you want to work with me, I think we could be an amazing team. If you don't want that, I still think we are amazing together. I'm sorry for pushing you away. I shouldn't have and it was a huge mistake. I've never asked anyone for a second chance, but I am now." Ben lowered to his knees and took her hands in his. "Maleah."

He stared into her eyes, and she couldn't hold back the overwhelming wave of emotion any longer. Her own eyes welled with tears, but they didn't spill over.

"I'm on my knees here. If I have to beg for your forgiveness I will. Or I can stalk you and wait until your next accident. Then before I rescue you, you have to swear to give me one more shot at being your boyfriend. What do you say? Do you want me back now or after your next mishap?"

She swallowed the peach pit that had suddenly lodged in her throat. A happy tear leaked down one cheek. She let go of his hand and swiped it away. "I'm not that accident-prone, so I guess I'll have to take you back now."

Ben stood and gathered her in close. "Good. We've already negotiated the first part of our contract. Second part. Do I get to kiss you whenever I want?"

"No!" She placed her palm against his chest and pressed, acting like she was resisting but in actuality, she was feeling him up. "I get to kiss you whenever *I* want."

"Oh, right. I'm trying my best not to be an asshole anymore, but you're going to have to remind me. Women get to choose when and how they are kissed... among other requested molestations. It's always the woman's prerogative."

"Exactly. And that sounds like the third clause of our new contract."

"Our negotiations are definitely leaning in your favor," he said but looked rather happy about it.

"As it should be." She infused more smugness than she was used to using.

"I agree. And your managerial skills have improved over the last month."

"Thank you for noticing." She kept up the façade of confidence. But Maleah felt herself softening and melting into the warmth and comfort of his embrace. "Ben?" she asked and snuggled her body closer to his.

"Yeah?" His hand moved to her face, and he brushed a lock of hair aside then tucked it behind her ear.

"I don't want to talk about business anymore."

"Okay, me neither. But I'd like to buy you dinner."

"Dinner would be nice. Where's Skyla? Will she be eating with us?"

"Skyla is spending the night at my parents' house."

Maleah nodded and realized that by accepting Ben back into her life, she was gaining a whole family. The idea filled her with pleasure and a level of contentment she had not known before. She suddenly had everything she never knew she wanted. A hilarious, fun, sexy, and thoughtful boyfriend and partner, a precious and unbelievable kid, a goofy dog who made her laugh almost as much as his master, and a cuddly kitten. That didn't even include his family, who she also adored. "Before we eat, I need you to kiss me."

Ben placed his palms along her jawline and dipped his head. He stopped and watched her face. "I would have made this work even if you'd stayed in Boulder. I haven't been able to do anything right without you. Thank you for coming back."

"I fell in love with Three Peaks and the remodeling work," she said. "I've never been so satisfied with my life before. I couldn't stay in Boulder, because everything I thought I wanted before no longer gave me anything to look forward to."

He blinked and his mouth softened into a small smile. Ben closed his eyes and inhaled.

But Maleah wasn't finished confessing. "And I fell head over heels in love with you, too."

With her final words, Ben's fingers tightened ever so slightly against her skin. His lips met hers in a kiss that sealed their fate and foretold of a beautiful and promising future together.

Six Months Later

"HOW MUCH TIME do we have?" Ben took her hand in his and led them toward the elevator of the Columbine Building.

Maleah stared at her phone screen, checking the time. "An hour? Maybe fifty minutes. That will give you ten minutes to get back to your job."

The elevator doors opened and they stepped inside. Maleah slipped her phone into her back pocket and took Ben's hand in hers once again.

They'd planned to have lunch together at Maleah's apartment and home office, the same apartment she'd been living in since she'd first returned to Three Peaks. Kiki had no intention of moving back in, since she and Grandpa Joe continued enjoying each other's company and both were happily living at the old folks' home.

The elevator doors closed and Ben swung around and backed Maleah against the wall, caging her in with his arms and placing one leg between her thighs.

"Lunch breaks" with Maleah were not always for eating. Food sometimes happened, but usually not. They could eat anytime, but they rarely had time alone. After-work hours belonged to Skyla or were eaten up by paperwork, mail, business administration, family dinners, and all the other long list of day-to-day responsibilities. There had been a kernel of truth to the time he'd had a meltdown and told Maleah he didn't have time for a relationship. But in that moment of weakness, he hadn't taken time to figure out how to work around his busy schedule.

Ben was still learning how to handle everything on his plate, but Maleah and Skyla were always at the top of his priority list. The lunch dates were often the best part of his week. He had Maleah to himself for an hour three or four days a week. There had been weeks where appointments or scheduling conflicts interrupted their alone time, but that was okay. Life happened. She accepted that Ben ran a thriving construction company. When he had to work out of town or on his brother's ranch, they would make up for their missed lunch by eating dinner together and often having sleepovers. But the sleepovers hadn't happened as often as Ben would have liked, and that was mainly because of Skyla.

Maleah wanted Skyla to be as comfortable as possible with their relationship. Ben was careful about bringing Maleah into their world too fast, but Skyla didn't seem to have any problem with Maleah's presence and even told Ben that his girlfriend was welcome to hang out anytime. The three of them did everything together: movies, shopping, cooking, skiing, trips to Durango or Denver. Ben couldn't be more relieved that Maleah and Skyla got along so well, but that left little time to have her to himself. He continued to work on this conundrum and adjusted his schedule whenever possible.

No words were necessary as he leaned in close and lowered his lips to hers. She circled her arms around his waist and accepted his kiss with equal longing and eagerness. Their tongues met and teased with increasing fervor. The ride to the second floor was all too short, and he reluctantly pulled his mouth away after the doors slid open, but he didn't move to leave.

Ben nudged his leg higher, pressing against her mound. "Takes too long to get to your apartment. I don't want to waste more time. Let's stay here."

"It's tempting, but I don't want to be filmed. I think we've had this discussion before."

"Damn cameras are everywhere these days."

"True, but not in my bedroom. At least as far as I know."

"Right," he said, then bent down in front of Maleah, wrapped his arms around her, and lifted her off her feet. She whooped in surprise.

"What are you doing!" Her question was more shriek than inquiry.

"I'm speeding this along," he said, as if it were obvious. "We're on a timer. I'm supposed to meet the new roofer in an hour. He has a reputation of being timely and impatient."

She squirmed against him, but Ben didn't let go as he punched the button to reopen the elevator doors. Ben took long, purposeful strides to the apartment. He turned so Maleah faced the door locks. "Key?" he asked.

"I think you have to put me down first."

He did but then scooped her back up the moment the door swung open. Ben kicked the door closed behind them and carried her straight to her bedroom. She'd done an excellent job with finishes and design, and Ben was so proud of the work she'd completed on the entire building. Maleah was also exemplary at managing the reconstructing and renovations of the Cinquefoil Building. Kiki was also incredibly proud of what Maleah had done over the last six months. Maleah had been a tremendous help to Ben with his court case against Kinsey and the changes to the custody agreement and visitation schedule. When Ben was consumed with stress, she was there to keep his eye on the goal of making a better life for Skyla. When he had to meet with his lawyer or be in court, Maleah fielded phone calls and appointments and kept his business running smoothly.

"We have actual business to discuss today," she said from his arms.

Ben tossed her onto the bed and her butt bounced against the mattress.

"Do we?" he asked with skepticism. Ben unfastened his belt buckle.

"Yep," she said as she undid the button of her jeans. "Hillary at All Your Flooring Needs sent an email letting us know they are having a summer sale starting on Monday and if we want the hickory then we should take advantage of the sale price because it's going to save us hundreds of dollars."

"Done and done. Do you want to go with me to place the order?" Ben lowered his zipper and stopped undressing. The damn boots always took forever to unlace and pull off. Maleah was likewise taking off her work boots. The right one dropped to the floor. "Are you going to tease me if I leave my boots on?"

"Probably," she said as her other shoe landed on the area rug and she pushed her jeans and panties over her hips.

His gaze followed the path of her descending clothes. Ben stroked his fingers along her exposed skin and watched the goose bumps rise on her creamy skin. His cock instantly followed suit and rose to attention.

She deserved the whole treatment. Even though they equally enjoyed spontaneity and the rough pleasure of a quickie, today he wanted to savor all of her. It'd been since sometime last week that he'd had her all to himself in a real bed.

Ben sat on the edge of the bed and made quick work of removing the boots and the rest of his clothes.

Maleah gave him another update about the progress of the tilework in the Cinquefoil Building, specifically the fourth-floor restrooms, but as she spoke, her hands roved over his torso as she kissed the back of his shoulders, and he forgot what she said as soon as it was out of her mouth.

Ben turned and slid farther onto the bed, taking her with him, then gathered her close. The mattress sank beneath their weight and the bedclothes swaddled them in a cozy nest. They stretched out, bodies pressing against one another as their mouths met and lingered for a timeless kiss. Maleah rolled on top of him, and he was all too aware of her peaked nipples brushing against his chest. Her hand snaked along his ribcage until she reached between his legs and massaged his member. He wanted their time to last, but Maleah was ready for more. Ben caressed the curve of her ass and slipped his finger into her heated center and found she was definitely ready for him.

He groaned as she put the tip of his head against her opening. He thrust as she sank against him and took his entire length into her warmth. Maleah's moan met his exhale of relief, the release of breath when finding exquisite pleasure of being with her, inside her, connecting on the most intimate level. She rose slightly, lifting her upper body and putting more weight on her knees, then moving against him in a rhythm all her own.

Her palms lay flat against his chest, squeezing her gorgeous round breasts slightly together as they bobbed and swayed in time with her hips. He was in fucking heaven, literally, and never wanted this to end. But in the building frenzy, his cock had other ideas. Even though his mind wanted to remain in a timeless vacuum, his erection was all about the grand finale. He gripped her hips, watching her endless beauty and reveling in the soft light that streamed in from the windows and cast her in the perfect shade of sunlight. And then he reached the peak of performance in perfect harmony with her own release.

Maleah collapsed on top of him and they lay together, hearts beating against one another's with a weighty yet buoyant tattoo.

Their breaths matched the quickened beat of their hearts, but as Maleah's body settled back into normality, she returned to the business side of their lunch date.

"After we go to All Your Flooring, we should stop in at Copper Valley Contractor's Supply. I need to look at sink fixtures again. I think I want to change styles from what I had picked out before."

"I want to fuck you again before we have to get back to work," he said, wondering how fast he could be ready for another round.

"Is that so? Do you want me on top again? I'm in good shape, but I need a little reserve of energy to get me through the afternoon."

Ben squeezed her butt. "I have plenty of energy. Lady's choice of course."

"Hmm…" she hummed. "Give me another minute. I'm still thinking about our schedule next week."

"Okay, but if you're thinking about work, then I am clearly not doing this right."

"Maybe," she said and slid to the side, keeping her arm draped across his chest. "Then again, I love my job and I love you. This is the best business meeting I could ever dream of."

"I still think I should be able to distract you from work for, I don't know, five minutes."

She pinched his chest. "That's fast. I think you can go longer than that."

"Challenge accepted." He turned, taking her in his arms and proving he could make their date last until the last minute of their lunch break.

Afterwards, they dressed and wandered into the kitchen to throw together sandwiches to take with them. Maleah spread peanut butter while Ben took care of the jelly.

"Will you come with me and Skyla to Alaska? Kinsey gets visitation for most of the summer. I thought we could bring Skyla to her mother's and then you and I can take a vacation."

Maleah's hands stopped moving and she turned to look at him. "Can we actually do that? I mean, not be in town with so much going on."

"We can. I'm my own boss, remember?"

"Yes, but—"

"No buts. Would you like to go on a real vacation with me?" They needed it and they deserved it. The winter had gone by fast, but it'd been snowy and cold. "We don't have to stay in Alaska. We can go someplace warm. Hawaii? Maybe that's too hot in mid-June. Baja? Florida? I'm open to suggestions."

"Brielle can give us some great tips about Ireland," Maleah said.

"I've always wanted to see Ireland."

"We could start looking online tonight," Maleah suggested.

"That sounds perfect," he said. "Come over after you're finished today. I'll even cook dinner."

"Does dinner include a sleepover?"

"You're always invited to stay the night. I'm sorry it's such a mess. Remodeling my house is a slow process when I have all the other jobs keeping me busy."

She laid her hand over his. "I know and I understand. Even if half the house is torn apart, I love that house. The disaster zones don't bother me at all. I lived here during all the construction and it was fine." Maleah glanced around at the apartment. "And yeah, a vacation would be amazing. So, yes, I'd love to take Skyla to Alaska and then explore the world with you. I couldn't think of anything that would make me happier. I'll come over tonight and we can start planning."

Ben put the butter knife down and placed both hands on the tops of her shoulders. "You know what would make me happier than I could ever imagine?"

Her hands moved to his waist, smiling up at him. "What's that?"

Maleah's skin glowed and her hair was slightly disheveled in the back. He'd seen her enough times after they'd been in bed to know he was responsible for the pretty pink flush of her cheeks and the messy hair.

"Since it doesn't bother you living in a construction zone, why don't you move back into one? Mine. I want you to move in with me, Maleah. I want to make sandwiches with you every day."

The smile stayed on her sweet and tantalizing lips, but her almond-shaped eyes widened. "Is spreading the peanut butter and jelly what we're calling it now?"

Ben grinned and nodded. "Spreading is good," he said with an eyebrow wiggle. "But I'd like to wake up with you every morning. And I just want you to be in my life. I want to take care of you for the rest of yours. Making you happy is what would make me the happiest man in the world."

"I guess I'm moving into your construction site then."

Ben's joy exploded and he kissed Maleah to seal the deal.

When he required air again, he held her in a tight hug. "I love you so much."

Maleah didn't say the words back to him. Instead, she said, "I'll start moving my things tonight, and I think we should keep this apartment for our business lunches."

"Oh, yeah, we're definitely keeping your office right here in the Columbine Building. The central location is ideal. I also think we need to cancel our afternoon and have an emergency meeting."

Maleah arched a suggestive brow. The tip of her tongue touched her lower lip as she entwined her fingers with his and they turned for the bedroom.

~*~*~

Thank you for reading.

If you enjoyed *Tease Me Once*, please help spread the word. The greatest compliment you could give is to leave a review on Amazon, Goodreads, or any other place readers might enjoy finding out about this book.

Reviews are incredibly helpful to authors and readers alike. A short sentence or two is all it takes and helps provide the social proof that this novel is worth reading. Thank you for leaving a review!

Subscribe to the newsletter for new releases, updates, and a free E-book copy of *The Call - An Angel Falls novella*. You can also find Jody A. Kessler on Facebook, Twitter, and Goodreads.

~*~*~

Acknowledgments

Thank you to my editors, Marianne Hull and Emily A. Lawrence. I appreciate your help in making this book the best it can be. To Barb from Coverinked, working with you has been so easy and your book covers are beautiful. Special thanks to my family and friends for their continued support. To the readers, I am humbled and honored that you chose to spend your time with these characters. I hope you enjoyed the novel.

About the Author

Jody A. Kessler is a USA Today bestselling and award-winning author. Her debut novel, *Death Lies Between Us*, is the winner of the Readers' Crown Award for Best Paranormal Romance. She writes contemporary romance, romantic comedy, historical time travel fiction, and paranormal fiction. She is the author of the An Angel Falls series, Granite Lake Romance series, The Night Medicine and more.

When Jody isn't navigating the terrain of her imagination and writing it down, she can be found exploring the wilderness of Colorado with her family and her three dogs, or in the kitchen baking cookies & brownies – and trying not to eat them all. She's passionate about continuing to learn and reads anything and everything that catches her interest.

Jody A. Kessler invites you to stop by her website and see what's new at: www.JodyAKessler.com. You can also connect with her on Facebook at Jody A. Kessler, on Twitter @JodyAKessler, and on Goodreads.

WWW.JODYAKESSLER.COM

Printed in Great Britain
by Amazon

41187565R10209